WTL 02/18

→ SOV

5/19

DS 02/21

THE
SECOND
WINTER

by Craig Larsen

 Other Press | New York

First softcover printing 2018
ISBN 978-1-59051-895-3

Production editor: Yvonne E. Cárdenas
Text designer: Julie Fry
This book was set in Berndal and Syntax by
Alpha Design & Composition of Pittsfield, NH.

10 9 8 7 6 5 4 3 2 1

Library of Congress Cataloging-in-Publication Data

Names: Larsen, Craig, author.
Title: The second winter / by Craig Larsen.
Description: New York : Other Press, [2016]
Identifiers: LCCN 2015039575| ISBN 9781590517888
    (softcover) | ISBN 9781590517895 (ebook)
Subjects: LCSH: World War, 1939-1945–Denmark–
    Fiction. | GSAFD: Historical fiction.
Classification: LCC PS3612.A765 S43 2016 |
    DDC 813/.6–dc23 LC record available at
    http://lccn.loc.gov/2015039575

Publisher's Note:
This is a work of fic
incidents either ar
ination or are use
to actual persons,
entirely coincident

A PORTRAIT OF POLINA

1.

East Berlin. August 1969.

The bus window framed the image with the geometric clarity of a camera lens. Beyond the glass, on the ground floor of a faceless apartment block, a pigeon was trapped in the sooty mesh of a torn screen. The boulevard had narrowed into a single lane approaching the border into West Berlin, and traffic had slowed to a crawl. On board the tourist coach, only one passenger noticed the stricken bird. Its wings were spread wide. Its scrawny chest was thrust out. In the blur of the woman's peripheral vision, for a brief instant the creature became a child — a girl, straining to free herself, her arms pinioned behind her back. Surprised by the violence of the image, the woman twisted in her seat to watch as long as she could. The pigeon's feathers were snared on the jagged wire. Beneath its claws, dust rose from the concrete windowsill like smoke. Threads of down fluttered to the sidewalk.

The woman's fingers slipped on the chrome handle on the seatback in front of her as the pigeon slid from view. It was a humid afternoon, and Angela Schmidt was suddenly aware of how sweaty her hands were. She barely smiled when she met the eyes of another passenger — the timpanist, Franck, wasn't it? — then faced forward again, allowed her gaze to return to the grim façades of the buildings passing outside the filthy windows. The other members of the symphony had changed back into their casual clothes before boarding the two coaches hired by the orchestra for this tour. She was still wearing the same formal dress she had worn for the concert the evening before. In the dense air, the charcoal gown was becoming as heavy as a soggy blanket. The woman next to her — a short woman with hairy forearms and olive skin — shifted and tried to catch her attention, but Angela ignored her. What was taking them so long? How much farther before the checkpoint? She tried to forget the trapped bird, she tried to make herself comfortable in her seat, but couldn't. Her stiff costume, she realized, stood out from her colleagues' more colorful outfits like a stone dropped into a field of grass.

Fifteen minutes later, the brakes squealed, and the bus lurched then trundled over fractured pavement as it followed the other bus off the boulevard into a parking lot. The Berlin Wall loomed beyond a chain-link fence crowned with rusty barbed wire. Angela's grip tightened on the chrome bar. She sat up to get a better view out the front, then instructed herself to relax. If she appeared too nervous, the border police would fasten on her. This wasn't Angela's first visit to East Berlin. She knew the drill. Usually, crossing back into the West, the inspections were cursory. Passport control was managed by a company representative. There were fifty people on this bus at least, half the symphony — too many to question. All she had to do was remain calm. She was a violinist with the Philharmonisches Staatsorchester of Munich. She had been playing the violin since she was five. She had been with the orchestra for six years, since she was thirty-one years old. She was respected, married to an industrial designer. She and her husband paid their taxes, they lived in an apartment with a spare bedroom, drove a 1967 Mercedes-Benz 250 sedan. All she had to do was relax. *Relax.* She wiped her hands on her thighs, folded them deliberately in her lap, shook the tension from her shoulders.

The diesel engine settled into an unsteady idle, sputtered, then came to an abrupt stop. The hydraulic system hissed, the door swung open. A man dressed in a green uniform climbed the stairs. His eyes darted up the aisle. Angela looked down at her fingers. The cheap ring Lutz had bought her five years before, when they were finally married, caught the diffused sunlight like a small chunk of plastic. Lutz was having an affair. They had never spoken about his infidelity, but Lutz didn't try to hide it. She didn't want him to. It was worse to lie to each other, wasn't it? *Relax, Angela, relax.* She reached for her throat, through the fabric of her dress touched a diamond and sapphire pendant dangling from a delicate platinum chain around her neck, made certain that it remained hidden beneath her collar.

When she dared to raise her eyes again, the border patrolman was three steps up the aisle, pacing slowly. Another soldier, shielded from view, was on board as well, speaking to the driver in German so guttural that he could have been choking. The patrolman's uniform was perfectly pressed. There was something fastidious about him, something precise. He was wearing glasses an engineer would wear. Even from this distance, Angela could see how immaculate the lenses were. His features were fine, his skin unshaven but smooth. The hair visible below the rim of his cap was clipped short, close to the scalp. When their eyes connected, Angela froze. She dropped her gaze, straightened the ring on her finger, forced herself to breathe.

Next to her, the olive-skinned woman ventured something in a whisper. The few words sent a wave of adrenaline through Angela's chest. Her skin tingled. It took her a few beats to understand the woman's question. *You don't think they'll go through the bags in the hold, do you?*

Angela offered the woman a curt smile.

"That could take hours," the woman said, "if they do it thoroughly."

Angela had to stifle herself. She wanted to whisper *shhh!* so forcefully that her lips twitched. She was still on edge. The dark streets of East Berlin still haunted her. After the concert had ended the night before, she had stayed behind in the symphony hall when the rest of the orchestra boarded the buses for the hotel. She had locked herself in a stall in the women's room until the voices receded and she was certain that the cleaning crew was finished with their work. Then — with the Adagietto from Mahler's Fifth Symphony still replaying itself in her head — she had felt her way across the stage and out of the pitch-black concert hall. At midnight, East Berlin was deserted. She hugged the walls, found cover in the shadows. Certain that she was being followed, she ducked into a bar, then detoured down an alley in search of the address she had been given by her cousin in Munich. Now, the echo of her frantic footsteps rang in her ears. *For God's sake, Angela, relax.* Her hands were squeezed into fists, and she told herself to loosen them.

Walking the length of the bus, the patrolman let his fingers brush over the top of the seatbacks. His footsteps paused.

Angela's gaze traveled up his arm, across the stiff collar of his shirt, to his thin, bloodless lips, the chiseled beak of his chin. He had taken notice of a particularly large bag in the overhead rack, and he appeared to be reading the tag on the handle. His Adam's apple ratcheted up and down, needle-sharp against the silk of his throat. "Amanda Christian," he said.

Two seats forward, next to the window, a blond-haired woman straightened in her seat.

"This suitcase belongs to you?"

"The black one," the woman said. "Yes."

The patrolman pulled it from the rack. "It is a large bag for such a short trip."

The woman shrugged. "I am a singer," she said. "I don't carry an instrument, I carry my costumes."

The patrolman hesitated, then shoved the bag back. He focused instead upon another, smaller suitcase next to it. "To whom does this case belong?"

No one answered, and the patrolman yanked the rectangular, varnished case from the rack. When it dropped from the ledge, it twisted on its handle with a jolt. The patrolman's arm flexed. He kept the case suspended above the row of passengers, dug out the name tag with his thumb. From her seat, Angela could see that the label was blank.

"Hmmm? Whose suitcase is this?"

Toward the front of the bus, a man looked over his shoulder. "Hey," he said. "That's mine. What's the problem?"

"No problem," the patrolman said. "I would like to open this case, that's all."

"It's a horn," the passenger said.

"Open it."

"It's a trumpet."

"I only see a trumpet case," the patrolman said.

"I'm a trumpet player."

The patrolman propped the case on the edge of a seatback. When he tried to unsnap the clasps, they were locked.

"You have no right —" the trumpet player began.

"Get up," the patrolman said.

"I —"

"Stand up."

The trumpet player's face reddened. Angela watched him pull himself to his feet, shuffle into the aisle. His jacket caught on the blue vinyl seatback. He pushed past the person seated next to him, unaware that he was knocking her knees sideways.

"Do you have a key?"

The trumpet player reached into his pocket. The key jangled against some change, then fell to the floor. Angela noticed how thin his auburn hair was as he bent to retrieve it. His mustache was much thicker.

"Here you are," the trumpet player said.

"Open it yourself."

From where she sat, Angela had a good view into the case. As the lid rose, the shadow inside fled, revealing the polished surface of a professional's trumpet, snug against a worn velvet cushion. The smooth contours of the instrument glistened like molten gold. "You see," the trumpet player said. "Nothing but my trumpet." Nevertheless, the patrolman lifted the instrument from its cradle and searched the well underneath.

Watching them, Angela's thoughts returned to her trek through East Berlin the night before. After losing her way, she had finally stumbled on the apartment block where her aunt lived with her husband. The garbage hadn't been picked up in two weeks, and she had had to step over bags of trash to enter the building. Martina Bloch was still awake, waiting. Even though the windows were blacked out with rags and newspaper, only a single lamp was burning. The old woman cracked the door open and peeked into the hallway, then grabbed Angela's hands. A thin silver bracelet slid down her bony wrist. She pulled Angela inside and locked the door behind her, then held her niece at arm's length in trembling hands. *You're so beautiful, my dear,* the old woman said, *so tall and slender, so much like your father.* Despite his own desire to see Angela, Martina's husband had already retired to the bedroom. He was seventy-six years old, and his health was failing. Through the thin walls, Angela had heard the creaks and whines and labored breathing of a fitful sleep. The smell inside the cramped apartment, of tinned sardines and weak tea, came back to her now with a sudden intensity.

"Which of these bags belongs to you?" The patrolman's voice shattered Angela's reflection. His eyes were on her, scanning her formal dress. She felt him pause over her bare shoulders, her breasts.

Outside, the rumble of engines became the whistle of wind — a sound Angela remembered from her childhood. Before he died in the war, her father had taken her sailing. The shrill, lonely rush of wind through the rigging and masts of the boats in the harbor had fascinated her. On the water, she hadn't liked the cold, or the way the boat tipped, but there had been something spellbinding about the sound. "I — my name is — I play the violin," she said. Although she was stuttering, the strength in her voice surprised her.

"And which bag is yours, Fräulein?"

"My suitcase is underneath with the others," Angela said. "That violin there belongs to me."

"This one?" The patrolman lifted the case.

Another bead of sweat slipped down Angela's temple, tickling her skin. Her thighs were suddenly moist, and she remembered making love to Lutz the very first time. When his fingers had found her vagina, he had entered her so roughly that it hurt. Despite the violation, or perhaps because of it, she had come immediately. When he had grabbed her by the neck, she had smelled herself on his fingers.

The case slid off the rack with a scrape. Angela wondered whether the patrolman would notice that it was heavier than it should have been. "Is it locked?" he asked her.

Angela couldn't find her voice to answer. Her body stiffened. Lutz's fingers had dug into her spinal column at the base of her skull. His thumb had clamped her jugular. Her head had become light, her vision had blurred, her thoughts had soared away from her like hatched butterflies.

"Open it," the patrolman said.

Angela couldn't move.

"Open it," the patrolman repeated. His eyes found hers.

"We're all Germans," a voice said, a few seats back.

"What's that?" The patrolman pivoted stiffly, located the man who had challenged him.

"You heard me," the man said. "We're all Germans here."

"There are laws," the patrolman said.

"Why are you harassing us?"

Angela recognized the director's voice. Had he realized that his violinist was smuggling something across the border in her violin case? He had been in the lobby this morning, drinking a coffee, when she had rushed into the hotel, just in time to grab her belongings and board the bus. She watched the patrolman's hand tighten on the handle then shove the case back onto the rack.

"Where is your suitcase, sir?" the patrolman asked the director. His fingers loosened on the handle, then let go.

"Here you are," the director said, proffering a small leather bag that had been resting at his feet. "I've already opened it. You can search my things. I have nothing to hide. None of us do. You're only wasting our time."

When the patrolman stepped past her, Angela shuddered. The lingering, antiseptic scent of his soap wasn't strong enough to conceal the stench of animal underneath. *Just like a dog*, she thought. *This man is no better than a dog.*

2.

Kraków, Poland. August 1938.

A young girl crossed a bridge on the outskirts of Kraków slowly, one hand trailing behind her, her fingers running over the rusty guardrail. In her other hand, the girl clutched a doll with black hair and a red dress. Mossy green, the Vistula rippled beneath her in the breeze, but the water could have been standing still. The river was low, barely flowing at the end of a dry summer. Beyond the sandy, stony expanse of the riverbank, reeds were drying into gray stalks. In the distance, through the heavy iron girders that supported the span, the spires of the Wawel Cathedral carved an ornate edge into the hazy afternoon sky — or perhaps it was the invisible weight of the sky, the young girl reflected idly, that gave definition to the stones of the cathedral. It was a long, hot day at the height of August. If not for the wind, the humidity would have been stifling. The high-pitched buzz of cicadas and crickets was so loud that the girl didn't hear the approach of a bicycle. The rattle of its wheels over the cobblestones penetrated her thoughts in the same moment that the rider called out to her.

"Hey there, little beauty."

Polina twisted around. Her hair, uncut and unruly, caught the wind and tangled in front of her eyes. She swiped at it. She had chipped a front tooth the week before, and when she squinted into the sun, her raised lip revealed a small gap. Her first thought upon hearing the voice was that it belonged to her uncle — her father's brother, Czeslaw — and this sent a twinge through her heart. But the man on the bicycle was a stranger. The dark stubble on his cheeks and a split in his dry lips drew themselves from the blur of movement. His eyes fastened on hers. They were black, but they shined like polished stones. The wind gusted, tossing her hair across her face again, wrapping her white linen dress against her thin body. Then the stranger had pedaled past. She turned on her heel to watch him, then once again started on her way. After a few paces, she reached for the guardrail, as before let her fingers trace its rough texture. She liked the feel of the rusty iron bubbling through the thick paint. The tiny holes had sharp edges, and despite the heat, the slick, mottled gloss was as cold as a slab of ice. It struck her that the metal was disintegrating. The bridge wasn't as solid as it appeared. If she moved slowly enough, she might step into a void.

At the far side of the river, she continued on the road, then dropped down onto a path that led through a thicket of birch trees into a field that was lying fallow. She walked listlessly, and the sun baked her through her dress. She stared at the rocky path at her feet, but her thoughts were elsewhere. She didn't look up until she was in the shadow of an old plaster barn. Catching sight of a boy dressed in clothing handed down from his older brother, she smiled, but the expression fled just as quickly. She hesitated, then took a few more steps, keeping herself hidden beside the barn.

Julian was lanky, as thin as a rail. He was about half a year younger than Polina, but already he was a few inches taller. This was a new development. Last summer, when they had played — which they often did, since they were neighbors and it was convenient for one of their mothers to look after both of them — Polina had hardly noticed him. His nose had always been runny, his hands were always dirty, his shirts had holes, he kept his pants up with a rope belt. She had begged her mother not to let him into the house. Now Polina found herself thinking about him even when he wasn't there. When she was close to him, she liked to stand on her toes to see if she could still match his height. Since he had become taller, his shaggy black hair had thickened, and she had noticed his eyes, his white skin, his too-red lips. At night sometimes she fell asleep wondering if he was thinking about her, too. She approached him slowly. His back was turned toward her, and he didn't hear her footsteps. In front of him, the chickens squawked.

Polina leaned into the wall of the barn. Bits of white plaster crumbled onto her bare shoulder like flour. She grasped a piece of embedded wood and squeezed until tiny splinters pierced her fingertips. Ten feet from her, crouched behind a fence post, Julian scooped up a handful of rocks, chose a black shard of flint, then took aim at the captive birds. Polina understood his intention, but when he raised his arm then jerked his wrist and sent the sharp stone hurtling into the coop, she gasped anyway. The missile struck the rooster, and when the rooster lifted its wings, a couple of feathers floated through the dusty air. It let out a shriek, leaped across the hard ground, pecked one of the hens — as if the hen had been the cause of its injury. When the rooster settled back down, Polina could see that the rock had left a gap in its feathers. A sliver of skin was showing, red with a trickle of blood. Julian was already weighing the next rock in his hand, getting set to whip it at the helpless bird.

Polina didn't think to shout. She bounded from the shadows, closed the distance to the boy, grabbed his arm before he could fling the stone.

"Hey!" Julian twisted around as if old Farmer Madeja, to whom these chickens belonged, had caught him in the act. His expression went from startled to terrified to flustered in the space of a second. "Hey," he said, more softly. "What are you doing?"

"What are *you* doing?" Polina asked him, without any pause.

Julian returned her gaze. He noticed how pale her eyes were. His own were bright. Their surface was as wet, Polina thought, as if he had been crying.

"Look at his wing," she said finally.

Julian didn't budge.

"*Look* at his wing," Polina said again. This time, she let go of her doll and grabbed hold of Julian's face and tried to twist him toward the coop.

"Stop it," he protested. Her fingers dug into his skin.

"Look," she insisted, "and I'll let go."

Julian capitulated, and Polina took her fingers away.

"You cut him," she said. "You made him bleed."

"He was hurting her."

"What?"

"The rooster," Julian repeated. "He was hurting her."

But Polina didn't hear him. The memory of her uncle Czeslaw's hands on her rib cage, lifting her, overcame her. She had left her house — earlier today, only one or two hours before — and she had started down the road to find Julian at the barn, as they had agreed. Her uncle had ridden up behind her on his bicycle and asked her to climb onto the bike behind him. She hadn't wanted to, but she hadn't resisted when he hoisted her up. As lithe as she was, she was too heavy to be carried like a child. The steel rack behind his seat gouged her skin. She hated the feeling of his waist beneath her fingers, but she didn't have any choice. If she didn't hold on to him while he was pedaling, she would have fallen. The cobblestones became a blur below the tires. They crossed the bridge, then wound through the streets on the other side of the river to the apartment where Czeslaw lived with his wife and two ugly sons. Her uncle squeezed her neck as he led her up the stairs. The rancid smell of dirty laundry assaulted her. The light had been dim. Czeslaw brought her through the kitchen into the bedroom where he and her aunt slept together on a mattress on the floor. She had never been in this room before, and it felt foreign to her, as if she had entered a different apartment altogether, one that didn't belong to this same city she knew as her home. There was a doll lying on the mattress that caught Polina's eye.

After that, the next thing Polina could remember was Czeslaw sitting in a wobbly chair beside the mattress, pulling on his shoes. He pointed at the doll, which was now on the floor. It had a face made of china, hair cut from a horse's tail, a body stitched together in silk, stuffed with cotton. When she didn't move, he picked it up, shoved it into her arms. *It's for you*, he told her. *Don't you want it? It's a little girl. See? Just like you are.* Then he had lifted the doll's red dress to show her the fabric body underneath, and his laughter had made her shiver. Beneath the dress, the doll's torso and legs had the clumsy shape of a cow udder.

"He was trapping one of the chickens against the fence," Julian said.

"What?" she managed.

Julian liked the way her lip stretched taut over her chipped tooth and uneven bite. The incisors on either side of her front teeth jutted into the skin, turning her upper lip white. It reminded him of Polina as he remembered her years before, with one front tooth missing, the other not yet fully developed. "He was pecking at her. Look."

She followed his finger to one of the hens at the far side of the coop. Its head and neck were bald of feathers where it had been attacked.

"He was going to kill her. If I didn't throw the rock, he would have eaten her, I think." Julian was still gripping the second rock. He had made his point to Polina. He lifted his arm again, took aim.

"Don't," she said.

Julian squinted at his friend. Hadn't she heard him? "He needs to learn his lesson," he said.

Polina shook her head. "Just don't," she said. "I don't care what he's done. Just don't hurt him anymore."

Julian let the rock slip from his hand. It landed on the hard, dry earth at their feet with a quiet thud. He fingered a small object in his pocket. "I was going to give you something," he said. "Now I don't want to."

"What is it?"

Julian tightened his fingers around the smooth chunk of raw amethyst at the bottom of his pocket. "I found it in the river this morning," he said. When he drew out his hand, the worn stone caught the sunlight like a jewel.

Polina took it carefully from his palm. She didn't thank him for the gift, but just slid it into her own pocket.

"I thought maybe you would want to keep it," Julian said.

Realizing that she had dropped the doll, Polina snatched it up by its arm.

"What's that?" Julian asked her.

Polina didn't answer.

"You're too old to play with dolls," Julian said.

"I'm going to call her Polina," Polina said.

"She doesn't look anything like you."

Polina shrugged. "She doesn't cry," she explained. "Neither do I."

■ ■ ■

That same night, Polina couldn't sleep. The smell of cigars climbed the stairs. Her father's voice shook the walls of the small house. Polina liked the sound, because it comforted her and she could picture his face and his eyes with the cadence of his words. An hour before, as the family was finishing dinner, Czeslaw had knocked on the door with a bottle of vodka, store-bought and unopened, and after he and his younger brother swallowed a few shots, he had pulled a box of cigars from his pocket, too. At the kitchen table, Polina had gone so quiet that her mother asked what had come over her. Her father grabbed her cheek between his index and middle fingers and gave her skin a soft twist. After so much sun earlier in the day, the gesture had lost its tenderness. Her skin felt chafed. *Ahhh, leave her alone, Ania. She just doesn't like to see her father drink. That's it, isn't it, sweetheart?* His eyes fastened upon her. *You don't like to see me drink and laugh and enjoy the company of my brother?* Polina didn't answer. *Here,* he said to her. *Why don't you help me with this splinter?* He held up a hand and showed her a long, thin sliver of wood that ran half the length of his finger beneath a thick layer of skin. *I can't reach this one myself—I need your little fingers.* She stared beyond the hand into her father's eyes. Then she ran from the kitchen, up the steep staircase to the small room she shared with her sister.

Through the walls, she heard her uncle's voice. *She's a strange girl, I think. When she's quiet, you can't really imagine what she's thinking.* Then her mother's. *She keeps her own company most of the time. Except for Julian. She doesn't even play with Adelajda.* Now, the rumbles through the walls had become less distinct. Polina listened with her eyes open, staring at the ceiling through the gray air, aware of her baby sister's shallow breathing in pockets of silence.

After some time passed, she slipped from beneath her covers and climbed into bed with Adelajda. Her sister was only five — there was nearly a decade between them, and Polina had little natural affection for her — but, suddenly, she wanted to be next to her. In her sleep, Adelajda shifted on the mattress, dropped an arm onto Polina's shoulder. Her hand squeezed her biceps, twitched. Her skin was damp with sweat. Polina lay still, concentrated on the feeling of her sister's fingers on her arm, listened for her father's voice, tried but wasn't able to figure out what he was saying.

When she finally closed her eyes, she was already asleep. She didn't wake when the front door slammed and her uncle stumbled out of the house into the unlit street. A few minutes later, her arm slid off the side of the narrow bed. Her fingers grazed the floor, but still she didn't wake.

December 1939.

The snow fell in flurries. At noon the sky was so dark that Polina thought that it was night. She sat beside the window in the kitchen and stared outside at the white blanket settling over the courtyard behind the house. A fire smoldered in the stove, remnants of the coal her father had lit at dawn.

Polina's mother was on her knees in the bathroom, scrubbing the floor. Her hair, covered in a kerchief, was coming loose from the bun, and she tucked a long strand behind her ear, then continued with her work. She was the firstborn child of a rabbi in Warsaw, but Ania Rabinowitz Dabrowa wasn't a practicing Jew. Outside the family, no one knew of her ancestry. Polina's father was Catholic, and that is how Polina had been raised. Her mother had never wanted to make things difficult for Aleksy, even before the occupation. She had fair skin and blue eyes, blond hair. There was no reason for anyone to know that her family was Jewish. When Aleksy was working and the Dabrowas had money enough for meat, Ania made a point of going to the butcher herself to buy pork. This morning, although there was nothing for Polina at midday, they had eaten well, and the air was still smoky, sweet with the smell of bacon grease from breakfast.

Polina listened to the scrape of the brush on the floor in the bathroom. She knew that she should be helping with the chores, but she had other things on her mind. Her mother had forbidden her to leave the house — it was cold, and she didn't have gloves — but, beyond the icy glass, the snow looked as soft and inviting as a thick layer of sugar. It was difficult for Polina to resist. When she caught sight of Julian, traipsing across the courtyard in his thin jacket, she made up her mind. She slipped into her coat, grabbed her mother's scarf, and, careful to latch the door behind her, ran to catch up to her friend.

"Which way are you walking?" she asked him, when she joined him at the side of the small house. The snow was deeper than Polina had imagined, and Julian was hugging the building under the eaves to avoid the deepest drifts.

He glanced at her without acknowledging her. Since his father had disappeared in September, he had become somber — this was only three months before — but he was still glad for her company. He shrugged. He was half a foot taller now than the adolescent girl next to him, and his coat was too small for him and his shoulders poked through the material like sharp branches. He had aged years, it seemed, since his father had gone. "Into town," he said.

"Why?"

"The market's today." His lips were even more red than they usually were. Polina had the impression that they possessed the only piece of color in the otherwise gray day. Even the tile roofs had turned to charcoal. "Anyway, my brother was picked up this morning to work on the road. I thought maybe I could find him."

"Are you going to help him?"

"Don't ask so many questions."

When Polina slipped, Julian grabbed hold of her arm, then held on to her until she found her balance again. The cobblestones were icy. Polina thanked him with a smile, but he didn't return it. She felt suddenly young next to him, even though she was older. She focused on the path in front of them. She didn't want to lose her footing a second time. In the distance, the rigid edges of the bridge emerged from the fuzzy whiteness like a shadow.

The snow had stopped falling and the sky had cleared a little by the time they reached the center of town. It was market day, but with supplies diverted to the German army, the square wasn't as busy as it usually was. Farmers with vegetables and staples had sold out their stock early, and most had already taken their carts and headed home. The merchants who remained were hawking wares no one wanted — the dregs of the harvest or cuts of meat that few could afford. A group of German soldiers stood huddled on one side of the square, smoking cigarettes, stamping their heavy boots, glancing at the Polish villagers. The tips of their rifles, strapped over their shoulders, poked above their heads like the strings of a marionette. As oppressive as the occupation was, Polina was barely aware of it. After the fighting had stopped, life had settled back into a routine. It wasn't the same as it had been, of course. From time to time, the family was woken by gunfire, and they didn't eat like they used to. Her father spent most days at home, her mother's face had become gaunt. But Polina was too young to appreciate the deeper effects of the changes, and she had seldom seen German soldiers up close. She stopped at the far edge of the square, grabbed Julian's arm. Even from this distance, she could see how foreign they were. They didn't belong here. Julian gawked at them, too. The two children stood still so long that their toes began to freeze.

"Come on," Julian said.

"Where are you going?"

"I'm hungry."

Julian slowed when they reached the first stalls. The farmers eyed the young boy and girl suspiciously. *Flour and spice*, one of the merchants said. *Meat, I've got meat, I've got pork, I've got sausage, I've got meat*, another repeated. The children paused to watch a woman in a heavy skirt and wool shawl haggle with a man for a large roll of orange fabric, then zigzagged through the stalls toward the center where there were more people. A fire was burning in a large steel drum, and smoke rose above the crowd in a dark, greasy plume. Its heat warmed their faces. *Bread and pastries, bread and cookies, bread and pastries.*

"Do you have any coins?" Polina asked.

Julian didn't answer. His eyes were focused on a cart that was nearly empty, except for a few soggy loaves of bread. The red cloth the baker had spread underneath had gotten wet in the snow, and it was covered with a sludge of crumbs and flour.

"I wish I had a grosz that I could give you," she said.

Julian was jostled backward. He had walked right into someone — his attention had been fastened on the scraps of bread. Polina hadn't seen the man either. He was wiry, barely taller than Julian, an elderly man with gray hair, dressed in a black jacket. Polina noticed the armband on his biceps first — the yellow Star of David — then his long, unkempt beard. His hands were like talons. He grabbed hold of Julian, gave him a shake. "Watch where you're going, eh?"

Julian pulled himself from the man's grip, then gave him a shove. The man slipped and nearly fell, but when he recovered himself, he didn't say anything more. He simply stared at Julian, and Julian looked back at him. Polina didn't breathe again until the old man finally let Julian alone and started back on his way through the crowd.

"Meet me in front of the school," Julian said.

"What?"

Julian didn't wait for Polina to understand. He squinted at the baker, made certain that his attention was focused elsewhere. Then he darted to the cart, grabbed whatever he could fit into his hands, and bounded off in the other direction. By the time the baker realized what had happened, Julian was already gone. Polina watched him disappear behind a line of stalls as the baker's voice rose into a shout. *Hey, you there, hey!* Worried that the commotion would attract their attention, she turned toward the soldiers, but they were laughing obliviously, engulfed in a cloud of steam and smoke. The baker, who had taken a few steps in pursuit, returned to his cart, and Polina started across town in the direction of the school.

When she reached the plaza in front of the schoolhouse, Julian was seated on a short flight of stairs in the building's shadow. A sliver of blue emerged between heavy clouds, and for a few brief seconds the streetscape was impossibly bright. Against the white backdrop, Julian's long and thin, hunched form stood out like a dab of paint on a blank canvas. His hands were cupped in front of his face, and he was blowing steam onto his fingers. As Polina approached, she realized that he was still holding the stolen bread in his lap, waiting for her. She didn't say anything. She simply took a small, soggy loaf from him, then sat down on the steps next to him and ate. The snow melted beneath her, wetting her skirt. She wiped her nose with her sleeve. Her fingers were nearly as red as Julian's lips.

Afterward, the two children lay in the snow and made snow angels. Polina hadn't expected Julian to join her. It had been some time since he had shown any interest in the games they used to play. Today, though, he had been hungry — it had been twenty-four hours since his last meal — and the food put him in a better mood. The bread hit his stomach like something sharp, but within minutes he felt almost giddy. He lay his head backward into the snow, looked up into the tissue sky, lifted his arms and legs. Lying next to him, Polina pretended to make an angel of her own, when really she was gathering a ball of snow. She sat up quickly and was about to throw it at him, when he stopped her with a question.

"So *now* it's okay for us to throw things?"

Polina smiled, because she knew that Julian was remembering that day, more than a year before, when they were standing in front of Farmer Madeja's chicken coop. "Well," she said, "this isn't a stone — it's only a piece of frozen air. And anyway, you're not a rooster."

Julian smiled as well. It was rare for him to win an argument with Polina. Then he rolled over and grabbed her arms. "No?" he asked her, looking into her eyes. "Aren't I?" The snowball she had made got crushed between them, and it disintegrated into powder.

Polina fought, but gave up when she couldn't move him off her. "No," she said, "you're not. At least not a terrible one."

This made Julian giggle, and he shoved her backward into the snow. Polina pulled him on top of her again. His eyes darkened as he hovered above her. She would have kissed him, perhaps, but he hesitated too long, and she let him roll off her onto his back. The two children lay still, their fingers touching. Above them, the sky opened up, and the crack between the clouds was so bright that Polina had to squint. Julian had stopped laughing. And in the aftermath of their brief tussle, Polina was aware of the rasp of his breath, and then of how quiet Kraków had become.

■ ■ ■

It was snowing again by the time they crossed the bridge on their way home. The sky had become dark, and Polina was pensive. When her parents saw how cold and wet she was, they would be upset. Julian, too, had fallen silent. After turning off the main road onto their street, they marched through the snow and ice without speaking, their eyes trained on the ground in front of them.

When they were just half a block from their houses, a single, sharp report echoed up the canyon between the buildings. Polina's first thought was that it was a gunshot, and she froze in place. Only in retrospect did the sound distinguish itself into the slam of a wooden door.

"Is that your mother?"

The wind was gusting, and the snow was blinding her, but Polina followed Julian's eyes. A woman, half naked — wearing a skirt Polina recognized, her shirt ripped and pulled down to her waist — stood uncertainly in the middle of the street. Her breasts were exposed. Her nipples stood out crisply, pinched by the cold into two tight, red circles. It took Polina a few seconds to comprehend the image. But Julian was correct. This was her mother. Polina reached for Julian's arm. Something kept her rooted to the icy street.

"What is she doing?" Julian asked. "Why is she standing in the road?"

The jagged tip of Polina's chipped tooth dug into the flesh of her lower lip. She blinked back tears as sharp as shards of glass. *Are we dreaming?*

Julian took a step forward, then stopped. "Who's that?" The mist was thick, and the snow was falling in a blizzard now. Behind Ania Dabrowa, the fuzzy outline of a man in a long coat emerged from the gloom, and then another and another.

"Mama," Polina whispered.

Ania pulled her shirt back up to cover her breasts, but the fabric was torn, and it slid off her shoulders again. She was more concerned with this than with the men taking shape beside her. She gathered the remains of the shirt, held it in place at her neck.

The heavy crunch of the soldiers' footsteps reverberated down the street. One of the soldiers — a man who wore a mustache like the Führer's and whose cheeks were black with stubble as thick as soot — grabbed hold of Ania's shirt and yanked it back down to her waist. He did this with a smile. A cigarette dangled from his lips, his rifle swung loose behind his arm. He twisted around for his comrades' approval, and they gave it to him. One of them shouted a word Polina couldn't decipher. Another whistled.

"Mama," Polina whispered again. Her voice was barely more than a hiss. Somehow, though, her mother heard it, and across the distance that separated them, their eyes met. Polina took a step forward. The soldier was fingering her mother's chin. Smoke from his cigarette was mixing with the mist, like a tincture of blood dropped into a glass of water. There was hair on his knuckles — black hair that Polina could see through the snow. His fingernails were as yellow as wax. She took another step, but her mother shook her head — no! — and Polina stopped. Ania wouldn't let go of her daughter's eyes. She was determined not to let Polina approach.

And then, from behind her mother, Polina heard her sister crying. She tracked the sound. Her sister's small body, writhing helplessly, was clasped in the arms of one of the soldiers. "Adelajda," Polina whispered.

Julian drew a sharp breath and held it. His fingers found Polina's shoulder. He wanted to shout, but he had no voice. Why wasn't Polina doing something? This was her mother. This was her sister. These soldiers were taking them.

The wind gusted, and in front of the two children the snow and mist began to clear. A transport truck parked against the row of houses lifted itself from the shadows, and in the same moment Polina became aware of voices. It struck her that she had been hearing them for some time now. Women crying, children sobbing, a man chanting prayers. The truck's engine turned over, and the large machine vibrated. In the cage behind the cab, through gaps in the wagon's sides, Polina glimpsed fingers and hands. A child's face was pressed into a crack — she could see a nose and a mouth and a wisp of hair.

The soldier twisted Ania around, then shoved her toward the rear of the truck. Adelajda screamed, and the other soldier extended his arms and carried her, kicking and struggling, behind the truck as well.

Julian, his mind made up, let go of Polina's shoulder, then — without any thought for the consequences — started running down the street toward the soldiers.

Polina watched him slide, catch himself, then trip through the snow, picking up speed as he ran. She shouted for him to stop. But he kept running. One of the soldiers turned at the sound of the approaching footsteps. His hand flew quickly to his gun, and he whipped it from the holster. "No!" Polina shouted. And then she began to run, too. "Julian — please — *Julian* — no!"

Julian reached the soldier before the man was able to aim his weapon. Clutching the pistol in his fist, clenching his jaw shut with a grimace, the soldier swung the steel butt across Julian's face like a club. Julian collapsed at his feet, unconscious. The snow beside his face turned as red as his lips.

Mama, Julian, Adelajda. Mama, Julian, Adelajda. As Polina ran, the three names resounded in her head like a heartbeat. The soldier's knuckles were splattered with Julian's blood. Everything else was out of focus. In the confusion of the moment, she didn't see the shadows shift in the doorway next to her, and before she could reach the soldier — before she could go any farther to help Julian or to rescue her mother and her sister — she was caught in someone's arms, yanked backward off the street. She fought blindly, but the man holding her was too strong, and he kept her pinned. When she realized that it was her father, she wanted to shout. *Papa!* He stopped her, though, with a hand over her mouth.

"Shhh," he said. "Shhh."

With her eyes, she pleaded with him to let her go. His hand, clamped over her nose and mouth, choked her, and she couldn't breathe. She grabbed his wrists and tried to free herself.

"Shhh," he said. "Polina — shhh." He held her even tighter. His eyes narrowed, and she read his fear. "There's nothing you can do, do you understand?"

She shook her head, squirmed.

"You belong to Czeslaw now, Polina."

She was suffocating. She tried to suck air through his fingers. Then she surrendered. Her body relaxed. Her father held her up, forced her to look at him.

"Do you understand, Polina? You can't be my daughter anymore. Listen to me, Polina. *Listen.* You can't have anything to do with me or your mother. Understand? You belong to Czeslaw."

Next to them, Polina saw her uncle, hidden in the shadows. His eyes were glowing like embers.

"*Understand?*"

When her father took his hand off her mouth, Polina didn't speak. She remained still, staring at her father.

"Good," her father said. Then he touched her cheek and raised his mouth in what should have been a smile. And then he let her go. Without more, he took a step out from the doorway and started walking down the street toward the soldiers.

"Papa," she said, but he didn't hear her.

When the soldier who had clubbed Julian pointed his pistol at him, her father stopped and raised his arms. The soldier shouted, and her father nodded at the truck. "My wife," he said. He gestured so that the soldier would understand — his hands over his heart, a finger pointed at the rear of the truck, where Ania had disappeared. "My wife," he repeated. He held his arms against his chest in the shape of a cradle. "My daughter." The soldier waited while the Pole approached, then grabbed him by the neck and shoved him toward the other prisoners. In the road, Julian was trying to raise himself onto his knees. Blood was still flowing from his forehead, but the soldiers left him alone. Polina watched her father climb up behind her mother and Adelajda, into the waiting cage. He had disappeared before she realized that Czeslaw's hands were on her shoulders. Her uncle's grip tightened. He pulled her backward until the shadows had swallowed them completely, and she let him.

January 1940.

It was after midnight. In the sitting room of Czeslaw's apartment, Polina's cousins were asleep on the cold floor. In the narrow bedroom behind the kitchen, her uncle was snoring. The sounds of lovemaking — the rustle of blankets on the hard mattress, her uncle's truncated grunts, her aunt's gasps — had long since quieted. In the kitchen, the cast-iron stove ticked as it cooled. The air was close with the smell of cheap tobacco and her aunt's horrible cooking — a veiny stew that had been simmering for more than a few days now. Polina lay in the hallway on a roll of blankets, her eyes wide open. As tired as she was, it wasn't difficult to keep herself awake. In the last few weeks, it had been impossible for her to sleep. She waited as long as she could. Then, when she was certain that no one would hear, she sat up and gathered her things. She didn't possess much — only the few pieces of clothing they had been able to recover from her house. She placed the doll her uncle had given her on her pillow, then stood from her makeshift bed as quietly as she could. She was already dressed — in preparation for her escape, she had even worn her coat to bed — so all she had to do was sneak from the apartment without knocking into anything or stepping on one of her cousins' hands. She let herself out the front door, then, when nothing moved inside, started down the stairs, running faster and faster the closer she got to the bottom.

Outside, the wind whipped fiercely through her clothes, but she hardly noticed the cold. She felt nothing but relief. She had the sense that she was breathing for the first time since the afternoon when her family had been stolen from her. She buried her hands into her small bundle of belongings, then set out in the direction of Julian's house. There was no moon, and the streets were dark. She walked in the center of the road until her eyes adjusted, then slipped into the shadows and meandered through the village toward the river.

As she crossed the bridge, the wind blew even harder. She bent her head down, but the cold bit her cheeks anyway. She closed her eyes and stopped, took a deep breath, then started forward again. Her toes had lost feeling, and she was having trouble with her balance. The blood was thickening in her veins. When the wind gusted, her vision blurred. She fastened on a memory of Julian's face, and it was this that kept her moving forward.

She was almost across the bridge before she saw the patrol on the other side, and by then it was too late to run. Two men in long coats approached like specters. Even before they reached her, she knew that they were Germans. She could smell the wool of their uniforms, the sweet scent of the machine oil they used to lubricate their weapons. When they were standing directly in front of her, she saw nothing but their eyes. Then she collapsed. The next thing she knew she was lying on the backseat of a German automobile and the engine was buzzing in her ears, the car vibrating beneath her, and dim streetlamps were gliding past, illuminating the interior with their yellow glow. Disoriented, she focused on the pulsing profiles of the soldiers' faces in the front seat, consoling herself with the thought that they would take her wherever they had brought her mother and father and sister. No matter what, even if she was interned with them in a prison camp, this would be far better than another day inside her uncle's apartment.

But the soldiers didn't bring her to her family. Instead, they drove her to a building in the countryside where other women were being kept as well. The man who had been driving stepped from behind the wheel and yanked her from the rear seat and led her inside, to a small, dank room without windows. Time passed. The door opened and closed, opened and closed, and Polina forgot about the sun and even the moon and let the dark surround her.

The dark had the weight of water. It reminded Polina of a pond where she and Julian would sometimes swim. The water was so murky that it was impossible to see beneath the surface. It clung to her arms and legs like oil, and it had the flavor of leaves and honey. She closed her eyes and kicked her legs and stretched for Julian, and she wondered if she would ever reach the surface again.

3.

West Berlin. August 1969.

In a single room at a nondescript hotel in West Berlin, Angela sat on a narrow bed, her hands in her lap, her chin resting on her chest. Her eyes were closed. She wasn't praying, but she could have been. She was reliving the relief she had felt, a few hours earlier, when the engine rumbled back to life and the bus finally started to roll forward again. The large tires sank into potholes and crunched over gravel on the way out of the parking lot onto the road that led through the checkpoint into the West. Even now, the syncopated idle of the diesel engine continued to reverberate in her bones. When she opened her eyes, she took the furniture in — the gloss of weak light on the nicked surface of the shabby desk, the way the desk legs rested on the nylon carpet — and wondered at the opulence of her country. The war, as distant as it felt here in this new world she inhabited, had entombed half her country in its wake. Behind the Iron Curtain, the citizens of East Berlin lived beneath the weight of so much oppression. The most common things — the basic accoutrements she took for granted — for them were luxuries. She had the sense that she had left her aunt far in the past, not merely a few miles behind her.

She stood from the bed and crossed to the window. The blackout shades were open, and she pulled back the sheer polyester privacy drape, too. A streetcar was sliding past four floors below. The metallic screech of its wheels on the tracks was muffled through the glass. She watched it round the corner out of view, then, remembering the necklace, slipped a finger under the platinum chain and lifted the sapphire pendant from her neck, examined it in the fading afternoon light. Over time, the setting had been damaged, bent, but the stones remained in place. A ring of diamonds formed a fiery circle around the edge. In their center, a large, pale sapphire glimmered, cut into a geometry of sharp facets. The priceless piece of jewelry confounded her as much as it thrilled her. Where had her father gotten it?

Inside the apartment in East Berlin the night before, Martina Bloch had led her into a dark utility room behind the kitchen, where the odor of rust and mildew had been thick enough to taste on her tongue. The plaster on the walls, saturated with steam from the unventilated stove, was as tawny as parchment. When her aunt bent down, Angela could count the vertebrae of her spine through the thinning fabric of her sweater. The old woman pushed aside a broom whose bristles were tangled with cobwebs, a pair of worn shoes, a pile of clothing that needed mending, then grabbed hold of a small cardboard box, pulled it free from the clutter. *Why don't you carry that into the kitchen, would you, dear?* Angela set the box on the kitchen table, waited while the stooped woman struggled with the flaps. The cardboard was beginning to disintegrate. Martina lifted an antique envelope from the shadows, and an object slid against the thick paper with the telltale slither of finely worked gold. The pendant and chain slipped into the old woman's hand. In the dim, incandescent light, the stones had sparkled with the brilliance of a flame. *This was sent to us after your father's — after your father was killed. It's very valuable, I think. Here, let me put it around your neck — that is the best way for you to take it across the border, like something you have always owned.* Around her neck, the platinum chain had seared then chilled Angela's skin.

Angela refastened the clasp beneath her chin and turned her attention to the violin case resting on the desk. She twisted the old-fashioned locks sideways, lifted its hard, shiny leather lid. The cool light from the window hovered above the polished wood of the instrument. This was an illusion, a trick caused by the parabolic curvature of the plate. The familiar smells of linseed oil and resin wafted into the room. The D string had broken in concert the night before. Had that been just yesterday? She gripped the neck of the violin that had been handed down to her when she was a child. Its heft was so familiar that she barely realized she was holding it. She twisted it out of the velvet, set it down on the desk. The strings resonated off-key, the snapped wire scraped the desk top. Her eyes settled on a sheaf of photographs hidden in the well of the case.

Her aunt's hands had been stained with age spots. The old woman's papery skin had stretched taut on her tendons as she grasped the photographs and worked them out of the box where they had lain hidden with the pendant for a quarter century. *These were taken by your father. During the war. That is how he avoided combat. He was a photographer — this you know already — decorated. Some of these are very good. They belong in a museum. Well, they belong to you now.* When Martina passed her the photographs, the old woman's fingertips had been icy, as if she had drawn her hands from snow.

Angela could barely remember her father. The last time she had seen him, she had been nine years old. What she remembered most strongly was his uniform — in her mind almost exactly the same green wool uniform the border patrolman had been wearing earlier today. The sweet odor of tobacco drifted back to her, so powerfully that she swiveled toward the door, to make certain that she was still alone. *Hermann Schmidt.* A fuzzy image flitted through her head of a blond-haired man with pale skin and translucent eyes, a nervous smile, perfectly clean spectacles. She flinched, remembering the feeling of his fingers on her cheeks, on her shoulders, in her hair, when she ran into his arms. *Daddy.* Standing in front of her aunt, lifting the photographs out of her cold hands, she had caught a glimpse of this man in his sister's face, and then she hadn't been able to hold on to the recollection any longer. *Daddy, Papa.*

The edges of the photographs dug sharply into her fingers. There must have been fifty of them. Somehow, her father had managed to deliver them to his sister, and Martina had kept them hidden all these years, secreted among her own belongings. Angela hadn't had time to look at them the night before. She brought them with her to the bed, sat back down, straightened them on her lap. The light was growing darker, but she didn't want to stand again to switch on the lamp.

The picture on top was dusty, grainy. The scene was inconsequential — a battlefield in the morning. A group of soldiers stood in a cluster next to a truck, distant, out of focus. She examined the photograph for a meaning, then lifted it off the pile, set it beside her on the bed. The next shot framed the same scene. Now, though, in the foreground, a young soldier lay in the dirt, a corpse. Half of his face was gone, and what remained was a pulp made black by the rudimentary chemicals of the old film. The stark contrast with the first photograph unnerved her. Had her father set the sequence up deliberately?

Farther down in the pile were a series of pictures taken in a concentration camp. The images were very nearly unreal. Jews herded into filthy barracks, dressed in rags stained with excrement. Behind bars, men so malnourished that their eyes seemed to plead not for mercy but for death. Children forced into labor. Well-fed soldiers smoking and playing cards in the midst of this unimaginable suffering. Angela lingered over the first few, then paged through the rest more quickly. A dull ache was beginning to cramp her stomach.

She stopped short when she reached a picture of a man in uniform, framed in a mirror, striking an oddly formal pose. "Daddy," she said out loud.

She lifted the photograph from the others. This one was developed on different paper. Most of the others had been matte. This photograph was heavier, shiny. Her own reflection floated on its surface next to her father's face. She held it toward the window, tilted it slightly to keep the refracted light from blocking her view, studied this man's strange but also familiar expression. As she remembered him, his mouth was tense, his lips were white, raised in a forced smile. Behind his spectacles, his eyes were lined with deep creases. The camera on a tripod next to him was nearly as tall as he was. He held a shutter-release cable in his right hand. His left was tucked smartly into his jacket pocket. Angela noticed the steel cross hanging from a ribbon looped through a buttonhole at the center of his chest. Had this been a proud moment for him? She couldn't tell, not from his demeanor. She took her time, then flipped the picture over, began to consider the next one.

Her heart wasn't in this exercise any longer, though, and she barely understood the scramble of pixels that described the burning shell of a factory in some northern European city.

As she reached the end of the pile, something continued to nag her. And then it struck her — the photograph of her father in the mirror was too heavy for a single sheet of photographic paper. Now that she had become accustomed to the weight of these photographs, she knew that this was true. Her posture stiffened. She found the photograph again, examined its edge. A second photograph was in fact stuck to the first, as if the two sheets had been set down together when they were still wet. She slid her nail between the sharp edges.

The second photograph didn't want to come unglued. Angela wasn't certain why — after all, this entire pile of photographs shared the same mystery — but her pulse had begun to quicken. She pried the two sheets apart, and at last they separated with a slight rip. The smell of acetic acid filled her nose. Her eyes sank into the texture of the forgotten picture underneath like fingers dipped into the cohesive surface of a still pond. At first, she was so overwhelmed by the sensuality of the photograph itself that she didn't see the image it captured. And then she brought the frozen saturation of dyes into focus.

Angela blinked. Tears blinded her. Embers lodged in her lashes. Staring back at her was the most arresting girl she had ever seen.

Reflecting on this moment later, as she often did, Angela wasn't able to explain the intensity of her reaction. What she would remember was the way the photograph assembled itself in front of her, piece by piece. Even in black-and-white, the girl's eyes were a nearly colorless shade of blue. Her hair was amber, her skin ivory. The symmetry of her nose was marred by a barely perceptible twist — perhaps it had been broken. She was biting her lower lip. One of her front teeth was slightly chipped. And then there was her long neck, and then her naked shoulders. She was covering her breasts with a forearm. Enough of her slender frame was visible, though, for Angela to appreciate how young she was — seventeen years old, sixteen? Her other hand held up a torn skirt. Her ribs were bruised. Slowly, the greasy marks on the girl's neck, on her shoulders, distinguished themselves into fingerprints.

Angela turned the photograph over. In pencil on the back, so faded that the scrawl was nearly gone, she read a name she hadn't noticed before. *Polina.* Angela didn't possess many things from her father. Her mother had left her some letters, though, and this was handwriting that she recognized. Her father had written with flourish. The corner of the photograph cut into her palm. She lifted it, weighed it, measured it as a physical object, turned it back over.

When she looked at the image again, some of its initial luster was already gone. Exposed to the air, the finish was relinquishing its vitality. But the girl inside continued to stare back at her with the same loss and the same defiance, and with the same profound beauty. As Angela looked closer, the background behind the girl began to take shape, and the opaque edge of a long mirror drew itself from the softer shadows. It came as a small shock to her when she realized that Polina was standing half naked in the same room where her father had shot his self-portrait.

When the gray plastic phone on the nightstand rang, Angela jumped. She touched her heart with her fingers. Then she picked up the heavy receiver and spoke to her husband. "Lutz," she said. "Lutz." And then she closed her mouth and her eyes and waited for the reassurance of his voice over the long-distance wire.

FREDRIK

4.

Jutland, Denmark. November 1941.

A tall farmhand stood alone in a harrowed field, contemplating the earth at his feet. The wind was howling, blowing from the east. Rain wasn't falling yet, but the sky was low. Drizzle hung like gauze in the air, then whipped sideways in horizontal sheets in the stronger gusts. It peppered the farmhand's face, swamped his left ear, stung his eyes. But he hardly noticed. The earth was soaked in blood. He lowered himself into a squat, lifted a clump of dirt from a furrow. Its tilled edge was as smooth as if it had been cleaved from a diamond. Squinting, he studied the bloody soil, then scanned the barren field for signs of a wounded animal. When he dropped the clod, a broken barley stalk scraped his fingers. He wiped his hands on his thick wool trousers. The blood was fresh — the wounded animal couldn't be far. Fredrik hoped that it wasn't one of the Nielsens' pigs, but he already knew that it was.

He patted the Luger in his pocket, set out over the dale toward the copse on the southern border of the farm. The rich land undulated in front of him like the swells of an ocean, steel gray, petrified into obsidian. His boots dug into the hard mud beneath the weight of his long, lanky body. As lean as he had become in the year and a half since the war had reached Denmark, he was heavy. Isabella, his favorite whore in Aalborg, had laughed at him and told him that he was getting fat. She was an immigrant, from Italy, and he didn't understand her well. Still, he hadn't liked her laugh. His blackened fingers had clamped her mouth shut, and he hadn't let go until she bit him.

Five minutes passed without much change in the landscape, and then he was standing in the shadow of the thicket. The naked birch trees swayed in the wind like seaweed. Above him, the iron blades of a windmill completed a turn, then swung sideways when the storm shifted direction. The rusty mechanism whined. He shielded his eyes with a hand and, as he had come to do over the years, without thinking read the sky. At last, rain was beginning to fall. The squeal of the pig barely reached him over the rush of sleet and hail.

Sheltered beneath the eaves of a shed, the farmhand's dog lay poised like a lion, panting despite the cold. Its eyes were narrowed, trained on its prey. Washed scarlet in its own blood, the pig was still on its feet. It had reached the end of the property, seeking refuge in the trees. The fencing prevented it from straying any farther. Perhaps it sensed already that it was running out of time. Its heart was beginning to fibrillate. Its breathing had become shallow. When it raised its head, its face mimed a scream.

When Fredrik stepped into view, the pig glanced at him, then — still hungry in spite of its imminent death — went back to sniffing the ground as if the shepherd-collie weren't sitting a leap away. It shoved its snout beneath a particularly large clump of dirt. Blood leaked down its front legs. The dog didn't stand. But its muscles tensed as it readied itself for the kill.

"You don't want to do that, Bruno," Fredrik said. The dog's face twitched. Fredrik noticed the dried blood matting the fur around its mouth. "A chicken last week, now a pig," he growled. "You're not just hungry, Bruno, are you? You're enjoying this." He met its stare. "Or perhaps you just don't like it anymore when I tell you what to do? You don't like being a second-class citizen —" Reflexively, he raised his left hand and contemplated a series of faint scars on his knuckles — the type of scars one might expect to find on the knuckles of a man who, as a child, had been disciplined with a ruler. "Maybe someday someone will tell me what that means, eh?" When he returned his attention to the dog, his right hand strayed to the pistol in his pocket. He wasn't thinking about the scarcity of bullets or the proximity of the Nazi barracks on the road to Aalborg. Still, he left the weapon where it was. "I knew your mother, you ugly mutt. Your father could have been one of the Nielsens' sheepdogs. Or maybe the mongrel that belonged to the old man who lived in Sulsted. What was his name? The old sailor from Sulsted. He was captain of a schooner, just like *gamle* Karl — a pederast, too, same as *gamle* Karl."

The rumble of its master's voice didn't soothe the rogue dog. It lifted itself onto its front legs. Its eyes became vicious, shiny slits.

"Old man Karl —" Fredrik muttered, alighting upon a distant memory. "He was a bastard, a real bastard, did I ever tell you that story? He used to invite the younger boys upstairs to play with his model ships — boys too little to cut his flaccid pecker off and stuff it down his throat. I tried to tell my father, but he always treated me like a fool — he wouldn't listen —"

When the dog pounced, Fredrik read the fear in its eyes even before its feet left the ground, and he knew that the hesitation would cost the beast its life. He sidestepped, caught the dog by the neck. Its fangs gnashed, but before the dog was able to bite, the farmhand snapped its windpipe, hurled it to the ground, crushed its spine beneath his knee. The dog let out a strangulated yelp, then went limp. When Fredrik stood again, both he and the pig examined the carcass with the same dispassion.

"Too bad," Fredrik muttered. He was still catching his breath from the exertion of the brief fight. "You were a good dog to have around." Then he shrugged, turned his attention to the wounded pig. "Come on home now," he said to the pink animal. He recognized the jagged bite of the gash in its neck. He had seen the same markings in the broken skin of the fowl and foxes the dog brought into the house from time to time. He untied a rope looped around his waist. The cold wind nipped his hands.

When he approached the pig, it took an uncertain leap away from him. Perhaps the animal remembered the farmhand's rough fingers, the pinch of his huge, powerful thumbs. It lost its balance on the uneven ground, and its front legs folded. As if it wanted to pray, Fredrik thought. And this made him smile. Then he grabbed the pig by its neck. The rope whistled as he cinched it tight. The pig squealed.

"Get up," Fredrik said. "Or I'll kill you here. Understand?" He gave the rope a fast jerk.

The pig bleated but acquiesced. It followed him into the wind. Sleet pelted its face. It cried. Exactly like a baby cries. With every hobbling step, it expressed the pain that was shooting through its body. Fredrik understood — it was pleading with him. *You're going to kill me anyway, aren't you, farmhand?*

You have a gun in your pocket. Why don't you use it? Why don't you kill me now and let me die a more noble death? But Fredrik ignored the argument. As long as the pig had power enough to walk, he would take advantage of its strength. The animal could carry itself to the slaughterhouse. That was what all the animals did. If he killed the pig now, he would have to lug it back to the farmhouse, almost a mile away, over the crest of the hill. He gave the rope another sharp tug. The pig shrieked again.

"Hurry it up," Fredrik said. "You don't realize how cold it is out here when a man's coat gets wet." When they left the loose shelter of the copse, the wind grew stronger. His feet sank into the mud.

■ ■ ■

From a distance, over the knoll, Fredrik was able to see that they had a visitor. A black Citroën was parked in front of the cottage the Nielsens provided for him as the caretaker of their farm. Recognizing the car, he started forward more quickly. Amalia was at the Nielsens' house, where she helped with the sewing and cleaning. Normally, Oskar, eighteen years old, would have been outside, completing his chores, but he had woken this morning with another headache. So it would be yet one more day where seventeen-year-old Amalia would carry more weight than her older brother — and Oskar was the only one at home. Fredrik wondered what his son would say to Johan Jungmann in his absence. Oskar couldn't be trusted, not in a situation like this.

When he reached the cottage, Fredrik hitched the pig to the fence at the front, then climbed the stairs. The porch shook under his weight. He pushed open the door, and the rush of wind receded into whispers. His grandmother's elaborate clock — one of the few heirlooms that had followed him to Jutland in the years after his father had tossed him from the family's house in Copenhagen — ticked audibly from its station on the wall in the cramped sitting room. The fire had burned down to coals. Of course Oskar hadn't thought to stoke it with another log. Fredrik threw an angry glance at his son, who was standing at the stove in the kitchen, then pushed past Jungmann to the hearth without a greeting, as if he weren't there at all, chucked a couple of wood scraps onto the grate. They had torn one of the barns down the month before, and ever since they had had enough fuel to burn. Losing the second barn hadn't meant much to the farm, not since the Nazis had appropriated half their livestock at the end of August.

"I was just leaving," Jungmann said. He had been fastening his coat in the vestibule when Fredrik entered. His hat was already back on his head. "Your boy told me that I missed you."

"What else has he been telling you?" Fredrik demanded.

Jungmann removed the black homburg, revealing a balding pate. "He's a polite boy, Gregersen. Polite but tight-lipped."

"What have you been asking him, then?" Fredrik approached the smaller man. The front hall was narrow. When the councilman took a step in retreat, his coat scraped the wall. "You don't have any right to come inside. Not when I'm not home."

"You have something here you don't want me to find, Gregersen?"

Fredrik wiped his long nose with the back of his hand. His nostrils were running from the cold. He could still smell the pig's blood on his fingers. "The last time I saw you, you were sitting at dinner in the Café Albert, eating sausages and mustard with a bunch of Krauts. You were the only Dane at the table, but I still had the impression you were brothers."

"If I don't talk to them, they only make the rules without me."

Fredrik grunted.

"I don't expect you to like what I do."

"It surprises me," Fredrik said, "how much you seem to like it yourself."

The councilman considered the taller man through dark eyes. He had anticipated Fredrik's animosity, but the farm-hand's wit was a small revelation. "Perhaps you are harboring fugitives here —"

"I can smell my tea on your breath," Fredrik said. He swiveled to take a look into the kitchen. Oskar had left the stove and wandered into the doorway. He was tall like his father, but his shoulders were narrow. Fredrik scowled. The boy was so lanky that he wore his sweater like a dress. His chest was concave.

"I offered him a cup of tea," Oskar said. "He was sitting for fifteen minutes."

"Biscuits, too?"

Oskar shook his head.

Fredrik returned his attention to the councilman. "Fugitives? What do you mean, fugitives?"

"People have been crossing the border into Denmark."

"Jews," Fredrik said.

Again, Jungmann assessed the man in front of him. This wasn't a political house. This farmer didn't care a stitch for anyone, as far as he could tell not even his own two bastard children. Before this war broke out, he wouldn't have been able to tell a Jew from a Chinaman. "I hear things. There are refugees in Aalborg."

"And you think I might be harboring them? Here? In this little shack. With my son and my daughter already sharing a room, and me keeping warm with kindling I steal from the Nielsens —"

The councilman allowed himself a look around the modest cottage. "Anyway, that's not why I'm here."

Fredrik faced his son. "Put the kettle back on. You serve this commissar tea, and you don't have any ready for your father?"

Oskar's cheeks reddened. He shuffled into the kitchen again.

"What does bring you to my house today, then?" Fredrik demanded.

"There was a fire last night."

Fredrik's eyes dropped. He hadn't had anything to do with the arson, but he had smelled the smoke, and he had snuck down the road far enough to figure out what was burning. He could easily surmise what Jungmann thought.

"Not half a mile from here," the councilman continued. "Maybe you can tell me something about it?"

"I don't know what you're talking about," Fredrik said.

"You didn't notice the smoke?"

"All the way from Jepsen's warehouse?" Fredrik asked. "Anyway, I was asleep."

The councilman removed his glasses, polished the lenses with his sleeve. "I didn't mention Jepsen or his property, did I?"

Fredrik looked away from the man, barely able to contain himself. "What kind of ass do you take me for, Jungmann? You think I wouldn't look out my window?"

Jungmann took his time, returned his glasses to the bridge of his nose, fitted the gold temples around his ears. "You said you didn't know anything about it—"

"And what would you have me say?"

"The truth, perhaps? I know the company you keep, and I know what you and your friends think of Jepsen. There was enough grain in that warehouse to see the German garrison through the winter. And barely half a mile from here—"

He gave the air a sniff. "You know, Fredrik, I believe I can still smell the smoke."

"Do you really imagine," Fredrik asked, "that I would be fool enough to shit in my own bed?"

"Your son told me that you were out late last night."

Fredrik turned on the councilman. His arms were still loose at his sides, but his hands had tightened into fists. "I won't have you come into my house, Jungmann, and interview my son without me here."

"I thought maybe you would want to help us, Fredrik. The Gregersens are a respectable family." This was true, Jungmann was thinking — they were. But they had disowned Fredrik years ago. Everyone in Aalborg knew that they had. This rough farmhand, a Gregersen! He continued to bring shame upon an old and venerable Danish family, even exiled to the north of Jutland. Still, it was worthwhile to remind this ruffian where he came from. Perhaps he had some vestige of filial duty left, and in any event he had more to lose than just his own tiny cottage.

"Get out of my house." Fredrik's voice remained calm, but there was no mistaking his fury.

"You would be wise to talk to me," Jungmann insisted. "The resistance isn't an illusion. German soldiers are getting killed. The brass will ferret out any rats until they find them. This isn't something to play with, Fredrik —"

Fredrik grabbed Jungmann by the lapels of his coat. A single hand was large enough to cover the smaller man's chest. He reached for the door with his other hand, yanked it open, then propelled the councilman outside. An extra push sent him tumbling down the stairs. Jungmann sprawled in the mud next to the dying pig. "You have my answer."

Fredrik was about to slam the door when the councilman shouted back. "You have made a mistake, my friend."

Fredrik stopped, spit a wad of mucus off the porch, then dismissed Jungmann with a snort. Again, he was about to slam the door, but now the pig, on its last legs, caught his eye. He let go of the door, started down the stairs. Misunderstanding his purpose, Jungmann scrambled out of the mud as Fredrik approached. The ground was slippery, however, and before he could escape, he lost his footing once more and fell, his arms splayed wide. His glasses got lost, and he had to dig for them. Fredrik reached past him for the pig. His fingers plunged into the gash in the animal's throat. The dog had done most of his work. The pig squealed. Blood pumped onto the wet ground. Its front legs shook. Then the pig collapsed. The councilman pulled himself to his feet and slid to his car, as if he were skating on ice.

Fredrik didn't wait for the Citroën to disappear. He hoisted the carcass onto his shoulder and headed for the barn.

5.

At two a.m., there was a knock on the cottage door. Fredrik's eyes shifted, glinted. The light inside the toilet room beside the kitchen emanated from a flame burning low in an old kerosene lantern. Shadows danced on the dirty walls, darkening his cheeks. Fully dressed — unchanged from earlier in the day — he was standing with one foot on the edge of the toilet, the lid closed underneath his boot. His left shirtsleeve was rolled up, above the elbow. A glass syringe with a shiny chrome plunger was sunk into a vein. There was another thump on the front door. Upstairs, Oskar rolled over in bed. Amalia's breathing sounded through the ceiling, raspy, disturbed. Fredrik didn't overreact. He slid the plunger into the tube, emptying the remaining amphetamine into his bloodstream, then gently withdrew the needle. A drop of blood followed the tarnished steel onto his forearm. The wall of the vein was shot — this hole would never heal again. A sharp, metallic pain traveled the length of his arm, lodged itself in his shoulder like an infection. A taste of clay coated his throat. The coarse particles of the stimulant flushed through his body like clumps of rust dislodged from a disintegrating bar of iron, snagging his organs, shredding his nervous system, then like fragments from an iceberg, cold, melting as they reached the darker recesses of his brain. Shivering, he wiped sweat from his lip, finally rolled his sleeve back down. A man's voice seeped through the front door, as soft as a whisper. *Fredrik.*

The farmhand let himself out of the toilet room. His boots thudded across the floor. He yanked the door open. "Shhh." His command was curt. As dark as the house was, it was even darker outside. The rain was an inky blur beyond the edge of the porch. "You're early," he said, peering into the eyes of the man at the door.

Axel Madsen, a foot shorter than Fredrik, shouldered his way into the vestibule. His coat was dripping wet. He pulled a wool cap off his head, unloosing a mane of yellow hair that didn't match the dark stubble covering his cheeks. "They're awake," he said. "A whole platoon. They're on the prowl — if we don't go now, we'll lose our chance."

Fredrik grabbed his coat off a hook. "Where are the Jews?" The cottage reverberated with the rustle of his long arms sliding into the coat's heavy sleeves, and he didn't hear the floorboards squeak behind him.

"Brandt's meadow."

"In the barn?" Fredrik reached for the door.

"I'll go with you." Oskar's voice stopped Fredrik short.

He twisted around, faced his son. Oskar had pulled on his work pants, but he was still in socks and an undershirt. "Get back to bed." Fredrik's reaction was instinctive, absolute.

Axel eyed the taller man. Fredrik's pupils were dilated. His fingers had left damp smudges on the edge of the door. "Maybe we should let him come. With the rain, the fields will be nearly impassible. I'm told that two of them are feeble — "

"This isn't a boy's work," Fredrik said to his son.

"I'm old enough," Oskar protested.

"Let him come," Axel repeated. "It's a long way to the crossing. He can help carry their belongings. And when daylight comes, it might be good to have a kid with us."

"You don't know this boy," Fredrik said. "We might end up having to carry him, too."

"I can help you," Oskar said. "You'll see."

Fredrik examined his eldest child's face, creased with wrinkles from his straw pillow. Oskar was a weakling. He would weigh them down, as heavy as a sack of bricks. But the drug was clouding Fredrik's judgment. Perhaps it was time for the boy to prove himself. His jaw was clenched so tightly that his teeth were beginning to ache. "Come along, then," he said. "But make it quick. Get your boots and coat. And you had better not wake Amalia."

Fredrik led Axel outside onto the porch. Two minutes later, when Oskar joined them, they started off on the shoulder of the gravel road that led across the southern edge of the farm, skirting the town of Aalborg. *I see there was a fire,* Fredrik said, *over at Jepsen's place.* Oskar lost track of the conversation. He remained a few steps behind the two men, his eyes fastened on the heels of Fredrik's boots. From time to time, he lifted his gaze and caught a glimpse of his father's profile, set off against the darker shadows beyond him. The tramp of their footsteps rang in his ears, louder and louder.

■ ■ ■

The barn where Farmer Brandt housed his livestock took shape beneath the low sky like the mouth of a cave. Oskar slowed his step. His heart was racing, though he didn't want to admit it. If they were caught, they would be shot on sight—he had overheard Axel say as much to Fredrik. In the last fifteen minutes, the two men had fallen conspicuously quiet, and despite the childlike invincibility Oskar had always felt in the presence of his father, doubt had begun to impregnate the silence. The closer they got to the barn, the less certain he was that they would find the Jews waiting for them there. Perhaps they were walking into a trap. He dropped behind another couple of paces. By the time Fredrik reached the door, Axel, too, had slipped into his wake.

From inside the building, Fredrik could hear the grunt of pigs, even over the incessant rush of wind. Bits of rotten wood flaked off the door onto his fingers. Jens Brandt had fallen on hard times. Fifteen years ago, he had been one of the largest landholders in Jutland. After the first war, he had begun to drink and then to gamble, and he had had to sell off his legacy, acre by acre, to pay his debts. This pathetic barn was just about everything that the farmer had left. Fredrik hesitated. He didn't like the feeling of decay on his fingers. He didn't like this fecal smell. Then he yanked the door open and stepped inside. Behind him, Axel waited a few beats. When the night remained quiet, he followed his friend into the void.

Fredrik withdrew an electric torch from his pocket. He had scavenged the apparatus off an infantryman whom he had found lying dead in a ditch a few weeks before. Since then the battery had become almost useless. "Brandt?" His whisper echoed hollowly at the far end of the barn. When there was no answer, he switched on the torch. The farmer's body emerged from the dark, supine on the dirt floor.

Oskar recoiled a step. Axel caught him in his callused hands, held him steady. Fredrik whipped out his Luger, peered into the shadows as far as the torch allowed. Certain that the farmer was dead, he knelt beside him, pulled the collar of his coat back from his throat, searched for a pulse.

The farmer opened his eyes.

Oskar yelped. Axel jumped. Fredrik grabbed the farmer by the lapels, hoisted him like he wasn't the three-hundred-pound slob that he was, tossed him backward onto the hard floor.

"What in God's name —"

The old farmer blinked, coughed, wiped the remains of his dinner from his gray beard. "I was feeding the cow. I must have passed out."

Fredrik noticed a broken kerosene lantern in the dirt. "It's lucky you didn't burn the barn down — it's the last thing you own, isn't it?"

The farmer hunched forward, coughed again. "How much time before dawn?" He raised himself onto a single knee, pushed himself up with a groan. From out of the shadows, a pig answered with a bleat.

"It must be three already," Axel responded.

"Light a flame," Fredrik instructed. "This torch isn't going to last much longer."

The farmer squinted at Oskar. "Who's this?"

"My son."

Fredrik had answered for him before Oskar was able to himself. "My name's Oskar," he said.

"Following your father into the family business?" Still dusting himself off, the farmer snickered, then found another lantern hanging from a hook on a post, struck a match. When he held the flame to the wick, Oskar saw how greasy his hands were. His knuckles were scabbed, and there was grime beneath his splintering fingernails.

Fredrik clicked off the tin torch. "Axel says two of them are sick."

"Not sick." The farmer took the match away from the lantern, extinguished it with a flick of his wrist, lowered the glass back down over the flame. "Old. But there are only three of them — not a lot to worry about."

Fredrik exhaled his frustration. "It's the same work for three or ten — "

"Don't worry," the farmer said. "These three can pay like ten."

"Where are they?" Axel asked.

The farmer jerked his fat head toward the back of the barn. "Keeping warm with the pigs."

"We had better get started," Axel said. "It's a long way, and the rain is getting worse. It's going to be slow."

"What are the arrangements?" Fredrik asked.

"You'll drive my cousin's truck to Agersted," the farmer said. "Then you'll walk the rest of the way to the coast."

"You've got the truck loaded?"

"Fifty bushels of barley, twenty casks of beer. My cousin's expecting the truck in Agersted. He'll be taking it to market himself. This war isn't all bad — we got a good price on the barley, let me tell you."

Fredrik rubbed his hands together. "Go get them, why don't you?" Oskar noticed how jittery his father was. His cheeks shimmered — the glow of the lantern revealed a beading layer of sweat. When the farmer disappeared into the recesses of the barn, Fredrik felt for something in the pocket of his jacket, then excused himself. "I'm going to take a leak," he said to Axel. On his way to the door, his boots hit the earth too hard, as if he was expecting a downward slope, Oskar thought. The shock of his weight telegraphed itself through his long limbs.

The latch was cold on Fredrik's fingers. Already, his body had begun to acclimate to the damp heat of the animals. When he pushed the door open, the wind smacked his face. Freezing rain stung his cheeks, blinding him. Normally, he would have simply popped a few pills. He had a vial in his pocket, and even though he wasn't a user, Axel probably would have wanted one, too. But Oskar was here with them — his presence was throwing him off. And Fredrik was fatigued. He had gone nearly a week without sleep. Last night, he had crept across the farm and burglarized the Nielsens' grain locker. He didn't like stealing from the Nielsens, because it only meant that they had less to pay him. But the grain locker was an easy mark, and he needed the money. And then the fire at Jepsen's warehouse had distracted him, and he hadn't gotten into bed until after two. The night before, he had been caught in Aalborg after curfew and had ended up staying with Isabella. The Italian bitch snored like a man, and the prostitutes in the next room had kept him up half the night whoring with German soldiers. The night before that, he had gone with Axel to Skagen to transport some contraband. The night before that — Fredrik closed the door behind him, found shelter on the side of the barn beneath the overhang. There wasn't much time. He removed the syringe from his jacket pocket.

When he switched on the torch, its weak glow encircled him in a small bubble of light. He knelt down, and his knee sank into the mud. He raised his trouser cuff, plunged the grimy, fetid needle into a vein just above his ankle. The torch flickered as the battery drained, and the bubble of light grew even smaller. Standing up again, he reached his hands for its smooth edges, expecting contact with a layer of film. The vial of pills rattled in his pocket. He uncapped the brown bottle without looking at it, dropped a capsule onto his tongue, then another. When he unbuttoned his pants, his hands were shaking.

He watched the uneven stream of dank yellow piss penetrate the edge of the filmy bubble then dig a ragged groove into the saturated earth. The urine burned, and he stanched the flow between his finger and thumb. He hadn't bathed since spending the night with Isabella. The smell of their sex wafted into his nostrils. The crude mix of chemicals ripped a gash into the lining of his heart, tore holes into his lungs, seeped like contaminated water into the marrow in the core of his bones. Behind him, the muffled voices inside the barn became the cry of doves.

■ ■ ■

When Fredrik stepped back through the rotting door, the Jews — an old man, his wife, and their daughter — were huddled around the lantern like moths, whispering to one another in proper German. At the sound of his entrance, they stopped talking, and all three turned toward him, their mouths poised in perfect circles. Rather than feel any pity for this family, Fredrik had to swallow a flux of disgust. The old Jew was so ugly that he could barely look at him. His eyes were dull brown stones behind the polished lenses of a pair of gold-framed glasses. He hadn't shaved in days, and he didn't carry his graying stubble well. But there was no question that he was filthy rich. His winter coat was cashmere. Cashmere! And underneath, he wore a sweater that was also cashmere and his collar was cinched with a tie. The old Jew's wife was equally repugnant, and like her husband she was dressed for the opera, not this trek. She wore a long wool skirt and stockings, shoes with heels — though, true enough, they were cloddish heels, as square and heavy as the head of a hammer. And then there was their daughter. Fredrik measured her breasts underneath her sweater — she wore it tight, as if she wanted to tantalize him. He saw how pale the naked skin of her legs was beneath her skirt. He noticed, too, the way this schoolgirl was looking at him, sideways, flushed — following him with her eyes. Though she was trying to conceal her interest, perhaps she had even favored him with a shy smile. The amphetamine coursed through his veins, and for a moment Fredrik pictured the prim bitch on her knees in front of him, her skirt yanked above her voluptuous ass, her head forced into the dirt. He would plant her face into the soil, he would clamp his fingers around her throat. But then her father stepped between them, as if he was able to read Fredrik's thoughts, and when Fredrik looked at her again, she was no longer the coquette he first imagined. Her face had become her father's. Her eyes were just as dull. Her nose was just the same shape. And her mouth — it was a thick-lipped, repellent hole filled with a jumble of crooked, coffee-stained teeth. "What are you waiting for?" he asked Brandt. "We don't have time to waste."

The farmer was standing a few steps removed from the Jews, engaged in quiet conversation with Axel. Oskar stood in the shadows behind them, watching. "This man is your driver," the farmer said in broken German to the Jews, raising his voice. "He will take you to the coast."

The old Jew's eyes had lit with a glimmer of hope upon seeing Fredrik, and he still clung to it despite his misgivings. He cleared his throat, addressed the tall man. "Perhaps you can help us." His German was distinguished. He spoke like a professor of mathematics at the University of Vienna, because this, until the Germans annexed Austria, was what he had been. "This gentleman here is telling us that we owe him fifty marks each for our last two nights here with him. Our contact told us that we were to pay him fifty marks — I mean to say, fifty marks in total — "

Fredrik shrugged. "We had better get moving," he said to Axel. "The storm hasn't let up. The roads will be muddy."

The old Jew turned to the farmer. "I was told fifty marks," he insisted.

"It's a hundred and fifty," the farmer replied. His German accent was thick, as if he was mocking the language. "Fifty each, or I instruct my friend here to drive you south again. He doesn't care which direction he's driving, isn't that right, Gregersen?"

Fredrik barely heard him. "Are these your things?" he asked the old Jew, speaking in Danish.

The professor glanced at him, then turned back to confer with his wife. He wanted to protest longer. "They're robbing us, Maria," he insisted. "They're taking advantage of our situation, when we will need every last mark we have." But the fear on his wife's face alarmed him. Her cheeks were taut, her eyes were stricken. They were at these people's mercy. They had left their home behind. They were running from certain slaughter. When her husband remonstrated, she shook her head. She had heard enough. She bent down to open an elegant leather satchel at their feet. Fredrik's eyes fastened on the suitcase. The old Jew touched his wife's forearm, knelt next to the bag himself. He dug around inside, then withdrew a small handful of German currency. "Here you are, then," he said to the farmer. "One hundred and fifty."

The farmer took the time to count the bills before pocketing them.

"Are these all your things?" Fredrik asked again.

"Yes," the young woman answered him, paying special attention to him still, Fredrik noticed.

He scooped up their belongings in his massive hands. "Get the rest," he said to Axel.

"I'll take this one myself," the old Jew said, pulling the leather satchel out of Axel's grip.

Fredrik's eyes met the old Jew's. "Sure you will," he said. Then he led the way out of the barn, into the storm. The rain drenched him as he shoved their carefully packed goods into a crude wooden crate. "You'll travel underneath," he said to the old man. "You and your wife and your daughter."

"Underneath?" The old man's glasses were slick with rain, and he couldn't see where Fredrik was directing him. He raised his voice to be heard, continued to speak in German. "I don't understand. Underneath what?"

"Shhh," Fredrik said. "Quiet, understand me?"

"Underneath the truck," Axel said, in German that was even worse than the farmer's.

"There," Fredrik said. He grabbed the Jew by the shoulder. Beneath his fingers, the old man's bones felt as light as a bird's. "There!" He shoved him roughly toward the side of the truck, directed him to a gap in between the oversize tires. From there, it was possible to climb onto a steel platform that had been hung from the truck's chassis.

"We can't climb in there," the old man started to protest.

"Yes we can, Papa," the young woman said.

"Yes we can," her mother said, at the same time.

The Jews were hesitating, wasting time. Fredrik threw the wooden crate into the rear of the truck, fastened the gate, checked the ties on the tarp. "You've got two minutes," he said. "There's room for eight people. You're just three. Climb in. Get your clothes dirty. I'll leave with you or without you, understand? Two minutes."

Oskar helped the young woman in first. As she slid into the gap, Fredrik disappeared around the truck. Axel climbed into the cab on the passenger side. The engine turned over with a guttural rumble. The lights carved tallow columns into the rain. When the girl's skirt caught on a spear of rusty metal and hiked up her leg, Oskar's eyes were drawn to the black hair matted against the white fabric of her underpants. He continued to stare until the girl had pulled herself onto the platform and her mother was climbing in after her.

"Are you okay, Rachel?" the old man asked his daughter. "Are you okay, Maria?" he asked his wife.

And then it was just Oskar and the old Jew standing in the rain together, and when Oskar reached out to help him into the gap, the old man shrugged the boy's hand off him as roughly as he knew how. "To hell with you, you dirty Danish bastard," the old man said.

Oskar waited until the old man was safely underneath the carriage, then climbed into the cab next to Axel. The overweight truck started forward through the slick mud with a lurch. Fredrik followed the weak headlights onto the dark road. The hard seat dug into Oskar's ribs.

■ ■ ■

By the time they reached Agersted, it was already after five. The sun hadn't risen yet, but farms were rousing themselves from sleep. Here and there in the dark, lit windows gave dimension to the landscape, and the salty air was tinged with smoke swirling from chimneys. The rain had stopped, but the wind was still blowing. The rich farmland was covered with a blanket of mist. They had two miles left to walk to the coast—at least half an hour across the pastures in between, probably forty-five minutes, an hour if the Jews didn't move quickly enough. At sunrise, when the air began to clear, the fisherman waiting for the Jews would set sail. To linger any longer would draw suspicion from any Germans stationed along the coast. Fredrik reached into the gap between the tires, grabbed the first arm he touched, yanked the old woman out. The bones in her wrist bent in his hand, and she tried to resist. "You're hurting me," she said, but he didn't let go. He dragged her clear of the truck, dropped her onto the wet, sandy soil, reached back inside for the girl.

Oskar helped the old woman to her feet while Fredrik pulled her daughter out. The girl was rattled from the journey, and her teeth were chattering. Her hair was splattered with mud, and it clung to her cheeks. Fredrik let his hands travel over her breasts — he was surprised at how firm they were. She didn't complain. She stumbled, fell to her knees, lifted herself up without help.

The old man was next. Fredrik reached into the gap. The cashmere coat was wet, but the fabric was still softer than anything the laborer had felt for many years. It triggered a memory — something dating back to his childhood at the family's villa outside Copenhagen — but just as quickly the memory flitted away. His fingers wrapped around the old man's feeble shoulder. The Jew wasn't helping him at all. He had gotten used to the truck. Maybe he didn't want to go any farther. "Come on, you old sow. If you don't get yourself out of there, I'll leave you here. Understand?"

Fredrik tugged, and the old man's head emerged between the oversize truck tires like a calf's head from the vagina of a pregnant cow, wet with its mother's blood. His glasses had slipped, and they bound his mouth like a gag. His thinning hair covered his forehead, thick with coagulating plasma. One eye was open, the other was closed. This made Fredrik snicker. The old man had become a clown — they would pay him well at Tivoli for a performance like this. He made sense of a gash at the top of the Jew's head. A rock must have kicked up from the front tires, clipped him across the pate. Fredrik deposited the limp body on the mud. He was calculating whether the cashmere coat could somehow be made big enough to fit him — Amalia was handy with a needle and thread, but no, it was far too small, it would fit Amalia better — when the old man coughed and opened both his eyes.

"Is he all right?" Axel asked from the shadows.

"What happened to him?" Oskar wanted to know.

"Harold!" the old woman said. Her voice emerged in both a whisper and a shriek.

"Hush!" Fredrik warned her.

"Harold," she said again.

"Papa, what is it, what is it?" The girl fell to her knees next to her father, pulled him free from Fredrik's hands.

"He's been hit by a rock," Fredrik said, stating what he thought was the obvious. "Didn't you notice when you were underneath? You must have heard something. A loud thud, I guess. Didn't he shout?" He straightened up, left the girl alone to take care of her father. He joined Axel at the rear of the truck.

In the dark, the door of a barn opened, and Farmer Brandt's cousin — who would take the truck from them and drive it to the market up north — stepped outside, punched into a silhouette by the soft, flickering light of a lantern behind him. Axel paused long enough to identify him, then reached inside the truck for the crate containing the Jews' belongings. "Olaf doesn't look so happy to see us this morning," he said to Fredrik.

Fredrik didn't hear him. Even as he helped Axel lift the crate, his fingers were remembering the texture of the old Jew's coat. The memory of a smell, of urine and wool, permeated his nostrils. Growing up in Copenhagen, though there were more than enough rooms in the house, he had shared a bedroom with his older brother. When Ludvig was ten years old, he was still wetting his bed. Fredrik was only nine, but he was already the taller and stronger of the two. The stench of Ludvig's piss had woken him. It was a sickly odor, but cloying, like the fragrance of a flower — not the smell Fredrik had come to associate with piss in his adult life. One night, he had gotten out of bed, gathered his brother's blankets, and, without having a clear idea of what he intended, shoved them into Ludvig's face. If Ludvig's screams hadn't brought their father into the room, he probably would have suffocated him. Those blankets of Ludvig's, the ones he had soiled with his piss, had been cashmere, too, every bit as soft as this old man's coat. Fredrik steadied his hands on the crate, squeezed his eyes shut, quelled the sensation of sleep rising from inside his chest. It was as insistent as nausea.

Olaf Brandt made a quick assessment of the old man's condition, then approached the two Danes behind the truck. "If he dies, you carry him." He was a short, stout man, but he wasn't intimidated by Fredrik's size. He placed a meaty hand on the taller man's shoulder. "Understand? You carry him." The rotund truck driver had woken up and filled his belly with fried fish. The stink clung to him like cologne.

Fredrik bristled, then focused on the crate, pried off the lid with his callused fingers.

"Understand?" the truck driver asked again. He gave Fredrik an extra shake, and Fredrik's body stiffened.

"He understands," Axel said.

The truck driver ignored him. "I don't want a corpse on my property." A cloth suitcase came undone in Fredrik's hands, and a few garments spilled. The truck driver tried to give them a kick. His boot passed through a silk scarf with so little resistance that the buffoon nearly lost his balance. "His things, too," the truck driver said, cleaving to his point. "If he dies, you carry him to Sulbeck. Dump his body in the sea. I don't want a shred of evidence he was here."

"Take it easy, Olaf," Axel said. He put an arm around the truck driver's shoulders, guided him away from Fredrik.

"They're becoming a real pain, these Krauts," the truck driver said. "They used to leave us alone. Now they're asking questions."

"Oskar," Fredrik said, raising his voice. "Bring them here. Tell them to hurry. They're going to have to carry their belongings themselves."

The old Jew stumbled toward him, on his feet again. His forehead needed stitches. Blood was oozing down his face. In the dark, it looked like oil. "I've been hurt," he said to Fredrik in German. "I don't think I can carry all these things. We'll need your help."

Fredrik shoved a handful of loose clothes at the old man. "All of it," he said. The old man didn't react, and Fredrik pressed the clothing into his scrawny chest. He found the Jew's wife over his shoulder. "All of it," he repeated to her. Thinking to intervene, Oskar bent to gather a few loose items himself. Fredrik gave him a shove. When he tried to continue — quietly, without protest — his father gave him another.

"Let him alone, Fredrik." Axel's voice was tentative. There would come a time this morning when Fredrik would snap. He could feel it. "If Oskar wants to carry these Jews' suitcases, let him."

Noticing a nerve twitching in Axel's cheek, Fredrik snorted. "You don't have to worry about me," he said. "We've done this before, haven't we?" He forgot about Oskar, pulled the vial from his pocket, slammed two pills back like a salute. After finding the saliva to swallow them, he held the small brown jar toward Axel, waited for him to open his hand, meted out a rough chunk of amphetamine.

The truck driver's eyes narrowed, but he held out his palm anyway when Fredrik offered him a pill, too. He examined the tablet on the tips of a greasy finger and thumb, held it to his nose, took a suspicious sniff. "Where are you getting this?"

Fredrik returned the jar to his pocket. His attention had already been drawn back to the Jews. The old man was clinging to his leather satchel, nothing more. The daughter had a suitcase in either hand. The wife had collected as many things as she could into an old lace tablecloth and had hoisted the lumpy package into her arms. The bundle, he noticed, clanked when she moved with the unmistakable twang of silver.

"This stuff will kill you, Gregersen," the truck driver said. "It will rot your bones from the inside out." Still, he shoved the tablet into his mouth and swallowed. The bitter taste made him grimace. "So you've got four hours," he said to Fredrik, wiping his hands on his coat. "My crew is waiting for me in Sindal. I figure we'll be passing back through Ulsted again at about ten."

Fredrik nodded. "Ulsted," he echoed. "On the side of the highway."

"We won't stop," the truck driver said. "It's too dangerous. If we see you, we see you. Otherwise, you're on your own." He lifted himself into the truck, slammed the door behind him.

The Jews' silver rattled in the old woman's arms. Fredrik shouldered past Oskar, gave the old Jew a shove, started leading them toward the sea.

■ ■ ■

Forty minutes later, the sky was laced with chalky phosphor. The mulched farmland rolled away from them beneath their feet, glittering here and there in the dark where slick stalks of scattered straw caught the first, nearly invisible rays of morning light. The old woman had long since abandoned her city pumps. After a hundred yards, the shoes were ruined. Another hundred yards farther, the heels had snapped off and the red leather had separated from the soles. Now her stockings were torn and her toes were bleeding. She dragged the bundle of silver behind her, no longer caring to possess it at all, only afraid that, if she let it go, Fredrik might lash out at her. The girl had stumbled more than a few times, and her feet and knees were bleeding as well. Like her mother, she hadn't once opened her mouth. Her father hadn't stopped complaining since they had begun the journey on foot. His litany had lost words, instead had become a series of groans and moans, squeezed from his lungs as if with every step another stone were being dropped onto his chest.

"Shut up, will you?" Fredrik gave the old Jew a push. The old man stumbled and caught himself with another groan. "The sun will be up soon. Keep moving, faster."

Oskar slowed a step to help the old man through a dense marsh. Fredrik would have chastised his son, but at last the fence bordering Olaf Brandt's property on the east stenciled the haze. They were almost at the coast. The wind picked up, blasting salt into Fredrik's eyes. Beyond the fence, the flat, steel-gray plane of the sea hovered in the mist, no more than a thousand yards in front of them. The rhythmic lap of waves penetrated the gloom, punctuated by the shrill cry of seagulls.

"That must be Johansson's trawler," Axel said.

Fredrik followed the direction of the shorter man's arm. Shimmering on the otherwise unmoving sea, a weak lantern cast a circle of light onto the water. Within the glow, tiny waves rippled. From this perspective, the pattern could have been the flutter of snow in a car's headlamp. Fredrik traced a line back from the small fishing boat to the shore, where he located yet another lamp burning, this one even weaker. The Swedish fisherman was waiting for them on the sand with his rowboat.

"Yeah, that's Johansson," Fredrik confirmed. In the distance, next to the rowboat, another flame sparked. The fisherman was lighting a cigarette. As far away as they were, Fredrik could practically smell the burning tobacco. The last time he had seen the one-eyed Swede, the fisherman had given him a Gauloises, something he had taken from a fugitive whom he had run across the straits. The cigarette had been as fat as a small cigar. He started forward again, allowing Axel to take the lead.

Arriving at the fence, Axel steered them sideways for about thirty or forty yards, until he located a gap large enough to crawl through. There, parting a tangle of broken wires and rotted stakes, he directed Oskar through first, the old woman next. When he reached for the girl, though, Fredrik grabbed him by the wrist, gave it a savage squeeze, shoved the old man toward the hole formed by the fallen posts instead. The professor's body was almost too battered to bend, but he was small and thin, and he fit through with only a little prodding. After that, Axel didn't wait for Fredrik. He had understood his intention. He followed the old Jew to the other side, then herded the group forward without Fredrik or the girl.

The fleshy young woman didn't protest. At first, she wasn't certain what was happening. She watched her father and mother dissolve into pixels, then raised her eyes to Fredrik. The handsome Dane who smelled like sweat brushed the suitcases and packages she was carrying from her arms. They hit the soil with a quiet thud. His hands tightened on her shoulders. Still, the girl didn't resist—she let this man whom she had dared to tease with an adolescent smile guide her downward. Then the gesture grew more violent. She slipped backward onto the wet soil. Mud oozed through her coat, through her clothes. The tall man didn't immediately follow her to the ground. He stood above her, his chest heaving—long enough for the girl to imagine that the moment might have passed. But then he knelt beside her, a knee between her thighs, and the girl knew.

The dark swallowed the man whole—everything except his lips, which had turned as white as his teeth. His hand found her vagina, and a sound escaped from her own throat that the girl didn't recognize. Her underpants tore with a rip. The huge man's fingers were made of concrete. His breath was hot on her cheek. She closed her eyes, clamped her jaw, waited. A belt slithered through a buckle. Heavy fabric separated from buttons with a series of muffled pops. His hands settled into the earth on either side of her. In her confusion, she clasped this brute's arms and pulled herself against him in an awkward embrace, as if she somehow believed that she could with tenderness entice this man whom she was holding to protect her from the beast who was on top of her. When the stubble on his chin dug into her skull, she twisted and tried to find his ear. *Don't*, she whispered. Her voice didn't belong to her. She had no idea what language she might be speaking. *Please, don't.* But the stone fingers wrapped themselves around her neck beneath her chin.

And then a voice interrupted them. "Father?" And in that same instant, the world fell completely still. The wind whistled, seagulls shrieked. The man had stopped breathing. Footsteps approached, slick on the muddy ground. "Father—where are you?"

The fingers softened back into flesh. The man shifted. "Stay back," he growled.

The flavor of her own oily hair permeated the girl's mouth. When she opened her eyes again, the boy emerged from the shadows in a blur. His face was stricken with concern.

"What are you doing, Father?"

The man let go of her, but she could nevertheless sense the tension in his body. It felt to her as if he was ready to explode. "What you should be doing. Eh?"

"Axel says you must come now. He says we must hurry."

The man considered his son. He yanked his trousers back up over his naked ass. Then at last he stood. The absence of contact left the girl suddenly cold. Her legs shook. The man lifted her off the ground, thrust her bags back into her arms. She lost her balance, but the boy gripped her elbow, managed to keep her upright. In the aftermath of her terror, even Oskar's gentle touch sickened her, and she felt herself retch. Mud slid down her thighs. Silently, madly, she began to weep. Her clitoris was vibrating like a string stretched too taut on the neck of a guitar, and the incongruity of this dysfunction blinded her. As Oskar directed her through the gap in the fence, all she could see was a series of geometric blacks and grays. Rusty wires snagged her skirt, scratched her scalp, pulled her hair. On the other side, Fredrik gave her a shove. His hand dug into her back. She tripped, caught herself, followed the rustle of clothes into the dark. A minute later, they had rejoined the group. Her feet sank into sand. Tears streamed down her face.

She wanted to reach for him, but her father didn't turn around. The old man's jaw was clenched. His shoulders were stooped. He saw nothing farther than the droplets and smudges on his glasses. The pain that racked his body was long forgotten. His face was contorted by a series of deep, symmetrical creases into the picture of grief. At the sound of the huge Dane's approach, his arms tightened around the leather satchel, which he carried now like a child against his chest. When his daughter bumped into him, he bent his head toward her enough to caress her shoulder with his cheek, but neither slowed. Once again, in the familiar presence of her father, silent sobs convulsed the girl's body. Her father closed his eyes and squeezed his hands into angry fists so tight that his knuckles captured the silvery light of dawn like moonstones or pearls. They kept on walking.

■ ■ ■

The sun peeked over the horizon, casting a narrow orange finger all the way from Sweden to the wide strand on the Danish shore. Small waves crested, and the froth sank into the golden sand at Ingmar Johansson's feet. When the crunch of footsteps broke the silence, the Swedish fisherman flicked his cigarette into the saltwater. It catapulted end over end in a fiery arc, then disappeared. The fisherman had lost his left eye in an accident with the rough edge of a fishing net some years before. When he blinked, the blind side of his face flinched, but it was only a sympathetic gesture — a remnant from the time when he possessed a second eye. He didn't wear a patch. The wound had healed into a twisted whorl of skin. As Fredrik approached, it took a moment for him to understand that the fisherman was smiling — his was such a difficult face to read. "Another minute or two, and I would have left," the fisherman said, with an accent that grated on Fredrik's nerves. Smoke streamed from the fisherman's nostrils.

"We had a rough night," Fredrik said.

"So this is what you bring me? Only three?"

"You were expecting more?"

The fisherman shrugged.

"Any sign of the Germans?" Axel asked him.

The fisherman thrust out his lower lip. Fredrik thought that he looked like a fool. "A frigate passed by yesterday night. But it's been quiet. I don't expect trouble."

"Put your bags in the boat," Fredrik said to the Jews. But when the old man took a step toward the beached craft, Fredrik grabbed him by the shoulder, stopped him in his tracks. "Not that bag."

"What do you mean?" the old man asked him.

"Put your bags in the boat," Fredrik repeated to the old woman and her daughter. The girl tripped against the side of the dinghy, dropped her bundle on the deck. Her shin hit the hull with a loud thunk. Her mother scurried through the dark to her daughter's side.

The giant's hand, the old man realized, had gripped the leather satchel. "What do you think you're doing?" he protested, wrapping both arms around the suitcase.

Fredrik stripped him of the bag without a word, sent him flailing backward toward the rowboat. The old man bumped into his wife, spilled onto the deck like a marionette. His head hit a steel fitting hard enough once again to tear the thin skin of his scalp. He scrambled back onto his feet. "You can't — It's stealing." He was almost too dizzy to stand. His wife and daughter pulled him backward, restraining him from attacking the huge Dane.

"Shhh," his wife said.

"Papa, don't," his daughter said. "Just don't." And the family watched helplessly as Fredrik weighed the small satchel with a shake.

"What are you doing?" the fisherman asked him.

Sensing an opening, the old man entreated the fisherman. "You can't let him. He can't just take our things."

Fredrik glared at the little man. "Shut your mouth," he told him. "Or I'll shut you up myself." The Jew's bleating would attract the attention of the other fishermen who were also heading to their boats on the sound. It was dark, but they weren't alone. Word had a way of spreading.

"You can't take that," the one-eyed fisherman said.

"Why not?" Fredrik asked.

"He can't," the old man repeated.

"Not until you pay me, anyway," the fisherman said. He grinned, but the concern didn't dissipate from his lopsided expression.

Fredrik grunted. He set the leather satchel onto the sand, knelt next to it, worked the brass lock in the dim light.

"You'll never figure out how to open it," the old man said.

This made Fredrik sneer. He slipped a finger under the clasp, flexed his arm, broke the satchel open with a quiet rip. When he pulled the bag apart, his breathing stopped. Beneath a few bundles of bills, the polished surface of a treasure of gemstones shimmered in the dim light. Reaching inside, a memory of his mother's jewelry chest blinded him. Her favorite piece had been a chain of diamonds interlaced with strands of precious, uncut blue and yellow stones that she had worn around her fat neck on special occasions. The scent of her perfume teased his nose. As a child, the powdery smell had reminded him of the barbershop.

"We can't take that." Axel was standing next to Fredrik, peering over his shoulder. "You have to give it back to them."

Fredrik's fingers tightened on the jewels. He pictured the tiny cottage he shared with his children, the empty larder. When was the last time he had eaten a pat of butter without sneaking it from the Nielsens? In the last few months, he hadn't been able to drink a simple beer without begging the barman to increase his tab. Oskar had outgrown his own clothes and was wearing his father's castoffs — this was becoming evident to everyone in Aalborg. The pittance of a salary that the Nielsens paid Amalia barely had time to grow warm in his daughter's palm before he had slipped it into his own pocket. What kind of life was this? The sharp edges of a few settings dug into his skin. Perhaps he could even return a handful of this plunder to the chest in his mother's room in Copenhagen. Imagine the look on her face! Fru Gregersen would never forgive him for stealing her most cherished belongings one by one and selling them for the price of a few bottles of whiskey and a couple of trips to the wrong side of town. But the war was taking its toll on everyone. The family was being brought to its knees by the occupation — this same proud, entitled family of strivers who had disowned him. It was only a matter of time before there would be no more artwork or other valuables left for the Gregersen family to sell. His mother would have no choice but to curtsy and accept his charity —

"We can't take that," Axel repeated. "Close it up, Fredrik — give it back to them."

"What?" Fredrik raised his eyes to Axel's. Even on his knees, he was nearly as tall as his partner. "What are you talking about?" He grabbed a bundle of cash — U.S. dollars bound into a tight roll with an elastic band — flung the green paper to the fisherman, squeezed the suitcase shut. "This is mine."

"You know we can't, Fredrik."

Unmoved, Fredrik lifted himself back onto his feet. "He wasn't born with this suitcase in his hands, any more than I was."

"How will we make the rest of the trip?" the old man asked him.

"Shhh," his wife said.

"Without that, we won't make it any farther. How can you expect us to make it without that?"

"Shush," his wife said.

"Please, Papa."

"Have I somehow fallen into your debt?" Fredrik asked the Jew. "Now get into the boat, and this man will bring you across the channel to Sweden. If it's meant to be, I'm sure you'll find your own way."

"When Gustav learns of this," Axel said, "he won't send me any more Jews."

The argument fell on deaf ears. After this, Fredrik would have no further need for Axel's Jews. He tucked the bag under his arm. "It's getting late," he said. Across the strait, orange flames were burning in pockets on the black water. "We have a long way back to the highway."

The old man broke free from his wife and daughter, rushed the tall Dane. "You cannot take that —"

"Get into the boat," Fredrik repeated. The discussion was finished. With one hand, he hustled the Jew into the dinghy. The old man's coat was soft on his fingers. Maybe he would take it, too, after all. He yanked it off his shoulders as the old man tripped over the hull.

"Leave him be," the fisherman said. He was growing worried that he would have to dispose of a corpse. "He'll freeze without the coat."

Fredrik took it in any event, tossed it to Oskar. "Give me a smoke for the road," he said to the fisherman. At his feet, the surf turned as blue as the stones in his mother's necklace. A wave broke against the sand and swallowed his heavy boots. Behind the fisherman, the family of fugitives huddled together on a bench in the rowboat, unable to do anything except watch as the tall Dane tightened his grip on the satchel then waited, his shoulders hunched, for the fisherman to light his cigarette.

Then the three Danes were on their way again. Sunlight touched their necks as they retraced their footsteps across the beach, over the dunes to the pastureland that bordered the shore. Their shadows led them back toward the fence bordering Olaf Brandt's property. The herbal tobacco singed Fredrik's throat, but he smoked the dense Turkish cigarette to a nub anyway. The roots of his teeth ached in his gums. He tasted blood.

6.

The cigarette was a memory by the time they reached the road. Ulsted lay in the distance, a smattering of gray buildings with red tile roofs. The clouds had parted, and steam rose from the saturated soil beneath the insistent heat of the sun. Oskar was two paces ahead of Fredrik and Axel, aware of their footsteps behind him but of little else. In front of him, the cracked asphalt had dissolved into a blur. Fredrik sucked on his teeth, spit, narrowed his eyes as he took in his son's lanky body, his bony shoulders. The boy's yellow hair was clumped in greasy strands that could have been a girl's braids. "You've been pretty quiet," the tall farmhand said.

Axel peered at him from the corner of his eye. He wanted to make certain that the observation wasn't meant for him. In front of them, Oskar didn't seem to hear.

Fredrik resisted the impulse to grab his son, give him a shake. If it had been up to this weakling, the old Jew's suitcase wouldn't be tucked under his arm. All they would have to show for the night's work would be the few crowns Axel had been promised. Maybe they would all three be inside Johansson's boat, helping him row the Jews across the channel to Sweden. Maybe Oskar would be looking for a safe place for the old Jewess to squat and take a shit. "You have something you want to say to me?"

Oskar woke to the threat in his father's voice. He had been far away in his own thoughts. What would happen to the family from Austria once they reached Sweden? The old woman had managed to lug her silver to the boat at least. His voice escaped from his mouth before he knew what he would say. "I thought that the Gregersens were a rich family." Behind him, his father stopped walking.

"What was that?" Fredrik was incredulous.

Oskar felt his heart touch his ribs. After a pause, his father's boots scraped the rough asphalt again, four or five steps behind him. The hair stood up on the back of his neck. "Your mother is a lady-in-waiting to the queen, isn't she?"

"Fru Gregersen is no more noble than a whore," Fredrik said.

"Your brother, Ludvig, is a bookkeeper at the palace."

"My brother is softer than you are," Fredrik quipped. "My mother still coddles him. Does it make him a stronger man if he counts the money in the king's pocket?"

"And your father was one of the king's huntsmen."

"My father?" Fredrik choked. "I don't speak ill of the dead, but my father was a bastard — what do you know about my father? So he took care of the king's horse and the king's spaniels. He also threw me out of his house when I was sixteen — " Not that Fredrik had blamed him, of course, when his father had finally lost patience. He hadn't left him any other choice. In fact, Nils Erik Gregersen had been a weakling. He had given Fredrik so many second chances that Fredrik could hardly take him seriously anymore — after he had raided his mother's jewelry box, after he drank all the liquor from the cabinet in the library, after he got one of the maids pregnant, after he beat up the mayor's effeminate son and tossed his prized pocketknife off the overpass into the smokestack of a passing train. To Fredrik, it had almost felt sometimes that his father took a perverse pride in his errant son's scandalous behavior, as if it befitted the scion of such a family and conferred its own status on him as patriarch. It had taken killing the Persian cat finally to force his father's hand. Miav, his mother had called it. It was Fru Gregersen's special pet — she doted on it, Fredrik had always thought, because it looked so much like her. He hadn't meant to kill it — all he was trying to do was slip its pearl-studded collar over its fat head, maybe give its ribs a little squeeze. But then the cat had scratched him, and its neck had broken so easily. If he had buried the carcass in the bog or burned it in the fireplace, no one would have been the wiser. His real mistake had been to try to feed it to his father's hounds. After that, his father had had no alternative. Sending him to Jutland to live on a farm and earn his own keep had been a fair compromise. His mother — who had herself discovered Miav's gory remains on the summer porch — would have had him locked in jail. The fact was, though, however justified he may have been, Nils Erik had been a bastard, if a weak one. As surely as Fru Gregersen was a haughty cow and Ludvig a spineless sycophant who had never done an honest day's work in his life. "What are you saying to me about my family?" Fredrik demanded.

Sensing the violence of his father's temper, Oskar remained silent. This, though, only infuriated Fredrik more. Oskar had poked a stick into the ass of dogs best left sleeping. How dare he hold his own mother and father up to him as paragons just because of their wealth and their name? Did it make them better than anyone else — these people who had renounced him and taken this same name back from him, their very own son — that they slept in beds their ancestors had made for them and walked in the shadow of kings? What did Oskar know about the Gregersens? They might not have had the luxuries he had had growing up, but Fredrik had never treated his children like fools, and he had never preferred one over the other. Once again, Fredrik's footsteps ceased. "Stop," he ordered his son.

Oskar faltered, but he forced himself to keep moving forward.

When his son continued to ignore him, Fredrik's cheeks reddened. "Turn around and look at me when you speak."

"We need to keep walking," Axel said. His eyes were focused on the bend in the road about half a mile in front of them, where the highway disappeared into a small copse. He wondered whether Olaf Brandt had already driven past Ulsted. If they had missed the truck, they had a long day in front of them, and he was nervous about the army patrols around the landing strips above Aalborg.

"Stop and face me," Fredrik repeated. "Do you hear me?"

At last, ten paces from his father, Oskar stopped. When he turned, the sun caught him in his eyes. It was glistening above his father's head as if Fredrik's scalp had burst into flames. At his sides, Fredrik's hands were gripped into fists that might have been forged from steel, and they, too, shimmered in the sun. In that moment, despite his fear, Oskar remembered an illustration from one of his childhood books. His father had turned the book's pages with him sometimes before he fell asleep. Thor had stood on a craggy, purple mountain, clasping a hammer with an orange handle and a shiny head. The glossy drawing had been separated from the other pages by a sheet of waxy tissue paper. When the tissue was flipped, the overhead light had flared on the drawing underneath with the intensity of a match being struck.

"Now tell me what nonsense you're speaking," Fredrik ordered. When he took a step toward him, Oskar felt his knees weaken.

"There's no time for a fight," Axel said.

"I figured you for a coward," Fredrik said, imagining that Oskar was too afraid to open his mouth again.

But a few more words did escape. "I didn't know that we needed to steal," Oskar said.

"*Steal?*"

Oskar nodded toward the bag clutched under his father's arm. "I thought that the Gregersens were the ones who had to worry about thieves."

Acid welled inside Fredrik's stomach, into his esophagus, strangling him as forcibly as a pair of hands beneath his chin. This soft-skinned, timid *boy* dared to lecture him? Where did every morsel of food he had ever tasted come from? Who had taught him how to walk? Who tolerated the very beating of his juvenile heart? Oskar had no right to judge him. Unlike with his own father — to whom Fredrik owed nothing — Oskar owed him a debt of gratitude with so many facets that it was impossible to contemplate. Did he not see what his father was doing right now to keep his family fed? How loudly would he still whimper if any of the horrors being suffered by the family of Jews were visited upon Amalia or him instead? Would any of the Gregersens or their dead ancestors come to their rescue then? Fredrik was blinking back his fury when the sputtering growl of an engine broke the stillness behind them.

Axel raised a hand to his forehead, squinted into the glare. "It's a truck," he said.

Fredrik took another step toward his son. "Shall I show you what it means to be a Gregersen?" he threatened.

"But it's not Brandt. Fredrik? It's a German truck."

The words penetrated Fredrik's anger. Behind him, the rumble of the engine was crescendoing. The truck was bearing down on them. From the pitch of the engine, Fredrik recognized it as a heavy diesel. He swiveled around. It was a military vehicle—a troop transport. The cab was painted olive green. The cargo bay was wrapped in black canvas.

"What do you want to do?" Axel asked.

"They've already seen us," Fredrik said.

"Are they going to stop us?" Oskar asked.

"Turn around," Fredrik commanded, still on the verge of exploding. "Keep walking."

"Should we run?" his son asked.

"Do as I say," Fredrik said, "or I will drop you myself. Understand?" His jaw worked as he sought to control himself. "We'll keep walking. We're three farmers heading back home from the market. There's no crime in that."

Oskar hesitated, then turned and began walking again.

"You can just relax," Fredrik said. "Act natural. It's normal to stop and look when a truck approaches you on an empty highway."

Oskar stopped when Axel and his father did, and the three Danes stood on the side of the narrow road as the dark truck bulked over their shoulders. Barely visible through the flat windshield, three blond soldiers stared them down as they approached, crammed together on the seat in the cab. Oskar met the gaze of one of the soldiers, and the German's scowl made him shiver. Then they had barreled past. The engine whined as the driver geared down. Catching a glimpse into the cargo bed through gaps in the canvas, Fredrik could see a few crates, a bundle of blankets. Otherwise, the truck was empty.

"There," Axel said, winking at Oskar. "Danger's passed."

"Bastards," Fredrik muttered. He was starting forward again when the truck slowed to a sudden stop. Its tires screeched on the asphalt. Its engine stalled, then rumbled back to life. Oskar glanced backward at his father, and Fredrik read his worry.

"They're going to question us," Axel said. He adjusted his sweater, hiked up his trousers. One of his shoelaces had come undone, but he ignored it. These boots were too small for his feet anyway. The shoe wouldn't come loose.

The truck's transmission squealed as the driver found reverse. The tires began to roll backward, and plumes of diesel exhaust spewed from the pipes. Oskar took a step off the shoulder into the mud. He was measuring the distance to the woods — not more than one hundred yards to their right. He could reach cover before the truck could backtrack the distance to them on the road.

"Stay where you are," Fredrik instructed him. "No reason to panic."

The three men stood their ground as the truck closed the gap. Fredrik slipped a pill into his mouth. One of Oskar's legs began to shake. Otherwise, no one moved. The thick, ossified rubber of the truck's tires chirped on the asphalt as the brakes ground the heavy vehicle to a halt. The engine settled into an idle. The passenger door swung open. A wool-clad leg emerged, booted in rich leather, followed by the thick robe of a long coat.

The soldier who dropped from the truck was a kid, barely older than Oskar. His hair was blond, his eyes brown. A scar disfigured his chin. His front teeth were prominent, separated by a gap. The soldier who stepped onto the asphalt behind him wore a sergeant's cap. He was taller, older. Maybe thirty, Fredrik thought. He spit onto the road, and his mucus was thick with tobacco residue. Ten feet away, Oskar imagined that he could smell it. The sergeant's eyes narrowed. "Do you speak German?" he asked.

Oskar didn't move. Axel shook his head. "No," Fredrik said.

The sergeant fiddled with his breast pocket, found a loose cigarette, shoved it into his mouth. His lips were cracked. He shifted his belt, lifted his pistol, located what he was looking for in his hip pocket. A lighter, made in America. He flipped back the lid with a clever flick of his wrist, dragged his thumb over the flint, lit his smoke, then dropped the lighter back into his pocket. When he took the cigarette from his mouth, he held it between his finger and thumb, cupped in a hand almost as large as one of Fredrik's. His fingertips were stained yellow with resin. The cigarette's ember glowed on his palm. "Which way are you heading?" he asked. Smoke streamed through blackened teeth. The tip of a purple tongue, coarse with veins, wetted his lips.

Oskar looked backward at his father. Axel shrugged. "Aalborg," Fredrik said.

"You have your papers?"

"My son is only eighteen," Fredrik said.

"Yours, then." The sergeant spit another wad of mucus into the mud.

Fredrik reached into his coat for his identification. His hand grazed the butt of his pistol. The soft suitcase under his arm shifted, and its contents tinkled. Oskar realized that he had been listening to this same music since they had left the shore. This, though, was the first time that he had actually heard it.

"What have you got in the bag?" the sergeant asked.

Fredrik's fingers tightened on the papers in his breast pocket.

The sergeant inhaled another breath of smoke, let it stream out through his nostrils. "Open it," he said.

Fredrik withdrew his documents. "Here are my papers," he said.

"Open the suitcase," the sergeant repeated.

When Fredrik shoved his documents back into his pocket, his hand was shaking. He wasn't afraid. It was the lack of sleep. His nerves were shot. He wrapped his fingers into a fist, squeezed. His nails dug into his palm. He knelt, set the soft suitcase onto the asphalt. Rays of sunlight glistened on the torn edge of the strap he had ripped loose when he couldn't figure out the lock.

The sergeant took a step closer, nudged the expensive leather case with the toe of his boot. "What have you got there?" He rested a hand on his Luger, with his other brought his cigarette to his lips for another drag. "This is a pretty fancy suitcase for a farmer to carry, isn't it?"

Fredrik's gigantic hands separated the top of the satchel. The shadow inside hid the jewelry from view. The sergeant craned forward, squinted. His curiosity was palpable. When he caught sight of the slick surface of the gems, he hiccuped, then let out a stream of rancid smoke. Behind him, the young soldier took a step forward, too. The sergeant's shoulders stiffened. Slowly, deliberately, he unsnapped his holster, slid his sinewy index finger behind the pistol's trigger guard.

Oskar was having trouble catching his breath. His vision had blurred. Panic gripped his stomach. He knew his father well enough to know that he wouldn't surrender the suitcase to the Germans. When he started running, his flight caught everyone off guard. He had reason enough, but it wasn't a premeditated decision to flee. His head was light, his legs started to move. He dropped the cashmere coat, pumped his fists, darted as fast as he could toward the trees.

A second passed. Oskar's footsteps resounded with a wet squish. Then the sergeant drew his pistol. He didn't issue a warning. He simply grabbed the toggle to cock the hammer and load a bullet into the chamber, straightened his arm. As much effort as Oskar was expending, he wasn't moving fast. His feet were slipping, the landscape was roiling. The small forest loomed in front of him. He saw a raven land on a twig then jump into the air and soar. A fern caught the sun like an emerald. A dead branch reached toward him like a blackened hand.

The German had the back of the boy's head fixed in his aim, blocked by the black, triangular edge of the front sight, when Fredrik took hold of his wrist. The sergeant's finger squeezed the trigger, but the round plugged the soil at Oskar's feet. Mud splattered Oskar's legs, the recoil vibrated up Fredrik's arm. His son kept running. The farmhand's fingers clamped the German's forearm, buried themselves into his muscle and sinew, and crushed his bones as easily as if he were sinking his fingers into a block of butter.

The young soldier watched from the corner of his eye as Fredrik snatched the pistol from the sergeant and swung his boot into the sergeant's shins. The leg splintered with a loud crack, the tall German dropped to his knees. His cigarette tumbled from his lips, hit the pavement with a shower of sparks. In the same motion, Fredrik let go of the sergeant's arm, ratcheted back the hammer, fired a bullet point-blank into the sergeant's head. With the crack of the shot, the smell of gunpowder permeated the cold morning. Blood peppered the young soldier. He barely had time to look directly at Fredrik before the gun was cocked again and a second bullet had found its way into his forehead. The force of the projectile sent him sprawling backward. His skull shattered against the asphalt. Then, except for the idle of the truck, it was quiet again. The two dead soldiers rested side by side in an unmoving heap. The sergeant's cigarette rolled to the edge of the road, where it lay smoldering, sending a weak finger of smoke into the still air.

"What the — " Axel spun around.

Fredrik was still moving. He took a clumsy step, knocked the suitcase flying, scrambled toward the cab of the truck. Jewels spilled across the road like liquefied amber. His eyes met the driver's in the side mirror. It registered that the driver was another soldier barely older than Oskar and was too stunned to react. The boy's hand shot not for his gun but for the gearshift. His left foot slammed the clutch, his right the accelerator. The engine screamed, the truck jolted forward. But Fredrik had already reached the open door. He hoisted himself up, then plastered the driver's brains onto the window next to him with a single bullet. The truck lurched, veered off the asphalt. Its tall, stiff tires sank into the mud.

Oskar disappeared into the woods. Axel shouted. At first, his words were indistinct. Then they took shape. "They'll kill us. They'll find us, Fredrik. They'll find us, then they'll kill us."

Fredrik dropped from the cab of the truck. An involuntary erection stabbed his trousers. He was kneeling, gathering the spilled contents back into the Jew's soft leather satchel when the distant hum of Olaf Brandt's truck broke the stillness of the morning. His fingers fumbled with a handful of glistening jewelry. When he spit, blood darkened the asphalt. He slid his tongue over his teeth. A front incisor was loose, but he couldn't recall banging it, couldn't recall being hit. He spit again, then tucked the suitcase under his arm, raised himself to his feet.

Quickly, he searched the sergeant's pocket for shells, dropped them into the suitcase as well, together with the Luger. The sergeant's green wool cap barely fit on his head. He was about to straighten up when he remembered something else, and, glancing at the approaching truck, he reached into the sergeant's pocket again. When he drew out the lighter, he flipped the lid back the same way the sergeant had. His thumb slipped on the flint, though, and he wasn't able to spark a flame.

Axel was yanking off the soldier's boots. "It would be better for us if no one sees us here," Fredrik said to him, snapping the lighter closed. "Even Brandt." The truck was taking shape in the distance. He took a step off the road, led the smaller man toward the trees.

Oskar was easy enough to find. He was sitting hunched against a tall birch, his head in his hands, sniffling. His father stopped in front of him, tossed the old Jew's cashmere coat into his lap.

"Come on," Fredrik said.

"I'm sorry," Oskar muttered. There was fear in his eyes when he looked up at his father. "I didn't mean to run." He flinched when Fredrik extended his hand. When he grabbed it, he was surprised by the tremor in his father's grasp.

"Come on," Fredrik repeated. The truck was getting closer. Fredrik let Axel take the lead, then, tearing the dead Nazi's cap off his head, gave Oskar a shove and followed him into the trees.

The shadows in the forest surrounded them. The wind picked up and rattled the branches. The sun vanished into a bank of heavy clouds. By the time they reached the other side of the woods, rain was falling again, pattering against the leaves. The three men lowered their heads and continued walking.

7.

Back at the Nielsens' farm, Fredrik stood at the mouth of the barn, peering into the hazy, unlit space. The rhythmic bite of a shovel's blade echoed inside. The sound swallowed Fredrik's footsteps, and he approached Oskar without being heard, grabbed the shovel from his hands. Oskar was digging a hole beside one of the posts supporting the roof, where his father had directed. The battered satchel was resting at his feet. The ground in here was packed and dry, and Oskar hadn't made much progress. Since returning home, he hadn't yet been inside the house, and he hadn't had anything to eat. The night was catching up to him. The gunshots continued to resound in his head. He recognized the dull ache behind his left eye. If he didn't eat something soon, he knew that it would spiral into another headache. "Give me that," Fredrik said. The farmhand was already wearing his work gloves.

"I can do it," Oskar said.

"Give me some room," Fredrik told him.

"The soil is hard as rock," Oskar said.

"Is it?" Fredrik positioned the shovel a few inches to the side of the shallow pit Oskar had dug. He clamped the handle with a practiced grip, placed a heavy boot on the lip of the shovel's blade. "This needs to be a deep hole," he said, glancing at Oskar. "Once we're finished, we should have trouble finding this suitcase again ourselves." Then he tightened his hands, balanced himself, drove the shovel into the ground. The blade plunged into the soil like a nail hammered into a plank. The scrape of metal against clay rang in Oskar's ears. The sound of the rain on the roof swept through the barn like the tide.

HERMANN

8.

Copenhagen. November 1941.

A dark blue Mercedes-Benz rolled slowly down a narrow street, in between stone and plaster buildings, through a drizzling rain. The wipers swept over the flat windshield in weak, uneven arcs. The rubber blades were old, and the chrome arms scraped the glass with a hiss. The city felt deserted. A fire was burning unattended in the gutter. Plumes of soot rose from the flames, swirled into the air, blended with the mist. A wooden crate filled with old clothing had been pulled into the road and torched. Orange shadows undulated on the windows, coloring the driver's cheeks. The putrid stench of the smoke filled the car. But the driver hardly noticed the blaze. His eyes were fixed on the street in front of him, over the long hood.

At the next corner, a German lieutenant in a green uniform was standing in the shelter of a doorway. The sky was low. At four o'clock, the day was already darkening into night. If the driver hadn't been expecting to find him there, he wouldn't have seen the lieutenant at all. Cautiously, scanning the sidewalk, he slowed the car. The idle was uneven, and the engine threatened to quit. The brakes squealed. He brought the car to a stop, kept the engine running by riding the throttle. The lieutenant darted from the safety of the doorway, circled the car to the passenger side. When he grabbed the handle, the latch wouldn't budge, and he rattled the door, knocked on the glass. The driver leaned across the seat to let him in. "Hurry up," he said to the lieutenant. He started pulling forward again even before the German had climbed inside.

The lieutenant yanked the door closed behind him, brushed the rain off his shoulders. Water pooled on the seat beneath his wet uniform. "It rains too much in Denmark," he said. He pulled off his spectacles to wipe them dry.

"In Norway," the driver said, "this rain will be snow."

The lieutenant shrugged. If this man thought that Germany's battles belonged to him, there was little he could say to defend himself.

"Anyway," the driver said, "it provides us with some cover. And that's what we want right now." He scanned the empty sidewalk again. He was every bit as afraid of being seen with this Nazi as the German was of being caught with him.

The lieutenant replaced his spectacles on the bridge of his nose, turned slightly so that he could examine the man behind the wheel. At first glance, Ludvig Gregersen did not appear to be a particularly powerful man. His hair was thinning, and the skin on his nose was pocked. He was somewhat overweight, and his posture was poor. But the hands on the steering wheel belonged to a giant. He sat folded in the seat with his arms and knees bent, as if this automobile was too small for him. And his eyes glistened with their own intelligence. He was not, the lieutenant decided, someone to underestimate. "Where are you taking me?" he asked the Dane.

Ludvig pursed his thick, red lips, but made no pretense of trying to answer. He stared out the windshield, gauged the accelerator under the heavy sole of his shoe. Except for the unsteady growl of the engine, the car remained silent. Five minutes later, when he finally responded to the question, the German had already forgotten that he had posed it. "You will see soon enough," Ludvig said, and it took a beat for the lieutenant to figure out what he meant.

On the southern outskirts of Copenhagen, the Mercedes-Benz rolled over two sets of railroad tracks and pulled to a stop in front of a large gray warehouse. The lot beside the building was empty, save for a couple of trucks parked at odd angles and a few stacks of wooden pallets. A single window was lit on the far side of the building. Otherwise, the structure looked abandoned. The rain struck the corrugated roof with a steady roar. From inside the car, the sound was the roll of a drum. The German looked up and down the wide street. He made a mental note of a tall grain silo a few hundred feet farther down the tracks — this was a landmark that he would be able to remember. Next to him, the Dane read his thoughts.

"This warehouse belongs to the Gregersens," he said. "So it was a convenient place for us to stash some of our belongings after your army invaded. But we are not foolish enough to leave our most valuable possessions here for any length of time. The paintings that I show you will not be here tonight after we leave."

The lieutenant's uniform rustled against the wet leather as he turned to face Ludvig. "This is a business for me," he said. "Not a heist."

"Your pistol, Herr Schmidt," Ludvig said.

Hermann Schmidt didn't resist. He unfastened the snap on the holster at his side, lifted out his Luger, handed it butt-first to the larger man.

"We will leave this here," the Dane said. He shoved the weapon under the driver's seat before unlatching the door. The hinges screeched. Outside, tilting his head back like a child might, he let his eyes travel up the quilt of interlocking planes formed by the slanting rain as he waited for Hermann to follow him.

The two men entered the warehouse with their jackets glistening. When Hermann stamped his boots on the floor, the smack of wet leather against concrete echoed through the cavernous hall. A single bank of windows, glowing almost violet in the late-afternoon light, provided the only illumination, and the rain streaming over the glass threw flickering shadows into the hazy air. Ludvig found a switch, and a series of bulbs lit the space. Except for a few random piles of clutter, the warehouse was empty.

Ludvig raised his hands palms up. "Most of what we had here was already seized."

"Was it a factory?" the German asked.

"I come from a family of traders," Ludvig said. "We used to be buyers. Now, unfortunately, we have no choice but to be sellers." He started across the warehouse. His shadow slid behind him on the concrete floor, then leaped ahead of him when he reached the first overhead lamp. Hermann hesitated. Somehow, he realized that they weren't alone. He hadn't heard or seen anything. He simply felt it — he was being watched. He suppressed a shiver, rubbed his hands together, followed the Dane. Ludvig led him into a dark corner. At first, all Hermann saw was an empty crate, shoved against the wall. Then he noticed a small stack of frames next to it, covered with a clean white sheet. Ludvig snatched the drape off the frames, carefully picked the first one up. When he swiveled it around in his palms, he revealed what appeared to be an important work, a Madonna and child, in the Baroque style. The paint was obviously a few hundred years old, and the saturated colors and sensual shapes were familiar.

Hermann reached for the canvas, but Ludvig pulled it back. "Is it a Rubens?" Hermann asked. "It couldn't be — "

Ludvig smiled. "You are very close. Anthony van Dyck, an apprentice of his — "

"I know who Van Dyck is," Hermann said, interrupting him. He reached again for the canvas. "May I?"

Ludvig didn't object, and, holding the painting by the frame, Hermann carried it into better light. The paint was cracked, but its condition was relatively good. The back of the canvas was smudged with glazed resin. As he evaluated the artwork, the incandescence from the bulb above his head surrounded him in a fuzzy, taupe cone. Stray rays of light carved shafts into the shadows.

"If you keep a masterpiece like this here in the cold and damp, you will destroy it."

Ludvig acknowledged the point with a tilt of his head.

Hermann couldn't hide his excitement. The white of the Madonna's skin was beginning to yellow and the varnish was losing its gloss, but there was no mistaking the painting's beauty. Or its value. In Germany, the market for it would be at least five thousand reichsmarks, maybe double that. "You take a risk bringing me here," he said.

"You take a risk coming here," Ludvig countered.

"How do you know I won't simply notify the authorities and have this confiscated?"

Ludvig shrugged. "A family friend tells me you can be trusted. And if you do betray me to the authorities, as you say, we both lose, don't we?"

At last, Hermann raised his eyes from the painting. "And the other two?" he asked, nodding toward the other frames still stacked against the crate.

Ludvig's expression didn't alter. He was watching the lieutenant without blinking. "Tell me about this one first," he said. "How much will you pay us for it? And how quickly?"

■ ■ ■

There was so much smoke inside the cramped bar that, behind his spectacles, Hermann's eyes were burning. The man in front of him, wearing a captain's uniform, was chewing on the butt of a thin cigar. When the captain exhaled, he made no effort to direct the smoke away from Hermann. On the other side of the counter, a lanky, empty-eyed bartender reached for a bottle, then turned it upside down over the captain's glass. A thin stream of clear liquid trickled from a chrome spout. In the far corner of the room, a scuffle erupted. Twisting on his barstool, Hermann looked. The captain didn't. A soldier crashed against a table, and a few glasses shattered on the floor. Another man yanked the soldier to his feet, then hustled him out the door. A welcome gust of fresh air rushed inside. Then the door closed again and the sounds subsided back into the usual cacophony of voices. Hermann couldn't breathe. The captain was squeezing his shoulder for more than a few seconds before he became aware of the pressure. He reached for his drink. He hadn't touched it yet, and already this was the captain's third.

"How long have we known each other now, Hermann?" the captain asked him. "Hey?"

Hermann shook his head. His eyes were drawn to a few wisps of tobacco smoke escaping through the captain's teeth.

"The irony is, my father worked for your father for twenty-five years. You went to the university — what did you study — it was art, wasn't it?" The captain made no attempt to mask his scorn — or the pleasure he took in his next thought. "Like my father, I became a mechanic. Now look where the two of us are sitting."

"I will pay you back, Fritz," Hermann said.

The captain swallowed half his drink. "I have no doubt."

"With interest," Hermann said. "The three thousand back into your pocket, plus twenty-five percent. This is a business proposition. I'm not asking for any favors."

The captain ran his tongue over his teeth, took another swallow of his vodka. "But you won't tell me what the money is for."

Hermann avoided the captain's intense stare. He knew Fritz better than he wanted to — well enough to know that, if he divulged the details of the deal he was working on, his old friend would no longer be happy with a profit of twenty-five percent. He would demand a share of Hermann's take from his buyer in Germany. He wished that he had somewhere else to turn for capital. If only he hadn't stretched himself so thin — But the Gregersens' paintings were as good as gold. Prospects like this didn't materialize every day.

"Three thousand marks," the captain repeated. His eyes roved the small, crowded bar in a squint, then settled again on Hermann's face. "Three thousand, and in cash. What does a photographer need with three thousand marks? Hey?"

"By Thursday," Hermann said. "I need it by Thursday — Friday at the latest."

The captain gave Hermann's shoulder a gentle punch. "And quickly. Hey?" When Hermann didn't respond with so much as a shrug, the captain thought of something else. "You never have told me, my friend, what a photographer is doing here in Denmark in a German uniform in the first place — "

"Does that matter?"

"I'm curious — "

"I'm as much a part of the Wehrmacht as you are, Fritz."

The captain gave Hermann's shoulder another gentle punch. "With your tiny camera, you mean?"

Hermann ignored the captain's derision. "Tomorrow I'm to use that tiny camera to take a photograph of King Christian riding his horse in the street, in front of the palace."

The captain smirked. "Are you hoping to impress me with that?" He spread his arms. "Do you really think anyone cares what happens in this pathetic little country? Every fool knows who that horse belongs to now anyway. The palace, too."

Despite his own lack of interest in the subject, Hermann's pride asserted itself. "The Ministry of Propaganda wants evidence — pictures, motion pictures even — to show the world what a German protectorate can look like. Reich Minister Goebbels himself issued the order for this photograph to be taken."

"Herr Goebbels himself, hey?"

Hermann assessed the captain's contemptuous smile. He had to resist the impulse to stand up and walk away. "About the money — " Behind him, a drunk bumped into his back, and he jerked forward. He glanced at the goon over his shoulder, then quietly lifted his glass to his mouth, took a swallow. The alcohol burned his lips, carved a path across his tongue, down his throat. "I need an answer from you. This opportunity — it won't wait."

The captain took his time, pursed his lips. He was still sneering. "You know, that much money, it will cost me something to get it." He picked up his glass, realized that it was empty, tapped the counter a few times with a stiff finger. Despite how busy he was, the bartender took a quick step over, grabbed the bottle, poured another refill. "Twenty-five percent sounds like a lot. But it depends, doesn't it?"

"It depends on what?"

"How long will you need it?"

Once again, the drunk soldier behind Hermann banged into him, this time causing him to spill his drink. When Hermann didn't react, the captain's brow creased. His eyes flashed, and he reached across his friend and gave the soldier a rough shove. The soldier twisted around. His eyes were bleary, his face was contorted. The moment he saw the captain, though, his expression changed. His jaw relaxed, and he licked his lips. His eyes darkened with confusion.

"Why don't you watch yourself, hey?"

"I —" The soldier fumbled for words, and this only seemed to infuriate the captain more. "It was an accident —"

"Hey?" The captain half stood from his stool, gave the soldier another shove. This one sent him reeling into the counter. The soldier caught himself, pulled himself back to his feet.

"I'm sorry," he sputtered.

The captain's face was livid. Hermann reached for his shoulder, but the captain shook his hand off him. "It's okay," Hermann told him. "The bar is crowded —"

"Sure," the captain said. The flush on his cheeks dissipated into a patchwork of purple stains and white splotches. "Sure." He sat back down, took a drag on his cigar. "Prost!" He raised his glass, waited for Hermann to do the same.

"Prost," Hermann echoed.

"You're a lucky man," the captain said to the drunk soldier, not yet ready to let him go. "You hear me? Consider this your lucky night."

"Forget about it, Fritz," Hermann said.

The captain took another swig from his glass, wiped his mouth with the back of his hand. "Answer the question, then. How long?"

Behind the captain, across the smoky bar, a door that led to a back room swung open, and a black-haired woman emerged. Hermann tracked her entrance over his friend's shoulder. She wasn't really a *woman*. She was just a girl — she couldn't have been more than eighteen. Hermann recognized instantly that she was a prostitute. This was clear from her makeup and the way she carried herself, the clothes she wore — a short skirt and fishnet stockings, a white jacket pulled tight over a red shirt. The jet-black hair was a wig. And then, a step behind her, the two girls holding hands as they entered the raucous bar, she was followed out of the back room by a second prostitute, younger still. This one was fair and thin, but taller. Her hair was her own, tied in a loose bun. Even from this distance, even through the thick air, through the shadows, Hermann was struck by how pale her eyes were. She was dressed like the other prostitute in a revealing skirt and stockings, but she carried herself differently. Hermann couldn't define his reaction to her. He simply felt a twinge in his heart. He fully intended to answer the captain's question. He hadn't forgotten Ludvig Gregersen or his paintings. He knew how much he stood to profit. He would double the money for himself, probably even triple it. But he couldn't pull his eyes from the girl.

"Hey?" The captain mistook his friend's hesitation for reluctance. He hadn't yet seen the prostitutes. "How long will you need the money? You have to acknowledge the point, Hermann — twenty-five percent for a week is a different proposition from twenty-five percent for a month."

"I —" Hermann began, but then lost his train of thought. "A few days maybe." An unshaven man with long, greasy hair emerged from the back room as well. He grabbed the slender girl by the elbow, then started with her toward the front of the bar. The black-haired prostitute followed. Hermann struggled to return his attention to the captain. "No more than a week —"

When someone whistled at the girls, at last the captain twisted on his stool to get a look behind him. He shifted forward again abruptly, fastened his friend with a scowl. "One would almost think, Hermann," he said, unimpressed, "that you have never seen a whore before."

"So what will it be, then?" Hermann demanded, still distracted. He was wondering what these two prostitutes and their pimp had been doing in the back room. He had heard of such things — The same door opened again, and now an officer in a German uniform stumbled out, tucking his shirt into his trousers. Picturing this animal with the prostitutes, Hermann felt suddenly flustered. He wanted to hurry the captain, to finish this discussion. "Will you lend me the money or won't you?"

"Three thousand marks for one week," the captain said. "Is that what you are asking?"

"One week," Hermann confirmed. "No more than that." The pimp shoved the front door open, and a fresh gust of wind reached Hermann through a crowd of anxious, hungry men who, like him, had fixed upon these women who could be had by any of them for a pocketful of coins. The rain was coming down in a torrent now. Splattered by the shrapnel of a few stray drops, the pimp paused long enough to flip up the collar of his coat. The heavy nylon tresses of the prostitute's black wig hardly rustled. Wisps of the other girl's hair caught the wind, and she had to swipe a few glistening, golden strands from her mouth. Even then, her focus never once wavered from an imaginary point in front of her face. Her expression remained somber, and she never returned any of the men's stares. Hermann had the impression that the night had spilled inside through the open door, stealing the light from her complexion. "At the end of the week, I return the three thousand to you, plus seven hundred and fifty for your trouble." The pimp pushed the black-haired prostitute outside first, then the other girl. And then, swallowed into the ink, they were gone. As the door slammed shut behind them, Hermann felt himself overcome with a sense of loss that he wouldn't have been able to explain.

"One thousand," the captain said.

"What?"

"I give you three thousand for a week. You repay me four thousand."

"That's too much," Hermann said. But his heart was no longer in the negotiation. His eyes hadn't yet left the front door.

"It's a lot of money you're asking," the captain said with a shrug. "You can take it, or you can leave it."

At last, Hermann returned his eyes to his friend. "Okay," he said.

"Okay?"

"But I need it by Friday, understand?" Then he couldn't restrain himself any longer. He tossed a bill onto the counter to pay for his drink, started for the door. Behind him, the captain chased him with a few words. *She's not worth it, Hermann — save your money, hey? I will want my three thousand back.* But Hermann barely heard him. A man wearing a hat barked something into his face. Another gave him a friendly shove — maybe this was a soldier he knew, though right now he recognized no one. He nearly tripped over a low table, stepped on someone's foot, caught himself on someone else's sleeve. As he made his way through the bar, he realized that every single person in the room — every last person — was a man. That was what accounted for this stink. That was what accounted for this noise. There weren't any women here. He stumbled to the door, reached for the handle.

Outside, he searched the street for the girl, but she was already gone. Leaning into the wind, he chose a direction and began walking. At the corner, there was still no sign of her. The neighborhood was empty. He twisted on his heel and started in the other direction. Hearing the echo of footsteps, he stopped to listen. In the distance, he imagined that he could hear voices — the growl of a man's voice, a girl's high-pitched titter. No streetlamps were burning, the city was dark. He peered into the grainy, tarnished haze of the rain but couldn't see a thing, not even any movement. When the pale-eyed prostitute had stepped into the bar from the back room, the rest of the faces surrounding her had blurred. Her own face — her ivory skin, her sharp cheekbones, her soft hair, her colorless eyes — had acquired the clarity of a photograph. The image began to assume the character of an object — like the memory of a painting — and it hovered in front of Hermann's eyes now, as distinct as a beacon. He started down the side street, following the voices.

The quicker he walked, though, the farther away the voices trailed. He was nearly running when he lost them completely. He came to a stop at an intersection, out of breath, held himself still with one hand resting on the corner of a building. His coat was becoming soaked. The wind cut through his wet uniform to his skin. He took note of where he was, one street away from the harbor at Nyhavn, then turned and, hunching his shoulders, his hands in his pockets, retraced his steps through the black.

9.

December 1941.

Sitting in the window of a small hotel a couple of weeks later, the pale-eyed prostitute stared outside at a commotion in the street. A German military automobile was parked half a block down the Nyhavn canal. A man in a lieutenant's uniform had left the car and crossed the cobblestone road to the next hotel over from this one, where, standing on the steps in front of the glass-paned door, he was engaged in conversation with a heavyset woman dressed in a morning coat. It was early December, and it was a gray day. It was cold — cold enough that it should have been snowing. Here in the harbor, though, the air gusting off the sea was laced with so much salt that the rain didn't freeze, and the girl's view was blurred through glass streaked with rivulets of rainwater. Her curiosity was piqued. It was not yet eight o'clock. In this rough section of the capital, it wasn't usual to see anyone outside, other than a stray sailor or two, until noon.

The other prostitutes would sleep into the afternoon. The girl had woken as she always did, exactly at seven. For years, she hadn't been able to sleep longer. And this was time she cherished — she could sit by herself with her thoughts, without a sound to disturb her, without another voice, without anyone's mouth, without anyone's fingers, without the stench of sweat, without the delirium of pills or alcohol. She knew how strange the other girls considered her. She couldn't remember feeling *normal*, not for as long as she could recollect. She enjoyed no connection to anything. Sometimes, the notion of stepping off the cobblestones into the harbor and sinking to the bottom of the cold green sea offered its own perverse comfort. Her breath fogged the window, but she didn't wipe the glass. She had been watching the German for about three minutes now, since he had first knocked on the door of the hotel. Maybe he was lost, or maybe he had forgotten something when he was drunk.

When the woman at the door couldn't help him, she called inside the hotel, and a few moments later a man with the beginning of a beard appeared, squinting in the dim morning light. He dropped the butt of a cigarette into the street, pulled his pajama top tight around his throat, shoved the woman back into the foyer behind him. The German asked him a question, and the man rubbed his scruffy, grizzled chin with stubby fingers. Even from a distance, his teeth were yellow from coffee and tobacco. Then he pointed down the street at the hotel where the girl was resident. There was no chance that she would be seen inside her dark room. Nevertheless, some instinct prompted her to duck backward, behind the curtain.

She watched with new interest when, following the hotelier's directions, the German started down the sidewalk, his eyes fastened on the sign posted above the door beneath her. It promised a hotel — but this, like many of these small inns lining the canal, was a brothel. His footsteps reached her ears through the glass. When she leaned toward the window, the light glistened on her forehead, and the pale skin of her cheeks became translucent. When she licked her lips, they brightened into the deep, rich color of a rose.

Two or three minutes passed before the German's knocking roused the brothel's pimp from his bed. A door slammed inside the building. The girl thought about running. She couldn't recollect ever having seen this soldier before, and she had no reason to think that he was coming for her. Still, she searched the room for her shoes. Her coat was crumpled under the bed. But she was only imagining things — and anyway there was, of course, no escape for her. She belonged to her pimp, and there was nowhere she could hide. Footsteps shuffled down the stairs, the locks twisted in the door. The German lieutenant's voice was a muffled series of indistinct syllables. Søren Pound's replies rumbled through the walls. *Yes, yes. But we are all asleep. You will have to come back later. Don't you know what time it is?* The meaning of the German's next words was unmistakable. He was not going to be put off. The girl stood from the rickety chair. When the curtain dropped, the air thickened. She crossed the room, sat down on the edge of the narrow bed she shared with another prostitute named Olga, touched her on her bony shoulder.

The Russian girl was only nineteen, but her skin was slack, her breath smelled like meat. Her hips were wide, and her arms were as thin as sticks, riddled with needle tracks. She had only fallen into bed three hours earlier, and she didn't respond when the girl shook her. A few seconds passed in silence, then she gasped for air like a diver coming to the surface with pearls, and after began to snore. The girl waited, then gave her shoulder another, firmer shake. When Olga opened her eyes, she focused on the younger Polish girl without recognition. "Oh — it's only you, Polina," she said, settling back into the bed. "What do you want? Is it time?"

Polina remembered the stink of her breath and the heat of her embrace from the middle of the night these last months since they had been sharing this bed, and her desire to escape translated itself into another impulse. She wrapped her arms around Olga.

"Is it already time?" Olga repeated.

Polina shook her head.

"What is it — what are you doing? Why are you waking me?" Olga spit the words like phlegm.

"I'm afraid," Polina whispered.

Olga pushed her away. "Leave me alone."

The patter of rain drummed the window. In the room above them, two prostitutes turned over in bed. Springs whined, floorboards creaked.

"They're coming for me."

"Who?"

Inside the hotel, footsteps shook the stairs. Their room was two flights up. Polina listened.

"What are you talking —" But Olga didn't finish her question. She fell back to sleep, snorted, stopped breathing completely. Polina held on to her and waited. The footsteps climbed the building to the second floor, then approached down the length of the hall. Søren didn't knock. A key scratched the lock. The knob twisted with a squeak. The door opened. Polina looked up from her awkward seat on the bed.

"Come with me," Søren said. When she stood, his fingers sank into her shoulder. She remembered this same grip from her first night in his hotel. The pimp had an enormous penis. Flaccid, it hung halfway down his thigh. He didn't become erect until he had beaten her. Then he was inside her, ripping her, and it took him forever to come. But it was his fingers that she remembered, gouging her shoulders, separating her arms from her body. She didn't try to resist him now. He twirled her toward the door like a puppet, and she tripped in front of him down the narrow hall. Safe in the uncomfortable bed, Olga hadn't woken again, and when she finally did, she wouldn't remember a thing about the morning. Another roommate would assume the Polish girl's place. Polina was taking these next steps alone, as she had so many before.

Hermann stood waiting for her at the bottom of the staircase, bathed in light as thick as paint. It glowed on his green uniform like an aura, shimmered weakly on his cheeks. In his spectacles, it shone with crystalline brilliance, as cold and crisp as rays refracted in the lens of a microscope. His lips parted when he saw her. He had spent the last week looking for her. And now she was his.

■ ■ ■

In the room above the bakery, nothing felt right.

The German army had garrisoned a number of city blocks just outside the old town. Soldiers were given makeshift barracks partitioned from the larger buildings. Officers occupied the apartments above the retail stores that lined the streets. In this industrial room, the windows were oversize, framed in steel. Hermann Schmidt had favored the apartment because of the light. Before him, it had belonged to a Dane who repaired bikes. Now it was his studio. He had salvaged a desk, which doubled as his dining table, a few filing cabinets, a bed comprised of a thin mattress resting on a rickety cot. A free-standing wardrobe stood in one corner, a mirror hanging from one of its doors. The rough-hewn floor was uncovered, stained with grease. A kerosene burner supplied the heat, but it was too small to keep such a large room warm. The bathroom consisted of a toilet and a sink, only a rudimentary shower. There was no kitchen. A hot plate was set up on the desk. Rats scurried through the walls at night, pilfering food from the bakery underneath. But it wasn't the austerity or the bleakness of the apartment that bothered Polina. It was something else, something that she could only feel in her bones.

Something wasn't right. *Nothing* was. Hermann had helped her gently from his car, shown her solicitously up the stairs. Now she stood in the center of the room hugging her own shoulders, trying to suppress a shiver, turning slowly about on her heel. And then it dawned on her. It was the very same thing that had attracted Hermann to the space. It was that which was making her uncomfortable — it was the light.

"I don't have anything to offer you," the German said in broken Danish.

Polina shook her head. Her Danish wasn't any better than his, though she had been brought to Copenhagen over a year ago now. "I don't want anything from you," she replied.

"I mean, I don't have any food. Some rye crackers, but nothing else. You must be hungry."

"I'm not hungry, no," Polina said.

"Would you sit down?" The German indicated the bed.

"No." Polina's fingers dug into her shoulders. "I prefer to stand."

The German took a step toward her, then stopped. "I want you to be happy here," he said.

Polina didn't answer, because there was nothing to say to this.

"I know it's not much, but — " Hermann followed her gaze to a dark corner of the room. Polina had the impression that he was seeing the apartment through her eyes. Perhaps he hadn't noticed the grease stains on the floor before. There was a layer of dust on everything, dirty plates stacked in the bathroom sink. The parts of a broken camera were scattered across the desk. A yellowing page torn from a newspaper was tacked askew to an otherwise bare, unpainted plaster wall. Everything inside the room was filthy and worn — except for the mirror on the wardrobe, which was polished to a bright shine. "What's your name?"

The German's voice broke into Polina's observations. She lifted her eyes from the mirror, dragged them back to the man's face.

"The gentleman at the hotel told me that they call you Polina, but he didn't give me the rest of your name."

"He isn't a gentleman."

"He said that you speak Polish — that you're from Poland."

"He's a pimp. He owns girls, that's what he does."

Hermann examined her through a squint. When he opened his mouth, she noticed the gaps between his teeth. Like a baby's teeth, she remarked, not yet fully developed.

"How much did you pay him?"

"What?"

"No one has ever paid to take me out before."

Hermann continued to stare at her, until the silence became unpleasant. Wind scratched the windows like fingers clawing the glass. The smell of baking yeast seeped through the floor.

"I'm wondering how much I will get."

"I don't know what you're talking about." Behind the crisp gleam of his spectacles, Hermann's eyes reflected his disappointment.

"Normally, I don't see much. Søren doesn't have to pay us anything at all, you understand what I mean? He has his hands on our throats, and he can squeeze them into fists whenever he wants to. I breathe because he lets me. I eat because he feeds me." Polina was listening to herself speak. She had never articulated these thoughts before, and they were as much of a surprise to her as they were to Hermann. "He only gives us a few crowns every now and again to keep us working. It isn't payment — it's a bribe. So I have a pocket full of coins I can't spend, and Olga has heroin in her veins. It's like that, you see? But I've never been taken out of the hotel before, not by a customer, only by Søren's partners, so I don't know what to expect — how much I'll get."

Behind his spectacles, Hermann blinked. This girl's pragmatism hadn't just caught him off guard, it sickened him. *He was saving her.* He wasn't paying her. Couldn't she see that? "How old are you, Polina?"

The Polish girl wrinkled her nose. Her eyes were so pale, in this light they lost their color. "How old are *you*?"

Hermann loosened his tie. It was cold in the room, but he was suddenly hot. He took off his coat, draped it over the back of a chair. From a few feet away, Polina could smell the sweat beneath his arms. He was nervous. "I'm thirty-five," he said.

"You have a wife." Polina had noticed the thin gold band on his finger.

"I have a daughter, too," Hermann admitted. His hands were still resting on his coat. The fabric pricked his fingertips. It wasn't luxurious cloth. It was durable, powerful. "Ten years old."

"My age," Polina said.

"What's that?" Hermann raised his eyes. This girl was confounding him. Was this a joke? He laughed, but it was an uncomfortable laugh. Beneath her heavy sweater, he could see the swell of her breasts. They were a young woman's breasts, yes, but they weren't undeveloped. Her hips gave shape to her skirt. Angela was a child. Angela had nothing in common with this girl —

"Who is Angela?"

"What?" Hermann was stunned.

"You were speaking the name," Polina said. "Just now."

"Was I?"

"Is she your daughter?"

"How old are you, Polina?" Hermann asked, repeating his question.

"To tell you the truth," Polina replied, "I don't know anymore. I turned sixteen. That's the last birthday I remember. But that might have been more than a year ago, I forget. Time doesn't run in circles for me anymore. It travels in a straight line now."

"What are you talking about?"

Polina considered the question. "I'm as nervous as you are, I guess."

"Come here."

Polina didn't move.

Hermann nodded toward the bed. "Come here with me. Sit down."

"I am comfortable standing."

"I told you. I want you to be happy here."

"How long will I be here?"

"What?" Hermann hadn't understood the question.

"Do you want me to suck you off now?"

"What —"

"Or are you going to fuck me?"

"You have it all wrong."

"Do I?"

Hermann straightened his spectacles on the bridge of his nose. "Yes."

"So you aren't interested in me."

Once again, Hermann felt confounded. "I didn't say that."

Polina held him in her gaze, then stepped across the room to the window. Smoke swirled from a brick chimney a block away. The sky was every bit as gray as it had been in the morning. On this side of town, away from the water, a light snow was falling. The façades of the buildings lining the street formed a colorless wall. Still, the light stung her eyes. Behind her, she was aware of this man's breathing. Shallow, through his nostrils. No, nothing felt right here in this room. She couldn't remember feeling safe. But here things were out of balance in a way that they hadn't been before.

"Take off your sweater." Hermann's voice was barely more than a whisper, but the command was clear.

Polina flinched, but she tried not to show it. She remained at the glass. A truck was rumbling down the road toward the bakery. When it reached the building, it came to a stop. The driver stepped outside, bundled himself in his coat, trudged to the back of the truck, yanked open the doors.

"Didn't you hear me?"

"So it is to fuck me," Polina said to the window. "That is why you brought me here."

"You don't understand."

"Don't I?"

"No."

When Polina faced him, Hermann had taken a couple of steps toward her. He stopped, returned her gaze. This reminded her of a game she used to play as a child, where your opponent could only approach when you weren't looking. Then his eyes dropped to her sweater. She could feel them on her breasts. A man had told her once that they were beautiful. That she had the most glorious breasts a girl could have. But that was a year ago, in her puberty. They were fuller now, she had noticed it herself. They were still firm, but heavy enough to want to drop a little. She thought about complying, but her hands wouldn't budge, they wouldn't lift the sweater over her head. Instead, she turned away again. Outside, the driver was carrying a tray of bread from the bakery to the back of the truck. She watched him load it then make his way back inside for another steel tray.

"I am going to take your picture," Hermann said.

"Why?" The question was so simple — there was so little inflection in Polina's voice — that yet one more time Hermann became confused. How could he impress this girl? Why didn't she appreciate what he wanted to do for her?

"I am a photographer," he explained.

"I can see this in your eyes," Polina said. "And in how carefully you maintain your spectacles."

Hermann took another step closer. "Take off your sweater."

"So you can see me naked."

"So I can take a photograph."

"Do you want a photograph," Polina asked, "because you don't trust your mind to remember? Or," she continued, now switching to Polish, "is it because you can't touch me with your fingers?"

"I want your photograph," Hermann said, "because you're beautiful." Another step, and he was directly behind her. Polina took a deep breath through her nose. Her body wanted to shiver, but she wouldn't let it. "Has anyone told you that before? How beautiful you are. I can't believe it — "

"I don't want you to touch me." Polina spoke the words abruptly and clearly. But, again, she spoke them in Polish. *Nie chcę, żebyś mnie dotykał.*

"What?"

"Stay away from me. Don't get any closer." She was speaking in a language Hermann could not understand.

"Let me help you."

"I'm warning you," Polina said, now in a whisper.

Hermann's fingers found the bottom of her sweater, clasped it, began to raise it. When the shirt underneath lifted, too, and he caught sight of her slender torso, his throat tightened. Her skin was made of paper, of silk, of ivory. It would be cold to the touch. Captured inside the lens of his camera, it would radiate. He raised the heavy wool fabric up to her armpits, stretched it to pull it over her shoulders. He gasped when he noticed the bruises that darkened her ribs and arms.

"No," she whispered, "I'm not challenging you, I'm begging you instead."

"Polish has a brutal tongue," Hermann said. "Like German."

The sweater got tangled in her hair, then slid off, over her head. Outside, the driver was climbing back into the cab of the truck. When the engine started, a plume of diesel exhaust shot from a pipe behind the cab, mixing with the snow like wine in water. Polina's shirt was crumpled, pulled up onto her breasts. Hermann's fingers were sweaty. He was fumbling with her bra. "Don't touch me," Polina said. Now she spoke in Danish again, so that this man would understand.

"You have a beauty that will translate onto film," the photographer said. "I can see it. I will show it to you, you will see."

"I won't let you touch me," Polina said.

Hermann stopped moving.

"Your fingers are sweaty," Polina said.

"A hundred and eighty reichsmarks."

Polina froze into a statue. The man's breath sank into her hair. She didn't have to ask him what he meant. She understood what he was telling her.

"That is how much I paid your pimp," Hermann explained anyway.

Polina's heart touched her ribs. His moist breath was continuing to warm her scalp, now to creep down her cheeks like tears, slide beneath the collar of her shirt, slither around her breasts. This was an absurd amount of money. Goose bumps pricked her arms. Sweat trickled down her ribs. *She wasn't going back.* She would never leave this place. This man had bought her from Søren.

"Now turn around," Hermann said. He managed once again to sound a tender note. "I want to see you."

When Polina still didn't move, he placed his hands on her shoulders. Gently, not like Søren had. Softly, so that she could feel how smooth his skin was — as smooth, she thought, as the feathers of a swan. He twisted her around to face him. If she had resisted, he wouldn't have been able to force her. But she didn't resist, and now she was standing beneath him, looking up into his eyes. His breath streamed from his nostrils onto her face, into her mouth. And she tasted him. "It's just you and me now," she said.

"What?"

"In this room," she said. "It's just you and me. Can't you feel how strange that is?"

Hermann didn't respond. His fingers slid from her shoulders, slipped beneath the collar of her shirt. He ripped the fabric off her. The buttons popped from their threads, landed on the rough-hewn floor like pearls bouncing on marble. The sound recalled a memory. *What do you think of her? Isn't she pretty?* In the apartment in Kraków, her uncle's fingers had directed her into the bedroom, where the black-haired doll was lying against a dirty pillow on the unmade bed. Her thighs were still tingling where the sharp, cold edges of the bicycle rack behind his seat had gouged her skin. *She's pretty, just like you are.* She had held on to the doll while her uncle undressed her. When she dropped it, its china face cracked. One of the ears had broken off and skittered across the floor — just like the buttons of her shirt now, on the floor of Hermann's apartment. Her eyes had tracked the broken ear until it stopped moving.

The German's clammy fingers traveled down the length of her arms, peeling off the sleeves of her shirt like a second layer of skin. Hermann stopped when he reached her hands, and he intertwined his fingers with hers. Specks of his spit flecked her cheeks, but when she looked at him, it was Czeslaw's face that loomed in front of her. When the German's hands found her breasts, her nipples didn't harden. They remained as soft as desiccated plums. He tried to touch her sensually, but she was only aware of his sweat and his eagerness and his breath.

When his hands dropped to her skirt and ripped the fabric, she slapped him. The violence was sudden and unexpected, and he reared backward. For a moment, Polina imagined that he would strike her back. Instead, his lips rose in another false smile. "Perfect," he said.

She didn't understand. She watched him straighten his spectacles on his nose, then take a step in retreat.

"Don't move."

One of her hands had found her skirt and was holding it up. The other was covering her breasts. She had no idea whether or not she was breathing.

He continued to stare at her, then turned and walked across the room. In the corner next to the wardrobe, he found his camera. It was a heavy piece of equipment. He hoisted it onto his shoulder by lifting the tripod, carried it back to her, set it down in front of her. "No — this won't do."

Polina couldn't understand what he wanted.

"Here — come this way." Hermann grabbed her naked shoulder, pulled her a few steps into the room, away from the window. "I need the light behind me." He set the camera in front of the window, aimed it at her. The mirror was behind her, and her reflection was visible in the glass. Still, she hadn't breathed. "Perfect," he said. "Absolutely perfect." His lips were raised in the same ugly smile when the shutter released. He snapped the photograph, then another.

AMALIA

10.

Jutland. December 24, 1941.

Amalia knelt beside the tub in the children's bathroom on the second floor of the Nielsens' house. Pushing her sleeve above her elbow, she submerged her hand into the bath. The hot bathwater stung her fingers. Between her knuckles, the skin was so dry that it was beginning to crack. The harsh detergents she used for the Nielsens' laundry had given her eczema. At night sometimes her hands bled onto her sheets. Naked in the white porcelain tub, twelve-year-old Christina Nielsen splashed her. A droplet of dirty water nipped her eye. The bar of soap Christina had lost slipped from her grasp. Her sleeve dropped into the bath. The milky water blushed red around her fingers.

Although it was the day before Christmas, Amalia had woken at four a.m., as she always did in order to get to work by five. This morning, she had allowed herself an extra few minutes under the covers. The wind had been blowing so hard that it whistled in the chimney. Amalia could hear the shrill sound through the wall. It had been difficult to pull herself from bed, knowing that she would have to cross the field to the Nielsens'. The soil had frozen into ice. There was a hole in the sole of one of her shoes, and the slush would pinch her toes. Before the war, Christmas had meant roast pork and red cabbage, marzipan cakes and candles and gifts in the evening. Seven years ago, Amalia had traveled with Oskar to Copenhagen to spend the holiday with Fru Gregersen, and the family had taken a sleigh ride in a park where the trees were made of sugar and the sky cotton. What she remembered from that day was the slap of bells tied to the leather harness and the breathing and snorting of the horse when the driver coaxed the animal into a trot. It had been so warm beneath the heavy blanket. Dry flakes of snow had melted into nectar on her tongue. Now Christmas meant something else. Christmas only reminded her how harsh life had become.

By eleven o'clock, Amalia's chores in the kitchen were complete. She had scrubbed the floor in the pantry, cleaned yesterday's dishes, carted the trash outside, unpacked the special linens. Setting up for the afternoon party belonged to Mrs. Nielsen herself and her personal maid. Amalia was too young to be trusted with anything so important. Normally, Amalia had nothing to do with the Nielsen children, either, but Alicia, the governess, had contracted influenza. This had happened two weeks before, and Alicia hadn't been allowed anywhere near the children since. Mrs. Nielsen had asked Amalia to look after Christina and Erik, to keep them out of trouble until it was time to get them ready for an early supper.

Christina giggled. Amalia's knees throbbed on the cold, hard tile floor. A twinge traveled up her thigh. She ignored the pain, leaned over the wall of the tub, reached into the water to chase the bar of soap. When she touched the girl's toes, the child squealed. She rubbed her legs together, sending another splash of water into Amalia's face. "It's not there, silly," Christina said, "or I would have felt it myself."

Amalia peered into the gray water. The soap was hidden beneath the film and froth. Giving up, she placed her hand on the edge of the tub, began to push herself to her feet.

"Not yet," Christina whined. "You haven't washed my back."

Only four years separated them, but Amalia had the impression that she was bathing a baby half her age. The contrast between them was stark. Christina was rail thin. Her arms were twigs. Her skin was translucent. Amalia was dark and heavy. She was on her feet all day, but she ate too much. She could barely fit herself into the new uniform the Nielsens had given her just a few months before — she didn't bother even trying to button the collar. Christina's cheeks were rosy. Amalia's were chafed from the weather. As far as Amalia could see, Christina danced from one delight to the next. Her own thick shoulders stooped. She had long since forgotten how to smile. "Does Alicia wash your back for you, too?" she asked the girl, pausing with one knee still on the floor.

When Christina laughed, her eyes caught the soft, gray light from the window and flashed liquid blue. Except for the cobalt accents in the corner of the floor tiles, Amalia had the impression that this was the only color in the room. Christina's laughter burst around her like an explosion. "Don't be so silly all the time," she said to the fat servant. "Alicia doesn't give me baths. She's my governess. She reads to me and teaches me to write and to do math."

"I'm sorry," Amalia said. She didn't understand why, but she felt suddenly stupid. "I didn't know."

"You didn't know because you didn't ask, because you're a silly girl."

Amalia's fingers turned white on the edge of the tub beneath the weight of her body as she stood. Water tinged red dripped down the slippery porcelain.

"Wait!" Christina insisted. "You haven't found the soap, and now you haven't washed my back either."

"Why do you want me to wash your back," Amalia asked the girl, "if Alicia doesn't?" Straightening up, pain radiated from her knees like heat, then dissipated. She stretched her neck and shoulders, arranged her shirt around her stomach.

"Because it feels good," Christina said.

"If Alicia doesn't wash it, who does?"

"Mama does, of course. Now wash my back, you silly cow, or I will tell Mama that you stole one of her brushes. The silver one with chestnut bristles."

Amalia blinked. The girl's words had stunned her. Though she had little experience with Christina, she didn't put the threat past her. The soapy lather on the girl's naked chest began to evanesce. Beneath the residue, her nipples were dots as faint as stains of raspberry jam. "How can I wash your back?" Amalia finally asked her. "You lost the soap, and I can't find it."

"Use a washcloth," Christina said. "Do I have to think of everything?"

Amalia took a small towel from the linen cabinet, sat down on the edge of the tub behind the girl. The porcelain rim dug into her ass. She waited for Christina to oblige by leaning forward, then dipped the cloth into the water and began to wipe the girl's back. It surprised her how sharp the child's bones were. The ridge of her spine jutted from her neck. Her tendons were sinewy cords, as taut as the wires in the Nielsens' grand piano.

Christina bent her head forward, rested her hands on her knees. Her shoulders, though, remained tense, raised. Without thinking what she was doing, Amalia let her fingers travel down the girl's rigid muscles. "Mama never does that," Christina said, closing her eyes.

Amalia dipped the towel into the bath again, squeezed out the excess water. Gently, she pressed the hot cloth onto Christina's slender back, let her fingers trace the channels and grooves, peaks and valleys, in the girl's frame. The bathwater stilled, and steam rose in small clouds that hovered above the surface. Drips pattered from the spout. The soapy brew sloshed against the porcelain. A minute passed and then another, before Amalia realized that the girl was working her thighs together. Slowly but deliberately, in rhythm with her own massage. She paused, and the girl paused. She dipped the towel one more time, lifted it again. Now the girl's small hand found the apex of her thighs and, silently, disappeared into the water. "You mustn't do that."

Christina froze. Her body was as tight as a coil.

"You have to stop that," Amalia repeated. "Now."

Christina's body stiffened under Amalia's hand.

"Take your fingers away."

Christina shook her head.

"Do you understand me? Take your fingers off your cunt." For this was the word that she had heard her father use, so this was the word that she knew.

Christina quaked. A quiver started in her core, then traveled up her spine. "My what?"

Amalia took a breath — almost, it felt, for the first time since she had started giving the girl a massage. Steam filled her nose. The cloth, she realized, had become tepid in her hand. The fabric gouged her fingertips, and she understood that her fingers were pressed into the girl's ribs. "Your cunt."

A second quiver rose through the girl's body. "Why?"

"What do you think you're doing?" Amalia asked, answering the girl's question with one of her own.

"I don't know." The girl squeezed her eyes shut. Her body was still flexed. And then her legs began to move again, as if she were swimming, only so slowly that — except for the surface of the water, rolling in small waves — Amalia could barely discern it.

Amalia let her eyes travel the length of the girl's arm. Where her fingers disappeared into the gray bath, she was able to see the top of the girl's small, hairless vagina. "Stop it."

Christina shook her head. Her fingers were moving faster again.

"You mustn't — "

Now the bathwater splashed against the walls of the tub.

"Stop it!" Amalia repeated.

"No."

Amalia grabbed the girl's forearm. In the same instant, the door to the bathroom swung open. The slosh of the water was so loud, so intense in Amalia's ears, that she didn't hear it. She wasn't aware of the footsteps or the change in the value of the light. Her grasp tightened on the girl's thin, bony wrist. Her fingers plunged into the warm water. She hadn't intended to squeeze the girl so severely.

"What's happening in here?"

The voice ricocheted off the tile walls like a hammer striking a mirror. The words reverberated in Amalia's head. Her scalp caught fire. She twisted toward the door. For a split second, Erik was a giant. Then he was nothing more than a ten-year-old child again. A reedy, blue-eyed, blond-haired boy with a puzzled smile creasing his face into an exclamation point. "Get out of here," Amalia said. Her fingers were crushed between Christina's thighs. The water surrounded her hand like the lick of flames.

"Why do I have to?"

"*Get out of here!*" It wasn't a shout. But the intention was clear. Erik hesitated. A shadow darkened his eyes. Then he backed out of the room, and the door closed behind him. On Amalia's hand, the girl's thighs had become a vise. She waited for the spasm to stop, then pulled her fingers away. Her knuckles bled. Her own thighs ached.

■ ■ ■

At eight o'clock that evening, Amalia was still in the kitchen of the Nielsen house. For families living in town, ingredients for a traditional Christmas dinner had been hard to find. Meat was scarce. Even butter was in short supply. It was so expensive that most shopkeepers couldn't afford to stock it. The risk that it would perish was too great. Here on the farm, there was an abundance. It had been a lean year, but that only meant less money coming in — and that meant little to a man like Jurgen Nielsen. There was not much that he wanted anyway. A new tractor maybe. A dress for his wife, to silence her nagging. They had everything they needed and more. For Amalia, this meant a long night, with hours of hard work behind her and mountains of effort still to come. Every pot, every pan, every plate in the kitchen had been used, some more than once. Standing in front of the sink, she had processed a river of cookware in a sea of dishwater. Her fingers were sore. Her back ached, her shoulders were numb. The skin on her hands was white and spongy. She had started with the roasting pans at four thirty, before the meal was served. Now more than three hours later she had been on her feet ever since, without a single break. And there was no end in sight. Plates from the main courses were piled next to the sink, and behind her, in the dining room, she could hear the scrape and clatter of silverware on dishes. The party would continue into the night.

She stopped to straighten her spine, dug her fingers into the muscles above her hips, leaned back and took a breath. When she closed her eyes, she was suddenly dizzy. After all, she hadn't herself eaten since morning. At ten a.m., she had taken a minute to swallow a few slices of bread. Watching the children, she had missed her usual lunchtime. And then she had gotten busy in the kitchen. A second maid, a girl named Birgit, whose family had come from Belgium to Denmark just before the war, entered the kitchen with yet another load of dishes. She set the tray down on the counter next to the sink. Amalia sighed, reached for the dishes to make sure that none toppled. This was the family's best china, the blue-and-white Royal Copenhagen that had belonged to Mrs. Nielsen's parents. They had to take extra care with these pieces. Mrs. Nielsen catalogued every plate, every cup, every saucer. "Another family joined them," Birgit said.

"Who?"

Birgit shook her head. She didn't know their names — she hadn't seen them before. "I don't think they'll stay long."

"I thought I heard the front door open."

"They sat down for a bite, that's all. I think there are twenty-eight at the table now."

"Twenty-eight?" Amalia lifted a stack of plates off the tray, set them down on the counter as close to the wall as she could. "It feels like fifty."

"A hundred," Birgit agreed. "I can barely stand. And they've asked for the roast pork again, and the potatoes."

Amalia finished emptying the tray. A cup teetered on the edge of the tallest stack. Rather than remove it from the jumble, she shifted the plates at the bottom to stabilize the tower. She had been doing this type of work for years now, and she knew how to get dishes clean. When Birgit carried the tray back out for another load, Amalia decided to steal a minute for herself. Fatigue was getting the better of her. She dried her hands on her apron as she stepped from the sink to the back door. Inside the kitchen, the air was so hot and steamy that she could barely breathe. The knob was cold on her fingertips. She twisted it, pushed the door open. A chilly blast gusted through the gap. She glanced over her shoulder, then reached into the pocket of her apron and grabbed three slivers of candied orange peel that she had lifted from the cook's basket a few hours earlier. The dried fruit softened on her tongue. She savored the flavor, milking the sugar from the rind, before finally swallowing the sweet pulp.

The food soothed her. She closed her eyes, let the fresh air fill her lungs. A spray of mist dappled her cheeks, her forehead. When she opened her eyes again, she was looking up into a black sky perforated by falling snow. She let her gaze stray across the field toward her house. The snow had begun to stick, and it was beautiful. The ugly furrows the farmers made to work the soil were hidden beneath a white blanket. All the violence was gone, all the hardness. Denmark was a soft, magical place, and here it was, Christmas. Amalia noticed the lights burning in the windows downstairs in her house, and she wished that she could run across the field and join her family. It looked warm and cozy inside the tiny cottage, with smoke rising from the chimney and snow collecting on the thatch roof. How nice it would be to spend Christmas Eve with her father and brother.

"What do you think you're doing, standing there?"

Amalia turned to face the middle-aged woman in the kitchen doorway. The woman's hair, normally gathered in a

CRAIG LARSEN

loose bun, had been lifted into an elegant coiffure. Her shape-less body had been squeezed into a regal black dress, which Amalia herself had let out the week before in preparation for the party. Her neck glistened with a string of tired, yellowing pearls she only brought out for special occasions, three or four times a year. "Mrs. Nielsen," Amalia said.

"You shouldn't open that door. We'll lose the heat. I could feel the draft all the way in the dining room."

"I'm sorry, ma'am." Amalia retreated from the doorway, pulled the door shut. The bluster of the icy storm outside was muted into a whisper. The close, steamy air choked her lungs again. The cottage across the field disappeared, replaced by Amalia's own reflection in the frosty glass panes.

"How long were you standing there?"

Amalia didn't respond. She straightened her apron around her waist, returned to the sink.

"I don't pay you to stand now, do I?"

Once again, Amalia felt overcome with dizziness. Her knuckles stung when she dipped her hands into the hot water.

"I'll want to talk to you about this rudeness."

"Ma'am?" Amalia was perplexed. She twisted around to get a look at her boss, but Mrs. Nielsen was already heading back into the dining room.

"If I address you," the middle-aged woman explained as she left, "I expect your attention."

Amalia reached for the next plate. In her confusion, her hand brushed the tower of china. The porcelain clinked and swayed. She managed to keep the pile propped up, but before she could react, the cup on top slid to the edge then tumbled. When it hit the tile counter, it shattered in an explosion of tiny, sharp pieces. One or two scattered to the floor. A few others skittered into the sink. The rest lay in a heap where the cup had struck, the fresh edges bright white against the kitchen's duller colors. Gertrude Nielsen reappeared in the doorway.

"I — I don't know how it happened," Amalia stammered.

Behind Mrs. Nielsen, Birgit entered with another tray of dishes. She stared at the remains of the cup. In the dining room, there was a dip in the conversation. Amalia took the tray from the Belgian maid, placed it on the counter. Her hands were shaking, and the plates shook and clanked.

"I saw how high Birgit had piled the china," Mrs. Nielsen said, breaking her silence.

"No, ma'am," Amalia said. "I did that — it was my fault."

Mrs. Nielsen crossed the kitchen. She began to pick up the shards of china, then, realizing that she was doing the maids' work, dropped them back onto the counter. "Clean this up, Amalia," she said. "We'll calculate the damage later."

"Yes, ma'am," Amalia said.

"And you make sure that you don't stack the plates so high, Birgit," Mrs. Nielsen said, now on her way back into the dining room. "Or it will happen again."

The two maids waited for the woman of the house to leave the kitchen before they breathed. "I'm sorry," Birgit whispered. "It was — she was right — I did it, I can't believe that I did, but I did it — "

Amalia shook her head. She couldn't otherwise respond. *It's not your fault — I got tired when I shouldn't have, and I bumped the plates myself.* Rather than waste the effort in explaining, she returned to the sink, unloaded the new batch of dishes from the tray. This time, she made certain not to pile the china too high. If she broke another piece — if she so much as chipped a single lip — she would lose her job, that was certain. She took the first plate, dipped it into the water, rinsed the smears of food from its smooth surface. Behind her, Birgit hesitated, then at last took the tray again and left the kitchen for another batch. Next to the sink, the shattered cup lay in shards, glistening in the weak electric light.

■ ■ ■

In Aalborg, in the library of a run-down house with a red tile roof, Fredrik sat on the edge of a velvet sofa, his elbows resting on his knees. A fire was smoldering in the fireplace. On the mantel, a round mahogany clock read a few minutes after nine. Heavy, sagging curtains were drawn over the windows, and only a single lamp was burning. A thin wisp of smoke rose from the lamp — perhaps, he reflected, the shade was too close to the bulb. Abruptly, he stood from the sofa, crossed to the fireplace, gave the wood a nudge with the toe of his boot. A flame licked the back of the chimney, then the fire died again. Upstairs, a woman yowled and moaned. Fredrik grabbed the last log from the hearth, tossed it onto the embers.

When the madam appeared in the doorway, neither she nor Fredrik smiled. She took him in with a glance, then wrapped the long end of a chiffon scarf around her flabby neck. The building was cold. Still, Fredrik noticed the film of sweat on her upper lip. "Isabella?" she asked the farmhand.

Fredrik grunted.

"Why don't you turn on the radio?" The old whore rolled her eyes toward the ceiling. "A little music wouldn't hurt."

Fredrik shrugged. "I've been here ten minutes already," he told her. He gave the log a shove with the poker, sending up a plume of orange sparks.

"Ane isn't busy tonight."

Fredrik didn't react. He was scowling, coaxing a flame from the fire.

"I don't know how much longer Isabella will be, but if you're okay waiting—" The madam started to turn.

"Who's she with?"

The madam smirked.

"A German?"

"Someone who can afford more than the two crowns you pay her."

"How much is Ane charging?"

"Tonight?" The madam was already halfway into the hall. She stopped with her fingertips on the doorframe. "I'm sure you could have her for a crown."

Fredrik reached a hand into his pocket. "Perhaps with the lights switched off," he muttered.

The old whore cackled. "You know where to find her," she said.

Fredrik counted out a few coins on his palm, then followed the madam into the hall, started up the stairs. His boots sank into a carpet scuffed threadbare by a decade's march of lonely men.

■ ■ ■

At ten thirty, the last dishes had been washed in the Nielsens' kitchen. Birgit was drying the remaining cups, Amalia was wiping down the sink with a rag, polishing the faucet, making certain that the counter, too, was spotless. The party had long since moved from the dining room into the library. Now it was up to the men to keep the fire burning and drinks poured. For the maids, all that remained was to rinse the crystal after the last nightcaps were finished. Apart from the distant rumble of voices and an occasional peal of laughter, the house had fallen quiet. Outside, the wind had picked up, and currents of cold air circulated through the kitchen. Amalia folded the wet towel, draped it over the front of the sink, then, patting her hands on her apron, crossed into the dining room to take one last look and make certain that they had cleared everything from the table.

The candles were still lit, and she stood for a moment in the flickering light, enraptured by the dance of shadows. Yellow flames reached for the ceiling, plumes of waxy smoke stretched, faded, disappeared, orange reflections kissed the walls. The polished surface of the large antique table glistened. Ornaments the children had cut from red and white construction and tissue paper over the last few weeks twisted slowly on threads hung from lintels and chandeliers. Already, the paper was beginning to droop beneath its own weight. Christmas Day was tomorrow, but these little bits of the children's imagination were halfway to the rubbish bin. A lone silver serving spoon, forgotten on the sideboard, shimmered like a splinter from the moon. The floorboards creaked beneath Amalia's weight. The voices ebbed then became louder again in the next room. She slipped the silver spoon into its velvet-lined drawer. Then she edged toward the doorway to the library. There, she hid herself in the shadows.

Now the Swensens are gone I can say it. This booming voice belonged to Jurgen Nielsen, master of the house.

Oh, now now, Jurgen, Gertrude Nielsen chided. *Save your unkindest remarks for my ears, wouldn't you?* Mrs. Nielsen was ashamed of her husband. Beneath a bushy mustache that had remained black even as his hair had begun to gray, his lips were rubbery and always wet, and his mouth was huge. He had nostrils like the barrel of a shotgun in a nose as formless as a potato. He inhaled a lot of air, and when he spoke his voice bounced off the walls. He had married into the farm, but it was his now, and he had made it everything that it was today. He might have been a boor, but he was a hardworking one. He didn't owe his good fortune to anyone. At heart, he was a kind man, but he spoke his mind without worrying what his wife or anyone else might think. *You know how you get after too much wine —*

Too much? I'm sorry, my darling, but I don't think I've had too much. I don't even think I've had enough yet —

Well — I don't think anyone wants to hear what you have to say about the Swensens.

Gisela was wearing wooden shoes, Mr. Nielsen boomed, unable to restrain himself.

Oh, dear. Mrs. Nielsen wanted to protest. *She's from Holland, darling. That's what they wear there, wooden shoes.*

And Peter —

Really, darling.

Peter had pissed his pants. Did you see it? I'm sorry, but he had pissed his pants!

The library broke into laughter. In the shadows, Amalia smiled. She couldn't help herself. Mr. Nielsen was a jovial, likable man. He was enormous — as tall as her father almost, but not thin like Fredrik, as barrel-chested as a cask. He held the world securely in his big, fat hands. She leaned forward to get a better view into the room, spied Jurgen Nielsen standing by the fire, draining the last of his wine. His crystal goblet was dwarfed by his fingers. Its contents disappeared, and he wiped his mouth with his sleeve. His eyes twinkled like they were made of glass. Amalia noticed that he was unsteady on his feet. He teetered, but gracefully, as if he were floating on the surface of the laughter his joke had provoked.

The laughter hadn't completely subsided before another voice chimed in. This was a weak, gravelly voice — an old voice.

It belonged to Mr. Poulsen, Gertrude's father. At eighty-nine years old, Viktor Poulsen had outlived his wife by nearly ten years. Ownership of the farm had long since passed to Jurgen and Gertrude. Old man Poulsen occupied a room upstairs in the attic. Every day at exactly seven fifteen, he made his way downstairs to eat his breakfast. He passed an hour in the study, then climbed the stairs back to his room, slowly, clasping the railing in long, silvery fingers. He took his evening meal by himself, sat in a chair with a book in his lap until he fell asleep, then at nine was woken for a bath, before being led back into bed. He was as much a fixture of the house as the old clock in the formal living room, and as little a part of the family. At the sound of his voice, the room fell silent. *And now,* he said, *and now — I — I will tell the last story.*

Amalia leaned farther out of the shadows. The old man was seated in a large white chair next to the hearth, cradling a goblet still full of red wine. Eyes glistening like a madman's, he raised the glass in a shaky hand and looked around the room at the guests. Some were seated, others standing. All were quiet, waiting for him to speak.

What do you have to tell us, Papa? Gertrude managed to sound protective and embarrassed in the same breath.

Yeah — what story do you have for us, old man? Jurgen guffawed, unaware of his own irreverence. *If it's your last one, you had better make it a winner —*

His hand still raised, the old man fastened his eyes on his son-in-law. His goblet gathered the light and cast it back out like a chandelier. The wood crackled in the fireplace. Jurgen swayed back and forth, his shoes squeaked on the polished floor. If a pin had dropped, Amalia would have heard it. *Will you raise your glass with me, Jurgen?*

Jurgen held up his empty glass. *Old man, I'm all ears.*

Poulsen appraised this buffoon who was his daughter's husband. Then at last he brought his glass to his lips and took a sip. The wine sloshed and dribbled down his chin. From her vantage point, Amalia saw a drop splash the edge of the white chair. It would fall upon her tomorrow to remove the stain.

So get on with it, why don't you, huh? We're all waiting. Jurgen raised his hands, gestured toward the gathered guests. *What about this story?*

Poulsen cleared his throat. *Did you know, Jurgen, that my father's father fought with Napoleon in Russia?*

Jurgen rolled his eyes and slapped his balding head with a hand the size of a frying pan. *Not this one again, no!* he shouted, and once again the room broke into laughter.

Yes, Poulsen said, intent upon continuing, as if Jurgen had expressed disbelief rather than impatience. *Yes, yes! He did, I tell you. He joined the Grande Armée as a grenadier, and it so happened that he was sent to the Russian front. One day — I imagine a very cold day — my grandfather's regiment found itself in battle with the Russians, and the Russian Campaign was a very bloody war, much more bloody than the battles we fight today. A cannonball landed at his feet — this should have killed him, it should have blasted him into a million pieces — but when it exploded, by some miracle, he wasn't touched — not touched, I tell you, not a hair on his head — except for a single piece of shrapnel no larger than my fingernail, which embedded itself into his chest next to his heart —*

Yes, yes, I know, I know, Jurgen interrupted, unable to stop himself. *He survived the blast, thanks be to God, and came home again in one piece, got married some years later, had a child — your father — and then one day, when he was playing with him on the floor, your infant father kicked your grandfather in the chest and dislodged the shrapnel into his heart, and he died like* that, *in his house, and what a strange world it is, am I right? Such a strange world, where a bomb can kill you half a lifetime after it explodes when you are safe inside the walls of your own home.* Jurgen had managed to repeat the entire, well-worn story in almost a single breath, and when he reached the end of his tirade, he bent double and held himself propped up on his knees and wheezed and enjoyed the room's laughter. Sparks flew up the chimney behind him, and the children — who were still awake, past their bedtime — began to chase each other in circles, caught up in their father's merriment.

Amalia took a step in retreat. The laughter and voices faded. The children's giggles trailed away. Once again, she surveyed the dining room. The candles had burned down, a few had gone out. There was nothing left for her to do but wait for the crystal.

■ ■ ■

Midnight was just a few minutes away by the time Amalia was setting the last of the goblets back into the display cabinet in the dining room. Mrs. Nielsen had come into the kitchen to send Birgit home an hour earlier. She had been planning to give them both a little present, two crowns each, but that was before the maids had broken the cup. The Royal Copenhagen had been in the family for two generations. Four crowns wouldn't begin to pay for the damage. Still, it was Christmas. If Mr. Nielsen agreed, Mrs. Nielsen would look the other way and wouldn't dock them any more than their Christmas bonus. Birgit had thanked Mrs. Nielsen and promised to return in the morning. Amalia, too — her hands clasped at the base of her puffy tummy, her eyes trained on the floor — had managed her own *thank you, ma'am,* just like Birgit. Now, she was stretching onto her toes. She slid the last glass back into

its place, made sure that the arrangement was properly symmetrical, then closed the cabinet door. The latch snapped
shut with a snug click.

Back in the kitchen, she took a cursory look around, then
crossed stealthily to the pantry, where she had stashed a small
package for herself on one of the upper shelves. On the floor
above, footsteps thudded across the heavy planks, voices
rumbled. Christina was still awake, and a peal of her laughter echoed down the stairs. The narrow pantry was dark,
cool. Once again, Amalia stood on her toes. Next to a large
sack of flour, her fingers found the cloth napkins she had tied
together into a bundle. She hadn't had time to wrap the bundle well, and the ends of the napkins began to unravel as she
slid the package of goodies off the ledge. Once it was safely in
her hands, she carried it to the counter. Loosening the knots,
she picked up a small pie she had stolen from the cakes and
treats the cook had spent the day preparing, set it next to the
empty drying rack. The fragrance of baked blueberries hit her
nose, mixing with the scent of soap from the sink. Underneath
the pie were three savory tarts — one for Oskar, one for her
father, one for her. She straightened them on the napkin, then
set the pie carefully back on top. Her mouth watered as she
tied the bundle back together, this time securing it properly.
Her hands were shaking. She couldn't remember ever going so
long with so little food.

"What have you got there?"

Amalia's heart burst inside her chest. She hadn't heard anyone approach. As she twisted around, she tried to hide the
package, and it slipped off the counter. The pie tin landed with
a loud twang, and crumbs jumped across the floor. In the dim
light, it was impossible to read Mr. Nielsen's expression. "I was
just leaving, sir," she managed to utter.

"I can see that. With your hands full, too." Mr. Nielsen started to chuckle, but cleared his throat instead. "It's been a long day, hasn't it?" As if to emphasize the point, in the living room the antique clock whirred then began to chime the twelve beats of midnight.

"Yes, sir."

Pursing his lips, Mr. Nielsen stroked his mustache as he appraised the mess on the floor. Floorboards creaked over their heads. "You had better clean that up before the missus comes downstairs. You wouldn't want her to see this. Stealing food from the party, she wouldn't like that."

Amalia's hands tightened into fists. "I didn't mean — I didn't get the chance to eat — "

The huge man knelt with a wheeze and snatched up the pie tin.

"No, sir, let me get that — "

"Don't panic." Still leaning over, he looked up at the girl with a red-faced smile. She froze where she was, uncertain whether to kneel down next to him. "I'm just teasing, Amalia. It's Christmas. You've been a real help around here. The sewing, the laundry, even farm work when I need it. Gertrude told me something about a cup. That's why I came downstairs." He set the pie tin on the counter. "I thought I would give you your bonus." He glanced over his shoulder, then dug his hand into his pocket. "You can't tell the missus, agreed?"

"No, sir, you don't have to do that."

Mr. Nielsen pulled out a few crowns, without counting them held them toward her. When she hesitated, he grabbed her by the wrist and shoved the coins into her hand. "Not a word to Gertrude, understand?"

Amalia felt her cheeks burn.

"Well, good night, then," he said. "You had better clean that up before you leave, though — not a crumb on the floor, or Gertrude will find it, you know how she is." He paused in the doorway. "And why don't you take a bottle of wine, too?"

"Sir?"

Mr. Nielsen opened the door to the pantry, grabbed a bottle from one of the shelves, set it down on the counter. "For your father. I know how much Fredrik likes a glass."

"Sir — please — I mean thank you — it's not necessary — "

"Merry Christmas, Amalia," Mr. Nielsen said. Then he left the kitchen. She waited until his footsteps reached the stairs, then dropped the coins into her pocket, bent to her knees, gathered together the pie and the tarts, bundled them carefully back into the napkins. The room was dark, but despite her fatigue, as Mr. Nielsen instructed she made certain that no crumbs were left hidden in the shadows. Then, grabbing the bottle from the counter, she switched off the light and let herself outside.

■ ■ ■

Across the white expanse that separated the two houses, lights were still burning downstairs in the cottage. The weak yellow glow coruscated on the smooth layer of snow in the pulse of the storm. The distance was deceptive. The cottage lay less than a quarter of a mile from the Nielsens' manor. But Amalia couldn't simply short-cut across the field. As soft as the snow looked, the ground underneath was uneven and rough. Sleet sprayed her face, stung her eyes. She brushed a hand over her cheeks as if she was wiping tears, tucked the bundle beneath her arm, set out up the driveway toward the gate.

As the huge house shrank behind her, the landscape swelled around her. For the first few minutes, the cottage only seemed to get farther away. With the moon hidden, shadows swallowed it until it was barely visible at all. The glow in the windows dimmed. The bottle of wine turned to ice in her hands. It would be warm inside, she told herself — and how good it would feel finally to get off her feet. And it was these thoughts, and the prospect of surprising her father and brother with the food, that tugged her forward through the cold. By the time she reached the front path, her shoes were soaked. She slid on the stairs, caught herself on the banister. When she pushed the door open, the heat from the fire seared her face.

From his chair next to the hearth, Fredrik looked up at her through bleary, drunken eyes. He had been dozing, and he nearly lost control of a bottle of whiskey propped on his knee. "Where have you been?" he asked. "I thought you were upstairs asleep already with your brother."

Amalia stamped the snow off her shoes in the vestibule. Her feet ached as they began to thaw. The cottage was abruptly quiet after having braved the long walk outside. "Isn't Oskar still awake?"

Fredrik shrugged his shoulders.

"I brought you something," Amalia said.

Fredrik turned away from his daughter, stared into the fire. He had just placed another log on top a few minutes before, and flames were clawing the tarry chimney.

"Are you hungry? Have you eaten?"

Fredrik located the bundle in her hands. "Something to eat?"

Amalia made sure that she wasn't tracking snow inside, then approached her father. "It's from the Nielsens," she said, offering him the food. "From their Christmas dinner —"

Fredrik snatched the package from his daughter. The movement was so rough and clumsy, and Amalia's fingers were so frozen, that she lost her grip on the bottle of wine, and it struck the stone hearth, where it shattered into a million green shards in a pool of liquid as dark as blood. Fredrik leaned forward to examine the mess, then tore open the bundle. When he saw what was inside, he snorted, then tossed the treats into the fire. Amalia's face flushed red. Tears stung her eyes. It had happened so quickly — she was too stunned even to ask her father *why*.

"I won't have you bringing me their scraps," he said. "Understand? And you don't need it either, do you? Look at you — look how fat you are."

A sob choked Amalia's throat.

"Clean this up," Fredrik said, gesturing toward the broken glass.

Amalia knelt at his feet. She gathered a few of the larger pieces, then stopped. She was on the verge of collapse. "No," she said. "No, I won't." Then she stood on weak legs and left the room and climbed the stairs.

■ ■ ■

Oskar was lying in bed, but he wasn't asleep. Fredrik's children shared a bedroom. It was divided roughly into two by a closet in one corner, which gave the room an irregular shape. On the side without a window, Oskar's narrow, steel-frame bed was pushed snug against the wall. A sheet nailed to the ceiling provided a privacy screen, but it didn't keep out sound. He listened as his sister pulled off her clothes. The coils of the mattress and the wire mesh beneath it squeaked when she sat down. He knew this series of screeches well. In his bones. He had heard these sounds in his sleep going on years now. They had become a reassurance to him. His sister was home, he wasn't alone. Her stiff sheets rustled as she lifted her legs off the floor. The bed groaned, she exhaled. A few minutes later, Oskar realized that she was crying. "You're late getting home," he said, in a whisper. "I was starting to worry."

"I have to wake up soon," she replied. "I had better sleep." Downstairs, the grate clanged when Fredrik threw another log onto the fire. The smell of smoke climbed the stairs.

"Are you okay?"

"I'm just tired."

Oskar's eyes had long since adjusted to the dark. He focused on his hands. His father had asked him to dig a trench inside the barn, to keep out the runoff from the accumulating snow and ice. A callus had torn off from the pad of his thumb, and the wound was throbbing. "Not much of a Christmas," he said. This was the second Christmas since the German invasion. In his memory, the first hadn't been quite as meager.

Amalia tried to stifle her sobs. "I didn't eat," she said.

Oskar picked at the ripped skin on his thumb. "When I was four or five, Dad gave me a tiny boat for Christmas — you probably don't remember, because you were still a baby. He made it for me himself — he split a walnut in half, then glued a bench inside, a small sail, too, cut out of paper." He was speaking softly. Amalia had to strain to hear him. And then he stopped. A memory teased his consciousness, almost too distant to grasp. He was squatting next to a stream of runoff on the side of a road, holding the walnut shell in his fingers. This had been long before the war, when the family still lived in town with their mother, too. He had dropped the vessel into the stream, then had started after it. When it reached a hill, it sped faster and faster, then, before he could reach it, abruptly cascaded into a storm drain, lost. A few days after, he had come upon the tiny boat again, perhaps a quarter of a mile away, floating serenely in a pool of water formed behind a dam of branches in a ditch. It hadn't occurred to him to marvel that the water that carried the toy made this very same trip every time it rained. His fascination lay with the miniature boat. He took a step into the icy water to retrieve it, then thought better of the impulse and let it go where it would. Maybe he would chance upon it again, somewhere else.

"I remember the dress Dad gave me one year," Amalia said.

"I got an air rifle that year," Oskar remembered. "One that really worked. I shot it with Dad, and I hit a bird."

"It was a white dress," Amalia said. "A big white dress, made of lace. I still have it, I think. But it's too small for me now."

Oskar, who had been thinking about the poor bird he had killed, thought about his sister instead, coming back downstairs, beaming, in her dress. "Do you remember," he asked, "what Christmas felt like then?"

"We were children," Amalia said.

"That was four years ago, wasn't it?"

"Six," Amalia corrected him. "That was the same year we moved here."

"We haven't seen Mother," Oskar said. "We used to see her, at least for Christmas. Or Uncle Lars, either — remember Uncle Lars? He used to bring us presents."

"I'm making her a sweater," Amalia said.

"Are you?"

"I haven't finished yet. It's red, but I'm not sure — I don't know what color she'll want."

"Red," Oskar said. "She has a red jacket. I remember how much she likes red."

Brother and sister stopped talking. Downstairs, the fire crackled. Their father settled backward comfortably in the large armchair.

"All you had to do," Oskar said, raising his voice suddenly, nearly into a shout — these were words directed at his father, "was tell her Merry Christmas. That's all. *Merry Christmas.*"

In the aftermath of the outburst, the house waited, as tense as a hound with its ears pricked. Outside, the wind gusted. The roof thatch ticked, the rafters creaked. Amalia stopped crying. What was Oskar doing? He had never challenged his father before. "Eh?" A few beats passed. Fredrik's boots shook the floor as he dropped his feet from the ottoman. "What's that?"

Amalia could hear Oskar take a deep breath. "She's been out working all day," he said. "Didn't you know that? All day on Christmas Eve, and she's seventeen, and all she wanted — all she wanted from you — was to hear you say Merry Christmas. No gifts. Just Merry Christmas."

"Shhh," Amalia said.

The strain of Fredrik's weight tested the chair's aging armrests. The floorboards complained as he gathered himself, pushed himself to his feet. When he reached the base of the stairway, his shadow darkened the room upstairs. The banister whined. The stair treads sagged beneath his boots. He was so tall that he had to bow to squeeze through the doorway. The smell of whiskey accompanied him into the small room, the sweet smell, too, of the fire. He took two uncertain steps, banged a boot against the corner of the closet, stopped at the sheet. A vague silhouette hovered on the thin cloth.

Oskar stopped breathing. The reprisal would be sharp and disproportionate. The back of his father's hand would bruise his cheek, maybe tear his lip. Only a few months ago, Fredrik had beaten him with his belt until his back had bled. Oskar watched as his father's gigantic hand approached the edge of the curtain. The sheet dipped backward, and in the dim light, Fredrik's cheeks glistened with the sheen of an oily halo. He rocked slightly, and the fabric began to tear from one of the nails. Oskar tried to swallow his fear. He readied himself for the lashes that would follow.

But Fredrik didn't approach farther. He stood where he was, staring back at his son, catching his breath as if the short climb up the stairs had winded him. Then he let go of the sheet, took an unsteady step toward Amalia's bed instead. "Is it really Christmas?" His voice was incredulous. He didn't sit down. He swayed in front of his daughter like a birch tree.

Amalia didn't answer. She drew her blankets to her chin. All her father could make out was the fuzzy outline of her shape, the tears glistening beneath her eyes.

"My little girl," the farmhand said.

Oskar raised himself onto his bony elbow.

"You know you're my little girl," the farmhand said. "Don't you? You've always been my little girl."

And you've always been my daddy. But Amalia couldn't speak the words out loud. They formed a whisper in her mind, a memory of what she might have said years before.

"It's Christmas, and I don't have anything for you."

"I don't want anything," Amalia whispered.

"Maybe a story," Oskar said.

Remembering his son, Fredrik swiveled, grabbed at the sheet, tore it from the first two nails. It dropped, opening a cavity into the small space Oskar considered his own. "What kind of story? What do you mean?"

"She always likes to hear the same thing," Oskar said.

"Does she?"

"You know she does."

Fredrik shook his head. His unwashed hair hadn't been cut in months — in a year, maybe — and it hung over his ears. "I don't know what you're talking about."

"About when she was born," Oskar said. "You know how it always makes her laugh. To hear how she wasn't breathing when she was born, how when the midwife handed her to you she was turning blue and you handed her back and the woman had to spank her and shake her to make her breathe."

"She looked like an angel," the farmhand said. "That's all I remember about that. She was the tiniest baby I have ever seen, and she looked exactly like an angel."

Oskar peered at his father. In her bed, Amalia looked at him, too. The fire downstairs was casting its shadowy glow all the way up here, and the light undulated on his shoulders and in his filthy, greasy hair.

"Anyway, I don't want to tell any stories," Fredrik said. "I don't like stories. I hate them. They make me dizzy, and I'm already dizzy enough. I have something else." He faced his daughter again. "I have something else for you." Then he twisted back around on his unsteady feet and left the room. His boots rattled the stairs, the front door opened then closed with a slam. From outside, Oskar and Amalia could hear the crunch of his unsteady footsteps in the snow.

"You shouldn't have done that," Amalia whispered.

Oskar laced his sore, aching fingers behind his head, stared up at the dark ceiling. It had been a long day for him, too. Five minutes passed, then ten. He listened to the rasp of Amalia's breathing, fought to keep himself awake. No doubt his father had forgotten whatever he had set out to retrieve. Or maybe he hadn't gone for anything at all. Maybe he had just moved his drinking to the barn, where he could enjoy his whiskey in peace. Then the snow crunched again. Oskar opened his eyes, pulled himself from the beginning of a dream. Fredrik slid, fell to his knees with a curse, stumbled across the porch. The front door opened and closed, and once again the farmhand made his way upstairs.

"Here," Fredrik said, as he appeared in the doorway.

Amalia sat up. "I can't see what you're holding," she said.

"Here," Fredrik repeated. He crossed the cramped room. When he sat down on Amalia's bed, the springs squealed like a dying pig, the frame nearly gave way. Something in his hand was sparkling. A delicate chain was draped over his fingers.

"Daddy — what is it?"

"It's for you," Fredrik said. He found Amalia's hand, in a rough gesture passed the necklace to her.

Amalia couldn't see the jewelry well, but she understood that this was something she couldn't own. Where had such a pendant come from? They barely had money enough to eat. "I can't —"

"Take it," her father insisted.

"But where did you get it? Is it really for me?"

"Just take it," Fredrik said. His voice was rougher than he wanted it to be. Frustration welled in his throat. Realizing that she probably wouldn't keep it no matter what he said, he stood from the bed, took a step into the center of the room. Oskar could see the outline of his brow and cheeks when he turned to face him — the rest of his body melted into the shadows. "It's time to sell the rest," Fredrik said to his son.

Oskar rubbed the sleep from his eyes.

"I can't do it myself. They're watching me. So it'll be up to you."

"I can do it," Oskar said.

"Not here. Not in Aalborg—not anywhere around here. In Copenhagen. I know a few people—you'll do it there."

Oskar met his father's gaze through the dark.

Amalia was studying the pendant. Even in the dim light, the tiny diamonds shimmered. The sapphire in its center was as large as a pebble.

"Put it on," Fredrik said to her.

"Daddy—"

Fredrik returned to her bed, grabbed the necklace from her, lifted it over her head. The chain tangled in her hair, then found its place around her neck. "There—jewels for an angel."

Amalia's eyes glistened. What had her father done? This pendant was worth more than anything she had ever seen in the Nielsens' house. Next to it, Mrs. Nielsen's pearls were a string of teeth.

"Now—" When Fredrik sat back down on Amalia's bed, the flask in his pocket sloshed, and he remembered it. He drew it out, twisted off the top, brought the bottle to his lips. "If it's Christmas, we sing songs, don't we?"

Oskar sat up in his bed, stared at the blurry figures of his father and sister across the room.

"That's what we do on Christmas, isn't it? We sing songs." And then the farmhand's voice, raised in song, filled the small cottage. And a few measures later it was joined by his daughter's, and then by his son's, and they sang the only song Fredrik knew, the only lullaby he could remember singing them, years before, when his daughter really was an angel and his son was a blond soldier too young for war.

Over where the road turns,
There lies a house so beautiful.

The walls stand crooked,
The windows are very small,
The door sags just a little.

Outside, the wind continued to blow. Downstairs, the fire collapsed into a liquid pool of orange embers. The dark thickened, a chill crept up the stairs. The night surrounded the small cottage, and only their voices escaped.

ANGELA SCHMIDT

11.

Munich. December 1969.

"How did he die?"

Angela Schmidt turned the question over. *How did he die?* The blood drained from his body. His heart fell still. He ceased breathing. At a specific point, his spirit fled. He hadn't been sick. If he had, then the answer could have been lung cancer, stroke, meningitis. Was this really what her husband wanted to know — how among the million ways to die had her father's life been extinguished? Ever since she had brought back those photographs from East Berlin, ever since she had uncovered that photograph of the girl — *Polina* — Angela's thoughts had become increasingly dark. What was happening to her? The fact was that only a single thing had caused his death. A bullet to the head. Still, there was no easy answer. The war had separated her from her father. And then the war had killed him. Over the years, the image of him to which she clung had become increasingly hazy, but in her recollection not only had he been the sweetest, gentlest man imaginable — the type of husband to her mother whom she herself would never find — he had been a hero. Not anymore. She turned Lutz's question over. He was sitting on the edge of their bed, using a bone shoehorn to squeeze his foot into a glossy shoe. He had stopped moving. He was waiting for her response, but — though she knew that none of this was his fault — she could barely bring herself to give him one. Her father's crimes had somehow contaminated her feelings for her husband. For all men, perhaps. If her own father could have harmed Polina — not just *harmed*, worse, he had *raped* her, Angela knew he had, she could sense it from the image of the girl in the photograph — then this man was certainly capable of the same cruelty, too. And as much as she wanted to forgive him, as much as she was desperate to preserve this marriage, she knew that Lutz hadn't been faithful. His transgressions weren't simply hypothetical stains. He had destroyed the intimacy of years without a moment's hesitation. "He was shot," she said.

Lutz remained doubled over. He finished working his foot into the tight shoe, tied the laces. When he looked up at Angela again, she remained frozen. She was seated on a low chair at her dressing table, in front of a polished mirror. A lamp was switched on next to her, illuminating her face, but she wasn't examining her reflection. Instead, she was focused on something in her lap. In her fingers was balanced the sapphire and diamond pendant her aunt had fastened around her neck in East Berlin. There was something special about this piece of antique jewelry. It had been abused, shoved into pockets, neglected. Over time, though, it had taken on a patina, and it had only become more beautiful. What secrets did it hold? Angela tilted it, and sharp refractions of light crawled up the side of the dressing table. "In battle?" Lutz asked her. And then, when she still didn't respond, "I mean—you never talk about it. I don't know anything about your father, except that he was a photographer."

"In Copenhagen," Angela said.

"There wasn't any fighting in Copenhagen, was there?"

"He was executed."

Once again, Lutz stopped moving. They were running late. Angela had to get ready. She was performing tonight in the opening performance of the *Nutcracker*. Afterward there was a reception. He was supposed to attend. It was black tie, and he had dug his evening wear out from storage in the hallway closet. The pungent smell of mothballs overpowered Angela's perfume. He fastened his wife with a stare. If she didn't get herself ready, she would be late. The other members of the orchestra were already there, rehearsing. "Darling?"

"Executed," she repeated. When she twisted the pendant on the tips of her fingers, the refractions cast a geometric pattern on her cheeks.

"Are you all right?"

"By the Danish underground," Angela continued, still focused on the impossibly valuable piece of jewelry. "That's what they told my mother anyway. I don't know what the truth is. I don't know why the underground would have wanted to kill my father. He wasn't in the infantry. He was a photographer. I don't know why a photographer would have been of any interest to anyone. There were other, bigger targets, there must have been—"

Lutz listened, then slipped the shoehorn into the next shoe, squeezed his toes into the opening. It was a cold December, and he was wearing wool socks. He watched Angela gather the chain into a bunch and place the necklace into a drawer in the dressing table. "You're not going to wear it tonight?"

Angela shook her head.

"It's a beautiful piece of jewelry, darling—"

"My father hurt a girl—a girl named Polina—" She knew that Lutz wouldn't understand. How could he? She hadn't shown him the photographs—she hadn't shared them with anyone yet.

Lutz stood from the bed. He lifted his wife's hair from her neck, stooped to give her a soft kiss. "I don't know what you're talking about. But we are going to be late."

"Would you—I mean, have you—hurt anyone, Lutz?"

"I don't know what you're talking about," her husband repeated.

"Have you hurt me?"

Lutz's eyes darkened. "What kind of mood are you in—"

"Do you really have to go tomorrow?"

His fingers touched her shoulders. "Is that what this is about?"

She twisted in her chair, looked up at her husband. There was a plaintive expression on her face that angered him. Why couldn't they both enjoy a little independence from each other, even if they were married? His fingers found her heartbeat in her neck. "I know about the secretary," she said.

"What secretary? What are you talking about?"

"In Stuttgart."

The mention of the city brought an image to Lutz's mind, of the offices at the factory where he would attend his meeting tomorrow. Zoë would be sitting outside the conference room in front of her typewriter. When people called, she would pick up her phone. Her red-painted lips would brush the receiver. He had met her half a year ago now. He hadn't tried to hide the affair. His wife's heart pulsed against his fingertips. It was a steady rhythm, belying the stress in her face. "This isn't the time," he said.

"Zoë," Angela said.

Lutz's own heart leaped. "Darling —"

"Her name is Zoë. Isn't it?"

Lutz didn't respond. Even if he had never told her about his various infidelities, he had never lied to his wife, either. This had been their explicit agreement, that so long as they were honest and didn't try to conceal anything from each other, they would each respect the other's freedom. If Angela wasn't able to stomach this arrangement, she never should have accepted it. She knew who he was when they were married. No rules had been broken. He inserted the post of a silver cufflink through the tight buttonhole in a stiff cuff and secured it with a snap. "You're as much to blame as I am."

Angela continued to look at her husband. She wondered if she would recognize him now — if she saw him on the street, as he was when they first met. Was he more a stranger now or then? She turned away from him, faced the dressing table, caught sight of her reflection in the mirror. Above the formal black dress she had chosen for the performance, her neck looked naked without the sapphire. When Lutz stepped away from her to slip into his jacket, she reached once again for the necklace, once again contemplated the pendant, balanced on her fingers. "Am I?" she asked him.

Lutz wasn't sure what his wife was asking him. He straightened the jacket on his shoulders. It fit him, he thought, with the snug precision of a military uniform.

"Am I really also to blame?"

Lutz adjusted the starched collar of his shirt, tightened the knot in his tie. He had an intention to respond. The sparkle in her hand distracted him, however. "Where do you suppose he got that?" he asked instead.

Angela didn't answer.

"Perhaps his death had something to do with that, don't you think? It must be worth a small fortune. If we were to sell it —"

Angela lifted the chain over her head, gently dropped the necklace around her neck. "I don't want you to come tonight," she said. The inflection in her voice hadn't changed. In the mirror, she admired the shine of the platinum against her skin, the placement of the glittering piece of jewelry above the swell of her breasts, then finally met her husband's gaze. Her lips parted to say more, but then she realized that she didn't have to. She simply continued to look at him until he understood, until he turned and walked away. By the time he reached the other side of the bedroom, as imposing as he was when he stood next to her, he was able to fit through the doorway, which, in the distorted scale of the makeup mirror's magnified reflection, perspective had reduced to a mouse hole. His footsteps echoed and faded. The front door slammed.

FRANZ JAKOBSEN

12.

Jutland. December 24, 1941.

Axel Madsen fell into his bed. The stench of the whore-house — the smell of sweat and cheap perfume, cigarettes and alcohol — still clung to his clothes. He had shit his pants on his way up the stairs, but just a little. He was too drunk to care. The floor was spinning. Someone in the room next door hit the wall with a fist — Fleming, a farmhand like Axel. Fleming's wife, Mathilda, also worked on the property. She milked the cows and did the washing for the house. They fucked once a month — but Axel couldn't sneer at that, he could only afford it once a month as well. Their bed would creak for four, maybe five minutes. The headboard would bang the wall. Mathilda would gasp, Flem-ing would let out a groan, and that was it. Not that Axel could sneer at that, either. The only pleasure he gave his whores was finishing early. He scratched his balls, pulled his pillow over his head. This wouldn't be the first night this week that he slept in his coat and trousers and shoes. His blankets stank like the pigsty. The base of the mattress was green with dried manure. The wind shook the windows. In the room next door, Fleming began to snore.

An hour later, after midnight, the nervous chatter of the pigs broke the stillness that had settled over the farm. The sharp click of the lock being forced on the front door echoed through the house. Careful footsteps climbed the stairs. The noises interrupted Axel's recurrent dream — a beautiful dream, about riding a galloping horse through a stand of tall white birch trees with bark as thin as paper — but not enough to wake him. At the top of the staircase, the footsteps paused, then continued down the hall. The doorknob turned, metal squeaked against metal, the latch rattled. Axel smacked his lips, tasted his last whore, returned to his dream. He had ridden a horse well when he was younger. If it had worked out, he would have joined the mounted police. But the war had intervened and here he was a day laborer, threshing wheat and planting barley and hops and shoveling slop for pigs. The horse galloped faster, and Axel tightened his grip on the reins.

A pair of polished leather shoes approached the bed. Despite the alcohol, something finally disturbed Axel's sleep. At the last second, he opened his eyes. Too late, though, because two hands were already clamped around his neck. A knee was planted in the small of his back, his spine was bent backward, about to snap.

"Axel Madsen?" The cool, dry fingers around Axel's throat reeked of tobacco. The man's breath was hot and wet in Axel's ear. He was wearing street clothes. His accent was rough, but he hailed from a city, not the country.

Axel choked. He wasn't certain how to answer, whether it was better to confirm or to deny his identity. His impulse was to lie. In the end, though, he was too much of a coward. "Yes," he managed, in a hoarse whisper.

The hands gave him slack to breathe. The man's lips touched his ear. The brim of his hat tickled Axel's scalp. "Gustav sends his greetings. You remember Gustav, don't you?" The knee found a crack between ribs. "Don't you? Answer me." Air rushed from Axel's lungs in a wheeze. "Quietly," the man said, and his fingers tightened once again around Axel's prone throat.

Axel nodded. The motion was truncated. His tongue slid farther down his gullet. "Gustav Keller," he whispered. "From Schleswig."

"That's the one." The fingers relaxed long enough for Axel to swallow more oxygen, then tightened again. Somehow, the man's skin remained dry and cool. The greasy sweat belonged to Axel.

"I can't breathe."

"Shhh."

"Let me go. I'll close my eyes. I won't look at you."

"Won't you?" The man twisted Axel's head to the side. Facing him, Axel could taste the tobacco on his breath. Expensive tobacco — American cigarettes. He squeezed his eyes shut. If this man allowed him to see him, it could only mean one thing. "Open your eyes."

Axel tried to shake his head. "Just tell me what you want," he pleaded.

The man's knee dug deeper into Axel's spine. His hands lifted his neck. Axel would snap in two like a wishbone. At last, he opened his eyes. The man's face was too close to see. He was a mouth, gleaming teeth, a pencil-thin mustache carefully groomed. Thick eyebrows, eye sockets as dark as charcoal, hollow cheeks dusted with black stubble. Axel's eyes began to tear.

"You stink like shit," the man said.

"I'm sorry," Axel said.

"You have something that belongs to Gustav."

Axel struggled, and the man tightened his grip. Softly, snow flicked the windows.

"Some weeks ago, Gustav was asked to make a delivery."

"I don't know what you're talking about," Axel protested.

"Three Jews."

"I don't know anything about any Jews," Axel said.

"Then maybe I should just kill you," the man said, "if there's nothing you can tell me."

Axel sputtered. Saliva bubbled from his lips.

"Don't spit on me," the man said. He dug a thumb into Axel's windpipe. Except for the slow, ticking whine of the bed-springs, the room fell completely silent until he let go again. Axel gulped for air like a dog lunging for a bone. "Three Jews," the man repeated.

"Three Jews — yes — I remember."

"Good. They were a family."

"From Vienna. I remember."

"A respected family. A professor and his wife."

"And his daughter," Axel said.

"A wealthy family."

Axel's tears were so hot that they burned fissures into his dirty cheeks. His legs had gone numb, his toes had begun to tingle. "We helped them. We did what Gustav asked us to — we took them to the coast, we put them on the boat."

"They reached Sweden, but they didn't make it farther."

"We did what we were supposed to —"

"In Gothenburg, the girl was raped and killed. Her mother died, too, trying to help her, the way any mother would. Our contact in Sweden only found the professor a week ago. He was holed up in an abandoned farmhouse with nothing to eat. Can you imagine?"

"We put them on the boat," Axel said. "We weren't responsible for them after that."

"He died, too. Last week. But not before he told his story — not before he was able to get a message to Gustav."

"I'm sorry," Axel said.

"Where is it?"

"I don't know what you're talking about."

"You think we couldn't have taken it ourselves? If we wanted to —"

"Please — I don't know anything —"

"Where is it, farmhand? Am I going to find it in this room?"

"I had nothing to do with it."

"That's better." The hands relaxed, though only a little. "Tell me what you know, and I will let you go."

"You have to let me go," Axel said. This glimmer of hope was enough to blind him. "You have to — I won't remember you — I won't say anything — nothing, I swear."

"Tell me what you know," the man said again.

"I told him not to take it."

"Take what?"

"It was in a bag — a leather suitcase."

"Exactly."

"Jewels — money — I don't know — there was a lot of it."

"And what happened to that suitcase?"

"I didn't take it."

The man waited. *Then who did?* His fingers, cramping Axel's windpipe, asked the question for him.

"He'll kill me."

The man chuckled, and Axel's blood ran cold.

"Gregersen," Axel said. And then the light was growing dimmer, the black was becoming thicker, the edges of the room were starting to close. "Fredrik Gregersen," he managed, and then the room was gone.

Franz Jakobsen didn't like the feel of the farmhand's sweat. The pulse of Axel's heart in his jugular made him sick to his stomach. This was only the fourth person he had killed, and with the first three he had used a gun. He had grown up in Aarhus — not a huge city but big enough. Before the war, he had been a clerk in a bank, down in Schleswig, near the German border. This job tonight put him closer to a farm than he had yet ventured in his life. He wasn't used to this much contact, with animals or people — and here in the country it was his impression so far that there wasn't much to separate the two. He grabbed hold of the Adam's apple. Its shape and texture reminded him of a chicken gizzard. He imagined that it would look the same, ripped from beneath this dirty skin. It had a joint like a crank. He pressed a little harder to investigate, and the snap of connective tissue echoed off the walls of the stuffy room. When Fleming sat up in bed in the room next door, Franz held himself still, listened. Then he tightened his grip again. His teeth dug into his lower lip. The body contracted underneath him in an unconscious spasm, then relaxed. A hand dropped over the edge of the bed frame. Axel's boots sank into the mattress.

When Franz slipped back outside, accumulated snow slid off the roof, landed beneath the eaves with a quiet, muffled thud. Upstairs, Fleming rolled over again, onto his side, suffocated his fat wife in his beefy arms. In the barn, the pigs huddled. The farmhouse fell back to sleep. The crunch of footsteps dissolved into the wind.

13.

December 25, 1941.

At ten o'clock on Christmas morning, the snow had turned into rain and sleet. The snow already on the ground was hardening into a layer of ice as the temperature dropped again. Fredrik was outside, beside the barn, splitting wood. His hair was soaked. His wool work shirt clung to his shoulders. The ax was dull, so he was using a sledgehammer and wedge instead. The clank of the hammerhead against the steel block reverberated across the frozen yard, all the way to the Nielsen house. Inside the barn, where the air was humid, Oskar was loosening hay from a bale, stripped down to an undershirt above his heavy winter trousers. The pitchfork's handle was cracked, and he had to clench it to keep it from splintering. The work was slower than it should have been, and the two cows at the back of the barn, hungry, were growing restless.

Amalia had left for the Nielsens' in the early morning. After getting out of bed, she had draped the necklace Fredrik had given her over her pillow. In the dim glow of dawn, the platinum chain had caught the light like the scales of a fish. The sapphire and diamonds scintillated. She gazed at the intricate piece of jewelry, ran her fingers over the glittering stones, then stepped out of her nightshirt and quickly squeezed into her uncomfortable uniform. She would decide what to do with the necklace later. Crossing the room, she tripped on an empty whiskey bottle. On the way downstairs, she found another, and she carried both with her and left them under the kitchen sink before letting herself out of the house. Oskar pulled himself from bed half an hour later. He and Fredrik only grunted their hellos. Neither mentioned Christmas. Oskar buttered a few slices of bread, and they washed the food down with unsweetened tea. Then Oskar had followed his father outside. *Don't be long in the barn,* Fredrik had told him. *I'm going to need help carting some wood to the house.* Now, Oskar's hands were bleeding on the handle of the pitchfork. Still, his father had the more difficult job, chopping wood. Oskar knew that he had no right to complain.

The muffled rumble of an engine interrupted Oskar's rhythm. Outside, the hammering ceased. Oskar stabbed the pitchfork into the bale and, wiping the perspiration from his face with his arm, crossed to the door. A low-slung automobile was rolling down the driveway toward the cottage. Oskar tried to catch his father's eye, but Fredrik had turned to track the approaching car.

Jungmann's face took shape behind the flat windshield. There was a man next to him, too, riding in the passenger seat — Josef Munk, the chief of police. Fredrik rested the hammer on its head, ran a hand across his brow, squinted into the sleet as the black Citroën pulled to a stop. The doors swung open, and the two men planted their patent leather boots, buffed to a shine, into the dirty snow. Up at the main gates, a Daimler truck slowed, then followed the councilman's automobile onto the property.

Fredrik glanced over his shoulder, found Oskar in the shadows, made sure that his son was taking heed. When he returned his attention to their visitors, the two officials were already marching toward him across the yard. His grip tightened on the hammer. This was the second time in as many months that Jungmann had surprised him with a visit. If this pompous little bureaucrat thought that he could intimidate him, he had a surprise of his own coming. And the police chief was an even more despicable man. The farmhand liked him less than the councilman. Jungmann was a sniveling coward. He cooperated with the Germans because he was afraid of them. Munk was a sympathizer. Two years ago, he had been assigned to a desk — and that would have been his future. He would have been passed over for better men. The German occupation had given him his job. If he had fangs, he would have been a snake. But he didn't even have teeth. He was a worm, nothing more. When Fredrik hoisted the sledgehammer, Munk's hand dropped to the holster on his belt. Fredrik snorted. He wondered how quickly this little man could draw his weapon. Not fast enough.

"It's too bad you have to work so hard on Christmas morning," Jungmann said.

"You, too," Fredrik replied. He flipped the hammer around, gripped it just beneath the head. Icy rainwater streamed down his forearm.

"Death doesn't always respect the holidays," Munk said.

The Daimler's engine growled as the driver steered the truck down the driveway. As it slowed, a couple of German soldiers leaped from the rear.

It took Fredrik a few beats to understand Munk's remark. "Did somebody die?" he asked. The two men were standing in front of him now. The policeman's posture was rigid, like a soldier's. Fredrik's own shoulders were stooped, but he still towered over the shorter Danes.

"An acquaintance of yours," Jungmann answered.

"Where were you last night, Gregersen?" Munk demanded.

When the driver of the truck killed the engine, the day fell suddenly quiet. Cables whined as the parking brake was yanked. The canvas tarp that enclosed the cargo bed flapped in a gust. Fredrik raised his chin at the soldiers. "What are they doing here on my property?"

"*Your* property?" Jungmann scoffed.

"I live here, don't I?"

"I asked you a question," Munk said.

Fredrik met his eyes. When the policeman was a child, his mother had dropped a pot of boiling water from the stove, and the liquid had scalded the young boy's face. The injured skin had healed, but its coloring was different. Normally, his cheek was too white, paler than his other features. In the cold, the patch of damaged skin turned crimson.

"Last night," Munk repeated. "Where did you spend Christmas Eve? Answer me, Gregersen."

Rather than respond, Fredrik swiveled around and scanned the yard. One of the soldiers — a boy with a pimpled face and a slight limp — was circling toward the back of the house, sniffing like a rat. The other had positioned himself at the front of the truck, awaiting orders. It crossed Fredrik's mind to wonder how thoroughly he had buried the satchel in the barn, after he had dug it up to retrieve the pendant for Amalia. He had been drunk last night. He couldn't be certain that he had packed the earth well enough to hide it. "Who died?" he asked again.

"I will ask the questions," Munk insisted.

"Madsen," Jungmann said.

"Axel?" The news came as a shock.

"Where were you last night?" Munk repeated.

"I wouldn't harm Axel," Fredrik said, quick to recover himself. "You know that."

"What I know," Munk said, "is that Axel Madsen was murdered in his own bed."

Fredrik took a step toward the policeman. Recoiling, the smaller man slipped on a chunk of ice and nearly fell. This made Fredrik smile. He bent to pick up a stray log, placed it onto the stack. Beside the cottage, the soldier had stopped in front of the doors that led to the cellar. Finding them padlocked, he lifted the lock, tested the hasp, dropped it again. The clank of the shackle drew Fredrik's attention. "What are you intending with these dogs, Munk?"

"We'll need to unlock those doors," the policeman said.

Fredrik glanced over his shoulder at the barn, looking for his son. Oskar was out of earshot, but he recognized his father's expression. Fredrik wanted something. Grabbing his coat, which had been lying in a heap by his feet, he started toward the group of men. Fredrik gave him a meaningful nod. "Make yourselves at home," he said, facing his visitors again.

"Is that your boy?" Munk asked him.

"Oskar," Fredrik confirmed.

Munk watched the tall boy advance across the icy yard. "Tell him to stay outside."

"He will unlock the cellar for you," Fredrik said.

Munk nodded.

"Fetch the key," Fredrik said to Oskar, raising his voice. "Upstairs in your room — you know where it is. They want to look inside the cellar."

Oskar considered what his father was telling him. The key to the cellar was in the kitchen drawer, next to the sink, where it always was. There must have been something else upstairs — And then it hit him, just as it had occurred to Fredrik. The pendant. He had seen it on Amalia's pillow early this morning, where she had left it. Out the corner of his eye, he watched a soldier edge toward him as he reached the stoop. *What is it you think I am hiding in my cellar?* His father's question followed him into the house.

Oskar closed the front door behind him, then climbed the stairs to the second floor. He was entering the room he shared with Amalia when the soldier's footsteps shook the porch. Downstairs, the front door opened, the hinges screeched. Oskar stepped around the curtain to Amalia's bed at the same time as the soldier's boots bowed the stair treads. The German was only steps behind him. Oskar snatched the pendant off the pillow. The chain slithered through his fingers. He gathered it, tried to slip the necklace into his pocket, but the sharp edge of the setting caught the fabric. He struggled to free it, yanked it from a thread. The soldier had reached the top of the stairs before he was able to shove it into his trousers. When the door swung open, Oskar was standing in the center of the room again. "I'm getting the key," he said.

The German fastened him with an uncomprehending stare. Their shoulders brushed as Oskar pushed past him. After Oskar was already halfway down the stairs, the soldier noticed the bloody stain Oskar's hand had left on Amalia's pillow. He fingered the pillowcase, then let it go, looked around the room. In the kitchen, Oskar grabbed the key from the drawer. He was outside again by the time the soldier had followed him out of the bedroom. From the edge of the porch, he tossed the key to the other soldier. Then he met his father's gaze. A cold wind blew, and the film of sweat that covered his body turned to ice.

14.

A few hours later, the storm had let up. At the train station in Aalborg, Oskar stood on the platform, clutching the old Jew's satchel. The train from the north was late, but with the severity of the weather, that was to be expected. He craned his neck to get a better view up the tracks. The silver edge of the steel rails glistened in the dim light of the early afternoon, punched from the snow and ice that blanketed the landscape. Except for an off-duty policeman and a well-dressed man smoking a cigarette, the station was deserted. Oskar watched the man out the corner of his eye. Clamping the cigarette in his lips, the man lifted a fedora off his head, smoothed his waxed hair over his temples, then set the elegant hat back down, gripped the brim front and back to pull it into place. The drizzle wet his cigarette, and he cupped it in a hand to protect the ember. Then, exhaling a stream of smoke, he strolled across the platform, stood idly in front of a kiosk, reading a bulletin. Oskar forgot about him. The rails began to hum, and he tightened his grip on the satchel and once again peered up the tracks. A single bright light pierced the mist, shadowed by the suggestion of a locomotive.

When the train finally arrived, Oskar waited for a few passengers to disembark before climbing into a second-class carriage. Descending from the next car, a woman in a long coat tried to catch his eye, but her face was nearly obscured by a thick scarf, and Oskar didn't see her. Coal smoke belched from the engine's smokestack. Steam jetted from vents beneath its belly. He grabbed hold of the guide bar and pulled himself up the tall first step.

"Oskar? Oskar Gregersen? Is that you?"

He glanced over his shoulder. The woman in the long coat was standing a few feet behind him on the platform. Next to her, a man with poor skin was holding a set of beaten-up, matching suitcases. "Elke," Oskar said. "Mother." He stepped back down, glanced up the length of the train, then stood in front of his mother with an awkward smile, unable to return her gaze. He didn't bend to give her cheek a kiss, and she didn't move toward him, either. "What are you doing here?" he asked.

"Ole has some business," she explained.

The man standing next to her shifted uncomfortably, and Oskar noticed how yellow and crooked his teeth were.

"Will you stay long?" Oskar asked his mother.

"Not long," the man said.

"Only a day or two," Oskar's mother said. "It's Christmas, or we wouldn't stay at all."

Oskar glanced again up the length of the train. The passengers disembarking in Aalborg had already gotten off. A conductor was walking toward him, closing the doors. "I have to go," Oskar said.

"Let me look at you first," his mother said. She pulled the scarf away from her face so that she could see her son better.

Underneath, her cheeks were red and chafed. Fine pieces of hay clung to her coat. "You've grown so tall — you know, I almost didn't recognize you."

"I have to go," Oskar repeated.

"Are you on your way to Copenhagen?" the man asked.

Oskar didn't respond.

"How is your father?" his mother asked.

Oskar only shrugged. At the base of the train, the conductor blew his whistle. "Well," Oskar said. "Goodbye, then, Mother."

"Merry Christmas," the man said.

Oskar grabbed hold of the guide bar, stepped up into the carriage.

"I would have seen you more," his mother called out after him, "if your father had let me."

At the top of the stairs, Oskar turned to look at her, and their eyes met. Next to her, the man was staring at the tracks. A conductor was waiting for Oskar to board. Growing impatient, he tried to usher him inside, but Oskar wouldn't move.

"Tell your sister you saw me," his mother said. "Your father, too."

The conductor reached past Oskar to tug the door closed. The train was pulling away from the station by the time Oskar was taking his seat. He looked out the window, but Elke Brink and her husband were already gone.

15.

Oskar's forehead rested against the cold window. Outside the train, the landscape passed in a blur. The satchel was on his lap. A fine layer of dirt from the barn floor still covered the soft suitcase. Before leaving the house, Oskar had wiped the leather with a wet towel, but not thoroughly enough to remove the soil from the grain. The dried mud darkened his fingertips. His trouser legs were stained with it. *You can spend the night at Fru Gregersen's house,* Fredrik had told him. *She won't be expecting you, but she won't turn you away. It's Christmas. Tell her that you bring holiday greetings from her son. She won't be too happy to hear from me, I don't imagine, and she won't know what to make of you, but no, she won't turn you away.* Oskar had taken his dress clothes from his closet. The shirt was wrinkled, but at least he could wear it. His feet barely fit into his old shoes. The trousers, though, were too short by inches, so he hadn't changed from the pair he had been wearing. Noticing the dirt on his thighs, Oskar brushed the rough fabric with his fingers. Then he rested his forehead on the glass again.

When the train crossed a bridge, the water underneath was so gray that it became part of the sky. The wheels rolled over the trestle with a hollow roar.

The train slowed as they approached the ferry terminal at Nyborg. In Odense, most of the passengers had disembarked, and the carriage was nearly empty. A man riding alone sat facing him a few benches away, partially hidden behind a seat-back. The only other people on board this car were a married couple across the aisle, dressed for Christmas, carrying a few wrapped packages in addition to their suitcases. The husband was worrying about the time, his wife was concerned about their children. They must have been wealthy, because the war didn't figure into their conversation at all. Oskar was only half listening. The flat farmland outside the train was lulling him to sleep.

And, too, he was distracted by the other lone passenger. Wasn't this the same man whom he had seen at the station in Aalborg? Oskar couldn't be sure, because he had only been vaguely conscious of him then, and he wasn't able to get a good look at him now. But Oskar remembered the fedora — the way this man wore it low on his forehead. There was nothing unusual about two men traveling to Copenhagen on the same train. Still, Oskar was aware of him. His eyes settled on the man's polished shoes, just visible under the seat. His trouser legs were folded into heavy cuffs. Beneath the wool, his shoes glistened. The dim light spilling into the carriage through the rain-dappled windows beaded on the lacquered leather like water. The laces were fastened into tight, precise bows.

When the conductor strolled past to announce their arrival into the harbor at Nyborg, Oskar decided to stand early and move to another car where there were more people. His palms were sweaty. The satchel had become a dead weight. At the top of the carriage, he looked back down the aisle and was reassured to see that the man in the hat was still in his seat, staring out the window at the darkening sky. Oskar caught a fleeting glimpse of his profile. He had lit a cigarette, and it rested in the limp grip of his fingers beneath a plume of smoke. Oskar passed into the next carriage, joined a group of passengers gathered in front of the door.

On board the ferry, he ducked into a restroom and bolted the lock behind him. His palms wouldn't stop sweating. It was hot, but that wasn't why. His hands were shaking, too. Oskar was determined not to disappoint his father. He set the satchel down at his feet, turned on the tap. Cold water spewed from the faucet with a sulfuric smell. He lathered his hands with a greasy bar of soap, washed his face. The grime from the satchel dripped into the sink, slid down the drain. In the mirror, his skin appeared green. His face looked stressed. He held his hands in front of him until they stopped quivering, then dried them with a dirty towel.

Voices passed the bathroom door, footsteps. Rather than rejoin the other passengers, Oskar entered the stall, shut the lid and took a seat on the toilet. He rested his head in his hands, closed his eyes. The floor vibrated beneath his feet. The hull of the huge steel ferry lifted and fell. The engine growled. The air was tinged with diesel.

THE FAMILY GREGERSEN

16.

Charlottenlund. December 25, 1941.

It was already after eight o'clock by the time Oskar reached the front gates of the Gregersen home in Charlottenlund. He had come to visit his grandmother before, but years ago. He had only a vague recollection of the estate on the coast a few miles north of Copenhagen — an incomplete image of a white plaster villa with striped yellow awnings, set back behind a wrought-iron fence on a bluff overlooking the Øresund. He remembered running as fast as he could across a lush green lawn, reaching the street, crossing blindly, then charging down the path to the beach. Even in summer, the seawater had been as cold as ice. He gazed at the house now, one hand resting on the painted metal railing. Across the manicured gardens, it loomed in the shadows with the grandeur of a palace. Had his father really grown up here?

The grounds were quiet. The windows were dark. Perhaps Christmas dinner was being held somewhere else. Perhaps the family had closed this house for the winter. He could return to the center of the city. It wasn't far, he could get a room at a cheap hotel — And then an orange glimmer lit the surface of a window. Oskar tracked the movement, focused on a fine, bright line of light. The windows were blacked out with heavy curtains, that was all. In the calm after a car passed, music trickled across the lawn, faint laughter. And then, too, he smelled the aromatic scent of burning wood. Making up his mind, he hoisted the satchel over the gates, then clambered over after it. His shoes landed on the crushed granite path with a scrape.

At the front door, he hesitated one more time. He tried to remember his grandmother, but all he could recall was an old woman with powdery skin and silver hair, rheumy blue eyes half hidden behind the tired folds of her eyelids. Her hands had been as velvety as rabbit fur. Inside the house, a child's shout bounced off the walls. Glasses clinked — someone was making a toast. Oskar's stomach rumbled. He hadn't realized how hungry he was. Screwing up his courage, he found the chime, gave it a firm tug. Behind the heavy door, the bell resonated across the foyer. He waited, then pulled the rod a second time.

Next to the door, a curtain was lifted to one side. Oskar peered back through the window at a man who reminded him of his father, though he was darker and heavier. The thick lead glass distorted the man's features, and only a sliver of his face was visible. But Oskar recognized his uncle. "Who is it? What do you want?"

"It's me, Uncle Ludvig," Oskar said. "Oskar. Fredrik's son."

"Fredrik's son," Ludvig repeated. He licked his lips as if he had tasted something foul. His one visible eye, though, widened and softened. He fooled with the locks, pulled open the door, stopped it short with his foot. "Are you alone?"

"Yes," Oskar reassured him. "I came by myself."

Ludvig examined him through the gap, then pulled the door open the rest of the way. Behind him, a small group had gathered at the mouth of the grand foyer. Oskar spotted his eldest cousin, Ralf, who was now twenty-two, Ralf's brother, Wilhelm, who was fourteen, and their sister, Lise, the youngest at thirteen. Next to them were a few cousins from another side of the family, whose names Oskar didn't know. "But we're not expecting you," Ludvig asked, "are we?"

Oskar didn't respond. His attention was drawn to the faces staring back at him.

Ludvig rested a hand on his shoulder. The affectionate touch surprised him. Fredrik's stories always described a cold and nasty man. "You've grown since the last time I've seen you. But it's been years, hasn't it?"

"Seven years," Oskar said.

"Yes — seven years. Well, come inside. Look, we're having a party here — it's Christmas — we're having Christmas dinner. There's plenty of food, that's for sure, and there's room at the table."

Oskar followed his uncle across the marble floor. His face flushed as he stepped into the salon. The family was throwing its own little gala. Flames caressed the bricks of a massive hearth, candles glowed. A woman wearing a gown was seated in front of an ebony piano, another beside a harp. A man in a tuxedo was holding a violin by its neck, as if he had bagged a goose. Oskar took in just how well-dressed everyone was. He had never felt more like a bumpkin.

"Where are you coming from today?" Ludvig asked. "All the way from Jutland?"

"Yes."

"And by yourself — you must be tired. Maybe you want to clean up a little, before you come to dinner — "

Anything, Oskar thought, to get away from this crowd.

"You'll be staying the night, I'm sure," Ludvig continued. "I'll show you to a room upstairs. But first you'll want to see your grandmother. She doesn't much like surprises, Mama doesn't. But this one will probably please her." As Ludvig led him into the center of the gathering, voices dropped, until — when they were standing in front of Fru Gregersen, who was seated like a queen on a divan, one hand in her lap, the other resting on a gilded armrest — the entire party had fallen still. The rough soles of Oskar's filthy, silly shoes scuffed the polished floor, and his footsteps alone, not his uncle's, echoed off the walls of the opulent gallery. Fabric rustled as people turned. The smooth swish of silk and the brittle crumpling of starched cotton swept through the room like a breaking wave.

Fru Gregersen had been speaking to a middle-aged woman seated next to her, and she wasn't accustomed to having her conversation interrupted. Her face concealed her displeasure. "You must be Fredrik's eldest," she said, even before the introduction was made.

Ludvig gave Oskar's shoulder a gentle squeeze. "Your mind is sharper than mine, Mama."

Fru Gregersen frowned. "The resemblance is unmistakable. At first I thought I was looking at my son."

"He came all the way from Jutland today, Mama," Ludvig told her. "By himself."

"Who are you?" Fru Gregersen demanded, reaching out abruptly to grab Oskar's dirty sleeve. "I've forgotten your name."

"My name is Oskar, ma'am."

"Oskar — so it is — Oskar. I remember now. You've been here before, haven't you, Oskar?"

"Yes, ma'am."

"And so polite!" Fru Gregersen gave his sleeve a shake, then let it go. "And you came all this way just to wish me a good Christmas, I suppose? Or did that worthless son of mine send you here?" She clucked her tongue. "What does he want this time? He's not in trouble, is he?"

"Ma'am?" When Oskar glanced at Ludvig, his uncle offered him an uncomfortable smile, nothing more. "I'm sorry, ma'am," Oskar said, and when he spoke, a couple of the younger girls giggled and his face turned red. He had no doubt that his accent was funny to them. It sounded rough even to him, against the proper Danish his grandmother and uncle were speaking. "I only need a place to spend the night." He was stammering. "I didn't mean to ask anything of you, I mean, I only thought I might be able to spend the night here."

"You can tell him," Fru Gregersen continued, "that he won't see another crown, not in my lifetime, not from me. That — that *woman* — your mother, yes, that's what she was, I suppose, your *mother* — she emptied his pockets. Did you know that?" A few of the guests exchanged glances. Next to Oskar, Ludvig cleared his throat. "Of course this was what we expected. She was a social climber, that's what she was. We tried to warn him, but Fredrik always had a mind of his own. He could never see past a pretty face — "

"Mama," Ludvig cut in at last, "I'm sure Oskar doesn't have any idea what you're talking about."

Fru Gregersen gave her son a stern look, then returned her attention to Oskar. "Well," she said, dabbing the edges of her mouth with a perfumed handkerchief, "sometimes the heart wants what the heart wants. And I do suppose that Ludvig is correct. There is no reason to visit the sins of the father upon a blameless child. Of course you can spend the night here. Of course — there is no question." She looked around the room. "Where is Ralf?" She raised her voice. "Ralf?"

"Yes, Farmor," Ralf said, addressing his grandmother in the traditional manner. He took a step forward, distinguished himself from the rest of the guests. His complexion was so clean, Oskar noticed, that it reflected the light. "I'm right here."

"Ralf is your age," Fru Gregersen said.

Oskar read Ralf's unease. At twenty-two, he was a full four years older than his cousin from the country. The last thing Ralf wanted was to be tossed into the same box with him.

"I am sure that the two of you will have much to talk about. You used to play outside here together, you know."

"I remember."

"But that was a long time ago. When you were little children. Anyway, I am glad that you can be here. Why don't you take a glass of wine, hmmm?" She twisted, stiffly, to look up at her eldest son again. "We can still afford to offer someone an extra glass of wine, can't we, Ludvig?" she asked him, as if continuing a conversation they had been having before. "You will allow me to lavish this extravagance on the boy, won't you?"

"Mama, please," Ludvig protested. "I never said — I only meant —"

"You know how thrifty you've become, Ludvig. Anyone would think we're destitute. What happened to all the provisions your father made for me?"

The room had grown even more quiet. Ludvig straightened his vest over his ample stomach with a couple of sharp tugs. "Now might not be the best time for this discussion, don't you think so, too, Mama?"

Fru Gregersen continued to gaze at him, then turned, abruptly, to face Oskar one more time. "Why don't you join the party and meet your cousins?" she said. "And make sure someone does find you a glass of wine. Now where is the music? What happened to the music? I was enjoying the piano."

The violinist slipped his instrument beneath his chin. The woman at the piano flipped a page in her folio. The music started. Then, slowly, one by one, the guests began to whisper to one another, then to speak, and once again the room was filled with voices and the sounds of a family celebrating Christmas behind windows sealed with velvet.

"My name is Lise," a tiny voice said.

Walking next to his uncle back into the front hall, Oskar slowed to greet the fine-boned girl who had approached him. Before he could speak, though, Ludvig barked at her. "You leave your cousin be, darling. There'll be time for an introduction later. Right now, I'm taking him upstairs."

"I can show him, Papa," Lise said. She placed herself in front of her father, forcing him to stop.

"That won't be necessary," Ludvig responded, too quickly. "You can say hello when he's had a chance to clean up."

Oskar smiled at his young cousin. "It's good to see you again. I remember you from when you were a baby."

"I don't remember you at all," Lise said.

Dismissing his daughter with a frown, Ludvig grabbed Oskar by the biceps, hustled him out of the room as if he might be contagious. The front hall was lit by an oversize chandelier suspended from the double-height ceiling. "It weighs over a ton," Ludvig said, noticing Oskar glance up at it. "It's more than two hundred years old, from a palace in Holland, I'm told. Your father went to the same school I did. Krebs School, perhaps you have heard of it? Our father attended the school, and now Ralf has graduated from Krebs as well. We all of us received the very same education. But can you believe that when your father was a boy he used to place a chair underneath that chandelier in the middle of the night, stretch up onto his toes, and steal the crystals? Not to sell them — though he might well have tried that first — just to skip them into the sea." As Oskar followed his uncle onto the wide marble staircase, his feet remembered this same Oriental runner from years before, plush through the soles of his shoes. "He was pretty good at it, too." Ludvig allowed himself to chuckle. "The pieces of glass were perfectly flat, you see? They leaped across the water like sparks. Myself, I was never brave — or wanton — enough to try."

On the second floor, Ludvig directed him down a long, spacious hallway to a bedroom facing the street. The room hadn't been made up yet, and it was cold inside. His uncle flipped the light switch, double-checked that the curtains were drawn tight, then showed Oskar to the washroom. "I'll send someone up to light the fire. In the meantime, I think you'll find everything you need. I would offer you a change of clothes from Ralf or Wilhelm or one of the other cousins. But I don't think there's anyone else as tall as you. Not by ten centimeters. And I'm too fat."

Oskar shrugged.

"Anyway, make yourself at home. Wash your face, perhaps, then come downstairs and get something to eat." Ludvig was letting himself out of the room, when he decided that he had more to say. "Right now, we only have family downstairs. But we're planning to have some guests stop by after dinner, beginning at ten. At that point, children will be asked to go upstairs. Adults only."

"I understand," Oskar said.

Ludvig forced a smile. "Well, then. I'll see you downstairs shortly."

Oskar waited for his uncle to leave. Then he walked to the center of the room and turned slowly around, all the way in a full circle.

■ ■ ■

At nine thirty, the men detached themselves from the party and followed Ludvig into the library. The doors were left open, and masculine voices rumbled through the house, indistinct by the time they reached the dining room. Fru Gregersen remained at the table, lingering over dessert. She hadn't touched the cake or rice pudding, but she had a taste for bitter coffee and sweet wine. So the rest of the women stayed with her, sipping from smudged glasses. Oskar knew enough not to follow Ralf into the library. His cousin would fit in with the men well enough. Oskar didn't look as if he belonged in this house at all, not even as a servant. Instead, he let Lise drag him away from the table, back into the main salon.

The musicians, who had been joined by a singer, were gathered in a corner, waiting to be summoned. Wilhelm was directing a group of the other children in a tame game of hide-and-seek. The piano was standing free, beckoning, and that is where Lise led her cousin, yanking him by his dirty sleeve, unaware of how foolish he felt in his grungy, mismatched out-fit and his worn, ugly shoes. "Sit down," she told him, position-ing him on the bench on the bass end of the keyboard.

Her coloring was unusual for the family. Not only was her hair copper, her skin was pigmented softly orange as well — or maybe it was the freckles that gave that impression, Oskar thought, because the skin itself was milky and translucent. Her long, unruly tresses had been gathered back into a band, but wisps of hair had come free at her temples. The freckles started on her scalp and stained her face like gold dust. "Do you play?" he asked her.

"I take lessons," Lise said. "Mother insists that I do. But I don't *play*."

"Then why should I sit down? I don't know how to play either." Over the raised top of the piano, Oskar caught sight of Wilhelm, who, from across the salon, had fastened him with an accusatory stare.

"Because I want to teach you something," Lise said. "Here." She sat down next to him in front of the treble keys, scooted him over a few inches to give herself more room. "Let me show you. All you have to do is this." She aligned her fingers on the ivory keys and tapped out a simple, repetitive tune.

"How can I do that," Oskar asked, "if you're sitting there?"

Lise laughed. "Haven't you ever sat at a piano before? You don't have to do it here. You can do the same thing down there. Don't you see how similar these keys are? These are called octaves. Just put your hands there — no, not like that. *There*." She grabbed hold of Oskar's long, battered fingers. "Oh — you're cut."

"It's nothing," Oskar said. "It's just from working on the farm."

"It doesn't hurt?" Lise waited for him to reply. When he didn't, she grabbed his hands again, more carefully, then positioned his fingers on the correct keys. "Now — watch me, and do as I do." She repeated the same simple melody. Next to her, Oskar felt more foolish and clumsy than ever. He couldn't seem to strike one key without banging another, and even when he did hit the right notes, he couldn't find Lise's rhythm. Lise giggled. "No, Oskar — not like that — watch." She played the tune more slowly for him. "See? You don't press the keys with both your hands at once — you do it one at a time, like this."

Oskar wanted to get this right. It was suddenly important to him that he didn't look too incompetent in front of his young cousin. He placed his left thumb on the single key Lise had shown him, then lined up the fingers of his right hand.

"Good," Lise encouraged him. "Now count it out in your head. Like this." She played the tune again, and this time he accompanied her. After a minute, they were playing it in sync, almost perfectly. "Good! That's it!" Lise squealed. "Now, you keep going, just like that, okay?"

Oskar kept the tune playing.

"Yes—perfect. That's right. Now, up here, I'll play something else."

After a few bars, Lise joined in with a simple, high-pitched melody on the treble keys. The ivory was cool and smooth beneath his fingers. The notes cascaded across the large room. And before Oskar could understand what was moving him, his eyes were glassy with hot tears. It must have been the most beautiful music, he thought, that he had ever heard.

"There," Lise said, continuing to play. "Do you like it?"

"What is it?" Oskar asked.

Lise treated him to another giggle. "It's from America," she told him. "I just learned it last week. It's called 'Heart and Soul.'"

"I don't think Farmor would like you to be playing on this piano." Wilhelm's voice was directed at his sister, but his eyes were fixed on Oskar.

A collection of thin silver and gold bracelets on Lise's wrist tinkled when she stopped playing. Oskar's half of the duet continued for a few notes, abruptly awkward without the cover of Lise's melody, then he stopped as well. "Why don't you leave us alone, Willie," Lise said. "I'm just teaching him a little song—I'm sure that Grandma wouldn't mind at all."

"This is a concert piano," Wilhelm said. "He'll knock it out of tune. I wouldn't even play it myself. And look, he's leaving blood on the keys."

Oskar felt his cheeks burn. His cousin wouldn't have lasted a day on the farm, but he knew that Wilhelm was right. He was out of his element here.

"I've been taking lessons since I was seven," Wilhelm announced. "I practice an hour a day."

"Why don't you play us something then?" Oskar asked him.

Wilhelm shook his head. "I wouldn't," he said. "Not without Farmor's permission. I told you, this is a special concert piano. Do you even know what that means?"

"What's going on in here?" Ludvig's voice boomed across the large room.

Lise twisted on the ebony bench. "Papa! I'm trying to teach Oskar a song, and Wilhelm's telling us not to."

Oskar stood from the keyboard, still confused by his own emotions. When he pushed past Wilhelm, he almost toppled him over. He hadn't meant to, but the shorter boy was thin and weak, his muscles were soft.

"Never mind that," Ludvig said. He was holding a fat cigar, and he brought it to his lips, took a deep, satisfied puff, exhaled through his nostrils. "It's almost ten. Time for you children to head upstairs for the night."

"What about Ralf?" Lise asked. "It isn't fair — "

"Tish." Ludvig took another drag on his cigar, patted himself on the stomach, straightened his vest, then his tie. Oskar noticed how rich the tie's silk was. The blue-and-black-checked fabric looked stiff, but it collapsed under his uncle's fingers with a hiss, without any resistance at all. "Our guests will be arriving soon. I want you upstairs." He faced the other children, who were gathered in a loose group on the far side of the salon. "All of you," he said, raising his voice. "And it's bed-time. Understand? I don't want you staying awake, and I don't want you talking."

Lise scowled. "Papa, please — " She wasn't tired yet, and she wasn't ready to let Oskar go.

"Come along, then," Wilhelm said to Oskar, unable to sup-press an arch smile. "You heard Papa, it's time for us to sleep."

Lise grabbed Oskar's sleeve and without another word led him from the room. Ludvig watched them disappear. "All of you," he repeated, shouting after them. "To bed! Sleep! Now!" Then, after he was certain the children were all upstairs, he crossed the foyer to the front door, let himself outside, and made his way down the long, crushed-granite driveway to unlock the gates in preparation for the arrival of their guests. His footsteps echoed through the unlit night.

■ ■ ■

At the top of the stairs, Lise slowed to let the other cousins go ahead of them. Most of the rooms occupied by the chil-dren were in another wing from the one where Ludvig had placed Oskar. Oskar hadn't realized it, but his uncle wanted him where he could keep an eye on him — and away from his own children. Lise squeezed Oskar's fingers as they watched the other cousins scurry down the wide hallway. The tall-est girl's blond hair bounced up and down as she ran. She shrank as she got farther away — that is how long the corri-dor was — and her voice receded into an echo. Only Wilhelm remained with them. He wasn't about to let his sister cozy up to this dirty peasant. Lise eyed her brother, then yanked Oskar closer. She stood on her toes to whisper in his ear. "I'm not tired yet. Are you?"

"What are you saying to him?" Wilhelm demanded.

Lise strained to bring herself closer to Oskar's ear. "I'll pretend to go to my room. Meet me back here in five minutes, okay?"

Oskar gave Lise a quick hug. "Good night, then," he said.

She looked up at him, uncertain whether he was rejecting her plan or furthering it with a ruse. "Did you hear what I said?" she whispered, loudly enough for her brother to hear as well.

Oskar gave a stray lock of her hair a gentle tug. "And good night to you, too," he said to Wilhelm. "It was good to meet you."

"We already knew you," Wilhelm said. "Our fathers are brothers."

Oskar shrugged. Then he turned and made his way down the wide corridor to his room. His cousins' voices faded behind him. Lise was chiding her brother, and her brother was lecturing her in return. By the time Oskar reached the door to his room, they were gone, and Oskar was glad. It had been a long and confusing day. He was ready for bed.

His hand was on the knob when the distant strains of the piano stopped him short. The music reached him barely louder than a whisper, but Oskar recognized the melody. It was the same one that Lise had just taught him. "Heart and Soul." Only now it was being played by a professional, and, though the salon was too far away for Oskar to hear the words, the singer was accompanying the piano as well. He hesitated, then, as drained as he was, started back down the corridor. At the top of the staircase, the singer's voice sharpened into lyrics. Oskar couldn't understand the English. He had studied the language a little as a child, but it hadn't stuck with him. Nevertheless enraptured by the song, he sat down on the top stair and listened.

The music was still playing a few minutes later when the doorbell rang. It was cold on the stairs, and Oskar had buried his hands behind his knees. Hunching forward, he peered into the foyer through the posts of the marble balustrade. His view was obstructed by the crystals of the gigantic chandelier, but he was still able to see the entryway in bits and pieces. A feeling of melancholy had gripped him. When the door swung open, he didn't much care whom the family had invited for a drink on Christmas, and he hardly took notice as a man dressed in a black coat and a formal hat accompanied another man in elegant evening wear through the front door. A couple of steps behind them, a bespectacled man wearing a green uniform paused in the doorway. It took a few beats for Oskar to realize that it was a Nazi lieutenant's uniform, and then to recognize that the three men were speaking German. Oskar felt suddenly exhausted. The day caught up with him in a rush. The morning had begun all the way back in Jutland, with the visit from Jungmann and Munk. The stress of carrying the jewels to Copenhagen had overwhelmed him. His family's apparent wealth had stunned him. And now this — *Germans*, invited into the Gregersen house for a Christmas dance.

When Ludvig met his guests in the foyer, Oskar dipped back into the shadows. Hidden from view, he watched his uncle, listening to the harsh cadence of the cultivated German he spoke as he welcomed these Nazis inside. And then, taking hold of the German soldier's arm, another figure — a woman, a girl — appeared in the doorway. And at first sight of her, Oskar felt his breath catch in his throat. His fingers tightened on the cold marble of the balustrade. A spike of adrenaline stabbed his heart, as sharply as if the hormone had coalesced into an actual dagger.

As she crossed the foyer, the sharp edges of the chandelier's crystals tore the girl apart, into a million kaleidoscopic fragments. Oskar pulled himself to his feet to get a better view. Her hair was coiffed into a lacquered bun. She was dressed in a bright red dress — silk, like something a Chinese girl would wear — and black patent high heels. Her legs and arms were uncovered, and just this peek of her skin was enough to give the impression that she was naked. Her eyes were blue, so pale that they were almost colorless — Oskar could see this all the way from where he stood. But what dazzled him most was her makeup. Her face was caked with powder. Her cheeks were thick with it. It was a mask, as white as milk. Her eyelashes were heavy black lines. Her mouth was a violet gash. Oskar took a step down the stairs, craned his neck to follow the girl as she strolled into the salon on the German lieutenant's arm.

Just as she was about to disappear, Polina's eyes darted up the staircase, and they locked with Oskar's. But she walked into the party beside Hermann Schmidt without a pause. If her expression hadn't narrowed, however slightly, Oskar would have imagined that she had looked right through him.

"You're here."

Oskar didn't recognize the voice behind him.

"I wasn't sure if you were coming."

He took another step down the stairs, caught a last glimpse of the girl's shoes. Then they disappeared, too.

"Oskar? Do you hear what music they're playing?"

He took yet another step down. But now the girl in the red dress was gone.

"Are you all right?" Lise hesitated on the top stair. She had changed clothes, though Oskar was slow to appreciate it. She had pulled on a nightgown. She was thinner than he had realized — a waif. "Oskar?"

"Yes — of course I am — yes, I'm fine."

Lise examined him, then, taking a few quick steps down, grabbed him by the hand. "Come on then."

"Come on where?"

"Downstairs," Lise said. "I know a way into the kitchen from the back. We can get another piece of cake. The cook is a girl named Patricia." She spoke the name with a French accent. "She's a nice girl, she's my friend. Come."

Oskar followed his cousin down the stairs. He was tired, and he didn't want to upset his uncle. But he might be able to get another look at the girl from the kitchen.

They were almost in the foyer when Ludvig reemerged from the salon together with his wife. Lise ducked behind the balustrade before Oskar could react, yanked his arm to pull him down next to her. She clenched her teeth in an excited smile, held her finger to her lips. *I think it's outrageous,* Oskar's aunt was saying. *And no, I won't play hostess to her, Ludvig — I wouldn't know what to say to her.* Their footsteps receded. Ludvig was leading her into a service corridor. *We can't afford to be rude, Grete,* he replied. *After all, they are more than just our guests.* Lise waited for her parents' voices to fade, then stood again and tugged Oskar the rest of the way down the stairs. At the entrance into the service corridor, she opened the door a crack and peered into the shadows, to make sure her parents were gone and the way was clear.

"Shhh," she whispered. She pointed at Oskar's shoes. "Take them off. They make a huge racket. If you don't take them off, they'll catch us for sure."

Oskar slipped his farmer's shoes off his feet, then followed his cousin into the corridor. They had made their way through the bowels of the house and were about to enter the kitchen, when a door swung open and Ludwig and his wife suddenly reappeared, both of them carrying a bottle of Fru Gregersen's precious wine in either hand, dusty from the rack in the cellar. Oskar recognized immediately how unhappy his uncle would be to see him there, caught like a thief in his socks, with his clunky, mud-caked shoes in his own hands, even before Ludvig's eyes darkened and his brow furrowed and he began to chastise them. Lise took a small step backward and, cowering, attempted to hide herself behind her taller, larger cousin.

"What is this?" Ludvig began. It took a few seconds for his fury to gather itself into words. His back straightened. His chest expanded. He rose up a little onto his toes, as if he was determined to make himself that much taller than his nephew. "So," he said, searching for the best way to articulate his indignation. "So — You're Fredrik's son after all, I see. It's not so hard to follow the rules, is it? I told you to go upstairs. I told you it was bedtime. This is a simple rule, isn't it? Or do you think I make the rules so that you can break them? Is that what you think?"

"Papa, please," Lise said, from behind Oskar, "we were just going to find Patricia and see if she would give us a piece of cake — "

As reasonable as this explanation may have been, it was lost on Ludvig, who bristled even more at the sound of his daughter's voice. His face reddened, and he took a deep breath. Although it was Lise who had interrupted him, when he began to speak again, he directed his anger at Oskar. "Rules are made to be followed, young man," he said. "Do you hear me? Of course, your father never understood this either. He didn't like to be called a second-class citizen, but that's what he was. That's what I was, too. That's what all children are until they're old enough to participate — second-class citizens. This wasn't something Father directed at Fredrik. The rules didn't just apply to him, they applied to all of us. But they did apply to him, too. Well, now, you see how angry you've gotten me. Lise, you stay here — your mother and I will talk to you separately. You, young man, up to bed! Now. And so help me, if I find you talking to my daughter again — if I find you outside your room again — I'll kick you out, onto the street. Understand? We've been kind enough to open our door to you. Be good enough to respect our rules now that you're inside."

Oskar didn't respond. Perhaps his uncle had a point. But they hadn't simply let him in — this house belonged as much to him in the end as it did to Ludvig. And as gracious as his grandmother had been, there had in fact been something dismissive about her attitude, he reflected, something just as patronizing in its own way as this display from his uncle. He let Ludvig finish his rant, which he suspected had little to do with this infraction of his rules, without speaking a single word at all. This was deep-seated anger, and there was no point in trying to defend himself. Then, freeing himself from his cousin, who didn't want to be left alone with her parents, he tousled her hair then followed the indistinct buzz of voices and laughter back down the dark corridor to the stairs.

In the salon, the beautiful song had come to an end, and now a German waltz was playing.

■ ■ ■

Forty-five minutes later, Oskar was standing at the window in his bedroom. The music downstairs seeped through the floor, so muted that he could barely hear it. The air was infused with the smell of Cuban tobacco. Oskar hadn't been able to sneak another glimpse of the girl, but her made-up face continued to haunt him. Ludvig had instructed him not to open the curtains, so he had switched off the lights first, then peeled them back carefully. They hadn't just been pulled closed. They were pinned together, and at the wall on either side of the window they were tacked to the plaster. Oskar pried out the pins from the bottom up, opened a slit large enough to slip inside. He had been standing at the window for ten, fifteen minutes. His legs were cramping. Fatigue was overtaking him. He was determined, though, to see the girl again, even if only for a second or two as she left the house. His breath fogged the glass, and his vision blurred. He wrapped his arms around himself to fend off the chill. After a few more minutes passed, he was beginning to nod off. And then, at the base of the driveway, he noticed a figure hidden in the dark.

He wouldn't have seen the man at all. It was a good distance from the house to the street, and it was a black night. The clouds were low, no streetlamps were burning. Shadows blanketed the garden. The faint ocher glow of a cigarette gave the man away. At first, it hung in the air a few feet from the ground. Then it swept upward, and when the man inhaled, the ember brightened enough to draw an obscure, russet face from the dark. Oskar saw only his profile, and then the hat he was wearing. The fedora.

Oskar's blood ran cold. He rubbed the glass with his sleeve, tried to get a better view. The man remained still. Two minutes later, when his cigarette had burned low, he flicked it into the street. When it hit the pavement, it sparked then was extinguished beneath the heel of a polished shoe.

When the front door opened downstairs, Oskar was so distracted that he didn't realize the girl had emerged from the house until it was almost too late. A chauffeur was helping her into the backseat of an elegant green limousine. Her face glowed like a ghost's in the dark. The silk threads of her red dress shimmered in the light shining above the passenger seat. And then the driver had shut the car door and the girl was a barely visible silhouette etched behind a sheet of opaque glass.

The limousine's weak headlamps lifted trees and shrubs out of the blackness lining the white granite carriageway, but there was no sign of the man from the train. The gates leaped starkly from the background. The asphalt beyond turned vaguely yellow. The taillights brightened then dimmed. Oskar watched the car until there was nothing left to see.

POLINA'S SKY

17.

Copenhagen. December 26, 1941.

It was still dark when Oskar woke. He was used to waking before sunrise on the farm, no matter how little sleep he had had. But the pitch dark in this room disoriented him. The fire had died during the night, and he couldn't see a thing. With the windows blacked out, he had no sense of the time. He sat up on the side of the bed, rubbed the sleep from his eyes. The house was quiet. A dank chill rose from the floor, and the air was stale with the odor of the cigars his uncle had smoked in the library downstairs the night before. He shuffled carefully to the window, found a gap in the curtains. Outside, dawn was only beginning to break. The dim light stung his eyes. Across the street, above the trees on the low bluff, the flat edge of the sound was lifting itself from the blurry haze of the sky. He let go of the curtains and found his clothes.

Tucking his shoes under his arm, he guided himself along the length of the wide corridor with a hand on the wall, then down the marble staircase. The entire household was still asleep. Above his head, the chandelier's crystals teased the dark. It didn't occur to him to go to the kitchen for something to eat. He felt bad for not saying goodbye to Lise—she would wake expecting to find him there, and he knew how disappointed she would be when he was already gone—but he put his shoes back on and, grabbing hold of the satchel, slipped out the front door. Like that, he disappeared as quickly as he had come.

At the padlocked gates, he scanned the street for any sign of the man in the fedora, then hopped the fence. This early in the morning, the strand was deserted. A breeze was blowing a salty mist across the roadway, thick enough to wet his face. From Charlottenlund he had miles to walk. He could have taken the train, but it was early yet. Every now and again, he swiveled around to make certain that he wasn't being followed. Otherwise, he kept his head down and tried his best to blend in to the gray morning. The long stretch of road in front of him hugged the coast as it meandered through the wealthier neighborhoods and small green parks and the rough edges of the woodlands and bogs on the northern outskirts of Copenhagen. The distant lap of waves accompanied him into the city.

When he reached the old town, the streets were still empty. The only people Oskar had seen since leaving Fru Gregersen's house had been a pair of soldiers riding in the cab of a transport truck. The heavy vehicle had bounced over the uneven pavement, its engine growling. Oskar had taken cover inside a doorway and watched the truck rumble past, then started on his way again. Once he spotted the Amalienborg Palace, he knew that he didn't have far to go.

When something squeaked behind him, he clasped the satchel, took a quick step sideways to hide himself against a wall. A silver-haired man on a rusting bicycle appeared out of the mist. The elegant old man was just as startled to see him. He veered to the other side of the road, cycled past with his eyes averted. Oskar noticed how fine his clothes were — and then the bundle of painted wood strapped to the back of the bike. The old man must have ventured out to steal kindling from one of the piers along the water. He needed fuel to keep his house warm, that was all. Oskar continued past Nyhavn, followed the edge of the canal, crossed the bridge to the narrow alleys of Christianshavn.

His destination was a crumbling brick apartment building, so run-down that it was difficult to believe it wasn't derelict. The front door was pulled shut, but the latch was broken. He pushed it open and, locating a name on the directory, entered the dim lobby. His footsteps echoed up the stairwell with the hollow ping of a stone dropped into a deep well. He climbed to the third floor, knocked on the door to the apartment whose address his father had given him. Inside, a pan clanged on the stove. A faucet was twisted off. Someone approached on the other side of the door. "Who is it?"

"You don't know me," Oskar said.

"Go away."

Oskar hadn't expected his nerves to flare. He took a deep breath. "Mika Rahbek?"

"So you can read."

"Fredrik Gregersen sent me."

There was a pause. "How do I know?" The man cleared his throat. "You sound like a kid."

Three stories below him, Oskar heard the scrape of the front door. His scalp tingled. "My name is Oskar. I'm his son."

"Fredrik's son?"

Downstairs, leather-soled shoes scuffed the dusty tile floor. Oskar controlled his voice. "I came from Jutland yesterday.

Fredrik, my father—he sent me to you." The footsteps began ascending the stairs. Oskar tightened his grip on the handle of the satchel. "Will you let me in? Please."

Finally, the lock clicked. The door swung open a crack, and an oily, puffy, discolored face appeared in the gap. Bulbous, veiny eyes examined Oskar, flinty with suspicion. Oskar noticed the spittle on the man's thick lips, the grizzled stubble on his fat chin. His pajamas were stained with coffee. He read the surprise in the man's expression—he hadn't expected Oskar to be so tall. "How old are you, boy?"

Oskar glanced over his shoulder. The footsteps had passed the first landing and were climbing to the second floor. "There's someone on the stairs."

Rahbek listened, then, his brow furrowing, pulled the door open and ushered Oskar into his cramped studio, shut the door behind him. "You were followed here?" He spoke in a whisper, but there was no mistaking his temper.

Oskar didn't respond. He had kept his eye out for the man in the fedora, and he had been certain that the streets had been empty the entire way from Charlottenlund.

Rahbek slid the deadbolt into place and leaned his ear against the door. Oskar could barely hear the footsteps. They reached the third-floor landing, paused, then slowly continued up the stairs. And then, above their heads, a door opened and closed. "It's old Fischer-Møller," Rahbek whispered, as much to himself as to Oskar. "That's who it is—old Fischer-Møller, out for his morning stroll." He sighed with relief, faced his visitor. "Well," he said, taking this son of Fredrik's in. "So here you are. About what I'd expect, too—Are you old enough for coffee?"

Oskar nodded his head. "Yes, sir."

"*Sir*—" Rahbek scowled. He wiped his sweaty hands on his filthy pajamas. When his shirt opened a couple of inches, his

belly jutted over the top of his trousers, pasty white and matted with long gray hair. "Do I look like a sir to you?"

Oskar didn't know how to respond without seeming
rude. He watched the fat man cross the narrow room to the
stove. Rahbek filled a pot with water, struck a match to light
the flame.

"Sit down."

Oskar assessed the small, disorderly room. There was only
a single chair next to a rickety table strewn with papers and
other clutter — nowhere else to sit. In the corner, the bed was
unmade. Otherwise the studio was unfurnished. Rahbek's
clothes were folded in loose piles across the floor. His books
were stacked in teetering piles against the wall. There were
cobwebs on the window, Oskar noticed, and even on some of
the clothing, but none on the books. Rahbek encouraged him
into the chair with a tap on its back, then pulled out another,
collapsible chair for himself from beneath the bed. The weak
light filtering through the window smeared the old man's face
with a layer of shiny grease.

"So tell me what you're carrying in that bag," he said, settling into the flimsy chair across from Oskar.

Oskar's cheeks flushed.

"You're holding on to it like your firstborn son."

"That's why I'm here," Oskar admitted.

"Of course." Rahbek found a cigarillo, half burned, on
the edge of an ashtray blackened with tar. He tapped off the
dead ash, stuck it into his mouth. "I have known your father,"
he said, lighting the stub, "since he was shorter than you are
now by half a meter. I don't know how much he told you about
me — Eh? But I was the one who bought his first piece of stolen jewelry." He glanced at the stove. The flame was engulf-
ing the small pot as if the pot itself had caught fire. "From Fru

Gregersen, did you know that?" Rahbek laughed, then began to wheeze, finally to cough. "From his own mother — he stole the jewelry from your grandmother, and he sold it to me. He wasn't patient enough to wait for his inheritance — in his mind, it already belonged to him, I suppose. Well, the fact is, by the time he was twelve his parents were already threatening to disinherit him — maybe the way he figures things, he didn't have any other choice — "

Oskar wasn't certain whether the old man was joking. "We didn't have much of a chance to talk," he said, "before I left."

"Anyway, it looks as if he's up to his old tricks." Rahbek nodded at the satchel. "It looks heavy."

"There's a lot of gold inside," Oskar said.

Rahbek's eyes lit, though dimly. "Is that right?"

"Bracelets, necklaces, chains. A few picture frames, something shaped like an egg — "

Rahbek licked his lips, and Oskar noticed how purple they were. "You know, you could be a target carrying something like that through these streets, eh?" He cleared his throat. "Of course you don't have to worry about me, because I know your father." Once again, he began to cough. When he took his hand from his mouth, the back of it was flecked with blood. "A man would have to be crazy — "

"Do you want to see it?" Oskar asked.

Rahbek harrumphed. "I'll admit, I'm curious, yes, of course I'm curious." When Oskar set the satchel down, the flimsy table rocked to one side beneath its weight. Rahbek stood to look inside it. "My god," he muttered. He grabbed the bag, pulled it from the kid, lifted out a handful of jewels. "My god," he repeated, "my god."

Oskar watched him appraise the treasure, piece by piece. On the stove, the water started to boil. The pot rattled on the flame. Realizing that he was wasting precious gas, Rahbek switched off the hob, then continued to examine the contents of the satchel. Five minutes later, he returned to the stove and ladled a spoonful of coffee grounds directly into two rusty steel cups, filled them with hot water, gave them a stir. The smell of coffee quickly replaced the stench of sleep in the small room. "You know what you have here, don't you?" he said, sitting back down.

"It's worth a lot, I think," Oskar said.

"A lot," Rahbek echoed. "Yes, it's worth a lot." He chortled to himself, then pushed one of the cups across the tabletop toward his guest. "I don't have sugar or milk."

"I like it like this," Oskar said.

The old man grunted. "Dirty as piss, you mean?"

Oskar wasn't certain how to react. "It will be my only meal today."

"If you sell any of this," Rahbek said, taking a quick sip of his coffee, "you can take a room at the D'Angleterre and eat as much as you want at the restaurant."

Oskar took the information in. He had guessed that the jewelry was valuable, but he hadn't expected a reaction like this. "Let me show you one more thing."

"There's more?"

Oskar reached into his pocket. He palmed the pendant, keeping it hidden beneath the plane of the table. He could see for himself how much more beautiful it was than the rest of the jewelry. When he lifted his hand, Rahbek's mouth gaped.

"My god," the old man whispered, smacking his lips. He reached for the pendant. It looked larger, finer, in his clumsy, fat fingers. "Where did you get this?" Rahbek met Oskar's eyes. "Eh? Where did you get this?"

Oskar shook his head. "I can't — "

"It's the work of a master," Rahbek said. "Look at the cut. This isn't something from your grandmother's house. Not even the Gregersens —" He turned the pendant over, grabbed a small magnifier from the clutter on the table, examined its back. "Russian," he mumbled. "Look — the imperial crest of the Romanovs." He set the magnifier back down. "Tell me, where did you get this?"

Oskar took a sip of his coffee. The grounds stuck to his lips.

"Ha!" Rahbek exclaimed, then leaned back in his chair. Oskar cradled his coffee, waited for the old man to explain. "Suddenly, you look exactly like your father. I see this — I look at you — and suddenly, there he is, Fredrik Gregersen, bringing me his mother's jewelry to supplement his allowance. To spend it on girls, did you know that? Whores and drink." The old man shook his head, remembering. "But not even the Gregersens, no, not even the Gregersens —" He held the pendant up to the weak light, let the sapphire's refractions play with his eyes. "Russian," he repeated. "No doubt about it." He grabbed Oskar by the wrist. "Did all this jewelry come from the same place? You can tell me that, at least."

"Yes."

Rahbek nodded, sucked on his fat lips. His next swallow of coffee nearly finished the cup.

"So tell me, then," Oskar said, "now that you've seen it — it's worth something, I suppose — hundreds, maybe thousands — how much will you pay us?"

Rahbek blinked. Then he shook his head. If he hadn't been belching, he would have snorted. His cheeks ballooned with gas from his bilious stomach. "Maybe you didn't hear me," he said, his voice distorted a little by the violence of the hiccup.

Oskar was confused — it was obvious that the jewelry was more valuable than anyone had thought.

"This jewelry belongs in a museum, do you understand? All of it."

Oskar received this as good news. "So how much, then," he prompted.

"Take a look around you," Rahbek said. "That's my bed there, do you see it? This is my kitchen — we're sitting in it — I don't have sugar, I don't have milk, didn't you hear me tell you? I'm smoking the butt of a cigarette I already smoked yesterday. Didn't you see me light it?"

It took Oskar a moment to realize that Rahbek was handing him back the pendant.

"Don't misunderstand me, boy. I'd like to buy this from you, the whole lot of it, and normally I could raise the money — in a day, in a week, something this large, maybe a month, I don't know. But this — *this* — Right now —" He spread his hands. "I don't have a crown to scratch my ass. And even if I did, it would be suicide for me if I tried to move something like this. I don't even like to have it in my house. I could try to take it off your hands cheap, but, well — you might as well offer me a suitcase full of explosives."

Oskar swallowed the dregs of his coffee, then shoved the pendant back into his pocket.

"Careful!" Rahbek snapped involuntarily. He chuckled, catching himself. "Careful with it," he explained. He watched Oskar return the rest of the jewelry to the suitcase, wincing a little with every handful. "You know — I haven't seen your father for more than ten years. And he hasn't seen me either. So you can explain to him — things aren't what they once were. There's a war going on, for god's sake. And I'm not the same man I used to be." He gestured, palms up, at the forlorn apartment. "I'm still in the same place — but look at me. Take a look at me, and tell your father what you have seen."

Oskar closed the satchel, stood slowly from the table. "Thanks for the coffee, then."

Rahbek didn't stand to show him out. He simply rested his hands on his thighs and, slumping in his chair, shook his head. "Tell Fredrik I'm sorry."

Oskar took an uncertain step toward the door. "I need to sell it —"

"There is only one man —" Rahbek began, then cut himself off.

Oskar turned to face him. He read the old man's hesitation. "We need the money," he said. "Things are bad. My father won't understand if I come back home with it, especially if all I can tell him is that it's too valuable." He shrugged. "I'll sell it in the street if there's no other way."

Rahbek studied him, critically, then looked away, drew a deep breath, belched again. At last, he relented. "There's only one man I know right now," he said, "who can fence this for you. Only one man. But it's dangerous. Understand? Dangerous. He's not a Dane. He's a German —"

Oskar waited.

"Okay." Rahbek's head sagged onto his chest. "For your father, then —" He took an old lead pencil, picked up a leatherbound book, scrawled a name and an address on the first page. "Okay," he said again. "Okay." And then he ripped the page from the book and handed it to Oskar.

Oskar was all the way downstairs in the lobby of the building before he noticed the book's title engraved on the page. *Captain Blood,* by Rafael Sabatini. He read the address, then set off across Copenhagen to the Nazi quarter. The satchel felt even heavier now. He had to tighten his grip to keep the oily handle from sliding through his fingers. The wind blew off the water, his knuckles turned red.

It was snowing by the time Oskar reached Hermann Schmidt's apartment building. The sky was low. The temperature was dropping. The road was icy, and within minutes it was covered with a thin white blanket. Oskar ducked into a doorway across the street, stared up at the bank of steel-frame windows that comprised the façade of the building's upper floors. This was his opportunity to prove himself to his father, and Oskar knew it. Fredrik hadn't expected any of this. He had imagined that Oskar would sell the jewelry to Rahbek and return straight home with his pockets full of crowns. Approaching this German wasn't a simple wrinkle in the plan, and it wasn't something a child would do. He was walking into a lion's den. He lingered in the doorway, thinking about his next steps.

Noticing a deep fissure in the wall, a sudden thought occurred to him. First giving the pocket of his trousers a tap to check that the pendant was safe, Oskar knelt, grabbed a handful of the jewelry from the satchel, shoved it into his jacket pocket. Then he worked the soft leather case into the cavity and covered it with a loose brick. When he stood back up, he felt elated, as if he had solved a difficult puzzle.

Across the street, shadows moved inside the apartment on the second floor. Someone was there. He leaned out from the doorway, made certain that the coast was clear. People were working in the bakery on the ground floor of the building. Otherwise, the neighborhood was quiet. If he was actually going to go through with this, the time was now. He screwed up his courage, took a step into the street. As he reached the center of the road, though, a face appeared in the window upstairs that stopped him in his tracks. His heel slipped on the ice, and he nearly lost his balance. His first thought was that he must be imagining it. But there was no mistake. It was *her* — it was the girl whom he had seen the night before at Fru Gregersen's. Her face was no longer made up. But Oskar would have recognized her in his sleep.

Polina looked down at him, and their eyes met.

The wind gusted, and snowflakes as soft and papery as ash swirled against his face. At the end of the street, a car emerged from the mist, led by headlights that flickered in the blizzard like candles. For a few beats, Oskar remained frozen. Then he continued deliberately to the entrance of the building. When he reached the door, his hands were shaking. He found the intercom, read Hermann's name next to a buzzer. The car rumbled toward him, its tires slipping on the slick cobblestones. Oskar pressed the button, listened to the faint buzz inside as the car plowed past. The intercom beeped, then a male voice sounded over the speaker. "*Bitte?*"

Oskar spoke no German. "Mika Rahbek sent me."

"Who?"

"Mika Rahbek."

There was a long pause. "Identify yourself." Hermann's Danish was so clipped that Oskar barely understood him.

"I'm sorry," Oskar replied. "I can't do that."

There was another pause. At the end of the street, the car's engine faded into the wind. Next door, the bakery's machinery whined and clanged. The aroma of baking bread charged the air. Then the latch clicked, and Oskar gave the door a shove.

The lobby was unadorned, grim, tiled in green porcelain. A metal staircase led upstairs. As Oskar approached the second story, a door swung open at the landing, and he was greeted by the barrel of a German pistol. His grip tightened on the banister. Behind the precise shape of the gun, Hermann hovered in the dim light. His spectacles glinted. His face—familiar from the night before—was a delicate nose, a thin mouth, a weak chin. His cheeks were slick, backlit by the windows behind him. As Oskar reached the top step, the floor began to spin. He hung on to the banister, met the smaller man's gaze.

"What do you want?" Hermann demanded.

"Mika Rahbek sent me," Oskar repeated.

"That is what you have already told me."

"I have something. Rahbek told me you might be able to help me sell it."

The German lieutenant glanced down the length of the narrow, unlit corridor. "Perhaps we should discuss this inside." He took half a step backward, gave the pistol a shake.

Oskar followed him into the apartment. He couldn't help himself — the moment he entered the barren room, he scanned it for the girl. She was seated at a small metal desk, facing the windows. Oskar recognized every contour of her face. As if, somehow, he had known her for years. He became aware of the rest of the apartment gradually — the uncomfortable bed pushed against a wall, the two or three lightbulbs dangling from wires tacked to the ceiling, the oversize wardrobe, tilting on its feet. The mirror hanging on the wardrobe's door cast a cool reflection onto the industrial floor. On a nightstand next to the bed, a red-white-and-black band of ribbon caught the light, drawing Oskar's eye to a small medal suspended beneath it — the previous year, Hermann had been awarded a War Merit Cross, and this was where he kept it, on display in a polished leather case beside an old, battered clock. Behind Oskar, the front door closed with a clank. The pistol emerged from the shadows. Its burnished steel absorbed the light like a chunk of coal. Beneath him, once again the floor began to spin, and his legs felt weak. Still, Oskar couldn't help himself — despite the danger, despite his apprehension, his eyes returned to the girl.

CRAIG LARSEN

"Now, what is it that you want?"

Oskar couldn't find his voice to answer. The hollow tip of the Luger was aimed at his heart. The German's finger was steady on the trigger. The sweet smell of machine oil, the faint odor of gunpowder, wafted from the weapon.

The lieutenant's lips whitened against his teeth. *Who was this standing in his apartment? My god, he was nothing more than a boy.* "What do you want?" he repeated. He was going to have to coax it out of him. The boy, he realized, was frightened. "You said you have something for me. What is it?"

Oskar struggled for his voice. "Yes."

"Show me."

Oskar reached into his jacket pocket. The lieutenant's grip tightened on the pistol. Oskar's fingers clasped the jewelry he had grabbed from the satchel. He hoped that he had been lucky enough to take some of the better pieces — he should have paid more attention at Rahbek's apartment. His hand unfolded to reveal the shimmering loot. A gold bracelet. A chain. A single earring studded with small red stones. A diamond ring.

Behind his spectacles, the German's eyes widened. He pointed the pistol toward the desk where Polina was seated. "There," he directed Oskar. "Set it down in the light."

Oskar felt out of sync. The closer he got to the girl, the more dizzy he became. He watched his hand place the jewelry on the battered desk as if these fingers belonged to someone else. The chain tangled with the earring. He couldn't separate the two pieces.

"Let me do that. Step away."

Oskar took a step backward. Hermann was mesmerized. Forgetting himself for a few seconds, he set the pistol on the desk, gently pulled the chain from the earring, laid the pieces out. Then he picked the pistol back up, nudged Polina on her shoulder, pointed with his chin at the narrow bed. She stood without a word and crossed the stark room. Oskar watched her, unable to focus on anything else. When she passed him, their eyes met for a split second. His heart leaped. *She had smiled.*

"Where did you get this?"

"I found it," Oskar said. The lie thrilled him. He had been thinking about it after his meeting with Rahbek — it was the perfect answer.

"You *found* it. I see." The German sneered. "And only this?"

"What is it worth to you?" Oskar asked.

"I asked you a question, boy — Only this?"

"And I will answer—" Oskar's voice emerged in a crushed whisper. "—when you tell me what it's worth to you." He was already certain that the German was going to want the rest. The hollow tip of the pistol traced a circle across his chest. It had been wise of him to hide the satchel.

"You have a big mouth for such a young boy."

"If you're not interested, then—" Oskar took a faltering step back toward the desk.

"I didn't say that, did I?"

"What will you pay me for it? How much?"

"How much I pay will depend upon how much there is."

"A thousand crowns," Oskar said. His father had told him five hundred.

"A *thousand?*" The German was incredulous.

"Do you have it?" Out the corner of his eye, Oskar was aware that Polina had turned her head. She was appraising him.

The German's mouth mimicked a tight-lipped smile. "Are you trying to play me, boy?"

"Play you?" Oskar wasn't certain what the lieutenant meant.

"You come in here with a few pieces of jewelry, you shake me down, find out how much money I'm holding, then you try to rob me."

If Oskar hadn't been so nervous, he would have smiled. The German's guess was so far off the mark. He held his hands out, palms up. "I came to sell you what I found."

Hermann's eyes narrowed. "Are you armed?"

Oskar shook his head.

Hermann turned toward Polina. "Come here," he commanded. He kept the pistol trained on Oskar as she stood from the bed. "Search him."

Polina didn't speak. She motioned for Oskar to raise his arms, then carefully began to pat him down. Her hands caressed the tops of his shoulders, then slid softly down his ribs. When she reached his pocket, her fingers fumbled with the sapphire pendant through the material of his trousers. Their eyes connected, but she moved on. Beneath the inseam of his trousers, her fingers grazed his testicles, and Oskar understood that this was intentional. *She was teasing him.* When she was finished, she shook her head.

"Nothing?" the German asked her.

"No," she said, speaking at last. "Nothing at all." And Oskar was struck by her strong Polish accent.

The German's hand relaxed on the pistol. He tucked it back into its holster, then directed Polina to the bed again with a nod of his head. "A thousand crowns," he repeated. "A thousand." He examined the jewelry, picked up the earring, set it back down. "You have the mate to this?"

"Yes."

"So you do have more?"

"Much more," Oskar said.

"*Much* more." The German straightened his spectacles on his nose.

Out the corner of his eye, Oskar was watching Polina. On the edge of the bed, she had dropped her chin onto her chest and was staring at her hands clasped in her lap. "Perhaps she would like this ring." The words were uttered before he realized that he would speak them.

The German turned to face him. "What's that?"

In his peripheral vision, Oskar saw that Polina had raised her eyes, too. "This ring," he said. He took a step to the desk, picked up the ring that still belonged to him. It was a diamond of five or six carats at least, set in an antique platinum setting. "It must be worth a thousand crowns by itself."

"Do you think so?"

"Yes. I do." Oskar wondered where this sudden courage was coming from. "And I think maybe she would like to wear it."

"As far as you're concerned, boy," the German said, "she isn't even here. Is that understood?" Hermann's fingers strayed once again to his pistol.

Oskar shrugged. He gathered the other jewelry into his hands, together with the ring. "A thousand crowns," he said. "Do you have it?"

"Yes," the German said. "I have it."

Oskar continued to look at the jewelry, but his attention remained fixed on the girl. "Then pay it to me, and I will give you the rest."

The German's mouth curled. "You don't expect me to hand you the money without seeing the rest of the jewelry first, do you?"

Oskar held his ground. "I do." Polina was gazing at him.

"Bring me the rest," Hermann said, "and then we will talk about payment. Not before."

Oskar was aware of the slightest movement from Polina. She had given her head a quick shake. *No.* "No," Oskar said, as if his voice was an echo. "If you want the rest, you will pay me now." Polina showed him the hint of a nod. "Otherwise I will walk away from here, and you will never see me again." He collected the jewelry into a single hand, then shoved it back into his jacket pocket.

"I wouldn't do that."

When Oskar faced the German, the gun was drawn from the holster again. The hollow point stared back at him like a dilated pupil. "Pay me first, and I will give you the rest."

The German gripped the pistol's hammer with his free hand, ratcheted it backward. A bullet clicked into the chamber with oiled precision. "Place the jewelry back on the table."

"The ring I just put into my pocket," Oskar said, "alone is worth a thousand crowns, isn't it? I am not a fool. I can see that it is. I can see it in your eyes. And this isn't the best of it. I only grabbed a handful. I have ten times more than this."

The German's jaw muscles worked beneath his cheeks. Then the tip of the pistol dropped. "You're telling the truth," he said simply. He nodded to himself, finally slipped the pistol back into the holster. *This boy was speaking the truth.* Oskar watched him cross the room and open the wardrobe. When the door stopped moving, Polina was framed in the mirror. The German pulled a small safe from the upper shelf, then carried the black metal box to the table, opened it with a key from his pocket. Oskar's eyes remained fixed on Polina's reflection while the German removed a packet of bills and counted them out onto the table. "There. One thousand."

Oskar's hands shook as he took the money from the German. Though he had no way of knowing it, this was some of the profit that Hermann had made from the sale of the

Gregersens' paintings. He began to count the bills, but almost immediately lost track.

"It's all there," Hermann said. "A thousand crowns — some of it in reichsmarks."

Oskar continued flipping through the bills anyway. He had no idea how much he was holding, but he didn't stop until he had touched every note. He shoved the money into his pocket on top of the pendant. "Okay. Here is what I will do. I will leave now, and when I get downstairs, I will ring the intercom, understand?"

Hermann nodded.

"You will answer yourself — not the girl. I will tell you where to find the rest."

"Agreed."

As much as he wanted to be gone from this strange apartment, Oskar didn't want to leave the girl alone here. He took an awkward step toward the door.

"Aren't you forgetting something?"

Oskar kept walking.

"In your pocket," Hermann said, raising his voice.

Oskar stopped, fumbled with the jewelry. Now that his business was almost concluded, his nerves were frayed. His palms were sweaty. He lay the jewelry onto the table again in a heap — the bracelet, the chain, the earring, the diamond ring — then at last left the room. The stairwell was a blur. His shoes slipped on the treads. He clasped the metal railing, kept himself from tumbling down the stairs. The clatter of his heavy footfalls followed him into the bare lobby. When he reached the bottom of the staircase, he leaned against the wall. He wasn't just breathing, he was panting. Slowly, he became aware of the porcelain tile against his temple. He pushed himself upright, shoved the door.

Outside, he barely recognized this street as the same one he had walked less than half an hour before. The intercom was as cold as ice on the tip of his thumb. He leaned into the button, closed his eyes to the swirling snow.

"Tell me," the German said. His voice was thin and weak over the cheap speaker. "Tell me where it is."

"Across the street—" Oskar said.

"Where across the street?"

Oskar interrupted him. He didn't wait for the German to finish his question, he didn't wait for him to understand. "—there's a doorway. If you look inside the doorway, you'll see a hole in the wall. That's where you'll find it—in the hole—in a suitcase in the hole." Then he let go of the button and began to run. His clumsy, ugly farmer's shoes slid on the slippery pavement. He caught himself on the side of a building, continued down the sidewalk in his awkward, loping gait. By the time the German had reached the bottom of the stairs, his footsteps were a distant swish.

■ ■ ■

It was already dark at five o'clock when Oskar backtracked through the Nazi quarter to Hermann's address. The huge windows that lined the German's apartment were lit, and the electric light hung in the snow. All day, the sky had crumbled into the streets, and there was no sign that the blizzard would let up. With the roads nearly impassable, Copenhagen had become a ghost town. Oskar took up sentry in the doorway across from the bakery where he had hidden the jewels, grateful for the cover of the storm. When the occasional pedestrian passed, he shrank backward, held his breath, found refuge in the shadows.

By seven, Oskar was frozen to the bone. His shoes were wet, his toes ached. He wished that he had gloves—he had lost feeling in his fingers. The wind was gusting, and the cold swept through his clothes and clawed its way beneath his skin. Still, no matter how uncomfortable he became, he knew that he wasn't going to leave until the lights were switched off inside. Not until there was no more chance that the German would leave the girl alone in the apartment.

When the door swung open across the street, Oskar dipped out of sight. Hermann emerged from the building, and Oskar's heart pounded. He had waited for this opportunity all day, and now it was actually happening. He watched until the German had disappeared down the sidewalk, then crossed the unlit street. The glow from the windows upstairs fastened a long, smoky shadow to his feet, which darkened as it trailed him over the snow.

When he touched the button to sound the intercom, the line remained dead, and he buzzed again. Finally, the speaker hissed. "Who's there?" It was barely a whisper.

"It's me," Oskar said, fumbling for words. "I was here earlier —"

"I know who you are."

Oskar listened to the open line, breathing, unable to think of more to say.

Ten seconds passed before the door clicked open. Oskar's hand was already on the lever. He stepped inside. The stairwell was dark. His shadow slid up the stairs in front of him. When the girl opened the door, the light chased it back down. "Stay there," she said from the landing, and he stopped. "What do you want?" His face was red from the cold. His lips were chapped and torn. His hair was thick with clumps of ice. "If he comes back, he'll kill you."

Oskar didn't speak. He wiped his nose dry with the back of a numb hand.

"What do you want from me?"

Oskar saw the huge diamond glinting on her finger. The German had given her the ring after all. *Perhaps she was happy here.* Perhaps he had misunderstood—perhaps nothing had passed between them.

"Why have you come back?" she demanded.

"How old are you?" Oskar asked her.

Polina peered past him, down the stairs. This late in the evening, the building was quiet. Most of the apartments were occupied by businesses. Upstairs, though, an old woman lived with her daughter and a boarder. Polina kept her voice low. "Your age, I think."

An emotion Oskar didn't recognize welled in his chest. "I came to help you," he said.

"What do you mean?" When he took a step toward her, she took a step in retreat. "Stay there."

"Are you in love with him?"

The girl shook her head.

"Where are you from?"

"From Kraków."

"In Poland?"

The girl didn't respond.

Through the dark that separated them, Oskar read her desperation. "Let's go," he said.

The girl's mouth formed the beginning of a nervous smile.

"Now," Oskar said. "Let's go now. I'll take you away from here. You can come with me — home — I can take you home."

"I can't leave," the girl said.

"Why not? Of course you can—"

"He paid for me," Polina said. "Do you understand? He is my — I belong to him."

Oskar thought about the money the German had paid him. It meant nothing to him. But was it enough to buy her freedom? And then he remembered the pendant. He pulled the necklace from his pocket.

"What is it?" the girl asked him.

In the shadow of his cupped hand, the jewels scintillated. "We'll give him this."

The girl considered the necklace, then made up her mind. "We have to hurry. He only went for a drink."

Oskar pushed past her, into the apartment. His first impulse was to leave the pendant on the desk, where he had placed the other jewelry that morning.

"No," the girl said. "On the bed."

This made sense to Oskar, because this in fact was the nature of the exchange. Crossing the studio, he lay the pendant onto the hard pillow. The girl stood next to him, looking at it with him. The large, pale sapphire captured the rays from the exposed bulbs and cast them back into the room, she thought, like pieces of an empty sky. Then she spit on the bed. The small wad of mucus landed beside the pendant on the pillow.

"My name is Oskar," Oskar said.

"Mine is Polina."

"Polina," Oskar repeated. It was, to him, a beautiful name.

"One more thing," Polina said. She took a step to the wardrobe, kicked the door with her heel. The mirror dropped in a single sheet, hit the rough-hewn planks, shattered into a thousand sharp pieces. The crash of breaking glass overwhelmed Oskar. A second later, a mosaic of small reflections dazzled him. He reconstructed Polina from among the shards, momentarily hypnotized by the jagged portrait. Then Polina's shoes splintered the broken glass. She was already leaving.

Oskar took one last look around the barren room, then followed her down the stairs to the street. They left the door open behind them, swinging in the wind on rusty hinges.

■ ■ ■

An hour later, when Hermann left the bar, his head was light. Fortune had smiled upon him, to be sure, and he had celebrated. A glass of champagne had turned into a vodka tonic and then another. He could still taste the oil of lemon on his tongue. Walking home, he hardly noticed the snow. He was turning over his conversation with his commanding officer. His request for a transfer back to Berlin would be considered favorably — that is what he had been told. In less than a month, he would be able to return with his newfound treasure to Germany. His future would be secure, his daughter's, too. The electric light flooding from the windows upstairs led him back to the building. When he reached the lobby, the door was latched shut again. He searched for his key, twisted the frozen lock, stepped inside.

He was halfway to the stairs when he realized that the lobby floor was covered in snow. Hermann was so used to it on the street that he almost failed to see it. He stopped, swiveled around. How had snow gotten inside? He squatted down to examine the seal at the base of the door, rubbed his eyes behind his spectacles with a finger and thumb. The buzz from the alcohol was wearing off. When he tried the switch on the wall, the lamp was out. He drew his pistol before climbing into the shadows.

At the top of the staircase, he fumbled with his keys, unable to shake the feeling that he was being watched. On the floor above, a door inside Fru Jensen's apartment opened and slammed. Hermann jumped, then relaxed. Fru Jensen or her daughter had left the door open downstairs, that was all, and now it had blown closed again in the wind. He slipped his pistol back into its holster, pulled off his gloves. Unable to find the right key, he tapped on the door. When Polina didn't respond, he tapped a second time, louder. The lights were burning. She was awake, certainly.

He was reaching for his pistol again when a leather sole scraped the tile in the dark behind him. His finger snagged the holster. The gun's barrel tangled with the flap. And before he could draw his weapon, a man emerged from the haze. A Luger was trained on Hermann's forehead.

"Don't move," the man said.

Hermann relaxed his grip on the butt of his own pistol. The Luger was cocked, aimed to kill. Hermann let his eyes focus on the man behind it. His arm projected toward him at a ninety-degree angle. His limbs were taut beneath his suit. His posture was stiff, tense. Still, there was something cool about him. He wasn't afraid. And then Hermann noticed the smile on the man's face, and his blood ran cold. *This man is a killer.* "Where is Polina?" Hermann asked him. That this was his first question of this assassin came as much of a surprise to Hermann as it did to the man in the fedora.

Franz Jakobsen shook his head. "You can hand me your gun."

Hermann complied. There was no point in trying to resist. This man wanted money, that was all anyone wanted — and he had money to give him. He had no use for it any longer. After all, he had the jewels.

"Now, open the door."

Once again, Hermann complied. Where before he had had trouble with the keys, his hands were steady. He turned the lock, opened the door. The broken mirror on the floor gave him a small start. The apartment was empty. "Where is Polina?" he asked again.

"You mean the girl who was here?"

Hermann led the man into the apartment. Their eyes met as the man closed the door behind him. "What did you do to her?"

Franz offered Hermann another smile. "You were in love with her."

Hermann noticed the use of the past tense, and once again ice ran through his veins. *This man will kill me.* "At least tell me that you didn't hurt her."

Now Franz's smile extended into his eyes. "She left with the boy."

"I don't understand."

"The boy who sold you the jewelry — I followed him here. Now do you understand? Those jewels didn't belong to him. They don't belong to you, either. They were stolen from a family of Jews whose passage we had guaranteed as far as Sweden. I'm here to reclaim them — I'm here because he led me here —"

Hermann barely heard the man. "And she left with him," he said.

Franz responded with a wink. His teeth glistened. "He came back to collect her just as soon as you left."

Hermann reached for the back of a chair, held himself steady. "I have money," he said.

Franz shrugged. "I'm not interested in that."

"I have two hundred reichsmarks here, but I can get more — a lot more —"

"Where is the suitcase?"

Hermann was still grappling with his thoughts. It had been too good to be true, that this boy could drop this jewelry into his lap without consequence. Of course it belonged to someone else. He would lose it now, just as he had already lost Polina.

"The suitcase," Franz said. "The jewelry. Where is it?" He surveyed the apartment. There weren't many places where the

German could have hidden it. "You can bring it to me, or I can look for it myself when you are dead."

Hermann felt his will collapse. "I will get it for you." He waited for the man's tacit approval, then crossed to the wardrobe. The satchel was sitting inside, tossed casually into a corner. When he pulled it out, the jewelry clinked. He carried the bag to the desk. "It's all here," he said. "All of it."

As Franz examined the satchel's contents, Hermann sat down on his bed. He began to bury his head in his hands. Then, on the lumpy pillow where Oskar had left it for him, he caught sight of the sharp, crystalline edges of the pendant. Eyeing the assassin, he picked up the necklace. This was the first time he had seen it, and the icy purity of the stones blinded him. Although he recognized how senseless the impulse was, it was suddenly important to him to keep this one piece of jewelry out of this other man's grasp. Stealthily, he lifted the small leather case where he kept his War Merit Cross from the nightstand, and he slipped the necklace inside.

The rustling noise pulled Franz from his contemplation. When he twisted around, though, Hermann's elbows were resting on his knees again. "You have what you wanted," Hermann managed to say. But he couldn't find the strength to look at the man, even as he approached the bed.

The man's footsteps rang in Hermann's ears, louder and louder, then stopped. The building fell completely still. Then the report of the Luger shattered the silence. Hermann heard the gunshot before the bullet reached his temple. A split second before it happened, he knew that the lead would spill his soul against the wall.

Afterward, Franz lay the corpse onto the bed. Hermann Schmidt was light in death, he thought. He had noticed how heavy some dead men become. The first man he shot had been short and insubstantial, but he had become a sack of bricks — he had barely been able to lift him enough to clean out his pockets. This German was as weightless as a bird. A puddle of blood was pooling beneath him on the dusty floorboards. Franz was careful not to let it touch his shoes.

After Franz was gone, the studio remained awash in electric light. Hermann's blood blackened. On Hermann's pillow, next to the indentation where the pendant had lain, Polina's wad of spit calcified into a scab of tiny alabaster crystals.

THE WALL

THE WALL

18.

Not quite a decade before Angela Schmidt would pay a visit to her aunt in East Berlin, Gerhardt Bloch packed the last of his books into a suitcase lying open on the sofa in the small sitting room of the apartment he shared with his wife. At the height of the afternoon on yet another humid day, the heat was stifling. A tall, thin man with long arms and a bony chest, he was dressed in an undershirt that was patchy with sweat, tucked into a pair of lightweight trousers. The air was so dense that it was difficult to breathe. Still, he didn't want to open a window, not even a crack. Their apartment was on the third floor of a large tenement, and the neighbors' windows were barely ten feet away. Their only view was of the narrow alley between the buildings — and not a thing happened in the Blochs' apartment to which their neighbors weren't privy. It was the same for everyone. He and Martina knew all their neighbors' secrets as well. The couple across the alley had been acting out the same argument for years now. The husband was convinced that his wife was unfaithful, and she was paying dearly for this imaginary slight. The melodrama was an ordinary one, so it was easy enough to dismiss these people as fools. It was important to remember, though, just how quickly information could find its way to the State Security Service. Gerhardt stopped to assess his work. The suitcase was nearly full. There wasn't room for anything else. Only his books. His collection of stamps and coins — though he had owned them since he was a child — would have to stay behind.

"Are you sure you need to bring so many?" Martina asked him.

Gerhardt hadn't heard his wife enter the room. He raised his eyes from the suitcase. The smile that creased his lips was a sad one. He didn't try to say any more than it expressed. He didn't even shrug. He simply looked at Martina.

"They have bookstores in Munich," she said.

Gerhardt returned his attention to the suitcase. He had read each one of these books, over and over, some of them until the spines were starting to disintegrate. He picked one up, flipped through the pages. "'That is no country for old men,'" he said, in English.

"If we had an automobile," Martina said, "we could take everything we will miss."

"*If* we had an automobile," Gerhardt echoed, closing the book.

"That is my point," Martina said.

Gerhardt shook his head. He returned the volume of poetry to the suitcase. His fingers lingered on the leather cover. "Perhaps you are right — I can simply leave them. Maybe there isn't anything I need after all."

"We agreed one bag each," Martina said. "We can't carry more. I only wonder if you think it best to take these books. They're heavy, too — "

"This one," Gerhardt said, still touching the book's cover, "I bought on the very same day that I met you — did I ever tell you that?"

"In 1936?"

"September 3, 1936."

Martina smiled. Her eyes dropped to the floor. "I wouldn't have guessed that you would remember the date," she said.

"After I met you — you were with your friend, Frauke, at the café, of course — I walked across town, on my way to the university, and I stopped at the bookstore. I was looking for something specific. In fact, I remember that, too. *Fear and Trembling*, by Kierkegaard. I ran across this volume, though — it was sitting on the table in front, it had just arrived from England — William Butler Yeats. I had never read him before. I picked the book up, and it fell open to a poem with a title that caught my attention. 'Sailing to Byzantium.' It was such a beautiful name."

The room fell silent. Martina's gaze was still directed at her husband's feet. She raised her eyes to the suitcase but didn't manage to lift them higher. "You're doing this for me," she said. "Aren't you?"

"It's the right thing to do," Gerhardt reassured her.

"We don't have to go," Martina said.

"Clothilde and Barend are in Munich," Gerhardt said. "They're expecting us tomorrow. Angela, too — I know how much you are looking forward to seeing your brother's daughter. I know how much Hermann's death still haunts you."

"Your life is here."

"My life is with you, Martina."

Once again, the room fell silent.

"And the Kierkegaard?" Martina asked at last.

"What?"

"The book you were looking for — *Fear and Trembling* — did you find it that day?"

Gerhardt tapped the side of the suitcase.

"Well," Martina said, "after all, it isn't that far to walk. From here to the Brandenburg Gate. Thirty minutes, not more. And it will be the last time we ever have to take that walk — "

"What about you?" Gerhardt asked her. "Have you already finished packing?"

"I'm ready to go," she said.

"You've made the tough choices — you've decided what you want to carry?"

Martina nodded.

"Well then," Gerhardt said. He closed the lid of the suitcase, fastened the clasps. "Let me get dressed, and then it's time. No reason to wait any longer."

"I'll get my suitcase," Martina said.

She was on her way into the hall, and Gerhardt was lifting his own suitcase off the sofa, testing its weight, when there was a knock on the door. It wasn't a soft knock — it was a rap, a staccato burst of five or six hard taps. Martina's footsteps ceased. Their echo, though, seemed to hang in the air.

"Gerhardt?" she whispered.

Gerhardt set the suitcase back down on the sofa, crossed to the hall, where Martina was standing transfixed, staring at the front door. "Are you expecting someone?" he asked his wife.

"Who could that be?" Martina whispered.

Gerhardt gave his wife's elbow a caress on his way to the door.

"Let's not answer it," Martina said, again in a whisper.

A second time, the rap of knuckles on the solid-core door reverberated through the small space. Gerhardt hesitated a moment longer, then reached for the knob. When he pulled the door open, Martina stopped breathing. A man in an olive uniform took half a step inside.

"Gerhardt Maximilian Bloch?" the policeman said.

"That is me," Gerhardt said, "yes — what can I do for you?"

The policeman took a cursory look around the small entry-way. In their preparations to leave, Martina and Gerhardt had made something of a mess. There were papers on the floor, and next to the closet there was a small stack of cardboard boxes, filled with clothing and other items that they imagined some of their friends and relatives might want to claim after they were gone. The policeman didn't seem to notice. He with-drew an envelope from his jacket pocket, handed it to Ger-hardt. "You're under arrest," he said.

"What?" Gerhardt said.

"What?" Martina echoed. "No!" she exclaimed. "No — what for? What can you possibly want him for?"

"You work as a clerk at the Babylon Cinema on Rosa-Luxemburg-Platz, do you not?"

"I am not a clerk," Gerhardt answered. "For the past fifteen years, I have worked as an accountant, at the bidding of the state. But I am a professor of philosophy. That was my training, and that remains my profession."

Behind him, his wife had turned pale. She raised her hands to her cheeks, then dropped them again. A thin silver brace-let slid from her elbow to her wrist. "No," she whispered. "No, you can't."

"You are under arrest," the policeman said, "for the crime of embezzlement. You are charged with the theft of fifteen thousand marks."

"The money belongs to him," Martina said.

Gerhardt turned around to face her. "It will be all right," he said.

"But the money is yours," she said. She looked past him, to the policeman. "My husband is sixty-eight years old," she explained. "He is ready to take his retirement in December. He only took what they would have paid him as his pension anyway. He has worked so hard. He has done everything they asked him to. Please —"

"Perhaps you want to put a shirt on first," the policeman said to Gerhardt.

Gerhardt lowered his head. "Thank you," he said to the policeman. "That is kind of you."

"Please," Martina repeated. "Please —"

"I'll only be a minute," Gerhardt said to the policeman. He stopped in front of Martina, took both her wrists in his hands, lifted them a little, gave them a gentle shake. "Shhh," he said to her. "It will be okay. Herr Hoffman will understand. I'll explain everything to him, and they will let me go. Surely."

"But Gerhardt —" Martina said.

"There will always be tomorrow," her husband reassured her. He squeezed her wrists softly, then turned once again toward the policeman. "I'll only be a minute," he said a second time. Then he led his wife back to the bedroom and, slipping it from the hanger, put on the shirt he had been planning to wear that afternoon for their passage into West Berlin. Martina had washed it in the sink just the day before, and the thick cotton was still slightly damp. The collar was stiff with the residue of hand soap. He buttoned the collar, pulled the sleeves taut, fastened the cuffs. Martina settled onto the hard bed. She sat as she always did, with her spine straight, her shoulders back, her hands folded in her lap. And that is how she remained as Gerhardt left the room and followed the policeman out the door and to the station.

August 13, 1961.

Early the next morning, a small crowd had gathered on the eastern edge of Pariser Platz. The grinding buzz of earthmovers had woken the city at midnight, and over the course of the last few hours the sounds had only intensified. Up and down the twisting length of the border between East and West Berlin, soldiers were wielding hammers and picks and shovels. Trucks carrying GDR troops continued to roll into the city center. The work crews were swelling, and in an impossibly long line front of them, before the foundation of the wall could be laid, the military had already constructed a human barrier that stretched over the north-south axis of the city, along boulevards and side streets and across bridges and train tracks without interruption. Martina had barely slept. Gerhardt had spent the night in jail, and she wasn't used to the emptiness of the small apartment. The foreign noises had scared her. She had gotten dressed before dawn and had let herself outside and crept stealthily through the dark, making her way toward the Brandenburg Gate. She was among the first to reach the edge of the plaza. By seven thirty, as sunlight slowly began to stain the streets, hundreds of other Berliners had joined her, and the crowd was quickly growing larger. Without the sun, it had been difficult to see exactly what was transpiring. Now, the majestic crown of the gigantic, neoclassical gate was bathed in an orange glow, and the four bronze horses of the *Quadriga*, and Nike, their charioteer, were looking down upon a massive, orchestrated operation to divide east from west.

What is happening? The voice sounded in Martina's ear. At first she didn't hear it. And then the words were repeated. "What is it? What are they doing?"

Martina put the speaker's face together. She recognized the woman, but she wasn't immediately able to place how she knew her. The best she could do in response was to shake her head.

"Where is your husband?" the woman asked her. "You look ill. Are you okay? If you need our help —" And then Martina noticed the man standing next to her, and she knew who these people were. She offered her neighbors from across the narrow alley an apologetic grimace, then turned back again and faced the activity across the plane of the square. Beneath the gate, the legions of soldiers were being joined by a flank of military trucks. From this distance, some of the vehicles appeared to be tanks, and it was clear enough that their guns were trained not across the border but back upon the people inside their own city. *What is happening?* The woman repeated her question, but now she had turned away from Martina and was asking it of someone else. *I'm only surprised,* another voice said, *that it took them so long.*

Martina stood silently a few minutes longer. Then, when the crowd was growing so large that she felt herself begin to panic, she pushed through these people — surprised not by their anger and shock, which was palpable, but by their polite acceptance — and made her way back home. As she walked, the city woke, and she found herself moving upstream in a trickle and then a flood of her compatriots, all of them caught in some invisible gravity, drawn west. She was glad when she was able, finally, to step inside her apartment and close the door behind her.

She sat down on the stiff mattress in the bedroom she shared with Gerhardt, uncertain what to do with the time in front of her. When she noticed the suitcase she had packed just the day before, a few hot tears sprang to her eyes. She blinked them away, then twisted the suitcase around, unfastened the clasps, lifted the lid. Her favorite shawl — a large rectangle of turquoise cashmere that Gerhardt had bought her for Christmas some years ago — was crushed on top. It didn't take up too much space, and she couldn't have imagined leaving it behind. She placed it on the bed next to her, revealing the stacks of keepsakes underneath.

Her hands went first to the photographs her brother, Hermann, had managed to send her over the course of the war. These she had kept in a box in the closet, and they were in remarkably good condition. The top few were covered with a thick layer of dust. Some of their edges and corners were bent. But for the most part, they were pristine. She hadn't had room for the box. She had simply stuffed the photographs naked into her suitcase, confident that they would survive the short trip she and Gerhardt had been planning to make. Except for a small leather case, which she had also packed in the suitcase beside them, they were the only objects she possessed that had belonged to her brother.

She lifted out the leather case next, ran her fingers over its sharp edges. It had been years since she had opened it. In fact, she had only opened it once, the day that it had arrived. It had been delivered to her through the regular mail, sealed in an envelope that also contained a letter informing her of her brother's death. Somehow, she had lost that letter. She had looked for it as she packed this suitcase, and it was nowhere to be found. How ever could she have lost it? She could still see the typescript, punched into the thick cotton bond by the stroke of a typewriter's keys. *We regret to inform you that First Lieutenant Hermann H. Schmidt has been killed while on active duty in service of the Wehrmacht.* She weighed the case absently, realized that she was still holding it, finally worked a fingernail under the small clasp in its center and spread its cover open. Inside, its single content — a war decoration, a steel cross displayed on a bed of silk — had come loose from its hook, and it slid out onto her lap. She had not held the medal before. In fact, the decoration had upset her — she didn't like what it implied, that her brother had served the Reich well in his capacity as a soldier. It had been sufficient to look at it inside its case. She picked it up now, ran her fingers over the old ribbon, pressed her fingertips against its sharp edges. Maybe she would throw it away. Maybe this wasn't something for her to keep.

And then, as she was preparing to return the medal to its hook, she noticed that the case wasn't empty. There was something else inside, tucked behind the folds of silk that cushioned the steel cross. Whatever it was, it slithered from one side to the other as she tilted the case. Noticing a small tear in the silk cushion, she stuck a finger carefully into the hole. A few seconds later, she was holding the necklace. The distant tramp of footsteps echoing in the alleyway outside her window, the quiet murmur of voices, faded into the steady pulse of her own heartbeat. The cramped bedroom was absolutely silent as she lifted the sapphire pendant and let it dangle in front of her, twisting in the shadows like a small fragment cleaved from a star.

OSKAR

19.

Sjælland, Denmark. December 26, 1941.

It was nearly midnight by the time Oskar and Polina reached the harbor in Korsør. With so much snow on the tracks, the train was rolling slowly. The last ferry for Nyborg had departed two hours earlier. Curfew had passed, and they were fortunate to have made it this far without being questioned. In Ringsted, a complement of rowdy German soldiers had boarded the car. Spotting them on the platform, Polina had shoved Oskar into the toilet compartment, and they rode as far as Sorø like that, cramped together, cold, the filthy steel trap rattling at their feet. At Sorø, all but two of the soldiers had disembarked, and the two who remained were drinking beer, too drunk to care who else was traveling with them. Still reeking of piss from the dirty toilet, Oskar and Polina ventured back out and were able to find seats in another carriage. Now, the train was nearly empty as the heavy wheels clanked over the rails and the pneumatic brakes pumped to slow the locomotive down.

The slither of the wheels on the steel rails echoed against the undercarriage over a section of track sheltered from snow. In the aftermath of the sound, Oskar realized how unusually silent the journey had been.

He stood as they approached the station, peered through the black window. Passengers were gathering at the door of the next car, waiting for the train to reach the end of the line. They appeared to be civilians, all of them — Danes — none of them a threat. Polina had fallen asleep, and she looked so peaceful that Oskar hated to wake her. Her head was resting on her forearm, and her mouth gaped in her sleep like a child's.

Oskar touched her shoulder. Her breath steamed onto his fingers, and this made him shiver. When she didn't stir, he shook her, then squeezed her arm. At last, she opened her eyes. As far away as she may have been in her dream, she was immediately back again. "Did you know," she asked him, "that you are the most handsome boy I have ever seen?"

Oskar flushed. He understood that she was lying to him. This was flattery that she had learned in order to survive. He was an awkward boy. His nose was too long, and it was bent where it had been broken when his father had slapped him at twelve. His hair was neglected and unwashed. In the past few years, he had become so thin that his ribs jutted from his chest. There was nothing handsome about him, and he knew it. Nevertheless, he *wanted* to believe her.

"Of course," she said, "I have never loved handsome boys."

It appalled Oskar to hear her use the word, though he wasn't certain why. *Had she loved at all?*

The train jolted. A lit sign glided past the window. "Korsør," Oskar said.

Polina pushed herself upright on the uncomfortable seat. She joined Oskar in the aisle, followed him to the front of the car as the train rolled to a stop. The brakes whined, and a conductor blew a single high-pitched blast on his whistle. Then, after a moment of silence, the doors swung open. Exiting the carriages, the tired passengers spoke in muffled whispers.

They had nothing to carry. Oskar hunched his shoulders against the wind. Polina lifted her collar to protect her face. She leaned into him as they followed the other passengers from the station into town. It felt natural when Oskar looped his arm around her waist. Her hair whipped into his mouth, and he tasted her. The lamps surrounding the small harbor blinked in the distance. Polina's hand found Oskar's pocket, and the cold touch of her fingers thrilled him. They chased the flickering lights without knowing where they were going, for one long moment removed from the passage of time. The series of steps that had brought them to this point had become a blur. And to Oskar, nothing lay in the future that could be better than these few minutes now.

They stopped at the first small hotel they passed. They were already soaked through, and there was no reason to go farther. Polina wandered into the bar, where a man with waxed hair was playing an upright piano. The hotelier at the reception counter narrowed his eyes as Oskar approached. He was more interested in watching Polina than in taking Oskar's money, and he seemed to know instantly what kind of woman she was. *This isn't that kind of hotel,* he said to Oskar. *If it wasn't so late and if we weren't so empty, if it wasn't storming outside, I would turn the two of you away.* Oskar took the key from him and found Polina in the bar. When the piano player winked at her, she winked back. Her fingers tightened on Oskar's arm as they climbed the stairs.

In the small room, Polina stood in the dark by the window. "Do you want me naked?" she asked.

At first, the question didn't make sense to Oskar. Then he felt his cheeks redden. From downstairs, he could hear the faint tinkling of the piano, and he remembered the way the piano player had winked at her, and then the look in the hotelier's eye when he first saw Polina. "I'm going to sleep," he said. She was still standing at the window when he pulled off his coat and his shoes and his pants and climbed into bed. The mattress was as hard as rock underneath him. Smells from the kitchen rose through the floor. He closed his eyes, and the room began to spin. Outside, the storm swept over the west coast of Zealand. Oskar had the sense that it would destroy everything in its path. By morning, nothing of this pathetic industrial harbor would remain.

When Polina slipped under the covers behind him, Oskar was already half asleep. For a brief instant, he imagined that they were sharing the bed inside the German's apartment. Then church bells chimed and the windowpanes reverberated, and he remembered where they were. She wrapped her arms around him, and he counted her fingers against his chest and thought about her face, masked in white makeup. The music downstairs melted into the bars of "Heart and Soul." "I have a sister," he said.

Polina's fingers tightened on his ribs. Her breath warmed his neck.

"I have a father, too. But not a mother. I mean, I don't know my mother anymore. I saw her yesterday, but that was the first time in three or four years."

Polina's breasts touched his back, and he could feel her heart beating. Slow and steady. His own was fluttering.

"I'm not sure what my father will think." And it occurred to Oskar how strange it was that Polina hadn't said a thing—she hadn't asked him anything, not a single question about his village or his house or his family. She had no idea where they were going, yet she followed him blindly. "About you, I mean. I'm not sure what my father will think when I bring you home."

"Shhh." And then her hand was on his hip, and her fingers were cold, and then her fingers were on his thigh. Oskar froze. Her fingertips traced a line to the waist of his underpants, then just as swiftly slipped beneath the elastic. Oskar's heart was suddenly pounding. When she felt him, he choked on his own breath. "Don't you like me?"

Oskar didn't respond. He was paralyzed. When her hand found his thigh again, he was relieved. He wished that he could explain. This wasn't what he imagined, and it wasn't what he wanted — not like this. He was still a virgin. He had never even touched a girl, not really. In school, before the war, he had seen a girl naked once, changing into her uniform in a classroom when she thought that she was alone. And one time when he had come for his father in Aalborg, he had found him passed out in the brothel, and there he had seen a woman's breasts. But when he finally figured out what he wanted to say — *You don't have to do this, Polina, not to make me happy, because I'm already happy right now, just like this* — by then she was already asleep, he could feel it in the weight of her fingers.

Oskar closed his eyes. He inhaled her smell, the sweet scent of her sweat, the fragrance of her hair, the pungent, lingering odors from the world she had inhabited in Copenhagen. And in two minutes more, he was asleep himself. When the church bells rang again sometime after midnight, neither one of them moved, not a single muscle. The silvery light of dawn captured them still together. Their hair was made of pearl and agate. Their faces were cast in china.

WHERE THE ROAD TURNS

20.

Jutland. December 27, 1941.

When Oskar and Polina reached the farm, Fredrik was in the barn, cleaning the pigsty. Denmark wasn't used to this much snow in December. The last two days had brought well over a foot to Jutland, and the wind was still blowing, the sky was still dark with heavy clouds. For the moment, the blizzard had stopped. But the temperature had dropped precipitously, and the wind was so strong that the landscape, blanketed in snow, was shifting like the floor of a desert in a sandstorm. The east side of the barn was nearly buried in a frozen bank. The livestock hadn't been aired for a week, and now Fredrik's work had disturbed the pigs' shit. The barn reeked. He paused long enough to cover his nose and mouth with the old undershirt he was using as a makeshift scarf, then continued shoveling. When Oskar returned, he would have him wash the pigs down. With this weather, even inside the barn it was too cold — the smaller animals would freeze. The crunch of footsteps in the snow interrupted him. He planted the shovel into the dirt. Glimpsing Oskar's face at the barn door, his eyes lit before his anger got the better of him. "You need to take better care of these pigs," he said to his son, yanking the rag from his face. "They're more important to me than you are."

They had eaten bread along the way, but only a little, and Oskar was so hungry that he felt faint. The walk from Aalborg through the snow had fatigued them both. It was already three o'clock, and he and Polina had been awake since five. All he wanted was to go inside and make a pot of tea. He met his father's gaze. "I'll change into my other clothes," he said. "These shoes are pinching my feet."

"Yeah — make it quick — " Fredrik mopped the sweat from his brow with a sleeve. "Because I'm done here, this is your job, and you've made a mess of it. I've got other things to do."

Oskar felt Polina's hand on his arm. His chest constricted. He had taken a risk bringing the girl here.

"Well, get a move on," Fredrik said, misreading his son's hesitation. Polina had remained hidden behind the door, and he still hadn't seen her. "There'll be time enough to tell me about your adventure when you've finished with this."

A slender, ivory hand touched Oskar's shoulder. The diamond ring sent shards of light into the dark barn. Next to Oskar, the shadows shifted. And then Polina appeared. "Aren't you going to introduce me to your father?"

Fredrik had been about to retrieve his gloves from the floor. Instead, he took a step toward the door, wiped his hands on his work shirt, squinted at the pale-eyed whore whom his son had brought home to their house in the middle of the day. Two or three seconds passed before he finally stooped to pick up the gloves. He beat the dust off them against his thigh. "It's my own fault," he muttered.

"I am Polina," the whore said into the silence. The rank smell was making her nauseous, but she didn't show it. Her voice startled the animals, and one of the male pigs bleated and jockeyed against the smaller ones.

Fredrik ignored her and faced Oskar instead. "You dare to bring a foreigner into our house?"

"She was in trouble," Oskar said.

"She's a stranger."

"I can explain, Father."

"No, you can't." Fredrik tightened his grip on his gloves, shoved them into his pocket. "No, you can't," he repeated, more softly. "I already know your explanation. I already know who this is."

Polina's eyes flattened. Her fingers found Oskar's sleeve. As incidental as her touch was, as gentle, he felt the tug sharply. "I won't stay," she said to Oskar, loudly enough for Fredrik to hear.

"It's my house, too," Oskar said, taking a step between his father and the girl. But Fredrik hardly heard him.

"I know a place in Aalborg," Fredrik barked, "where they're looking for girls like this one." Isabella had complained to him just the day before that they needed more women to keep up with the demand the occupation was placing on their business. The soldiers had an appetite for whores, and unlike farmers they had the means to satisfy it.

"You haven't even met her yet," Oskar said.

"Go inside," Fredrik said. "Change your shoes. The pigs are waiting."

"You haven't even talked to her."

"I've seen enough," Fredrik snapped. He grabbed the shovel again, hoisted it as if he intended to take it outside and find a use for it there. "I've met her before."

Oskar felt his resentment rise in his throat. He wanted to confront his father, but Fredrik had already turned away, and he lacked the resolve to chase him. Polina's fingers sought his. Rather than take her hand, he grabbed her by the elbow and led her out of the barn. Their feet sank into the slush as they crossed the field toward the cottage.

■ ■ ■

Upstairs, Amalia was standing in front of the sink in the narrow bathroom. Her blouse was undone, and her uncovered breasts hung slack from her chest when she leaned over the basin to look at her reflection in the mirror. The door was closed. When she heard footsteps downstairs, she assumed that they belonged to her father. It had been another long day, and she was exhausted. With the New Year approaching, there was yet another party for which she had to prepare — the Nielsens' friends and family would come to the house on the thirty-first to kick 1941 in the teeth. Amalia had spent the day polishing the silver. Her fingers were still black from the chemicals. The footsteps on the stairs barely registered. When the door swung open behind her, she quickly covered her chest. She was startled to catch sight of Polina in the mirror. "Who are you?" A current of colder air had followed the girl in, and Amalia felt her nipples harden in her hands.

"I'm sorry," Polina said. But she remained where she was.

Oskar's footsteps creaked on the floorboards. When he leaned his head into the bathroom, Amalia protested. "What are you doing, Oskar? Get out."

Oskar retreated to the bedroom, sat down on his bed to take off his shoes.

"I met Oskar in Copenhagen," Polina said.

Flustered, Amalia waited for the girl finally to leave the bathroom before she fastened her blouse.

Polina found Oskar in the bedroom, bent over his shoes. "Your sister is beautiful," she said, and this surprised him. Not because he disagreed — he had always thought that Amalia was beautiful, whether or not she was his sister — but because he had expected something else from Polina. She didn't seem to care if Fredrik sent her away to become a whore again in Aalborg, and she wasn't aware of how Amalia would perceive her. It had been a mistake to bring her back here. Now that he was home, he wondered what had moved him to steal her away from the German in the first place. Wrestling with these thoughts himself, Oskar had expected Polina, too, to show some concern for their predicament.

He looked up from his shoes. "Give me the ring," he said.

Polina faced him, not quite comprehending.

"The ring," Oskar repeated, nodding toward her hand. "Give it to me."

She studied the diamond, then pulled the ring off her finger, weighed it in her hand as if she might keep it, finally tossed it to him as if he was mugging her. "It's yours anyway. I don't own anything here that you don't want me to."

Oskar pulled a dirty shoelace from one of the shoes, slid it through the band, tied the ends into a knot. Then he stood from the bed and placed the necklace around her neck. When their eyes met, she looked away from him quickly. "It's better like this," he said.

Polina gathered the lace, slipped the ring under the collar of her shirt. Oskar noticed the curve of her neck and how smooth her skin was. Wisps of loose hair glistened above her shoulders.

"You can sleep in Amalia's bed," he said.

"Hmmm?"

"That's Amalia's bed, there." Oskar gestured toward his sister's side of the room. "You can sleep with her until we figure something else out."

Outside, the afternoon was becoming darker, the clouds were growing heavier. The sun was beginning to fall somewhere beyond the horizon. Oskar noticed the way the light collected in the girl's eyes. The same way the sun's rays sometimes become trapped inside a brook, he thought. "I had better hurry up," he said, realizing the time. He slipped out of his trousers, grabbed another pair, searched under the bed for his work boots.

Polina remarked how skinny his legs were. The muscles were sinewy and strong, but his knees protruded over his calves. The dim light gilded his skin, severing his silhouette from the shadows. She watched him dress, then sat down on Amalia's bed after he was gone. The sheet separating Oskar's half of the room from Amalia's rippled in an invisible current. She peered past it, to the corner of Oskar's unmade bed peeking beyond its edge, then swiveled around to assess the simple arrangements. It was so cold inside that her breath turned to steam. She passed a hand over Amalia's pillow, then, remembering the ring, pulled it from beneath her shirt to examine it again. After testing the strength of Oskar's shoelace, to make certain that it was secure, she dropped the ring back between her breasts. Then she reached into her pocket. Her hand remained hidden there for a minute, before she finally drew out the small, smooth piece of amethyst that Julian had given her years before.

The violet stone retained the heat of her body. She balanced it on her fingertips, ran a fingernail over a few glassy ridges where the semiprecious mineral darkened into obsidian. *I was going to give you something. Now I don't want to anymore.* Downstairs, the front door slammed, and Oskar's footsteps beat a path across the porch and into the yard. The house, Polina noticed, felt empty without him.

■ ■ ■

It was after seven by the time Oskar finished shoveling the pigsty. Once again, the work had chafed his hands. The shovel's wooden handle had opened up old blisters and created a few new ones as well. Oskar hardly noticed. He returned the shovel and rake to the utility closet, then carted the last wheelbarrow of waste out of the barn. The ground was too icy to roll it to the usual heap around back, so he brought it as far as he could, then emptied it on top of the previous loads he had already carried outside. When the snow thawed, he would have to scoop it back onto the flat barrow and bring it the rest of the way to the dump. Until then, the cold would keep it frozen. He tilted the barrow up against the wall, then emptied a bucket of slop into the pigs' trough. One of the smaller pigs — a runt that hadn't made it beyond its first year — had died the week before, and Fredrik had ground it up in the feed grinder. Everything except the intestines. Blended with barley, the soup would last the pigs a few more days. As Oskar headed back to the cottage, except for a few contented grunts, the pigs were quiet behind him.

Halfway across the icy yard, he was joined by his father. Fredrik had been working outside, scraping snow off the roof of a shed. He had been working in the light of a kerosene lantern before the fuel had run dry. He would finish tomorrow in daylight. When he fell into step beside his son, he was winded from the effort, and his breath billowed in front of him. "It sounds like you fed them, too," he said.

Oskar nodded. "I did."

"Animals are always happier when they've eaten."

Oskar remembered his own hunger, but he kept his mouth shut.

"A famished pig becomes a lion. Starve him and he bites your fingers off." When Fredrik placed a hand on Oskar's shoulder, his son was surprised by the touch, and he was surprised even more when his father left the hand resting there as they walked. "Feed him, and he becomes a meal himself."

Oskar stamped his boots on the porch, and dirty chunks of frozen turf skittered across the painted wood planks.

"I suppose you brought back something else from Copenhagen," Fredrik said. He stamped his boots, too. "Other than the whore."

His father was only expecting five hundred crowns for the whole of the treasure. He would be happy, Oskar thought, with two hundred and fifty. There was no reason to tell Fredrik the truth. The day before, Oskar had wanted nothing more than to impress his father with his success. Now the thought occurred to him that he might have his own use for the money. He opened his mouth, ready to deceive, but found he couldn't. "More than you thought."

Fredrik took one last whack with his boot against the side of the house. A chunk of ice disintegrated like a diamond beneath a hammer. "Oh?"

"A lot more," Oskar said.

"How much?" Fredrik wanted to know. It had been a long year, and this was going to be a difficult winter. Even with the food from the farm, his family was suffering. Fredrik wondered how much longer Amalia would be able to continue working like this. He saw how tired she was.

"A thousand."

Fredrik allowed himself a smile. It was no wonder that the old Jew had clung to the suitcase so tightly. "Why don't we bring some wood inside," he said. "You can light a fire."

It was clear from his father's words that at least a few crowns were already spent. *You* can light a fire. Fredrik would head into town to find Isabella. It might be a day or two before they saw him again. "Will you have dinner with us?"

Fredrik jostled his son's shoulder. "You did well, Oskar," he said, choosing not to reply — perhaps because he didn't know the answer yet himself. "In that at least, you did well." He chuckled, but there was no mirth in the sound. "Still, I noticed you put a ring on the girl's finger."

Oskar thought about explaining, but he didn't know how. He remembered pulling the ring from his pocket, turning it over in his hand, suggesting to the German that he might want to give it to Polina. The smell of baking bread came back to him with the memory, strong enough that the thought crossed his mind that Amalia might have the oven on inside.

"You could have gotten more," Fredrik said. "Eh? If you hadn't kept the ring for yourself — "

Oskar shook his head. This wasn't true — he had sold the ring to the German, then had stolen it back from him again — but the story was too complicated to relate. He glanced up at his father, realized that he would never understand.

Fredrik surprised him with another smile. "Anyway," he said, "at least you're finally acting like a man." Then he led his son inside.

In the kitchen, the kettle was on the stove, and the water was boiling, forgotten. The metal was nearly dry, and the room smelled of scorched iron. The pot was so hot that it would crack under running water. Polina was seated at the table, holding a cup of tea to her lips. She had found the sugar in the cupboard, and a spoon was sticking out from the small paper bag. Oskar had been expecting to find his sister there. Normally, Amalia would have had the kitchen clean from the dishes left over from their lunch. The table would be set, the counters would be clear, food would be roasting in the oven or simmering on the stove. There was little doubt how Fredrik would react to this disarray. And the sugar was for special occasions. Only Amalia was allowed to touch it, for she alone knew how to apportion it to get the most from the bag.

But Fredrik crossed to the stove and turned off the flame himself. He set the glowing kettle onto a hob at the back where it would cool down slowly. Then he stepped behind Polina and took the cup from her hand. The liquid inside was still scalding — she had only poured it a couple of moments earlier — but he swallowed half in a single mouthful, as if this indeed was the way he liked his tea, boiling hot and as thick as syrup with precious sugar. His Adam's apple bobbed beneath the gray stubble crawling down his neck from his chin. He wiped his lips with his sleeve, offered the cup back to Polina. He was already drunk, Oskar realized, on the thousand crowns. "Where's my daughter?" he asked.

"She was tired," Polina said. Within the walls of his own house, Oskar was more aware of her accent. "So I told her to lie down for a while. She fell asleep, I think. Upstairs, in her bed."

Fredrik looked around the small kitchen. Polina had made herself at home. She had cut herself a slice from the bread, leaving crumbs that would feed the mice. She had found a tin of cookies left over from Amalia's birthday, and even though they had been rationed until they were stale, she had treated herself to a few. She had tried to saw a chunk off the salami, but it was too hard, and she had left it where she had laid it, on the counter. Fredrik smiled — he had been right about this girl, that much she had already proved — but it was a tolerant smile. There was something compelling about her, wasn't there — There was a reason why Oskar had fallen under her spell. She wasn't an ordinary person. Well, they never were, he thought. They always had their stories to tell if you let them. "Now," he announced, nodding his head at the mess on the counter. "I was planning to eat in town anyway. I'll be leaving before it gets too late, and you can clean this up after I'm gone."

Oskar saw the kitchen through his father's eyes. Taking a step past him, he wrapped the bread in its foil, set it back inside the box, put the salami away, brushed the crumbs into the sink. "I'll light a fire," he said. "The house is cold."

Fredrik grabbed the tin of stale cookies and set it squarely down in the center of the table. As if he were serving them cake and champagne. "Let's have a little celebration before I go," he said. "After all, it's almost the New Year, isn't it?"

Oskar crossed the small cottage into the sitting room, where he stacked a few logs onto the grate in the fireplace. "I can make us some coffee," he said, "once the kettle cools back down."

"Forget the coffee," Fredrik said. "I'll open a bottle, eh? And you know what I'd like to do then?" He reached into the cupboard, found what he was looking for. "Play a game of cards."

It had been years since his father had wanted to play with him. Those had always formed some of Oskar's fondest memories — the few times when his father had sat with Amalia and him and taught them hearts. In front of the hearth, he stopped still, bewildered by the recollection. When he looked back into the kitchen, the deck of tired blue cards was splayed in his father's gigantic hands like an Oriental fan.

■ ■ ■

When Amalia stumbled into the kitchen an hour later, the bright light stung her eyes. She took in the cards on the table, the open bottle half empty next to her father, the three glasses in front of them. The smile on Oskar's face perplexed her, as did the amount of flesh on display below the unbuttoned collar of Polina's blouse. The diamond ring dangled from the shoelace around the Polish girl's neck, cradled in her exposed cleavage. Candles burned on the table. Wax had melted onto the cloth. The house was as hot as an oven. It was this that had woken her — the heat, and the rumble of her father's voice and the tittering strain of Polina's laughter. Polina was still laughing as Amalia stepped through the doorway. When their eyes met, she quieted, but forced a smile. Amalia stopped where she was, blinking, trying to make sense of the scene.

Fredrik's back was to the door. "What," he said, "did the police come inside?" He swiveled in his chair to see what had dampened the cheer. When he caught sight of his daughter, he opened his arms and offered her his lap. "Come," he said. "Get yourself a glass, then have yourself a seat."

Amalia wasn't keen on letting her father know how relieved she felt to be included. But she obeyed and pulled the last of their four glasses from the cupboard and took a careful seat on her father's thigh. "I fell asleep," she said, "before I could make dinner."

Fredrik filled her glass with an ounce or two of whiskey. "Nonsense," he told her. "You're working too hard anyway. Those bastards — what are they paying you? Fifty øre a day, isn't it?"

Amalia took an experimental sip. Her father had never poured her a glass before. The liquid burned her lips and tongue, then cut a swath down her throat. Almost immediately, the alcohol went to her head. Now the expression on Oskar's face made more sense. He wasn't used to it either.

"Eh? Fifty øre a day?"

Amalia didn't answer. Fredrik knew exactly how much they paid her, because he counted her earnings himself every week. Three crowns that went straight into his pocket. He would take the coins from her with a scowl on his face, as if he was doing her a favor letting her remain in his house for so little.

"Maybe it's time to tell the Nielsens what they can do with their lousy fifty øre, what do you think?" He gave his daughter a squeeze. "Maybe then you can spend a little more time on yourself, the way a girl your age should. I know I haven't been the best father, but things are going to change, I can promise you that." He finished the whiskey in his glass, poured himself another. "Things are going to change."

"I don't want anything to change, Papa," Amalia said.

"No?" Fredrik let out a guffaw, as if she had made a joke. "You hear that?" he said to Oskar and Polina both. "She likes to wake up at four and clean the shit off other people's underpants."

Amalia pulled herself from her father's lap, but he grabbed her back again. She acquiesced and collapsed into him beneath the weight of his arm.

"Why don't you sit down at the table with us?" Oskar suggested. "Amalia plays hearts better than anyone else," he said to Polina.

"She's beating us," Fredrik told Amalia. "We taught her how to play just an hour ago, and already she's beating us." He pointed to the score, which he had been tallying on the tablecloth with a lead pencil. "Oskar and I almost have a hundred each already, and she only has twenty-three." Amalia struggled to stand again, and this time Fredrik let her.

"I'll deal you in," Oskar said.

"Yes, sit down," Polina said. "I think it will be much more fun when you are playing."

Oskar dealt the cards, and Amalia sipped her whiskey. Her mood lightened, despite her reticence. Every candle they owned was lit. Some were burning on the counter, others on the table. The electric lamp over the sink was glowing, too. The room had never been so bright. She could not recall a moment like this one before in the little cottage.

"Give her twenty-three," Oskar said to his father. "Like Polina. She should come in with the lowest score."

"I'll give her ninety-three," Fredrik said. "The same score I have."

"Give her sixty, then," Oskar said. "In the middle."

"I'll give her ninety-three," Fredrik repeated.

"That's okay, I'll take ninety-three," Amalia said. "I don't mind — I'll take your score, Papa."

"You're a hard man," Polina said to Fredrik, "aren't you?"

Fredrik looked at her, and the room fell silent. Then he picked up his drink and held it toward Polina, waited for her to clink glasses with him. "*Skaal,*" he said, taking a swallow. He wiped his mouth. "A man who leads a hard life," he told her, "turns into a stone." He spoke the words somberly, as if he thought that this insight might excuse him for his brusqueness. "Of course, there isn't much good in a stone. You can't plant it and expect a statue to grow. Eh? You can only bury it."

"Flowers blossom on top of graves," Polina said, "don't they?" She took a drink, too.

Fredrik's eyes narrowed. He thought for a moment, and it looked as if the alcohol was going to take him to a darker place. Then he chuckled. "Okay, then." He leaned forward onto the table, once again picked up the pencil. "You win. I'll give her twenty-three." He scratched out the score he had

just written beneath Amalia's name, wrote in another number. "Just like you. So now we'll see who the better player is,
eh? It'll be between you and her." He picked up his cards and
began to arrange them.

Polina realized that Oskar was staring at her, and she
met his gaze. When her face flushed red, she looked down at
her cards, too. She couldn't remember the last time she had
blushed. But his eyes were so intense. She remembered the
sensation of his flaccid penis in her hand the night before, at
the hotel. His skin had been hot, moist. But he hadn't shown an
ounce of desire.

"And another thing," Fredrik said, losing interest in his
hand. He leaned across the table toward Amalia. "When I say
enough of the Nielsens, that's what I mean, understand?"

Amalia didn't know what to make of her father's behavior.
As far as she could tell, he wasn't that drunk. The bottle was
half finished, but she had seen him drink much more, and his
movements were controlled, his words weren't slurred. The
only difference tonight, as far as she could discern, was this
girl at the table.

"They're working you like a dog," Fredrik continued.

"They're not, Papa —"

"Who will start?" Polina asked, having finished sorting her
cards.

Fredrik's face broke into a clever smile. "And you know
what happens to a girl if she works like a dog and eats and
sleeps like a dog?" He lifted his whiskey to his lips, finished the
glass. "She starts to look like one, too."

Amalia blinked as if she had been struck.

"Now," Fredrik said, grabbing the bottle by the neck and
tipping it over his glass with a slosh, "I didn't mean it like that.
It was just a joke."

Amalia set her cards onto the table. She tried to hold her emotions in check, but two tears rolled down her cheeks, cutting red lines into her chafed skin. "I don't know what you mean, then," she said, "if you don't mean it like that."

"All I mean," Fredrik said, filling Oskar's glass as well, and then Polina's, "is that you used to be my little girl, eh? Don't you remember? You were my little girl. When you were born, you could fit inside my hand. Did I ever tell you that?" He tilted the flask over Amalia's glass, too, but there was no more whiskey left, not even a dribble, and he tossed the empty bottle into the sink, where it broke into three clean pieces. "I picked you up like this —" He demonstrated, cupping his hand palm up, as if he were weighing a heavy piece of fruit. "And your legs were shorter than my fingers, and your toes were tiny as, tiny as, I don't know, tiny as grains of sand. They were pearls, that's what they were, pearls. And your fingers, too, they were a centimeter long, and they were soft as cotton, even the nails. If I put my finger into your hand, you know what you did? You closed your hand around it, just like that, you squeezed, I didn't have to teach you that, and it felt like I was sticking my finger into a flower."

Amalia slid her chair backward. "You think I want to wake up so early and burn my hands in boiling water to clean their sheets and prick my fingers with needles to sew their clothes and stand all day in front of their sinks and stoves?" she asked.

"Don't, Amalia," Oskar said. "It's okay. He doesn't mean it so badly —"

"I do it for you, Papa. That's why I do it. I do it for you and for Oskar —"

"Hey, what's this?" Fredrik sat back in his chair, as if he was somehow surprised by his daughter's reaction. "All I mean to say is you work so hard you don't have time to take care of yourself like other girls do —"

"You mean like *she* does," Amalia said.

"So now I want you to stop — that's what I'm telling you — I want you to stop, it's time to tell the Nielsens that you're not coming back, eh?"

"And then what will we do?" Fredrik's bluster had touched a nerve, and all the anxiety Amalia had accumulated in the last years, which normally she was able to conceal, came rushing from her in a torrent. "What then, Papa?" Her eyes blazed. She stared her father straight in the eye. "What will we do when there's no money for us?"

"You let me worry about that," Fredrik said. "Eh, little girl?" In his mind, the thousand crowns might as well have been a million. "If I tell you we're going to be all right, then that's the way it is, we're going to be all right. I'm your father — "

"Are you?" Amalia demanded. "Are you my father?"

Fredrik looked stunned.

"All you do is drink," Amalia continued. "All you do is spend the money I bring home. If you're my father, why don't you act like it?"

"Now that's enough," Fredrik said. His fist slammed the table, and two of the candles toppled over. Droplets of red wax splattered the cloth. Amalia stood. Her chair scraped the floor, and she tripped on it as she fled. Her hip hit the table, and yet another candle fell. The light seemed to flee the room with her.

"You can be very cruel," Polina said, in the aftermath.

"Enough!" Fredrik shouted. Behind him, Amalia was shuffling up the stairs. His fist pounded the table a second time. Oskar jumped in his chair. "I said *enough*!"

Polina continued to look at the farmhand. Oskar gazed at her, then lowered his eyes. His leg was bouncing on his chair. They had been having such a good time together, and then everything had fallen apart so quickly. His father sat silently, daring Polina to speak. Oskar was certain that she wouldn't hold her tongue. But the room remained still.

At last, Fredrik stood from the table. He walked from the kitchen, then from the house. The door swung open, hit the side of the cottage, then slammed shut. Afterward, Oskar became aware of the sound of sleet tapping the glass. Amalia's footsteps creaked on the floorboards above their heads.

"Your hands."

Polina's voice penetrated Oskar's thoughts slowly, like water through sand. At first, he wasn't certain what she meant. Then he saw the red stain spreading out beneath his fingers. He had been squeezing the lip of the table as if he would snap it. He relaxed his grip, turned his hands over, examined them. A couple of the blisters had burst again, and a few of the deeper cuts were oozing. "It's nothing," he said.

"It must be painful," Polina said. She reached for his fingers.

But Oskar didn't let her touch him. He pushed his chair backward, stood from the table. The heat inside the house was suddenly too much — the walls were as hot as the iron walls of a furnace. His face was bathed in perspiration, his stomach was knotted. The whiskey had torn a hole in his gut. He walked from the room, followed his father outside. It was as he had told her — these cuts, these blisters were nothing. He had grown up with pain, and he would feel it again and again. When it stopped, it would only be because he was dead.

He stood on the porch and listened. Inside the house, the stair treads creaked beneath Polina's faint weight. In the distance, his father cut an uneven path through the slush. When he reached the edge of the property, the gate opened and closed with a rusty squeak. Closer, the wind blew. It cried in his ears, and it blew and blew.

■ ■ ■

In the middle of the night, Oskar woke in a sweat. His first thought was that Polina was under the thick, stiff covers with him. He had been dreaming of her. Polina had been lying on her back in a field. The sun was burning, there was no wind, no rain, no snow, just the sun and long, green grass and a clear, blue sky. Naked, he had floated on top of her, then he had been inside her, surrounded by her, embraced. And then they were standing together, and she was pushing him backward onto a bale of hay, and stalks of cut, drying grass were poking into his skin, and she was still on top of him, he was still inside her, undulating with her as if the two of them were swimming. In his half sleep, Oskar's body remembered the feeling of her arms around him at the hotel in Korsør the night before. His penis was erect, tangled in his undershorts. The hard, lumpy pillow took shape under his cheek, and he realized that he had to urinate. His arm had become numb underneath him, and his head ached from the raw, cheap alcohol. He opened his eyes.

Behind the curtain tacked to the ceiling, the dark was impenetrable. He tried to peer into it, but couldn't distinguish anything beyond the gauzy veil, not even the outline of any shapes. Only very slowly did he become aware of the whispers emanating from Amalia's bed. *How long have you been the only woman in the house?* This was Polina's voice. *My mother used to live with us, too,* Amalia told her, *but my father found a letter to another man.* Oskar wanted to distinguish more words, but couldn't. The hushed conversation continued for a while, then subsided. He closed his eyes again, concentrated until he was able to separate Polina's shallower breath from Amalia's. The rhythmic pulse of the two girls' breathing began to hypnotize him, holding him on the verge of his own sleep. Blackness surrounded him like water. He opened his mouth, but there was no air. His arms were bound to his waist. He couldn't swim. He felt himself drown.

■ ■ ■

Just before dawn, the silence in the children's bedroom was disturbed by heavy footsteps. Fredrik was still wearing the same clothes he had worn the day before. His feet were clad in his boots, icy from the trek home from Aalborg. He made no effort to tread softly, but neither Polina nor Oskar woke. Both were exhausted from the exertion and stress of the journey from Copenhagen. Oskar rolled to the other side of his bed and pulled his blanket over his head. Polina didn't stir at all. Opening her eyes, Amalia found herself clinging to this stranger lying next to her, in the same position in which she had fallen asleep. One hand was tucked under her own cheek. The other lay over Polina's ribs, hanging loosely at the base of Polina's firm breasts. The footsteps approached, and she peered up at her father. In the gray light, his face was a blur.

"What is it you're doing there?" Fredrik asked.

Amalia was confused by the question. "Is it time to get up?" she responded.

"What kind of behavior is this?" her father demanded.

And then Amalia realized that the skin beneath her arm was naked, and when she pushed herself away from Polina, she saw that the covers had fallen off and they were sleeping outside their shirts. Her face flushed, though the dark concealed this. "I'm only sleeping," she said. She found the lapels of her nightshirt and yanked them over her slack breasts.

Fredrik hovered above her for a few beats longer, then finally withdrew. "It's already almost five," he said from the doorway. "You overslept." Still, neither Polina nor Oskar woke.

Amalia waited for her father's footsteps to recede, then pulled herself from bed. She passed a hand over Polina's thigh as she stood, perhaps with the hope of waking her. But the Polish girl only turned over on the mattress, then gathered the blankets around herself and began to breathe even more deeply.

Downstairs, Fredrik was waiting for Amalia in the kitchen, standing with a hip propped against the counter, his arms folded across his chest. The flame burning under the kettle provided the only light in the room, and soft shadows darkened his eyes and danced across his cheeks. Amalia stopped in the doorway, uncertain what her father might be thinking, especially after the words they had exchanged yesterday. Again, her cheeks flushed. This time, Fredrik was able to see it.

"She's very sweet," Amalia said, tentatively.

Fredrik didn't say anything in return. His expression didn't change.

"She's very young, I mean," Amalia said, as if to correct her observation. She waited for her father to say something. On the stove, the pot began to rattle. "She told me that her mother is Jewish — her parents were taken away — "

Fredrik's eyes narrowed. In the dim light, Amalia thought that he looked angry.

"Father?" She took a step into the kitchen, then stopped and tried to read him, and father and daughter continued to gaze at each other like this as the water began to boil.

"Make us some tea," Fredrik said to his daughter. "And make it strong — I haven't slept." He pushed himself away from the counter, and when she passed him on her way to the stove, the unfamiliar scent of this other girl who had shared her bed with her circulated through the air, mingling with the smells Fredrik had brought home with him from the brothel. Instead of thinking about this, Fredrik gave consideration to the day in front of him. The chair's legs scraped the floor as he sat down. "Yeah," he said, as if they were in the middle of a conversation, "there's so much snow this year I can't reach the fence to fix it. I've never seen so much snow. Not as long as I can remember."

"She's very beautiful," Amalia said. "Isn't she?"

But Fredrik ignored her. "It will stop soon enough," he said, as though she hadn't spoken. "I'm sure it must — it always does. The sun wants to shine. It feels different this year, though. Doesn't it?"

When Amalia extinguished the flame, the kitchen was plunged into darkness. She waited until her eyes adjusted, then filled the teapot and carefully poured out two cups of tea. As she handed one to her father, the touch of his fingers on her arm gave her a small jolt. Her heart melted in her chest, and she thought about embracing him. But then she realized that he simply wasn't yet able to see. He fumbled for the cup, and she passed it into his hands, then took a seat at the table across from him.

■ ■ ■

An hour later, when Oskar opened his eyes, he couldn't remember falling back to sleep. His dream returned to him. The scrape of threshed wheat against his back felt so real that he thought his skin might be torn. He was still facing his sister's bed, and he stared at the curtain, slowly lifting the smooth rectangular plane out from the dim light. Outside, a rooster was crowing in the coop. The sun hadn't risen yet, and he wondered whether Amalia had already left. Holding his own breath, listening, once again he became aware of Polina's gentle breathing on the other side of the room, and then, when he inhaled, of the vague, soapy scent of cheap perfume.

PAPER HEARTS

21.

Polina became aware of the stiff pillow before she opened her eyes. Bristles of straw pierced its rough slipcover, poked her cheek, scratched her skin. During the night, the air inside the cottage had been redolent with smoke. Now she woke to the smell of Amalia's sweat and the dank, ferrous odors that rose from the kitchen and the cooling bricks of the hearth. The dusty, grassy scent of the pillow reminded her of her house in Kraków. She had slept on a pillow stuffed with straw there, too. She remembered this fragrance, this texture. She remembered waking and running her fingertips over the lines and indentations imprinted in her cheek after a long sleep. She rolled onto her back and stared at the ceiling. It had been years since she had slept so well. Dangling from the shoelace, the diamond ring slid between her breasts, and a forgotten emotion stirred inside her. Perhaps there was something special about this house. Perhaps there was a place for her here.

She tried to fasten down the feeling. And then it struck her that, for the first time since the war began, her thoughts were tinged with hope.

Downstairs, there was a sudden crash, and the small house shook. Clutching her nightshirt to her chest, Polina sat up on the mattress. She had woken at six when Oskar stepped from behind the curtain and stumbled from the room, then had fallen back to sleep again. She could tell from the light filtering through the window that it was already eight or nine. She had assumed that she was alone. Had this been the sound of a door being slammed? No — the noise was too violent for that, too sustained. Her feet touched the rug. She pushed herself up from the bed, tiptoed to the door.

On the floor below, nothing moved. She crept to the stairs. At the landing, she waited, listening. A man snorted and groaned, and, as uncharacteristically weak as it was, she recognized the voice as Fredrik's. Holding her nightshirt closed, she hurried the rest of the way down the stairs and peered into the kitchen. The giant farmhand lay sprawled on his back beside the table. Blood was oozing from a gash on his scalp, over his ear. Polina took a tentative step toward him.

His eyes opened just a crack, but Fredrik saw the fuzzy outline of someone approaching him. His head was reeling from his fall — his vision hadn't cleared. The taste of amphetamine was so strong in the back of his throat that he wanted to gag. He scrambled backward, clawing the air, half raised himself against the cabinet beneath the sink. His boot hit the table and knocked it sideways, sending everything on the tabletop — the salt cellars, a couple of stray glasses, a plate of bread that Oskar had left for Polina, some silverware — splintering onto the floor in a broken heap. By the time he recognized the girl, he had squeezed himself into the corner. The fear in his eyes dissipated, but not before Polina had seen it. He pushed himself up, stood to his full height, held himself steady with a hand on the edge of the sink.

"You're bleeding," Polina said.

Fredrik grunted. He fingered the wound on the side of his head. This wasn't the first time that he had blacked out like this. In fact, the spells had become more frequent than he wanted to admit. The amphetamine he was consuming was to blame. His body needed to sleep — it almost felt as if he had forgotten how. This was the first time, though, that he had actually harmed himself.

"You're hurt," she said.

"I don't need your help."

Polina took a step closer. "Let me take a look." Reaching for his wrist, to move his fingers away from the cut, she wasn't prepared for the swipe of his knuckles. The blow glanced off her forearms. Still, the contact nearly knocked her off her feet.

"Stay back," he barked.

Now Polina kept her distance. Her eyes dropped, and she wondered whether to stay or to go.

"Clean this up," Fredrik told her, gesturing at the mess on the floor. He found a towel on the counter, pressed it to the side of his head, took it away to measure the amount of blood. The cut was deep, almost to the bone. The wound wasn't dangerous, but it would be difficult to stanch the bleeding. He clamped the towel to his head, pushed past Polina toward the bathroom. "Save the salt if you can," he instructed her. "It wouldn't do to waste it."

She waited until he had disappeared into the bathroom. The pipes whined as he opened the taps. Then she knelt on the hard, cold floor to gather the scattered kitchenware and pick up the broken pieces of glass. When she dropped the debris into the trash, it hit the bottom of the empty container with a shrill, vitreous clank.

■ ■ ■

There was tea steeping on the table for him when Fredrik emerged from the bathroom. Polina had poured a cup for herself as well, and she was carrying it with her as she left the kitchen and headed for the stairs. "Sit down with me," Fredrik told her. Then, when she hesitated, "Oskar is in the barn with the pigs."

"I'm cold," Polina objected. She wasn't only making an excuse. She was wearing nothing else beneath her nightshirt, and her feet were uncovered. The fire hadn't been lit since the early morning. It was no more than forty degrees inside the cottage.

"Sit down," he repeated. "Drink your tea with me." He took a seat at the table, then waited for her to join him before picking up his cup. "My daughter is across the way at the Nielsens' house."

Polina sat on the edge of a chair and blew on her tea. She had filled the pot with too many leaves, and the brew was sour. It crossed her mind to begin a conversation herself, but she had little to say. If he didn't mind the silence, neither did she. She was finishing the dregs, already preparing to stand from the table and leave the kitchen, before Fredrik finally decided to open his mouth.

"I don't understand," he began, taking his time — leaning back in his chair until the wood creaked underneath him, narrowing his eyes as if he were contemplating something that would perplex a man with a far larger mind, "why it is that Oskar brought you back here from Copenhagen. And, to tell you the truth, I don't understand either why you came back here with him."

Polina set her cup down. There was a draft in the kitchen, and she suppressed a shiver. Her cheeks, though, were warm. "Perhaps," she responded, "he realized if he didn't, he wouldn't be able to forget me."

Fredrik rocked forward in his chair, reached for the pot of tea. The girl's candor hadn't surprised him. She wore it naturally, as many whores did. She had been stripped of artifice, just as she had been stripped bare of everything else. He poured himself another cup. By the time he thought to refill hers, too, there were only a few drops left. He let them dribble from the spout, then set the pot back down with a clank. "And you?"

Polina understood the question. She simply wasn't certain how to answer it.

"Do you spend your time thinking about him?" Fredrik prompted her, mistaking her silence for confusion.

"I think that it takes a woman longer," she answered at last, "to come to know a man."

Fredrik acknowledged the parry with a sniff. He started to take a sip of tea, then stopped. "You're not interested in him," he said. "He's still a boy, and you're not the innocent he thinks you are." He was lifting his cup to his lips when the cut on his scalp opened again, and a large drop of blood rolled down his cheek. He didn't react quickly enough to keep the drop from tumbling off his chin and splashing onto the rim of his cup. The blood mixed with his tea and splattered onto his lap.

"Do you have a needle and thread?" Polina asked him, ignoring his last accusation.

"The bleeding will stop," he said.

"It needs to be stitched."

"In the drawer," he told her. He nodded toward the cabinet next to the sink, then watched her as she crossed the kitchen to retrieve the sewing kit. Polina had been eating well in the weeks since she had left the hotel on Nyhavn to live with Hermann. There was evidence of this in the luster of her hair, and she had filled out a bit. Still, her limbs were long, and they were thin. Her shoulders were slender at the top of her sleeves. She was younger, Fredrik thought, than he had realized.

The only thread she could find was coarse and black. When she lit a match to sterilize its point, the needle turned red in the flame, which flared around the steel as if the metal refused to be touched. "Bend toward me," she instructed him. "You're too tall, even if I stand."

Fredrik rested his elbows on the table and tilted his head. The blood was still flowing, and she tamped the gash with the towel, then separated its edges with her fingers. His hair fell in her way. When she combed it backward with her fingers, the flap of skin lifted, and the blood flowed even faster. "We will need to clean it first," she told him.

"There's whiskey in the cupboard."

After she had poured enough to soak the towel, he grabbed the bottle from her and drank a swig before allowing her to continue. She knew how much the alcohol would burn, but the farmhand didn't flinch. He didn't flinch, either, when she penetrated his scalp with the point of the needle. Closing the wound was no different from mending a ripped sock. Perhaps his skin was somewhat tougher, and the blood oozing from underneath the stitching was bothersome. But in the end the result was identical. "I used to do the same for my father," she said, as she tied the last knot. She pulled the thread tight, bent forward to grab it in her teeth. When it snapped, it left a thin line of blood on her chin.

Fredrik ran his fingers over the stitching. "I've had worse cuts."

"It should be okay now."

"Heat up some more water," he told her. "There's enough tea in the pot for another cup each." He combed his hair over the gash while he waited for her, then wiped the blood from his fingers and his cheek with the towel. "And where was this?" he asked her, when she had taken her seat again.

Her forehead creased with puzzlement — she wasn't certain what he was asking her.

"You said you did the same for your father," Fredrik explained. "Where?"

Polina took the bloody rag from him and folded it onto the tabletop. "His hands, mainly," she replied — and this made Fredrik snicker. "He was a carpenter," Polina said, misconstruing Fredrik's reaction. "When he could find work, at least. He worked with his hands, just like you do — so his hands were often cut — his arms, too."

Fredrik's smile broadened. Polina's answer had reminded him of a joke. He decided that he might as well tell it to her. "A man walks into a brothel," he began, then he remembered some detail he had forgotten, and he started again. "A whore takes a man's hand and leads him into her room in a brothel. He sees a bed on one side of the room and a chair on the other. So he turns to the whore and he asks her, where is it you prefer to have sex?"

Polina's eyes had dropped.

"And the whore answers, in the ass." Fredrik chortled, but Polina didn't look up again or even smile. "In the ass, do you understand?" He grabbed the bottle and took another large swallow. His scalp was throbbing. The whiskey would take the edge off the pain, certainly. "I meant to ask you where your father lived," he said, in between gulps. "Not where he cut himself when he was sawing wood." Polina remained quiet, and he decided to prod her. "You're a Jew, aren't you? A Polish Jew — a refugee. The Nazis brought you here from Poland, I suppose."

Still, Polina didn't raise her eyes. "Why don't you tell me something instead?" she said.

"Hmmm?"

Now she did meet his gaze. "Why don't you tell me about your wife?"

Her presumption surprised Fredrik, then pleased him. This she could see in the series of expressions that crossed his face. "I have no wife," he answered. "It's better for a man like me to live alone."

"The children's mother, then," Polina said.

Again, her boldness surprised him.

"The children have a mother, don't they?"

"Children?" Fredrik grinned. "They are older than you, aren't they?"

"Are they?"

Fredrik grunted.

"Anyway, they are still your children, and they still have a mother. Why won't you tell me about her?"

On the stove, the water had begun to boil. Fredrik used this excuse to stand from the table. He grabbed the kettle, filled the pot. Polina had added so much tea before that the water colored brown almost instantly, despite the fact that this was the second steeping. By the time he sat back down, he had recovered himself and figured out how to answer her. "You want to know about their mother?" He gave the pot a little shake, filled his cup first, then hers. "Their mother — she was also a whore, just like you."

Polina lifted her cup, once again blew on the tea to cool it. When the steam hit her forehead, she shivered. "Maybe I would believe that if there weren't two of them."

"What?"

Polina shrugged. "A man only makes a whore pregnant once."

Fredrik's surprise melted into mirth. This time, though, his laughter was directed at her observation rather than at her. He settled backward in his chair. "I don't talk about these things," he told her.

"No?"

"No."

"Why not?"

He set his cup back down, toyed with it for a moment, then changed his mind, decided to speak. "I made the mistake of falling in love with someone who couldn't love me in return."

"Why couldn't she?"

Fredrik raised his hands, palms up. To anyone in the room, in the presence of this gigantic, rough man, it was enough of an answer. *Just look at me.*

"So you tricked her, then," Polina said. "Or at least you seduced her. Is that what you would have me believe? You let her imagine you were someone else long enough to father two children with her — "

"I told you," Fredrik responded. "I don't talk about these things."

"I have always believed," Polina said, "that marriage is a sacred vow."

"This from you? You're a whore, aren't you? What does a whore know about marriage?" Fredrik examined her more seriously. For a few beats, she returned the stare. Then her eyes dropped. Her cheeks flushed. "A man gets married," Fredrik said at last, "to lock the demons out of his house. Elke opened the door and invited the devil back inside."

"She wasn't faithful to you?"

Fredrik ignored the question. "All she wanted was my name. Anyway, I never said we were married."

"Did you hit her? When you found out — "

He snorted. "I should have."

"But you didn't?"

Again, Fredrik examined her, this time shifting forward in his chair, closer to her, placing an elbow on the table. "Is that what I really am to you?" he asked.

Polina managed not to fidget beneath his scrutiny. "Does she live close to you now?"

"Enough of this — "

"Does she?"

"In Skagen," he answered, reluctantly. "On the northern coast, about an hour from here by train. The children never see her — not too often. I took them from her so that she could marry someone else."

When Polina finally raised her eyes to his again, his face softened into a sudden, incongruous smile. He leaned across the table and with a long, nicked finger touched her cheek. She didn't understand at first, until he came away with a tiny, downy feather on his fingertip, perhaps from her bed, which, when he flicked it, fluttered into the center of the kitchen. She fumbled for her cup, and the tea burned her lips and then her tongue, but she took a swallow anyway. "Still," she said quietly, carefully, "you can't punish them, no matter what their mother did to you."

"Hmmm?" Fredrik looked at her as if he hadn't understood.

"She is the one who doesn't love you."

"You think I am punishing them?"

Polina was still trying to reconcile her first impressions of Fredrik with this new one. Perhaps she had judged him too quickly — perhaps there was more to the man than his fists. "I think you're pushing them away from you before they leave you first."

Fredrik thought about this. "It doesn't work to hold on to people," he said. "The tighter you hold them, the less you find yourself holding." Then he grabbed the whiskey and pushed his chair backward and stood from the table. He took a swig from the bottle, wiped his mouth. "Tell Oskar that I won't be home until after midnight." He was halfway out of the kitchen when he stopped. "It was a mistake for Oskar to bring you here," he told her.

Polina returned his stare.

"This talk," he said, "you realize it hasn't changed anything, don't you?"

Polina considered what he was saying. "Yes," she said, when he still didn't move from the doorway, "I realize that." But she knew that it had.

22.

Polina hesitated at the threshold of Fredrik's bedroom. The small cottage was so quiet that the tick of the clock in the sitting room reverberated up the stairwell. She placed a hand on the cold brass knob, then, glancing over her shoulder, pushed the door open.

Once inside, she stopped again. She had been expecting something else — the lair of a beast. Instead, the room, however spare, was surprisingly kempt, even inviting. A window had been left open a crack, and the air was fresh, sweet with smoke from the chimney. Though the bed wasn't made, it was pulled together, and Fredrik had covered it with an old yellow bedspread. The edges of the cloth were frayed, but the material was a luxurious damask linen, evocative of a grander past. Flanked on either side by a matching mahogany nightstand, the bed itself was a four-poster, too large for this cottage. The Oriental carpet, too, belonged in a different house, and it was centered precisely at the base of the bed. Soiled clothes were tossed into one corner, but carefully, all in a tidy heap. A lone antique armchair, which was missing a leg and had been flipped onto its side, constituted the sole piece of disarray. Fredrik had attempted to fix it, but the wood had split, and he hadn't been able to figure out yet how to glue the leg back together. The tools he had brought upstairs for the project — a screwdriver, pliers, a drill, and a bundle of rusty wire — were laid out in a neat row beneath the window, but had since been forgotten and were collecting dust. There was no other furniture except an aging dresser, and the room, as small as it was, felt empty somehow. On one of the nightstands, a painted metal alarm clock sounded out a heartbeat in tandem with the tick of the wall clock downstairs. Otherwise, Polina realized, there wasn't a single object on display, not on any surface. A shiver constricted her shoulders. She hugged her arms to her chest, then, taking another glance behind her, ventured into the enigmatic room.

The rickety dresser creaked as she tugged on the top drawer. Its frame gave beneath the force, and it wobbled as the drawer finally jerked open. Polina lifted out the garments inside — a shirt so badly torn that it was useless except as a rag, a lone sock, a singlet stained with blood. She dropped these onto the floor, then pulled the drawer out farther, searched it inside all the way to the back with her fingers to make sure that it was empty. She repeated this exercise with the next drawer down. The third drawer didn't want to budge. Its contents were heavy, and she had to lift it and cheat it from side to side finally to pry it open just an inch or two. The musty smell of decaying paper wafted from the gap. She pried it open farther, revealing a cache of leather-bound books. The names of the authors, stamped in gold on the spines, meant nothing to her. Tolstoy, Flaubert, Zola, Dante. She picked one up, lifted the cover, ran a finger over the engraved lettering of the title.

Anna Karenina. As worn as the edges were, the pages were still crisp. The novel hadn't been read. She mouthed the first line, softly, fumbling with the written words. *All happy families are alike; each unhappy family is unhappy in its own way.* Closing the book, she set it down on the floor, then emptied this drawer, too. The last drawer, again, was stuck and didn't want to give up its secrets. Spying an old boot peeking out from the closet, she used it to bang the drawer a few times in order to loosen it, then was able to pull it forward. The drawer, however, proved to be empty, save for a bundle of old pencils and three or four chipped and bent lead soldiers.

Standing back up, hands on her hips, she surveyed the room. Downstairs, something creaked, and she held herself still, listened. But it was nothing — the house reacting to changing temperatures outside, perhaps. In the faraway distance, she could hear the sawing of wood, closer, the quiet howl of the wind. This was a constant sound in Jutland, and she had already become used to it. She swiveled on her heel, pursed her lips. At last, her eyes settled on the broken, overturned chair. The wool upholstery, which had once been white, was now so grimy that it was gray, especially in a dark patch next to a hole in the chair's side. The hole itself, Polina remarked, wasn't a tear but a slit, sliced cleanly. She crossed the room, reached her hand inside. A smile creased her lips. She pulled out a notebook first, then a bundle of paper crowns.

Sitting down on the edge of the mattress, she opened the notebook in her lap and began leafing through it. A few sheets seemed to keep a tally of Amalia's wages, others to track the balance of various loans. For the most part, though, page after page, it was nothing more than a list of sundries and figures. *Ham for Easter, 1.25. Sugar, .15. Another pair of shoes for O., .50. Remainder, 28.85. Plus October, 43.85.* When she reached a page in the middle of the ledger that contained only a few sentences, she stopped. Fredrik's handwriting was very precise, and she had no trouble reading it. The first three words were written large. *NO MORE DEBTS*. Underneath, the lettering was smaller but no less resolute. *A man only owes who he wants*. Polina pondered the words, then flipped the page. The rest of the notebook was filled only with numbers reflecting Fredrik's meager household account, no further cryptic notes.

She closed the ledger and was about to turn her attention to the roll of bills, when something fluttered from the last pages — a small scrap of fading red construction paper, cut with scissors into the crude shape of a heart, the way a child would fashion it. She picked it up from the floor, turned it over. There was nothing written on either side to identify it. It could have been inconsequential. It could have been a Christmas decoration that had found its way between the pages of the notebook, or something that one of the children had given to their father. But she knew that it wasn't. She brought it to the base of her nose. The faint scent of expensive perfume made her shiver again, as she had when she first entered the room. She examined the heart a second time, front and back, as if she might somehow have missed some writing that could establish its provenance, then slipped it back into the ledger.

After replacing the notebook in its hiding place inside the broken chair, she counted the money. The thought, to tuck a few bills into her pocket, never crossed her mind. She rebundled it, then returned the money into the hole, too, and, after stuffing the clothing and books back into the dresser drawers, left the room.

23.

"A man walks with a whore into her bedroom." Fredrik's voice carried over the other voices in a dimly lit bar in the village of Aalborg. It was already late, nearly ten o'clock, and the patrons were drinking up before curfew. Conversations were growing louder. Fredrik held an empty shot glass in one hand, with the other was propping himself up on the oak counter. Even slouched, he was head and shoulders taller than anyone else in the room. The man standing beside him was sipping the froth off a mug of beer. The next man over was lighting a cigarette, listening as Fredrik began his joke. "There is a chair on one side, a bed on the other—"

The man lighting the cigarette blew smoke through his teeth. "You're an idiot, Gregersen, an idiot—you know what an idiot you are? I was the one who told you that joke. Don't you remember? That's my joke." He grabbed the shorter man standing between them and shook his shoulders hard enough to spill his beer. "Steen here heard me tell the joke to you, didn't you, Steen? Hell, even Svend heard me tell the joke—"

He twisted to get the attention of the bartender. "Isn't that right, Svend? I've told this joke to all of you — to everyone here — haven't I?"

"A hundred times," the bartender agreed.

"A thousand," Steen said.

Across the room, a farmer with slack cheeks and a gray beard raised his glass in a salute. Another man seated at the same table shouted over the noise, "Her ass, eh? She likes it in the ass."

The man with the cigarette grabbed his whiskey, returned the farmer's salute. "You see? It's my joke. And everybody's heard it already."

"No?" Pedersen arched his eyebrows. The cigarette dangled from his lips. He was a lanky, gregarious man who looked significantly more intelligent than he was — a favorite of the other customers at the bar.

Fredrik shook his head. "No," he said. "This time the woman is your mother."

Steen choked and snorted a mouthful of beer through his nose. Pedersen cleared him away with a push, and the smaller man, still drowning, took a step backward to wipe his face clean. Behind the counter, the bartender was filling Fredrik's glass, and he laughed, too, silently, but hard enough to sprinkle the oak counter with whiskey. *Cheers to that,* someone else said. *Did you hear that?* another man chuckled. *Pedersen's mother takes it like the Greeks.*

Fredrik lifted his whiskey, drank it in a single swallow, slammed the glass onto the counter. "Another," he said.

"Easy, there," the bartender told him, though he was already filling the glass. "Who's going to pay for all this?"

Fredrik stuck his hand into his pocket, dug for a few crowns, slapped them on the counter next to the whiskey. "I am," he said. "In fact, I'm paying for drinks all around."

Skaal! someone shouted.

Skaal! the rest of the bar echoed, and to a man everyone in the room bent their heads into their drinks.

Fredrik knew that he was being foolish. The bundles of crowns were burning a hole in his pocket. He had never bought a round of drinks before, not once in his life. Behind his back, his friends liked to remark how difficult it would be to pry a single øre from his fingers. Still, he felt light tonight, and it was nice to relax a little.

Pedersen took a deep drag on his cigarette, then draped an arm over Steen's shoulders and leaned toward Fredrik. "So what do you think about this business with Vilfred?" he asked.

Steen shook Pedersen off him long enough to take a careful look around the room. "Shhh," he warned. "No need to shout."

"Why *shhh*?" Pedersen was suddenly belligerent. He wasn't used to so much whiskey. "We can talk, can't we? Vilfred's our friend, there's no more to it than that."

"Shhh!" Steen hissed again. "Don't be a fool."

"You're both fools," Fredrik said. "That's what I think."

Pedersen faced him. Steen's brow furrowed. Behind the counter, the bartender filled their glasses. "Almost closing time," he said.

"Sure, sure," Fredrik said. "If the Nazis tell us to go home, we go home like good children. Who are we to decide how much we can drink or how late we can stay up?"

Pedersen's eyes sharpened, despite the alcohol. "And yet you call us fools," he said.

Fredrik shrugged. "Vilfred wasn't alone that night, was he? You set fire to Jepsen's warehouse last month, sure as he did. I call that stupid."

"Christ," Steen said. "I'm telling you — quiet."

"Jepsen's a Dane," Fredrik said. "You probably went to school with him, didn't you?"

"Jepsen's a traitor," Pedersen said. "And to tell you the truth, I didn't like him any more when he was sitting in the front row with the answer to every question. He was every bit the weasel then that he is now." He tried to make this into a joke with a laugh, but Fredrik didn't join him.

"That might be," Fredrik said with another shrug. "But the three of you set fire to a warehouse full of Danish grain. And now Vilfred's in jail."

"The grain was only feeding the Nazis," Pedersen countered. "And Vilfred knew the risks. We stand up and we fight — or are you happy cowering like a baby, Gregersen?"

Steen looked over his shoulder, met another man's stare. "I'm telling you," he said, slapping his friend's chest with the back of his hands. "Quiet." He thought about giving Fredrik a small punch as well, but decided better of it. "The walls in here have ears."

Fredrik sneered. "You know what will happen to Vilfred? He will be shot — executed without a trial. Are you going to tell me that the small fire you three set was worth it?"

Pedersen swallowed his whiskey, set his glass on the counter. Fredrik held his glass toward the bartender, too. Rather than pour the drinks himself, the barman slid the bottle down to them. He had heard enough of the conversation to know to keep his distance. Steen nursed his beer, eyeing the crowd in the mirror that hung behind the counter. Pedersen leaned in close to Fredrik's ear while Fredrik filled their glasses. This time, he spoke in a whisper. "We're going to get him out."

Fredrik exhaled through his teeth and shook his head, still unconvinced.

Pedersen gave the counter a firm tap with the tip of his index finger. "He's our friend, isn't he?"

"A friend worth dying for? You don't have the guts, either of you."

Pedersen leaned even closer. "Tonight."

Fredrik swallowed his whiskey. At last, the alcohol was going to his head. He palmed the glass, appraised Pedersen, waited for him to tell him more.

"They're going to move him tomorrow," Pedersen said. "That's what we've heard — tomorrow our man Munk is going to sign him over to the Germans, and you know what that means. They'll take him to the base in Aalborg for questioning, and we'll never see him again."

Fredrik smirked. "So that's what it is, then."

"What's *it*?" Pedersen asked him.

"You're afraid he's going to talk. That's why you want to spring him — you're afraid he's going to finger you, too, before they shoot him."

Before Pedersen or Steen could respond, the door to the bar was pushed open, and a man in uniform entered. Steen spotted him first, and he gave Pedersen a sharp nudge.

"Speak of the devil," Pedersen said.

When Fredrik caught sight of the Danish policeman in the mirror behind the counter, his mouth tightened into a frown. He swiveled, raised his voice. "What's this, Brink? Haven't you heard about the curfew? Or perhaps you think it doesn't apply to you?"

The policeman was closing the door behind him. "Does it?" he snapped. Conversations lulled. He glanced around the bar at the men seated there, then tracked Fredrik's voice to the counter. When he met the farmhand's eyes, he half smiled, as if the two of them were in on a small joke. "Anyway, curfew or not, I see you've still got a bottle for yourself." He made his way across the room between tables, approached the counter, offered Pedersen and Steen a curt nod. "How are the three of you tonight?" he greeted them.

"I was feeling much better," Fredrik said, "just before the door opened."

The policeman sniffed, as if Fredrik had meant something funny. The farmhand didn't yield an inch for him, and the policeman jostled Steen to make space.

"I don't remember asking you to join us," Fredrik said.

"Do I need an invitation?" the policeman retorted. He signaled the bartender. "A shot of vodka," he ordered, "and a glass of water."

"On your way home from the precinct, Brink?" Pedersen asked him.

"Hmmm?" The policeman assessed Pedersen out the corner of his eye. "Me? No — I have the late shift — I'm just on my way in."

"So you're standing watch tonight," Pedersen said, "are you?" Except for a few scattered voices, the bar had fallen quiet.

"It's my job," the policeman said.

"And we're all grateful to you," Fredrik said, "for keeping us safe."

"What's that?" The policeman cleared his throat nervously, threw a glance over his shoulder at the hushed room. "You don't like the job I'm doing?"

"Is it your job," Fredrik pressed him, "to turn a Dane over to the Germans?

The policeman swallowed his vodka, then followed the shot with a few large gulps of water. He held the empty shot glass toward the bartender, waited for him to refill it. "Vilfred Thiesen?"

"That's who we're talking about," Fredrik said. "Isn't it?"

"Is it?" The policeman drank his second vodka, then placed the glass back down on the counter, so gently that it slid sideways in a small pool of whiskey and beer. "I thought maybe you were asking me about his accomplices." He pulled a few coins from his pocket, dropped them next to the glass. "Thiesen didn't set fire to that warehouse by himself. Did you know that? Jepsen was there that night. He saw the gasoline being poured. He said there were others. At least two others. They should be found and interrogated, too, alongside Thiesen. And I'm sure they will be."

Pedersen froze. Steen couldn't resist a frantic glance at the taller man. Fredrik harrumphed. "What do you think will happen to you, Brink," the farmhand asked, "when your friends pack up their guns and their tanks and leave the country?"

The policeman shrugged his burly shoulders. On his way back through the bar, he raised his voice. "They're not my friends, the Germans. Any more than you are, Fredrik."

"You take care of yourself, Lars," Fredrik said to him.

The policeman paused at the door. "I would say the same to you." Then he let himself out.

When the door clicked shut behind him, a few people laughed, but the mood had darkened, and everyone had become much more somber. Fredrik waited for voices once again to fill the room before leaning toward the other two men. "I'll do it," he said. Now he was the one to speak in a hushed tone.

Both Pedersen and Steen understood, but neither could quite believe it. "You'll do what?" Pedersen asked, also in a whisper. He wanted to hear Fredrik say it.

Fredrik's eyes met Pedersen's. "I'll get Vilfred out," he said. "Tonight."

"He's your brother-in-law," Steen said. "Isn't he?"

"Lars Brink?" Fredrik shook his head. "I never married the woman," he said. "I only made her pregnant."

Pedersen lifted his glass. "*Skaal*," he said. He waited for Fredrik and Steen to raise their glasses, too, then the three men drank.

■ ■ ■

Two hours later, Fredrik sat crouched in an unlit doorway across the street from the police station. Snow was falling, and the temperature had dropped. His chest was cramped with a sharp pain he hadn't felt before. Still groggy from the alcohol, he found himself fading in and out, focusing on the snow rather than the building behind it, and then the station house would begin to float like a helium balloon against the black sky. Once or twice, he caught himself falling asleep. He was holding himself up with a hand pressed against a brick façade, and his fingers were so cold that they were beginning to bleed. The staff sergeant from the evening shift, whom Lars Brink was supposed to relieve, hadn't yet left to head home. Perhaps he was lingering as long as he could in a building with central heat. Fredrik wasn't afraid — he wasn't sober enough to worry about one more policeman. But he had no quarrel with the staff sergeant. He didn't even know who he was. Perhaps the man had a wife and family. He lowered his head, fought to keep his eyes from closing.

When the door finally swung open across the street, Fredrik roused himself. The staff sergeant stood in the doorway, peered up at the sky to measure the fall of the snow, then started ambling down the sidewalk. Behind him, the yellow light fled back into the station house. Fredrik watched the man until he had blackened into a wisp of smoke and his footsteps faded into the tick of a clock. Then he pulled himself to his feet and started across the street. The ground was icy, and Fredrik's legs had become tight. He stopped in the middle of the road to place a few tablets on his tongue, then staggered the rest of the way to the precinct door. There, he paused to look up and down the street for signs of trouble. But Aalborg was asleep, buried beneath a blanket of snow. The only sound was the distant rumble of an engine in the direction of the air base. He yanked open the door.

Seated behind a reception desk a few steps up from the entry, Brink started at the commotion. His hand shot to his pistol. When he saw Fredrik, his face relaxed, but he didn't let go of the Luger. He set it on the desk in front of him without taking his index finger off the trigger. "Oh — it's you."

Fredrik stumbled into the lobby, stopped below the desk, found his balance with a hand on a polished wood railing. The amphetamine was hitting his bloodstream, reviving him, but he was dizzy. His legs tingled, his toes ached in the sudden heat. He swayed from side to side no matter how hard he tried to hold himself still. "Yeah," he said, "it's me."

"What do you want?"

Fredrik's vision blurred. He tried to remember how many whiskeys he had swallowed. The tab had come to seven crowns eighty — almost eight crowns. Of course that had included drinks for Pedersen and Steen, too, not to mention the round for the bar, but he had drunk more than his share. And what a waste! *Seven crowns eighty.* He wouldn't be so careless again.

"Come along," Brink said. "What is it you want here, Fredrik?"

Fredrik squinted over the policeman's shoulder. Behind him, a hallway led to the jail. The lights were switched off, though, and the corridor was dark. All Fredrik could see was a series of shadows. When he focused on the policeman again, Brink had taken off his cap. Elke's brother had lost so much hair in the last few years that he was almost bald. The cap, its rim shiny with grease, was lying on the desk next to the Luger. The weapon was sitting loose. "I want to talk to you," Fredrik said, "that's why I'm here."

"Talk to me?"

Fredrik shook his head. "That's not true, no." He climbed a step, once again stopped, clasped the railing. "I am here to deliver a message to Elke."

"You're drunk." The policeman's face registered his disgust. He turned away with a sneer, ready to dismiss this intoxicated lout. In the same instant, before he knew what was happening, Fredrik had climbed the next stair and was leaning over him, and his hand was covering the pistol. It had happened slowly, but so unexpectedly — and with so much surprising grace — that Brink hadn't had a chance to react.

"I never noticed before," Fredrik said, "how much you look like your sister. Even without your hair." Then he yanked the Luger from the policeman. It was landing on the marble floor with a metallic clatter as Fredrik's hands were sinking into the policeman's uniform. He lifted Brink from his chair as if he were as light as a pillow, slung him onto his back on the hard surface of the desk. Brink managed to grab Fredrik's wrist, but Fredrik was too strong to be stopped. He pinned the policeman down with one hand around his throat, with his other reached into his jacket pocket and found his favorite hunting knife. "You knew she was seeing Ole Henriksen behind my back — you all did, the whole lot of you — didn't you — " He brought the knife to Brink's jugular.

CRAIG LARSEN

When the door swung open behind him, Fredrik swiveled clumsily, but he didn't let go of the policemen — he only gripped him tighter. Pedersen and Steen burst into the station house. Fredrik acknowledged them with a grunt, then returned his attention to the policeman, crushing him to the desk beneath his elbow. The tip of his knife formed a pointed depression in the soft skin of the fat policeman's cheek. "Keep an eye on the street," he thought to tell the two men as they jostled inside. "Make sure no one else joins us." Beneath him, Brink's eyes were open wide. Spittle was bubbling from his lips. His face was turning red. He wrapped his hands around Fredrik's arm, struggled to free himself. Perhaps he was trying to say something. Fredrik gave his throat a little slack.

"For god's sake, Fredrik," Brink gasped. "Have mercy."

"Suddenly there's a god who cares if you live or die," Fredrik said.

"You can't let him live," Pedersen said.

"What?" Fredrik turned slightly, brought Pedersen into view. As obvious as it was, this eventuality had not occurred to Fredrik as he had contemplated this confrontation.

"Please, Fredrik." Brink fought for his breath. His face had become scarlet. His eyes were bloodshot. "Please — we've known each other for twenty years."

"Have we?" Fredrik renewed his grip on Brink's throat. "We're strangers, Lars, complete strangers you and I. You never knew a thing about me." The man underneath him writhed and kicked his legs, then at last gave up. His body went limp. A raspy moan emanated from his chest.

"If he lives," Pedersen said, taking a step forward, "the three of us die."

"Hang on," Steen said, grabbing his friend by the elbow. The smaller man's face was stricken with panic. He had known

| 312 |

what they were planning, but he still wasn't ready for it, not when he saw what it meant.

Pedersen shook himself loose from Steen, bent to pick up the policeman's Luger from the floor. "It must be done — let's get on with it." He sniffed the Luger, as if this might inform him if it was loaded. "You think he would spare us? Look what he plans to do to Vilfred —" He slid his finger over the trigger. "He will throw us to the wolves just as easily if we let him go."

"Please, Fredrik," Brink pleaded, "please. I won't turn you in. I won't —"

Fredrik blinked. His grip tightened, then loosened again. "I can't," he muttered. He shook his head. "I can't do it." When he twisted enough to face his two accomplices, the tip of his knife carelessly squeezed a drop of blood from the policeman's cheek. "My son calls this man uncle."

In that same moment, the policeman made one last, desperate attempt to free himself. He reached for a second pistol, hidden beneath his shirt, and he was quick enough to draw it and even to grasp the butt in the palm of his hand. Before he could find the trigger, though, Fredrik had slammed his arm backward, and once again he immobilized the weaker man with his elbow. Their eyes met. Pedersen had time to ratchet back the hammer and draw a bullet into the Luger's chamber. Steen took an uncertain step up the short set of stairs, raised a hand toward Fredrik as if to grab his arm. *Wait, wait a moment* — "God damn it," Fredrik said. "*God damn it.*" He tightened his grip on the hunting knife. "You had better go get your friend," he said to Pedersen. "If you stay, by god I'll kill you, too, for this." Then he was alone with the blubbering policeman. His fingers were as white as dried bone as the blade drew a line of blood, even whiter, like snow, as the cold, gray steel sank into the other man's throat.

Two minutes later, Pedersen and Steen were leading Vilfred Thiesen through the village in a mad dash. Muffled on the frozen ground, their footsteps receded into the wind. Fredrik started down the street in the opposite direction. The same hands that had just stabbed Elke Brink's brother were shaking uncontrollably. He shoved them into his pockets as if they didn't belong to him, bent his head, continued on his way home to the Nielsens' farm.

24.

Polina lay still beneath the covers. Amalia was warm in her sleep. Polina didn't mind her sweat. The room was cold, and she was grateful for the heat. Without their father at home, Oskar and Amalia had chosen not to light a fire. They knew how little coal they had left and how precious the remaining wood was. Anything they burned, Oskar himself would have to replace. For him, the fire wasn't worth the effort. Polina's eyes were open. She had long since become used to the lack of light. Outside, the sky was gathering weight, the earth was turning to ice. But beneath the covers, next to Amalia, she was safe. She listened to Amalia breathe. Across the room, Oskar was quietly snoring. Still, she couldn't find sleep. She stared at the ceiling, and she waited.

When she heard Fredrik's footsteps outside, her heart thumped against her ribs. He was moving quickly. His boots were slipping in the snow. The porch stairs creaked, then his boots pounded a hollow beat across the stoop. The front door swung open with a squeal. A current of cold air whipped through the cottage, then just as quickly died. Next to Polina, Amalia continued to sleep. Her fingers tightened on Polina's shoulder, that was all. Behind the sheet that divided the room in two, Oskar continued to snore. Polina barely breathed as Fredrik stumbled into the kitchen. His footsteps were heavy, and the bedroom door rattled in its frame. She waited as long as she could, then lifted Amalia's arm off her and slid from beneath the covers. "Stay," Amalia whispered. But when Polina turned to her, Amalia was still breathing softly, her eyes were still closed. Polina peered through the dark at the thin curtain, listened to make sure that Oskar hadn't woken either. Then she let herself out of the room and tiptoed down the stairs.

She stopped in the front hall. She wasn't certain what had brought her downstairs — she wasn't certain yet what she intended. She glanced up the stairs behind her, then continued to the kitchen, where, unseen, she came upon Fredrik.

He was standing in front of the sink, running the taps, bent over the basin. Her footsteps were so soft that he didn't hear her. She paused when she was close enough to see his profile. His expression was strange. His jaw was slack, his brow was wrinkled. His eyes were pained but luminous, even in the dim light. She had taken another step before she saw the blood on his arms. He had thrust his hands under the faucet, and the water spilling off them into the sink was as red as if he were emptying a bottle of wine. "Oh!" Polina gasped.

Fredrik twisted toward her, startled. "You —" He didn't manage more.

Polina's face reflected her concern. It was instinctive, almost primal. She closed the rest of the distance to him, grabbed his hands. "But now it's your hands — your hands, you're bleeding," she said.

Fredrik pulled his hands from her, once again thrust them under the faucet.

"Let me see," Polina insisted.

"Leave me alone," Fredrik said.

"Please," Polina said. "Let me help you, let me see." Her hands joined his under the water.

Fredrik extended his forearms into the stream. "It's not my blood."

This stopped her. But she didn't let go of him. She continued to wash his hands and wrists with him, until they were clean. As she ran her fingers over his forearms, his eyes darkened, then closed. His arms became limp, and he let her scrub the blood off him without his help. His body, she realized, was quivering. She thought to ask him what had happened, but she couldn't find her voice. When she sought to pull his hands from underneath the faucet, he wouldn't let her. They were thoroughly rinsed now, but he wanted to wash them more. Then, beneath the water, his fingers began to intertwine with hers. Her heart pounded in her chest.

"You have to leave me alone," he said.

"I don't want to," she managed.

"You must," he said. His body continued to tremble, but he had found his resolve. His fingers released hers. His arms stiffened. "You must," he repeated, turning on her. "Do you hear me?" He yanked his hands free. "You must!"

Polina took a step backward, remembering how he had struck her before.

"You've seen who I am now," Fredrik said. "You've seen what happens when I touch something."

"You're not who you pretend to be," Polina said.

"No?" Fredrik's eyes narrowed. He stood away from the sink, reached a wet hand into his pocket, pulled out a handful of coins. "How much does it cost," he asked, "to pay you to leave? Eh? What's your price? Do you charge the same on the way out of a bed as the way in?" He rattled the coins, then thrust them toward her. When she didn't take them, he grasped her by both wrists, forced them into her hands. "What's the matter? My money is as good as anyone else's, isn't it?"

Polina stared at the coins long enough to count them. "Is that really who I am to you?" she asked, throwing his own words back at him.

Before Fredrik could answer, there were footsteps on the stairs. *What is it? What's going on down here?* The shadows shifted, and Oskar appeared in the doorway. Polina let the coins drop, and they were still skittering across the floor when the flat of her hand swiped Fredrik's cheek. She had slapped him so quickly that he didn't have time to react. His head jerked sideways on his neck, but only a little. The smack resounded through the kitchen. "What is this?" Oskar asked, taking a step closer.

"Get out," Fredrik growled. "Do you hear me? Both of you. Leave me alone. Get out!"

When Polina turned, Oskar was unable to make sense of the bloody handprints that stained her nightshirt. She pushed past him. Her bare feet slipped on the stairs.

"You, too," Fredrik said, facing his son. "*Now.*"

Oskar hesitated, then followed Polina from the kitchen. The water was still running in the sink as he climbed into his cold, lonely bed. "What happened?" he asked into the dark, but Polina didn't respond. He listened to her breathing quietly beside Amalia, who was snoring softly, somehow able to sleep. At last, downstairs, the faucet stopped whining. Fredrik's footsteps crossed the house to the toilet room. A drawer slid open. The night fell silent as he filled his syringe. Oskar closed his eyes.

Polina let Amalia drape an arm over her shoulder. The girl's clammy fingers settled on her breast, and for some time she counted the beats of her heart in the rough fingertips, with the same measure of precision Fredrik applied to the tally of the figures in his notebook. A sweet, foreign scent teased her nose. It was almost dawn before she placed it. A faded red butterfly, cut from an old scrap of construction paper, floated in the dark in front of her, just beyond her reach, leading her slowly but inexorably into another room — a room, slowly shrinking, empty of everything but shadows, a box, once shrunk, containing nothing but pale dreams.

A PAIR OF GLOVES

25.

Jutland. December 29, 1941.

The blade of the shovel sank into the snow. A layer of ice cleaved off in a chunk, revealing a stack of firewood trapped beneath. Oskar used the shovel to loosen a log. The handle vibrated, but today his cut, bruised hands didn't complain. Fredrik was gone from the house. At midday, Oskar had slipped into the master bedroom and searched his father's closet for his gloves. He had found them shoved into a pair of boots like used socks. Wearing them made an enormous difference, and he was making good progress. The log separated from the ice, and he started on another. They had burned almost everything else, and the Nielsens were running low, too. Now even this stack was almost gone. In the next week they would have to chop some more from the branches stockpiled at the side of the barn.

"You should use a pickax for that. Not the shovel."

Oskar hadn't noticed his father approach. Taking a short-cut across the field from the road, Fredrik had reached within a few yards of him without Oskar hearing. At four, the light was already fading, a heavy sky was descending toward the ground. His father was wearing a new wool scarf around his neck, which he had wrapped over his face to protect himself from the wind. His hands were deep in his pockets, his shoulders were hunched against the cold. Oskar returned to the task in front of him. The shovel was doing the job well enough. "I'm okay," he said.

"Give me the gloves," his father said.

Oskar continued working, until his father was standing in front of him. When he stopped, he propped the shovel next to him, held the handle in a loose grip. "I'm okay," he repeated nonsensically.

"I'll go feed the pigs if you want to keep working here," his father said. "You haven't fed them yet, have you?"

Oskar shook his head. "I've been busy today. There was a lot to do with you gone."

"Give me the gloves," Fredrik repeated. "And the shovel. Come with me, get the pickax for that, it will work better."

Again, Oskar shook his head. He tightened his hands on the shovel, then picked it back up, shoved the blade into the woodpile. "My hands are hurt," he said, grunting. "I need the gloves."

Fredrik studied his son.

"You can use the bucket to feed the pigs," Oskar said, in between thrusts. "That's how I always do it." He expected his father to say something else, but he didn't. He expected the back of his father's hand. These were Fredrik's gloves after all. In the morning, this was their routine — to leave the house together, to pick up their tools, for Fredrik to stop and pull on his gloves while Oskar began his chores without any. It was something that they never once spoke about, this disparity. But Fredrik simply watched his son work. Then he started toward the barn, his hands still in his pockets, his shoulders still tensed against the cold. "How much is left?" Oskar called out after him.

Fredrik stopped. "What are you asking me?"

"How much have you spent already?"

Fredrik didn't respond. Finally, he continued to the barn. The pigs were waiting for their dinner, and this was a farm, there was more work to be done than could be performed by a single man in a day.

Oskar paused long enough to see two billows of his father's breath steam through the new wool scarf, then he lifted the shovel again. He put his back into the work. Icy sweat gathered on his brow. His hands perspired and bled inside his father's gloves. And in a few minutes more, the rest of the woodpile was unearthed from the snow.

■ ■ ■

Oskar was still thinking about his confrontation with his father that night when he sat down on the side of his bed and pulled off his boots. Amalia was already sound asleep on the other side of the room. New Year's Eve was only two days away. Today she had worked late to prepare the Nielsens' house for the party. Fredrik was downstairs, asleep as well, in front of a dying fire. Polina was in the bathroom, cleaning her face, sponging off her body. Oskar untied his laces, then kicked the heavy boots from his tired feet. His toes were wet and cold, and he reached down and squeezed them until they thawed. The pain melted into warmth.

When Polina stepped through the doorway draped in a towel, he was still bent double. Her shadow slid across the sheet that divided the room. The only light emanated from the fire downstairs. The smell of soap wafted across the room with her, and with it came the memory of her perfume from the middle of the night. She moved without a sound, as light, Oskar thought, as a breath of wind. The sensation of her arms around him through their first night together, in Korsør, tickled his shoulders. "Sit down with me," he said.

Polina paused behind the sheet. Her shadow undulated on the surface of the cloth.

"Sit down with me," he repeated.

She took a step to the edge of the curtain. *Why should I do that?* In retrospect, Oskar wasn't certain whether or not she had spoken.

"Sleep here tonight," Oskar said.

"I might be bleeding," she said.

"I was wrong before," Oskar said. "I want you in bed with me."

When she approached him, as gentle as she was, their first embrace was clumsy. It was nothing like Oskar's dream. She misjudged the distance, and her hand poked his eye. Then she giggled, and when she leaned toward him to apologize, her mouth hit his forehead. She slowed herself down, clasped his shoulder, sat next to him on the bed. It took Oskar more than a few beats to realize that she was nervous. She had been so sure of herself since he had met her, and then so indifferent. Now he was seated next to a child. A girl barely eighteen. The temptress had vanished. This prostitute had hands that shook, a heart that beat loud enough for him to hear. Her fingers faltered as they climbed his chest. And Oskar, inexperienced himself, had no way to lead her. Their hands became tangled. He lost her face in the dark. When he leaned into her to kiss her, he found her ear, then her cheek. What he remembered afterward was the taste of her hair, and then the damp heat of her breath on his neck.

When he pulled his shirt off, the smell of his sweat displaced the soapy fragrance lingering from her bath. He slithered out of his undershirt, too, then stood to unfasten his belt. His trousers slid to the floor. He stepped out of them, then climbed into the bed with his underpants still on. He was so thin that the sharp edges of his pelvic bones nearly punctured his skin. "Lie down," he said. "Here. Under the covers — next to me."

Polina obeyed. He lifted the blankets for her, and she pulled herself onto the narrow, lumpy mattress. Her towel crumpled between them. He yanked it out awkwardly, dropped it onto the floor, found her naked body. She had entered the covers with her back to him, and he pulled her against him. In the small bed, the gesture was rough. The stiff sheets grabbed her shoulders. The straw pillow snagged her hair. His hands explored her body, and she was aware of the gnarled cuts and calluses on his fingers. "I might be bleeding," she repeated.

Oskar didn't understand. Of course he knew about a woman's menstruation. But what difference did this make to him? She felt his lips on the back of her neck. Her hair caught in his mouth. He tried to kiss her. His teeth pinched her skin. The firmness of her breasts fascinated him. They were small and as hard as apricots. "I haven't been able to escape you," he said, though even he wasn't certain exactly what he meant.

"I know, love," Polina said. "I know."

Her words were a whisper, and then the room fell silent again. Downstairs, a log broke apart into embers inside the fireplace. Another log popped, perhaps because the wood was still wet and the fire was having trouble consuming it. Fredrik rolled his head to one side, and the armchair groaned underneath him. Across the room, Amalia continued to breathe steadily. Her sheets rustled when her hand twitched.

When Polina reached behind her and took hold of him, she understood how much Oskar wanted her. She slipped her hand below the band of his underpants, pulled his erection free. Just this friction was enough to excite him further. She shifted her ass and guided him toward her. The dirty fabric of his underpants blocked his path, and she yanked the cloth out of the way, then repositioned herself. Her breasts ached. The smell of his sleep trapped in his blankets and pillow wouldn't dissipate. His bony hips gouged her back. The ring around her neck formed a sharp lump between her ribs and the hard mattress. Knowing that the penetration would be a painful one, she bowed her head, waited.

But then Oskar stopped.

The house remained silent. The smell of smoke climbed the stairs. Polina lay still. When Oskar didn't insist, she squeezed her hand around him, decided to finish him off that way.

Oskar wasn't certain what had stopped him. He tried to silence his breathing, then found himself gasping. An instant later, the pressure of her fingers was too much for him. His eyes were open, but when he thought about this moment, he would remember them closed. He saw nothing but black. The taste of Polina's hair suffused his mouth.

And then it was over. Just like that. The ejaculation gave Polina a small start. His penis was already becoming flaccid again. She held it firmly in her hand. "Are you finished?" she whispered.

Oskar's heart was still pulsing in his ears. He was rolling in an undulating ocean, floating in the sun, washing toward the shore. The sensation, he realized, felt exactly like the elation of his dream. Softly now, he held her. His lips found her neck, nuzzled her spine. The glint of dim light reverberated in her hair. "Stay here," he said.

"Your father —" she replied.

Oskar breathed in her smell. She was his. *His.* "It's okay," he said. "I want to sleep with you."

"We shouldn't."

"I want you in my bed tonight."

She didn't move.

"Every night," he said. Already, he was drifting off to sleep.

And Polina let him. She lay in his arms, listening. Across the cramped room, Amalia was still breathing softly. Downstairs, Fredrik reclined in his chair, master of the house, asleep in front of a dying fire, waking from time to time with a grunt. Mice scurried in the walls. Outside, the wind gusted, whistling in the eaves. The windows rattled. The buzz of a German airplane whined overhead, then faded, disappeared. The country slept, the house slept. But Polina's eyes remained open.

She could count the steps to the sitting room. She could feel the cold, painted floorboards on her feet, the warmth of the fire on her face. And there was Fredrik, in his chair, his chin on his chest, his long hair shaggy, uncombed, hanging over his eyes. She couldn't erase his image from her mind. She remembered him pounding the table. *Enough!* And then the feeling of her fingertips on his scalp and, later, of his gigantic fingers intertwining themselves with hers under the faucet. The memory was so real that her skin tingled. She tightened her grasp on Oskar's hands, pulled them against her chest, then up to her lips. They were damaged hands, but they were good hands. She tasted his skin, recalled his smell, recollected him as she had first seen him, and then at the hotel in Korsør. The shoelace became a chain around her throat. This was the man to whom she belonged now — wasn't it? And then she capitulated and allowed her thoughts to return to the beast sitting in the chair downstairs, absorbing the last heat from the hearth.

AN OVERDOSE

26.

Jutland. December 30, 1941.

Fredrik sat with his head in his hands. He was alone in this room. The bed's metal frame sagged underneath him. The scent of Isabella's perfume rose from a dark, indistinct heap on the mattress behind him. At three o'clock in the afternoon, the whorehouse was quiet. Music crackled on a speaker downstairs, barely audible through the oak planking. In the room next door, a whore was shouting angry words. Her voice carried through the thin wall separating them, but Fredrik didn't hear what she was saying. His eyes were focused on the floor just beyond his bare feet. A heavy curtain covered the window. As low and threatening as the sky was, where the curtain was snagged on a loose nail the gap glowed white with an intensity that burned. Nevertheless, the room was dim. Shadows camouflaged the filth.

On the edge of a throw rug lay a syringe, half filled, a length of rubber cord, a spoon with a blackened bowl. At the sound of footsteps in the hall, Fredrik's eyes darted to the door. A shadow flickered across the crack at the threshold. The footsteps receded, and his eyes returned to the rug. A shaft of light reached into the room from the bright edge of the curtain, bathing the steel syringe in a soft, luminescent pool.

A few minutes passed. Then Fredrik stood from the bed. His torso was clothed only in a singlet, tucked into the waist of his trousers. His arms were sinewy and strong, marked with cuts and bruises. His left shoulder was disfigured with a pink scar. He crossed to an ornate dresser. Its top was covered with a square of dirty lace. There was a pitcher with a couple of inches of water remaining in its reservoir, and he poured himself a glass. He swallowed too slowly, and water escaped on either side of his mouth, streamed down his chin, spilled onto his shirt. The singlet clung to his chest. He set the glass back down, stared blankly at the pitcher, then returned to the bed. Once again, the frame sagged beneath him. Once again, he lowered his head into his hands.

Half an hour earlier, when he had knocked on Isabella's door, Fredrik had been holding something in a hand behind his back, and he was nervous when she let him inside. He had visited the small lingerie shop in Aalborg on his way to the whorehouse. The shopkeeper hadn't restocked her inventory in more than a year, and Fredrik didn't have much of a selection. He had considered stockings, but he wanted something special. There were a few sweaters and robes, but they didn't feel appropriate. Finally, he settled on silk panties and a matching chemise. He didn't like the color. Isabella had dark skin. But there was nothing else as beautiful in the shop. The shopkeeper wrapped the present in tissue paper and tied it with a ribbon. Fredrik shoved the package into his pocket and trudged across town to the brothel.

When Isabella opened the gift, she said nothing at all. Fredrik hadn't expected this reaction. He had never bought her anything before, and he thought that she would be pleased. Sitting on the side of the bed, she pulled the tissue apart, picked the delicate silks out from the paper, held them up to the light. Fredrik wanted her to try the lingerie on. She had large breasts, and he wondered if they would fit inside the chemise. Instead, she folded the undergarments onto her lap. When she met his gaze, she didn't smile.

"Wash yourself first," she said.

Fredrik stood above her, propped against the headboard of the bed. His arms were crossed over his chest. He looked down at the whore. Since when had she told him what to do?

"Go on," she said. "Wash yourself."

The gift meant nothing to her. He had spent three crowns on the weightless bits of shiny fabric, but the gesture had been ignored. He pushed himself up from the bed frame. The bathroom was at the end of the hall. He grabbed a towel from the back of a chair. The cloth was still damp, and the smell of mildew wafted into the air. Out the corner of his eye, as he closed the door, he saw Isabella slide open the drawer of the night table.

In the hallway, he heard music rising through the building. Someone was listening to the radio with the volume turned so high that the sound from the speaker was distorted by static. The song was something that Fredrik had never heard before, something in English broadcast over an Allied station. He paused to listen. He had received the beginning of a classical education in Copenhagen, and the melody cleaved itself into words he could understand. *When you look at me, it's easier for me myself to behold.* Behind him, in Isabella's room, he heard the floorboards creak, then the scratch of a match against flint. He imagined that he could smell the pungent, sour scent of heroin boiling in the basin of a spoon. He stared at the closed door, then followed his shadow down the corridor to the shower.

Now, sitting on the side of Isabella's bed, he squeezed his temples with his thumbs. His hair was still wet. He drew a deep breath through his nose. When he exhaled, his breath caught in his throat. He let go of his forehead, raised his eyes, once again fastened on the syringe. Thirty seconds passed, then a minute. Then he leaned forward, hooked the chrome plunger with the tip of a finger. He stared at the amber liquid still inside the tube, measured the volume. The steel and glass caught the weak light, and the glint became a reflection on the glazed surface of his eyes. His left hand curled into a fist. With his right hand, he gripped the hypodermic with a practiced motion. His fist tightened until his fingers became white. He didn't bother with the rubber strap. He placed the needle against a bluish vein, pushed slowly until the steel point punctured his skin.

■ ■ ■

At the Nielsens' house, Amalia was carrying a bundle of soiled linens down the length of the hallway upstairs. Her foot scuffed the carpet, and she tripped and lost her balance. As she fell, she tried to catch herself on a decorative table. Her hand struck a porcelain bowl, and the pottery skidded across the tabletop. If it had hit the floor, the bowl would have shattered, certainly. But by some miracle, when it left the table, it landed instead on the laundry Amalia had been cradling in her arms. Her knee scraped the carpet, her wrist wrenched backward. Her gaze remained fastened on the bowl. She heaved a sigh of relief when it didn't break. Tears stung her eyes. No one in the house seemed to have heard.

Picking herself up, she returned the bowl to the tabletop. Her hair had come loose, and she collected it back into a bun. Then, glancing up and down the hallway first, to make certain she wasn't being watched, she reached into her apron. Her pocket turned inside out in her haste, and she stuffed it back into place. After another quick look behind her, she slipped a chunky tablet she had stolen from the vial in her father's coat onto her tongue. Even as she swallowed it, she told herself that this would be the last time. She wouldn't let this become a habit.

She gathered the laundry, started once again down the hall. Behind her, a door opened, but she didn't hear it. Old man Poulsen leaned his head into the hallway, peered at Amalia's retreating figure. Light was streaming into the house through an oversize window at the end of the corridor. Despite the clouds outside, this light burst into the hallway and sur-rounded Amalia in a halo so bright that the old man had to squint. He watched her shrink as she walked. The light grew brighter. At last, he had to shield his eyes with a hand. At the base of the hall, when she turned to glance behind her, he couldn't see her face. She had become a black silhouette, flat and featureless. The bundle of laundry in her arms had become indistinct, and the old man wondered if she was carrying one of the children.

Amalia noticed the old man, and she smiled. The old man didn't return her greeting. She opened the door to the rear stairs, carried the laundry down to the kitchen. Dropping the bundle into the utility sink, she twisted on the taps. Steam from the faucet billowed into her face, and she closed her eyes. The water was nearly overflowing when she remembered to open them again.

■ ■ ■

In the barn, Oskar had dropped the shovel and taken a seat on a crude bench Fredrik had fashioned from two logs and a splintered plank. Slivers of wood pierced the fabric of his trousers. He was suddenly out of breath. He had woken this morning at five and had been busy all day without a single break. A pig had escaped, and he had found it half frozen on the far side of the property. After that, he had had to cross the farm a second time to repair a fallen section of fence. He hadn't eaten breakfast, and now he was missing lunch. His heart was racing. If he didn't sit, he might tumble.

He took a few deep breaths and steadied himself. Behind him, the pigs were bleating. They needed to be fed. The hens squawked. He twisted on the bench to see if something was disturbing them, but the barn was empty. He faced forward again, leaned his elbows onto his knees, let his head hang. At his feet, he noticed a few stray feathers. He picked one up and examined it in the dim light. When he held it at a certain angle, its barbs turned from gray to purple. He gripped it by its quill, brushed the soft tip of the vane against his chin. This made him shiver. He let the feather drop, watched it flutter to the hard floor of the barn.

A few minutes later, after a rest, he was feeling better again. He stood from the bench and crossed to the barn doors. The air was thick with mist. Across the icy yard, the windows of the cottage were dark. A thin trail of smoke was rising from the chimney, and he breathed the sweet smell into his lungs. He narrowed his eyes and tried to see inside through the plaster walls.

■ ■ ■

Upstairs in the cottage, Polina was standing next to the window beside Amalia's bed. When Oskar stepped into the light at the crack between the barn doors, she took a quick step backward, hid herself in shadow. His face was pensive. His eyes were focused into a squint. His mouth was raised in a loose circle. His front teeth showed white beneath chapped, cracked lips. Not for the first time, Polina remarked to herself how beautiful he was. He had grown up on this farm, a slave to his father. Fredrik had worked him from morning until night, seven days a week. His hands were bloody despite how callused they were. His face was weather-beaten. His nose had been broken and was misshapen. He only cut his hair when it tangled. He hardly ever bathed. But there was still something soft about him. His mother must have been a beautiful woman. He had Fredrik's height, Fredrik's arms, Fredrik's build. But he had a woman's eyes, he had a woman's lips, a woman's cheekbones. *That was it.* He must have resembled his mother, and yes, Fredrik must have fallen in love with the woman for good reason. Polina took another half step backward. She didn't want him to see her.

Behind Oskar, the shadow inside the barn formed a black background without any depth. The longer Polina stared at him, the less connected he became to the objects surrounding him. She had the impression that he was floating.

Then Polina caught sight of her own reflection on the surface of the window. It had been a long while since she had paid any attention to herself. She had seen her reflection in mirrors, but only in passing. Now she noticed how broad her forehead was becoming. Her nose had grown longer. She didn't recognize the expression in her eyes. Her lips were fuller than she remembered, and she could see how red they were, even in this nearly translucent likeness. No, she hardly recognized herself at all. She felt her cheeks flush, though she wasn't certain why. Blinking, she let go of the image on the glass, focused once again on the barn.

Oskar, though, had disappeared from the crack between the doors, and there was nothing there for Polina to see any longer except the blank canvas of the barn's dark shadow.

■ ■ ■

In Isabella's room, Fredrik was slumped on the floor next to the bed. He had emptied the syringe into his arm. His back was pressed against the sharp edge of the metal bed frame. His breath was so shallow that his chest wasn't moving. His arms were resting on his thighs, his hands were open, palms up. His legs were splayed, his feet were bare. The light was seeping slowly from the room. Maybe the air was seeping from the room as well. The walls were moving closer. The gap between the curtain and the wall was shrinking into a dot. When voices were raised downstairs in the whorehouse, Fredrik didn't move, not a single muscle. His cheek twitched, but this happened so briefly that it might not have happened at all.

There were footsteps on the stairs, punctuated by the squeak of polished leather. The swish of heavy wool echoed down the length of the corridor. In a room across the hall, a woman was moaning and a bed was creaking. The footsteps approached, then stopped on the other side of Isabella's door. Knuckles rapped the door, and the door rattled in its frame. *Isabella?* The customer spoke the name softly, but with the unmistakable accent of a German. He knocked again, waited. The doorknob moved. The latch clinked. Still, Fredrik didn't wake. The door fell still again. Isabella's disappointed customer found another whore. Music floated through the building like down that has escaped from a pillow.

When Fredrik opened his eyes, it was dark. On the bed behind him, a black-haired woman with olive skin was lying on top of the covers. She wasn't moving. One arm hung limply at her side, the other was draped behind her head. Her breasts had been heavy, and they lay flat on her chest and rolled off her ribs, half hidden by the thin fabric of her shirt. Her mouth hung open, and her chin was scabbed with dried mucus. A small stain of blood darkened the arm by her side, just beneath the fold of her elbow. Fredrik pulled himself to his feet. He didn't look at the bed, not once. He had known that Isabella was dead from the instant he returned from his shower. There had been no reason to feel for a pulse.

He gathered his clothes, pulled on his boots, then let himself out the door. Outside, the snow didn't melt when it touched his face. Behind him, the music crackling on the radio's tinny speaker faded. He didn't know which direction to walk.

POLINA CAPTURED

27.

Jutland. December 31, 1941.

Johan Jungmann stood in front of his bathroom mirror, a razor in one hand. His other hand was resting on the rim of the washbasin. Without his glasses, he looked like a different man, even to himself. The brass frames, the slivers of crystalline glass, had become part of his face. His vision wasn't so poor that he couldn't bring his image into focus. A drop of blood was rolling down his cheek an inch beneath his eye. He had nicked himself with the razor. He watched the red liquid thin as it mixed with the water on his skin, then vanish into a foamy mass of shaving cream at the base of his jaw. Another drop welled from the cut, then followed the first, and a diluted, pink sheen spread across his cheek. He looked into his reflection, struggled to define just what it was that was so different about him without his glasses. Perhaps it was how naked he seemed. Without the corrective lenses to shield them, his eyes became organs.

He splashed his face with hot water, then tore a ragged square of tissue from the toilet roll and stuck it to the cut. Then he picked up his glasses from the edge of the sink and placed them back onto his nose, wrapped the thin metal temples behind his ears. The water drained from the basin with a hollow gurgle.

In the hallway, he paused at the door to his daughter's room. It wasn't yet seven. Mia, his wife of eight years, was still in bed, and he hadn't expected any sound from Kirsten's room either. The quiet patter of his daughter's voice filled him with emotion. Resting a hand on the knob, he tried to make sense of what she was saying, but he couldn't decipher a word.

When he opened the door, Kirsten was sitting on the floor in front of her bed. Dressed in her flannel nightgown, the little girl was holding something in her hands, playing a child's game. Behind her, the curtains were pulled back from the window. Although it was early, enough light was streaming inside to throw the four-year-old's face into shadow. She looked up at her father. Only the tip of her nose glistened in the light. Her hair shimmered as if it were spun from gold. They had given her a new dollhouse for Christmas. It had been an extravagant present. Jungmann had intended it as much for Mia as for Kirsten, indirectly, at least. He knew that his wife would be reassured by the display of confidence the gift represented, despite how difficult their circumstances were becoming. If the Germans dissolved the Danish government, there was no telling what would happen — not just to his income but to him. Kirsten, though, had mostly ignored the toy. She had lost interest when her father tried to show her how to move the dolls about inside without upsetting any of the furniture. By the end of the evening, she had dug her old cloth doll out from the closet where Mia had hidden it, and this was what she was cradling now.

When Kirsten raised a hand to point at his face, her arm burst into the light. The shadow surrounding her assumed the weight of water. "What's that?" she asked her father.

"These?" Jungmann let go of the doorknob, touched the frames of his glasses with his fingertips. "These are my glasses, Kirsten, you know that."

The little girl shook her head. "No — that." She continued pointing at her father's face.

For an instant, Jungmann felt shaken, as if his daughter was able to see something terrible about him. Then he remembered the nick on his cheek from the razor. He tapped the piece of toilet paper, made certain that it was still stuck to the cut. "It's nothing, darling."

Kirsten continued to point at him. Then she dropped her hand, found her doll again. A few seconds later, she had forgotten that her father was standing in the doorway, and she resumed her game. *Rikke doesn't like the sound, Rikke wants to run away, Rikke is afraid. Oh, it's okay, Rikke. There's nothing to be afraid of. Those are only airplanes.* Jungmann watched his daughter, then took a step backward into the hall and closed the door again.

Downstairs, he didn't pause in the kitchen for anything to eat. He would stop for a coffee on his way. This murder of Lars Brink had thrown the administration into chaos, and he wanted to get to his office. The Germans, of course, were most upset by the escape of Vilfred Thiesen. Yes, it was the Christmas season. But how could the local police have left their prisoner in jail with only one guard on duty, the night before he was to be transferred into their custody? The Danish townspeople were running scared, but now they were fighting back. Like the rest of the city council, Jungmann had found himself trapped between the Nazis and his own countrymen. He pulled on his coat, slipped his hands into his gloves, let himself out the front door.

On the stoop, the crisp white corner of an envelope pro- truded from beneath the edge of the bristle doormat, and he bent to pick it up. He had to remove a hand from a glove in order to open it. He tore the seal, lifted out the letter. His fin- gers were red by the time he had unfolded it.

You will find a Polish Jew in hiding in Fredrik Gregersen's house.

Jungmann's expression didn't alter as he read the note. He folded the letter again, inserted it back into the envelope, sur- veyed the street. A light snow was falling. Smoke was rising from a few chimneys. The village was quiet. Remembering the deadbolt, he slipped the envelope into his jacket pocket, then found his keys and locked the door before starting down the sidewalk.

From his vantage point in a doorway halfway up the block, Franz Jakobsen watched the magistrate disappear. Gustav Keller would be happy with this twist. Franz's instructions had been to track down the stolen jewels and punish the bastards who had lifted them from the Jews. A business such as theirs, providing illicit passage through Denmark to Jews and other refugees fleeing Germany, couldn't survive such treachery — it depended upon their clients' faith that their person and prop- erty would be kept safe, when they had no outside redress through the law. A message had to be sent. So Franz had exe- cuted Axel Madsen. He had assassinated Hermann Schmidt. He had recovered the stolen jewels. Now he was taking care of Fredrik. Gustav would appreciate the cleverness of turn- ing his own Danish compatriots against the farmhand. Let the police do their dirty work, especially as Fredrik appeared to be a dangerous man to subdue. Before the war, Gustav had been the general manager of the bank where Franz had been a clerk. Just before the invasion, Franz had been caught ambushing another one of the bank clerks — the husband of a woman with whom Franz was having an affair. Gustav had fired him, of course. Franz had beaten the man senseless. *What job do you think you hold?* Gustav had asked him. *This is a bank, sir. A bank.* A couple of weeks after the Germans stormed into Denmark, though, Gustav had knocked on Franz's door. *I have a job for you,* he had said, *that I think you might like.* Franz waited until Jungmann's footsteps receded. Then he pulled a small blue pack from his pocket, lifted it to his mouth, clamped his lips over the butt of a cigarette. In the past few weeks, he had developed a taste for American tobacco. He struck a match with his thumbnail, drew a deep breath of smoke into his lungs, then headed up the street in the opposite direction.

■ ■ ■

At ten o'clock, Fredrik hadn't yet returned home. At the side of the barn, Oskar was sawing a plank. A few boards had begun to rot on the barn door, and they needed to be replaced. Fredrik had started the project a few days before, but he hadn't gotten far.

At the top of the driveway, Amalia was letting herself out the gate, on her way to a neighboring farm to trade some sugar for flour and yeast. She noticed that the latch was still broken. Mr. Nielsen had himself asked her to remind her father that it was waiting to be fixed. She had told Fredrik twice already, but he had ignored her. Mr. Nielsen would be upset. After all, if the gate didn't stay closed, the animals could escape. She pulled it shut behind her, propped it against the post to make sure that it stayed in place, then tucked the five-pound bag of sugar under her arm, buttoned it inside her coat. It was a two-mile trek to the Hartmann farm. The wind was gusting, but at least the snow and rain had let up for the moment. After the exchange, she would carry ten pounds of flour back to the Nielsens'. Perhaps the Hartmanns would offer her a cup of tea first. Across the road, birch trees planted to screen the crops were swaying in the wind. She peered between the trunks into the hidden recesses of the copse, then set off down the side of the highway in the direction of Aalborg.

A few minutes later, the growl of a truck's engine broke the silence. Amalia shielded her eyes. At first, she saw nothing. Sound could travel farther than light on a day like today. And then the faint outline of a black Citroën sedan appeared, trailed seconds later by the larger, looming shadow of the truck whose engine she could hear, rumbling over the frozen asphalt. She recognized Jungmann's car, even from a distance. Hanging from the rear of the truck, a German soldier with scarlet lips, his long coat flapping in the turbulence, grabbed his crotch and leered at her as the vehicles passed. The truck's engine geared down as they reached the Nielsens' driveway, then quieted into an idle. Worry creased Amalia's face, but she bent her head and continued walking.

Oskar had long since given up hope that Fredrik would return today to help him with the chores. His back was aching. He had stopped sawing to watch Amalia trudge up the driveway to the gate. When she turned around halfway up the path, he had waved at her, and she had waved back at him without a smile. Then he had continued his father's work. Chunks of wood dropped from the saw's teeth. Fine particles of sawdust stung his eyes. When the grind of the truck's engine rode to his ears on the back of the wind, he twisted to look up toward the gate again. Still bent over the half-sawn plank, he watched as Jungmann's car circled down the drive toward the cottage, followed closely by the German truck.

Inside the house, Polina turned off the tap at the kitchen sink. The window was frosted with a layer of steam. She wiped it clear with her fist — her skin left a smear on the pane — then peered outside in time to see the convoy emerge from the mist at the top of the property. She dried her hands, stepped back from the glass, switched off the lamp. She was half naked in a sheer undershirt and a silk slip that Hermann Schmidt had given her — for these were her only underclothes. For a moment, fear paralyzed her. Then she hurried to the stairs. In the room she shared with Fredrik's children, she slunk to the window and pulled back the corner of the curtain as the car and truck trundled to a stop beneath her, in front of the cottage.

Beside the barn, Oskar stiffened. Across the field, through the thick, swirling mist, he had seen the curtain move upstairs. When Jungmann stepped from the Citroën, the magistrate spotted the boy next to the woodpile. Even from this distance, he could smell his fear. "Where's your father?" he called out to him.

Oskar watched the soldiers jump from the rear of the truck. He counted five, all of them armed.

"Where's Fredrik?" Jungmann repeated, when Oskar didn't answer quickly enough.

Oskar shook his head. "He hasn't returned home. Not since yesterday."

The magistrate pivoted on his heel, studied the cottage. "Is anyone inside?" Without waiting for an answer, he started around the side of the house toward the cellar. Finding it locked, he turned back toward Oskar. "Get me the key."

Oskar's mind was spinning as he headed for the cottage. Perhaps he could reach Polina before Jungmann did — but even so, how could he protect her? His feet slid on the ice, and he nearly tripped with every step. The soldiers were watching him. He bit his tongue and tasted blood.

"I want this door opened," Jungmann said.

But Oskar didn't hear him. His attention had been drawn to some movement on the other side of the house. Fredrik was letting himself inside through the back door. Halfway across the yard, Oskar's feet rooted to the earth. As relieved as he was to see his father, a premonition of what might follow left him suddenly cold. An icy wind nipped his ears.

"Get me the key," Jungmann repeated, raising his voice. "Do you hear?" When Oskar didn't move, he let the lock go and circled back toward the porch himself.

Inside the house, Fredrik didn't waste any time. He twisted the bolt to lock the front door, then took the stairs two at a time. He tried to move quietly, but his boots pounded the treads. When he burst into the children's bedroom, Polina was standing in a corner, clutching a cut-glass pitcher as if it was a weapon. Her face was contorted with panic, but this dissipated the instant she saw him. Her lips parted, her brow relaxed. The pitcher slipped from her fingers and landed at her feet with a thud. "Come with me," Fredrik said.

His eyes swept over her body as she passed in front of the window. The weak light pierced the pearly material of her slip, her undershirt dissolved into gauze. The diamond ring sparkled between her breasts. "Who are they?" she asked him.

Fredrik didn't respond. "There's an attic," he said. "Hurry."

Polina followed him into the hallway at the top of the stairs, where he pointed to a trapdoor in the low ceiling. He was tall enough to reach up and, without standing on his toes, to slide it clear of the opening. The hole the panel revealed was pitch-black. The whistle of the wind intensified, the musty smell of mold wafted into the house. Outside, there were footsteps in the snow. *You told me that there was no one in the house.* Jung-mann's voice penetrated the walls.

Oskar forced himself forward again. "Maybe my father came home," he said, striding toward the cottage. "I've been working by the barn —"

Jungmann, though, had already reached the porch. "You stay outside," he commanded, cutting the boy off.

"The key to the cellar," Oskar reminded him.

"Stay where you are." The magistrate grabbed the railing, started up the stairs.

In the hallway on the second floor, Fredrik let go of the trapdoor, turned toward Polina. "You're going to have to climb up, hide yourself there."

Polina repeated her question. "Who are they?"

"There's no time. Come." Grabbing her by the waist, Fredrik was surprised at how insubstantial she was. His rough fingers caught on the fabric of her undershirt, tugging a few threads loose. He slipped his hands underneath, and they very nearly ringed her torso. He hoisted her as if she were made of balsa, lifted her into the dark. Below her, his gaze was fixed between her legs, in the shadows beneath her slip.

"Wait." She searched for a ledge where she could set her hands, then pulled herself into the attic. The rustle of rats scurrying to the walls sent a chill down her spine. She squirmed into the cramped hiding place beneath the thatch, drew her legs up behind her.

"Okay?"

Downstairs, the door rattled in its frame. The light shifted when Jungmann pressed his face against the glass.

"Yes," Polina answered, in a whisper.

"Don't move, then. Stay there until I come back for you, understand? *Don't move.*"

The hole beneath her closed like the aperture of a camera, and that was it, Polina was encased in blackness. She choked on the odor of rodent feces and piss. Only a thin layer of thatch shielded her from the wind, and she shivered, unable to wrap even her own arms around herself for warmth. Rats ventured back out from the walls. She could hear them, but it was too dark to see. And then, tracking the scrape of their claws and the slither of their bellies, she glimpsed the shiny glint of their eyes. Beneath her, Fredrik's heavy footsteps shook the stairs, then the bolt on the front door clicked, the hinges squealed. A breath of air ruffled her hair. The beams creaked, the rats circled. Looking down, Polina realized that there was a tiny crack between the boards of the trapdoor, almost too small to notice. She leaned toward it. If she concentrated hard enough, she could just make out the top stair and then a sliver of the hallway. It was, she thought, like looking through the window into a dollhouse — and, focusing like this, she hoped she might also forget about the rats.

"What do you want this time?" Fredrik asked, pulling the door open. "Eh, Jungmann? Axel is still dead, I suppose. And the Jews are still slipping through your fingers like sand?"

As long as the magistrate had known him, Fredrik had never appeared so nervous before. He sniffed the air. The house smelled different, too. *He had him.* He could sense it. The wind gusted against his back. Beneath the brim of his homburg, the mist climbed his skull like icy fingers. "May I come inside, Gregersen? It's cold today."

The farmhand took a step back from the door — an uncertain step, Jungmann remarked. And again the thought crossed his mind. He had him. But what was different today? Fredrik was chewing his lip — as if he was trying to bite a piece of chapped skin off it. As if his skin was too dry. *Or like an addict.* The magistrate measured the light inside, peered into the shadows, at last followed the farmhand into his shack. If Fredrik hadn't been a Gregersen, he would have dispensed with him long ago. He didn't like him, not one bit. He was a savage. Now he had him. But he mustn't get too confident. Cornered, there was no telling what Fredrik might do. Jungmann pulled his gloves off his hands. Watching him, Fredrik noticed how dainty his fingers were. His nails were cut, buffed like a woman's. "You've already searched the house a few days ago," the farmhand said.

And Jungmann thought, *The tip is correct, he's harboring someone here. That's what is different today — Fredrik is scared.* "You know," he said, "you're not fooling anyone, Gregersen."

Fredrik had been on the cusp of asking the magistrate if he wanted tea. It wasn't in his nature to kowtow — but he saw the importance of distracting him. Now bile rose in his throat, and he changed his mind. "What do you mean, fooling anyone?"

"Your pupils are so dilated," the magistrate said, "that I'm surprised you can see anything at all."

"What's that supposed to mean?"

"Show me your hands."

Fredrik didn't react.

"You're shaking like a leaf."

"What is it you want, Jungmann?"

"You're an addict, aren't you? A thief and a junkie."

"What is it you want?" Fredrik repeated, unable to modulate his voice. His fingers twitched. It would be so easy to snap this man's gizzard.

Upstairs in the attic, through the crack in the trapdoor, Polina saw the shadows shift beneath her. *An addict.* Of course she had known. How many had she come across in the last few years? Too many to count. Somehow, though, she had thought that this man was different.

"I have already told you everything I know about Axel Madsen," Fredrik blustered. "You searched the house — what more do you want?"

Jungmann was enjoying the farmhand's discomposure. He wasn't used to it. This was a new sensation for him. If he prodded this unsophisticated man, he would come apart into pieces. "I haven't mentioned Axel Madsen to you today, have I?"

A feeling of foreboding overcame Fredrik. Equally, he wasn't used to this man's confidence. "Maybe a cup of tea," he said, stumbling over the words.

In other circumstances, Jungmann might have felt sorry for him. Scoffing at the offer, he turned on his heel, leaned his head out the door, whistled. The soldiers had gathered in front of the truck. He pointed around the side of the porch, and two of them began circling the cottage. Then he snapped his fingers, signaled for another to approach. The soldier who had given his crotch a lewd squeeze passing Amalia in the road trotted toward him. "We're here on a tip," the magistrate said to Fredrik.

"A tip from who?" Fredrik asked. He couldn't resist the question, as pointless as it was.

Jungmann sniffed. "A tip," he repeated. "Just a tip."

"You can go to hell," Fredrik said.

"Can I?" Jungmann twisted around to face him again. He was still holding his black leather gloves, and he shoved them into a pocket, then, unbuttoning his long coat, deliberately unsnapped the holster on his belt. "You're harboring someone here, Gregersen," he said.

Fredrik paused too long. "You don't have any right — " he said. "You can't just come into my house and search it whenever you please."

"No?"

On the porch, the soldier's footsteps shook the cottage. His shadow darkened the doorway. When he appeared at the threshold, Fredrik seethed. This soldier was a kid. A pimple-faced boy not yet twenty years old. He probably had pimples on his ass, too — his dick was probably as bald as a girl's twat. He could take him apart with one hand and worry about Jungmann with the other.

Outside, Oskar had retreated to the side of the barn, uncertain what else to do. The saw still sat in the cut he had been tearing in the plank, and he lifted it out, set it down on the boards. The mist made it difficult to keep track of the activity across the yard. Two of the soldiers had disappeared around the cottage. Oskar watched as a third followed Jungmann inside. The boots this soldier wore were polished to such a gloss that they rippled in the gray light as he passed through the doorway. The last two soldiers stayed with the truck. One cupped a hand over a match lit by the other, leaned forward with a cigarette in his mouth to dip its tip into the flame.

On the side of the highway, Amalia stopped walking when the growl of another engine broke the silence. Something was wrong. Jungmann had turned off the highway onto the Nielsens' farm. They were coming for her father, she knew that they were. Weak headlights burned holes in the mist, then a small black Opel followed them into view. Munk, the chief of police, hovered behind the windshield, his gloved hands clamping the steering wheel. The Opel's tall tires spit chunks of ice backward in its wake as it slipped past into the mist. Amalia waited until she heard this car, too, gear down and turn off the road onto the farm. Then she pulled her coat tight and bent her head into the wind again. She had no choice but to keep walking. The Hartmanns were expecting her. The Nielsens needed the flour.

"I have heard," Jungmann said to Fredrik, "that you have come into some money recently."

"What business is that of yours?"

"A new scarf, a round of drinks at Albert's, vodka from Russia, lingerie from Mathiesen's. Where does a man like you get the money for such indulgences? This is my business, Gregersen. *This* is my business."

Fredrik squared his shoulders, blocked the young soldier from entering beyond the vestibule. His jaw was clenched. He was grinding his molars, breathing through his nose.

"I am going to have to ask you once again," Jungmann said, "for the key to the cellar." Fredrik barely heard him. "The key," the magistrate repeated, "to the cellar. Or I will simply break the door down."

Fredrik's teeth felt loose in his gums. He rubbed his tongue over them as if they were foreign objects. Stones. "You searched the cellar already. And you came up empty."

"The key." Jungmann's hand moved to his holster. It felt better, grasping the butt of his pistol. When Fredrik took a step toward him, he yanked the gun out — but Fredrik raised his hands, nodded toward the kitchen. Jungmann eased the weapon back into its sheath, let the huge man pass.

Fredrik opened a drawer, found the key. He weighed it in his hand, then tossed it to the magistrate. The glint of steel in the bottom of the drawer caught his eye. He had sharpened the carving knife himself just a few days ago. The blade's new edge hadn't yet begun to oxidize.

"Search the house," Jungmann barked to the soldier. "Upstairs, too." He made certain that the German had understood him, then returned his attention to the farmhand. "You stay inside, understand?" He glanced across the driveway at the soldiers smoking in front of the truck. "I've got the house covered. If you follow me outside, they'll shoot you, Fredrik. Do you hear me? And nobody will shed a tear."

Fredrik watched Jungmann descend the stairs to the yard. The magistrate's boots crunched on the frozen snow as he skirted the cottage. The key slid into the padlock on the cellar doors.

The soldier glanced into the kitchen at Fredrik, then crossed into the sitting room. His attention had been drawn to the small items on the mantel — a single photograph of Oskar as a baby in a white christening gown, a few blue-and-white porcelain figurines that had been given to Amalia by the Gregersens when she was a child, a silver matchbox that had belonged to Fredrik's father. The soldier picked up the matchbox, opened it, closed it again. Fredrik's face hardened as he watched the German shove the heirloom unceremoniously into his pocket. The soft tramp of Jungmann's fancy boots descending into the cellar barely disturbed the silence. When the soldier emerged from the sitting room then headed for the stairs, Fredrik's hand dropped to the open kitchen drawer.

In the attic, the rats were growing bolder. Their claws scratched the rafters, only inches from Polina's fingers. Their whiskers caressed the wood. They were hungry, testing her, getting set to attack. She focused on the narrow fissure in the trapdoor. Her arms were beginning to ache. The rafters splintered into her skin.

Beneath her, the soldier appeared at the top of the stairs, barely visible through the crack. Polina could feel his every step in her bones. When he glanced up at the trapdoor, her head jerked backward involuntarily. Her scalp flamed, her arms tingled. She suppressed a scream. She was certain that he could see her, too. But he passed underneath without pausing, into the bedroom she shared with Oskar and Amalia.

Two floors below, voices drifted up from the cellar. The magistrate had leaned his head outside and was calling to the soldiers at the truck to bring him a torch. The light from the open doors only lit a small arc at the cellar's mouth. There was someone here, there was someone hidden inside, Jungmann was certain of it. Boxes scraped the floor. The scent of a cigarette rose through the house.

A rat's whiskers grazed Polina's fingers. Polina jumped, and the rafters creaked. The sound was loud enough to give her away. Another rat scurried toward her through the liquid blackness, but she didn't flinch a second time. She held herself entirely still, too afraid to breathe. Beneath her, the soldier retraced his steps from the children's bedroom. What had he heard? His boots resounded on the floorboards. In Fredrik's room, the bedposts whined when he placed a hand on the mattress to peek under the bed. The closet door squeaked. He kicked a pile of old shoes over, then returned to the hallway.

When he spotted the trapdoor, Polina's eyes met his through the crack. His fingers stretched toward her, then stopped short, two inches from the panel. Fredrik was taller than the mousy-haired boy by at least a foot. Even on his toes, the soldier couldn't reach the panel. He gritted his teeth and strained — all he needed was an extra inch — then gave up, dropped his arms.

Beside the barn, Oskar watched as Munk's black Opel pulled through the gates at the top of the property then wound its way down the driveway and rolled into place next to the truck. The remaining soldiers stood at attention to greet the chief of police. One of them saluted, the other squared his shoulders. Munk slammed the car door behind him, spoke a few muffled words.

Inside the cellar, Jungmann heard something move in one corner. He raised the battery-powered torch, directed its beam into the shadows. The yellow light penetrated the dark, growing dimmer as it reached for the far wall. His heart pounded against his ribs. He drew his pistol and pointed it toward the sound. When Munk appeared behind him, his finger very nearly yanked the trigger. He kept his aim steady, called to the police chief over his shoulder. "Is that you, Munk? Come down here, I think I've found someone."

The police chief drew his own pistol as he descended the stairs. His eyes followed the weak beam. "Where?" he asked. "I don't see anything."

"In the corner." Emboldened by the smaller man's presence, Jungmann took a step forward. The torch lit the back wall. Cobwebs scintillated like silk. And then a rat, as fat as a pregnant cat, scurried through the yellow light.

Munk scoffed. "Is that your fugitive, Johan? A rat?" He returned his pistol to its holster. "Come with me — there's been a development in town. We caught Vilfred Thiesen — he was hiding with the chickens behind Torben Pedersen's house. I think he might talk, but he insists upon speaking to you first. He wants your word that we won't hand him over to the Germans if he fingers Brink's killer."

Underneath Polina, the soldier reappeared from Fredrik's room, now carrying a couple of old boots from the closet. There wasn't a single chair upstairs except for the one next to Fredrik's bed, which had a broken leg, not a crate, nor anything large and sturdy enough to hold his weight, or he would have retrieved that instead. He set the boots onto the floor beneath the trapdoor, on their sides so that he could stand on the stiff edges of their heels. Polina watched him straighten up, then balance on the shoes. As his fingers stretched toward her, the light shifted in the very corner of the crack. Polina's heart pulsed. Fredrik was creeping slowly up the stairs behind the soldier.

As cold as it was in this attic, a bead of sweat gathered on Polina's forehead. The soldier was reaching for the panel, wobbling on the shoes. The bead of sweat slid down to her chin, dropped onto the trapdoor, splattered next to the crack. Fredrik was nearing the top of the stairs. Something in his hand glimmered — a long-bladed carving knife, which he held loosely at his side. As he approached the soldier, he raised the blade to the height of his chest. Another bead of sweat dropped from Polina's forehead. This one landed on the crack, blurring her vision just as the soldier's fingers touched the wooden door. The plank shook, lifted from the frame, began haltingly to move. And then Jungmann's voice exploded through the cottage. "Bauer? Where are you? Come!"

The boots flipped sideways under the soldier's feet, and he lost the extra height he needed. The trapdoor dropped back into place. On the stairs, Fredrik tucked the carving knife into his sleeve. The soldier gave the boots a kick, sent them tumbling down the hallway, then pushed past the farmhand on his way downstairs. In the attic, hot tears seared Polina's cheeks.

"Outside!" Jungmann barked to the soldier. Then to Fredrik, "We'll be back. Hear? You think you can hide from us, but you can't, Gregersen, you can't."

At the side of the barn, Oskar watched the soldier and the magistrate file from the house. Jungmann and Munk disappeared back into their cars. The soldiers climbed back into the rear of the truck. Metal doors slammed, engines rumbled to life. Exhaust steamed into the roiling air.

28.

By the time Oskar reached the cottage, Fredrik was raging at Polina. She had waited for him to open the trapdoor, then had lowered herself into his hands. Her anxiety was streaming down her face in tears. Fredrik was furious. In another second, he would have grabbed the German boy. He would have had no choice but to finish him. Oskar heard his father's shouts as he approached the house. *I want you out, tonight, do you understand, tonight!* Oskar slipped as he climbed the front stairs. He clasped the railing, crossed the porch. His arms were still shaking. His muscles were stiff with cold, his legs were clumsy. He yanked open the door. Inside, shadows were shifting on the stairwell wall. He bounded up the stairs to the second floor three at a time.

Fredrik was snarling like an angry dog. Polina had raised her hands to push him away from her, and the farmhand grabbed her forearms, bent her elbows, pulled her forward onto her toes. His fingers dug into her skin.

Oskar slowed at the landing. "What's going on?" he demanded. The sprint inside had winded him. "Tell me, Father," he said, raising his voice, "what are you doing?" His nose was dripping, and he wiped his face with the back of his hand. He had brought the cold into the cottage with him.

Polina's arms were bruising beneath Fredrik's fingers. "You were wrong to bring her here," the farmhand said to his son, without taking his eyes from Polina's.

Oskar ascended the last stair onto the second floor. "Let her go."

Fredrik snorted. "They know she's here, they'll arrest us if she stays."

Oskar took another step toward his father. "I said, let her go."

Fredrik gave Polina's forearms a final squeeze. Her thin bones bent, her face registered the pain. When the farmhand released her, she dropped from her toes back onto her heels, caught herself against the wall. Fredrik turned away — not from her but from his son. "She won't spend another night in this house," he said, controlling his voice. This was a statement of fact, no more. He wouldn't tolerate dissent. "I won't have it."

Oskar reached for Polina, pulled her protectively into his arms. His hand slipped under her shirt. The gesture was accidental, but his fingers remembered her skin. "This wasn't her fault. There's no reason to blame her."

Polina pulled away from him. After the terror she had just experienced, she didn't want to be touched. "Please," she said. "No —" But in the narrow hallway, there wasn't anywhere to escape.

When she jostled into Fredrik, the farmhand gave her a little shove, pushed her back into Oskar's arms. Fredrik sneered at her, not yet able to swallow his anger, and their eyes connected as Oskar's hand found her waist again. "There's no reason to shelter her either."

"You're right, Father," Oskar said. "It's too dangerous — she can't stay."

Polina stiffened, uncertain whether she had heard him correctly.

The capitulation stopped Fredrik. He examined his son. The hallway was dark, lit only by the window in the children's bedroom. Still, Oskar could read the relief in his father's eyes. "You understand it's for the best."

"If they know she's here," Oskar agreed, "they'll come back."

"They said as much. It won't be safe. Not for Amalia. Not for you."

"So there is no choice, then." Oskar pulled the girl closer to him. The smell of her hair was so strong that he could taste it. He was gripping her too tight, he knew that he was when he felt her ribs flex beneath his fingers. But he couldn't let her go. The realization that he would speak the next words stunned him, but they tumbled from his mouth anyway. "We will leave tonight."

Fredrik's brow creased. He met Oskar's gaze as he considered his words. "You, too?" He wanted to make certain that he had understood what his son was telling him.

Polina twisted away from the tall, bony boy. "This is your home, Oskar." She clasped his arm, tried to confront him. "You know you can't just leave — "

Oskar ignored her. His eyes hadn't left his father's. He didn't really mean to leave, did he? The threat had slipped out so impulsively. Now the words were uttered, though, he recognized their truth. *He was going to leave this house with Polina, and he was going to leave it tonight.* "We'll leave Denmark," he said.

"Where?" Fredrik asked. It wasn't really a question, and the word wasn't spoken in disbelief. He simply wanted his son to lead him to the next step of this discovery. "Where will you go?"

"To America," Oskar said.

Fredrik nodded slowly. He had heard that this was where the Jews would go, too, when they escaped the Nazis. To America.

"I'll take the money," Oskar said.

Again, his father nodded.

"It will be enough to get us to America, and once we're there, it will be enough to keep us both safe, at least for a while."

Fredrik gazed at his son. "This is something you've thought about?"

Oskar's eyes dropped. The audacity of his declaration had stolen his breath.

"Oskar?" Fredrik reached for his shoulder. "I'm not saying I don't understand. But you're a fool if you think you will make her happy." He gave the shoulder a squeeze. He wanted to seize his son's attention. "Eh? You hear me?" He tightened his fingers until Oskar raised his eyes again. "You're a fool if you think you'll find more than a minute of happiness with her."

Oskar tried to shrug his father's hand off him, but the man's grip was too strong. "I'm in love with her, Father," he managed.

"You think so?" Fredrik's lips formed a smile that his eyes didn't share. "You can't even see her, Oskar. You think you can? You'll never be able to. Eh?"

"And *you* can see *me* so well?" Oskar tried again to wrest his father's hand off him. "You think you know me well enough to tell me how I feel now?"

"Who is she to you? Eh? Think about it, Oskar. All you see when you look at her is what you want to see."

"Isn't that the way it always is?"

Fredrik shook his head. He had no answer to this.

"I tell you I love her, Father." The next words, Oskar had to force from his mouth. "She loves me, too."

Fredrik raised his other hand to Oskar's other shoulder and squared him in front of him. "Is that what you think? Eh?" When Oskar turned away from him, he gave his son a small shake. "If that's what you think, then you're an even bigger fool than I thought." He tried to find Oskar's eyes but couldn't. His son's chest, he noticed, was still heaving. "She's been beaten, Oskar. Don't you remember that stray you tried to feed? She'll draw blood if you get too close, just as surely as that bitch did. Oskar?" He waited for the boy to lift his eyes, but Oskar only glanced at him. Fredrik studied him, and the house fell still. "But I understand — I can't say I don't." At last, the farmhand let go of his son. His fingers slid from his arms. He could feel Polina's eyes on him, but he avoided her. "Come downstairs with me, why don't you?" he said to Oskar. "Let the girl pack her things. Have a drink with me at least before you leave."

Oskar mastered his breathing. Was this really happening? His words rang in his head. *We will leave tonight* — He had spoken rashly. In anger at his father, in relief after the soldiers had left the house. But his father was taking him seriously — his father was ready to let him take the money and go. And if he didn't go, if he stayed, it was Polina who would have to leave, on her own. And then what would become of her?

"Yes," he heard Polina say, "have a drink with your father, Oskar. It is better for you to talk this over, it is better if the two of you think about this some more."

"Okay," Oskar said. He tried to smile. "We'll have a drink. Then Polina and I will go."

Fredrik found his son's shoulder again. This time, it wasn't to demand his attention. He had the impression that he had never touched his son before, and now that he was touching him, he simply didn't want to let go. Like Oskar, he hadn't seen this moment coming. But perhaps it had been inevitable. Perhaps it was for the best. "Now," he said. "Okay. I will go downstairs and set up a few glasses. If you're leaving tonight, you had better see about your things, too. Come down, join me when you're ready." He gave the shoulder a final clasp, then turned away. His head still felt giddy after the narrow miss with Jungmann and the soldiers. His footsteps were slow and heavy on the stairs.

Oskar followed Polina into the bedroom. He ripped the sheet from the ceiling, then sat down on his mattress and leaned his elbows on his knees and watched her get dressed in the silvery light filtering through the window. The wind gusted against the cottage, the roof thatch shivered above their heads. His father was right. This girl, he realized — this creature with amber hair and ivory skin and narrow hips and breasts as hard as unripe fruit, this child who now owned his innocence — was a stranger.

■ ■ ■

Downstairs, Fredrik pulled the last whiskey bottle from the cupboard. There were barely two glasses in it. He uncorked the bottle, lifted it to his lips. The whiskey burned his tongue, warmed his chest. He set the bottle down, thinking to save the rest, grabbed two tumblers from the shelf. Then, impulsively, he lifted the bottle again, took another swallow. The alcohol cut a hole in his stomach, flowed through his veins. A memory of Jungmann inside the house rekindled his rage. His hands tightened into fists. Something had to be done about him, because *he* was the problem. Not Polina. Jungmann, the Germans. He sat down at the table. His jaw was clenched. He slipped his hand into his pocket, found a pill, swallowed it with another mouthful of whiskey.

By the time Oskar stepped through the doorway, Fredrik was finishing the bottle. He lowered it from his mouth, sat it onto the table at an angle, let the neck roll back and forth between his finger and his thumb. "It's Jungmann," he said. "Jungmann and Munk. They're the ones who need to go."

Oskar stepped past his father to the cupboard, searched for another bottle, came up dry. "I'll go to the Nielsens'," he said. "I'll see if they'll spare us a bottle. After all, it's New Year's Eve."

"Is it?" Fredrik asked.

Oskar crossed from the kitchen to the vestibule. "If they don't want to give me a bottle," he said, "I suppose I can buy one from them."

The pill was hitting Fredrik's bloodstream with the alcohol, reviving him but disorienting him as well. Perhaps it was the stress from this afternoon, but he hadn't felt this euphoric in some time. He envisioned the syringe in the drawer in the bathroom. The sores on his arms and legs where the needle had punctured his skin ached. His eyes glistened. "Sure you can," he said. "We have the money now. Buy one."

Oskar glanced upstairs as he pulled on his coat. He thought about calling to Polina, but she was fatigued from the ordeal and had decided to lie down for a rest before they started on their journey. There was no point in disturbing her.

From his chair in the kitchen, Fredrik watched his son leave. Upstairs, the girl shifted in Oskar's bed — her hair was spilling over her face, she was propping herself up on an arm, licking her lips, perhaps she was touching the soft tuft of hair he had seen between her thighs as he was hoisting her into the attic. Outside, Oskar's footsteps receded. Fredrik waited until they were gone. Then he stood from the chair. He paused for a moment at the base of the stairs, wavering, then stumbled into the cramped bathroom, shut the door behind him, quietly pulled open the cabinet drawer. The steel and glass syringe glimmered in the dim light.

■ ■ ■

Fredrik's hands shook. One foot rested on the toilet. A pant leg was drawn up to his knee. He ran two fingers along the side of his calf, then decided upon a puncture hole that had scabbed and was nearly healed. Gritting his teeth, he clasped the steel syringe, slid the needle's hollow point into the wound. The pain was sharp, but in the very same instant it was forgotten. He stood upright. The pant leg dropped back onto the top of his boot. He spread his hands out flat on the edge of the sink, stooped forward, closed his eyes. From the moment he had first seen her, he had known that the girl would be his. He had tried to forget her, but to no avail. And now she was about to disappear. An image of her face began to draw itself in his mind. The cold from the porcelain radiated up his arms. The amphetamine gathered itself into a tiny ball in his chest, then made itself tinier still, centered itself like a chunk of ice in his heart. When the small, poisonous ball detonated, the explosion obliterated everything else. Fredrik felt himself sliding backward. He struggled to hang on to the picture of Polina but couldn't. The room darkened, and it slipped through his fingers like a wisp of smoke as he blacked out. Then he was opening his eyes again, sitting up on the floor, wondering how long he had been unconscious. He took hold of the doorknob, pulled himself to his feet, stumbled from the bathroom into the hall.

The stairwell was a blur. The next thing he knew, he was in the narrow passage on the second floor, squeezing through the doorway into Oskar and Amalia's room. He stopped when he saw Polina, but only for a second. Long enough to catch her eye. Long enough for her to read the violence of his thoughts in the weak, late-afternoon twilight. Long enough to smell her. Then he crossed the room, dropped onto his knees in front of her, grabbed her around her narrow waist. Her eyes were colorless. Her lips were only faintly pink.

When Fredrik raised a hand toward her, Polina thought that he was reaching for her face, and she lowered her chin toward his fingers. In itself, this surprised her, and she felt her chest heave. Instead, though, his fingers found the shoelace around her neck, and he lifted the ring from beneath her shirt. The piece of jewelry looked small in his giant palm. He examined the diamond, then tightened his fingers into a fist around it. The shoelace dug into her neck. When he let go, his hands slipped back down to her waist. Polina's fingers sank into his greasy hair. His breath was hot and moist on her legs. His unshaved chin scraped her skin. But he held himself apart from her with a tenderness she didn't expect.

"I don't want you to go," Fredrik said to her, and as he spoke his lips tickled her. Her skirt, she realized, had ridden to her hips. "Please," he said, louder. "Please don't go."

Polina understood the words for what they meant. He was howling. This wasn't an invitation to stay. "Shhh," she said. That was all. "Shhh."

"I recognized you," he said, "from the first moment."

The way one animal recognizes another, she thought. Her fingers clasped his skull, and she wasn't certain herself whether she was holding him away from her or simply holding him.

In her lap, Fredrik's breathing slowed. In the fading light, she saw that his cheeks were wet with tears. The farmhand was crying. "Why are you doing this?" he asked her. The drug was coursing through him in waves. In one instant, it was holding him aloft, permeating him with power. In the next, it was dangling him over a precipice, ready to drop him into a void. "Tell me, Polina. Tell me why."

A shiver ran down her spine. Her fingers dug into his temples. *This was the first time that Fredrik had spoken her name.* His hands tightened around her waist. She concentrated on the sensation as his thumbs sank into her ribs. Her breath caught in her throat. She reminded herself that this man was capable of great violence. She remembered him, made small through the narrow crack in the trapdoor, sneaking up the stairs behind the soldier, wielding the carving knife. In that moment, he had been ready to throw away everything to protect her. His son, his daughter, his own life. Just to keep that soldier from discovering her. Yet a moment later, when that danger had passed, he had been equally willing to toss her out of the house to protect his son, his daughter, his small world here in the middle of this frozen, windswept, godless wasteland. This man's heart beat, she knew, in the grip of that contradiction. She forced herself to exhale, loosened her fingers, let her fingertips touch his cheeks.

Fredrik continued to gaze at her. "Why him?" he asked her.

"Shhh," she repeated.

His voice grew more urgent. "Why?" he asked. "Why him and not me?"

He hung on to her eyes as long as he could in the weakening light, until her face became a singular blur, until the pounding of his heart wouldn't let him think any longer, and then he succumbed. His hands slipped from her waist to her thighs, then eased her legs apart. He was engulfed in darkness, there was nothing else but this taste, this pressure of her thighs, this softness of her hips in his hands, this texture on his tongue.

The taste shocked him. Of course he knew this taste. But there was something unexpected in the flavor, too. There was fear. There was anticipation. There was desire.

Her spine arched. She leaned her head backward, held on to his skull, pulled him into her. Her body began to tremble. But she held her eyes open and stared him straight in the face. She gasped for air. It struck Polina in this moment that, for the first time in her life, she wasn't yielding. There was no memory of Czeslaw to terrify her. There was no thought of resistance, no yearning to escape. Then she silenced her thoughts. *This* was what she wanted. Nothing more.

Time passed, how much she couldn't say. She was present, but, too, she was far away. The sounds that echoed through the small room were too foreign to have been uttered by her. And then, as footsteps shook the stairs, she wriggled backward and, when he wouldn't let her go, fought to push this man away from her.

■ ■ ■

When Oskar returned, he understood that the kitchen was empty even before he had let go of the door. He heard their voices upstairs as soon as he entered the house. He didn't close the door behind him. There was no explaining his reaction — it was instinctive, not controlled. The small cottage lost its geometry. The bottle of whiskey that one of the maids had carried to him from the Nielsens' pantry was still clasped in his hand as he started up the stairs. He stumbled, fell, picked himself up again.

Fredrik didn't hear him enter. Oskar crashed through the doorway, teetered above them in a daze. The light was nearly gone from the day, but the gathering dark couldn't hide them. Polina's skirt remained fastened around her waist, hiked above her hips. She was pushing herself backward on his bed, caught in Fredrik's grip, unable to escape. Off his knees now, Fredrik was grabbing her, pulling her onto her back as if she had no weight at all. In his hands, Polina was no longer the girl Oskar knew — she was a bundle of disconnected bones and pale flesh. The pillow was as white as milk in splinters and crescents beneath the wild mass of her hair. Disheveled like this, he did not recognize her at all.

The bottle of whiskey dropped from Oskar's fingers, tumbled onto the floor. He took hold of his father's shoulders with both hands, yanked him backward. His arms had never felt so powerful. He had never known such fury. He was blind. He didn't see his father anymore. He simply attacked.

The farmhand was surprised by Oskar's strength. His son lifted him off the girl, and he wouldn't have been able to stop him. Fredrik, though, had spent his life chopping wood and shoveling dirt, pounding nails and sawing boards. He weighed twice as much as his young son, and he was infinitely more vicious. Oskar couldn't imagine the violence of which his father was capable. Had he chosen to, he could have collected himself and silenced his son. But Fredrik didn't fight back. He let Oskar's blows rain upon him. He made no move to protect himself. He didn't even wince.

Polina's face contorted. She picked herself up from the bed but didn't think to straighten her clothes or cover herself. She screamed. Her fingers dug into Oskar's shoulders. But she wasn't able to budge him, and Oskar didn't stop. He reveled in his strength. He would destroy his father. He would tear him apart. He would *kill* him. And he could do it. Because this man whom he had feared so much was nothing more than a man just like he was. He was nothing more than a mean laborer on a desolate farm. His fist connected with Fredrik's cheek, and, his legs buckling underneath him, Fredrik dropped to the floor. He was too strong for this single blow to fell him, but it had. He looked up at Oskar, saw the girl, saw his son raise his boot above him, then closed his eyes. When Oskar's boot dug into his ribs, he didn't feel it. He was no longer there. He was no longer in this room. He was somewhere else. *The day had come.* Yes, the day had finally come, and he was nowhere at all.

And then Polina had found the whiskey bottle on the floor, and she had smashed it into the back of Oskar's skull like a club, the last rays of light had scurried and leaped from the room, the day had fallen completely still.

FREDRIK'S WANT

29.

January 1, 1942.

In the early morning, Oskar left the house carrying a small suitcase. He only possessed a few extra pieces of clothing, so the case wasn't heavy. He stepped outside onto the porch and measured the weight of the sky through a squint. Polina was inside the narrow vestibule behind him, lacing her shoes, and she followed him out a moment later. Amalia had given her a wool sweater, and before leaving in the morning for the Nielsens' house, she had taken in the waist of one of her heavier skirts. Polina carried her old clothes in a bundle under her arm. They were nicer than the garments she was wearing now, but they were too thin to offer protection from this cold. She gripped Oskar's arm, marched with him down the icy stairs. When they reached the driveway, their feet sank into the slush. During the night, the snow had turned to rain. The frozen layer of ice that covered the earth was beginning to thaw. Muddy water soaked their shoes. Leaning into the wet wind, they set out together in small, slippery steps across the field toward the barn.

Fredrik looked up from his work on the woodpile. When the door slammed, he paused long enough to take stock of his son and this Polish girl, moving in step, arm in arm, carrying their belongings with them. Then he wiped his brow and bent over the woodpile again and continued to work the saw. His jaw throbbed, his cheekbones were swollen and bruised, his ribs pinched his lungs, but he refused to be hobbled. The drugs and alcohol he had consumed in the last days had left his body weak. It felt good to sweat and to breathe, to labor like this through the tremors. His eyes focused on the metal teeth ripping shards of oak from the trunk of a sapling. He lost himself in the rhythm of the cutting. The long blade sank lower into the wood. When their footsteps became audible, he paid no attention. Perhaps they would stop to say goodbye, or perhaps they wouldn't. What did it matter? In either case, they were leaving, and this was work that had to be done. Without more wood, he and Amalia would freeze. There were only a few shovelfuls of coal left in the cellar, barely enough to get them through a single night. And after this, a fence needed repairing. The pigs were hungry. He was just at the beginning of another long day, and he didn't have time to spare. Sentiment was a luxury that this farm couldn't afford.

Oskar and Polina passed out of view, entered the barn. The smell of mildew and rot drifted down from the ceiling. The roof needed replacing, just like the roof of the cottage. This was something that he and his father had meant to undertake in the spring, once the weather cleared. Now Oskar wouldn't have to. He set his suitcase down, grabbed the shovel, sank the blade into the dirt floor to the left of one of the posts, beside the pigs' trough. The money Oskar had taken from the photographer lay about two feet under the surface, wrapped in newspapers, bound in twine. He dug the last few inches carefully, then knelt to scrape the soil out by hand. When he picked up the bundles of notes, they emerged in a cloud of dust. He shook them clean, and clumps of earth scattered across the hard floor. Polina ran her fingers through his hair when he bent over his suitcase. This tenderness confused him in retrospect, when he thought about it afterward. He stopped to look up at her, then snapped the case shut, stood to his feet. It would be wise to get started.

Outside, they paused in front of Fredrik. The farmhand stopped sawing. Oskar remarked that he wasn't wearing his gloves. His fingers were red, clamped around the edge of the cut log, gripping the handle of the saw. Then — just as Oskar was wondering why — his father reached into his rear pocket, found the gloves, handed them to his son. They were a workman's gloves, but they would keep his hands warm, too. It was cold, and Oskar had a long way to travel.

"Thank you," Oskar said.

When Fredrik smiled, his lip cracked, and his mouth began to bleed. He noticed because of the warmth and the flavor, and he swiped at the mess with the back of his hand. Polina tugged Oskar's sleeve, and he understood that it was time to leave. He tightened his grip on the suitcase. It was a little heavier now with the money inside it. Then he started to walk. Polina held on to his arm. He concentrated on the soft grip of her fingers there, and then on the splash of her footsteps in the dirty snow next to him. Behind them, the saw worked itself back into a rhythm.

At the top of the property, a voice called out Oskar's name, and he stopped, turned back around. The rain was coming down so steadily now that it was difficult to see. He squinted, held up a hand, searched for Amalia. She had been running for five minutes already, all the way from the Nielsens' house, and she was out of breath. Her cheeks were flushed. She ran with one arm across her chest, with her other hand lifting her skirt so that she wouldn't trip. Her hair was soaked, and so was her shirt. She had dashed out of the house without a coat. "Oskar, Oskar." Her shouts caught up to them before she could. Her breath steamed from her mouth in billows. She could barely take another step. "Oskar, wait, Oskar!"

Oskar waited for his sister. When she reached them, her eyes were thoroughly red. Her face was so wet from the rain that they wouldn't have otherwise known that she was crying. "You don't have your jacket," Oskar said.

"Were you going to leave without saying goodbye?" Amalia choked on the words. She could barely see her brother through her inflamed eyes.

Oskar looked at her, and this was the way that he would always remember her face. "Why don't you come with us?" he asked her.

She shook her head. "I can't," she said.

"We have enough money," Oskar said.

Amalia was biting her lip. "You're going to America?"

Oskar nodded.

She shook her head again. "It's not for me, I don't think. I wouldn't belong there. I belong here instead, with Father."

"Okay, then," Oskar said.

"You know — I don't know what he would do without me."

"By the way," Oskar said, "I forgot to tell you — I saw Elke the other day."

"You did? You saw Mama?"

"It was on my way to Copenhagen — at the station — she was looking well."

"You saw Mama — " Amalia repeated.

"She said to tell you that she misses you."

"Did she?"

"She said she wants you to come visit her," Oskar lied.

"Yes," Amalia said. "I will."

"Soon, she said."

"I will. I'll go up to Skagen to see her."

"That's good," Oskar said, and brother and sister fell silent.

"Well — " Amalia lurched forward and grabbed Oskar's shoulders. He was so tall that she had to bend him toward her to give him a kiss. It was an impulsive gesture. She had never kissed him before. Her lips brushed his cheek, and he noticed both how hot her breath was and how cold her lips were. "Goodbye, Oskar," she said into his ear. "Will I see you again?"

"I don't know," Oskar said.

Amalia's fingers dug into his shoulders. She held on. Then she let go. When their eyes met, they each felt slightly bashful, even in this moment, as they were saying goodbye. And then Oskar turned and stepped through the broken gate and started with Polina down the highway. He didn't turn back again to look at the cottage where he had grown up or at his father working next to the barn or at his sister standing still at the top of the driveway, unable herself to move, watching her brother disappear into the slanting rain.

■ ■ ■

When they reached Helsingør, on the sea above Copenhagen, they checked into a small hotel on a side street — a boardinghouse for sailors and journeymen and prostitutes where no one would question what they were doing. Oskar left Polina by herself in the room and, pocketing one of the bundles of crowns, went into the village to find his father's contact.

This close to the sea, the air was laced with salt, and the mist off the water stung his eyes. It was already after sunset. The narrow streets were as dark as unlit alleys. Shivering, pulling his coat tight around him, he made his way to the address Fredrik had given him. The cobblestones were slippery, and, crossing a street, he tripped on a curb. Spying him from a doorway, mistaking the reason for his disorientation, a beggar wondered whether this boy might be drunk enough to roll, but decided better of it when he realized how tall Oskar was. At the next corner, Oskar stopped to read a street sign, then, gathering his disparate thoughts, continued through the quiet town.

Fredrik's instructions led him to a pub. The echoes of people speaking and eating met him as he approached. Shadows shifted in the windows. He felt for the packet of crowns in his pocket, screwed up his courage, then stepped inside. It was a small, dark bar, frequented by locals. If a tourist was going to stop for a drink or a bite to eat, it wouldn't be here, on this narrow alley five or six blocks from the strand. All eyes turned toward him as he entered, and when the patrons didn't recognize him, their voices dropped. The ceiling was so low that Oskar had to stoop. He ignored the few groups at tables, the two or three men at the counter, and approached the bartender instead. "I'm looking for Mads Knudsen," he said.

At the counter next to him, a couple of men exchanged a glance through the smoke of their cigarettes. Behind the counter, the barman smiled. "Can I get you a drink?" he asked the boy.

Oskar shook his head. "Mads Knudsen," he repeated. "I've been told I can find him here."

"Who wants to know?" the barman asked him.

"My father's name is Fredrik," Oskar said. "Fredrik Gregersen."

The barman studied him. "And what's your name, then?"

"Oskar."

"Okay, then, Oskar." The barman looked down the length of the wooden counter, then back at the boy again. The patrons were still listening, the room was still silent. "I can't tell you if your information is good or bad. But let me put it this way—if a man named Knudsen is here, and if he wants to speak to you, he'll speak to you. If he doesn't want to—" The barman shrugged. Behind Oskar, a few men chuckled. Conversations resumed.

Oskar twisted around, looked through the hazy air at the men in the dark, stuffy room. For the most part, they were sailors. This was apparent from their gnarled hands and leathery skin, the deep creases beside their eyes. The bar itself smelled of the sea. "All right," Oskar said. "You can give me a beer."

The barman pulled him a pint. Oskar paid with a loose coin, then lifted the thick glass and took a sip. This he would remember as his first taste of freedom. At eighteen, Oskar had never entered a pub by himself, he had never yet ordered himself a beer. The liquid was tepid and flat. He filled his mouth with it and swallowed anyway. If these men were going to rob him, there was little he could do about it, sober or drunk. In any case, he wasn't ready yet to leave. He couldn't give up so easily.

"Where are you from, boy?" the man standing at the counter next to him asked.

Oskar set down the heavy glass, took a look at the man. He was older than Oskar had first thought—fifty or sixty. His face was swarthy. His blue eyes were cloudy with cataracts. Over time, his ears had sagged and his nose had grown. He wasn't tall, but he was as broad as an ox, and his shoulders were thick from years of labor as a longshoreman. "From Jutland," Oskar said.

"Yeah? Jutland. That's an easy answer. It's a big place. You might as well say Denmark."

"From Aalborg," Oskar said.

"Hmmm. And your father's working there?"

"He's a farmer," Oskar said. "We live on a farm."

"And here you are, all the way in Zealand. By yourself?"

The old man's breath stank like tobacco, and there was something shifty about his eyes. Oskar wondered how wise it was to speak so openly to him. Perhaps this man was trying to trick him somehow. If he found out how much money Oskar was carrying, he might even try to steal it. His hands were misshapen, but they were powerful. Despite his age, he could probably best him in a fight, if that was what this came to. But this man had asked him a question, and Oskar was young and inexperienced. He felt compelled to give him an answer. "Yes," he said at last. "I came alone."

"And you say you're looking for Knudsen?" the man asked him. "Why?"

"Do you know him?"

The man shrugged his heavy shoulders, twisted his lips in a noncommittal frown.

"Is he here?" Oskar asked him. "Do you see him?"

"Buy me a drink," the man said, "and maybe I will tell you."

Behind the counter, the barman was smiling. Oskar took another swallow of his beer. "Sure," he said. "I'll buy you a drink if you want."

"A whiskey," the man said to the barman. "And one for my friend Oskar here, too."

Oskar felt his face flush red. The man had remembered his name. He watched the barman fill two small shot glasses with amber liquid. When the man grabbed his, a third of it sloshed onto the counter. He drank the rest in a single swallow, then waited for Oskar to do the same. When Oskar set his glass back down, the man was extending a hand toward him. At first, he wasn't certain what the man intended. Then he took the hand and gave it a shake. The man's skin was warm and dry, his own was clammy.

"Mads Knudsen," the man said.

Oskar's face flushed a second time.

"Another whiskey," the man said. "This time, I'm paying." The barman poured their shots, and the man finished his without a pause. When he slammed the empty glass back down on the counter, droplets of spilled whiskey splattered Oskar's face like the spray of surf. "Now," the man said, "tell me why your father sent you to find me. It's been a while since I've done any business with him."

Oskar swallowed his drink, then followed the old longshoreman to a quiet corner and told him about his desire to find passage from Denmark to America.

■ ■ ■

When Oskar returned to the hotel, Polina wasn't in their room. The curtains had been left open, and the windows, encrusted with a thin glaze of frost from the polar wind blowing off the sound, glowed softly gray, casting enough light inside to give shape to the dark. Oskar's first thought upon opening the door was that Polina had left him. He felt himself blanch, and he froze in the doorway, the knob still cold on his fingers. But then he noticed her things on the floor where she had set them. The shirt she had been wearing was laid out on the mattress. And he became aware, too, of the trickle of water from the communal bathroom down the hallway. She was preparing herself for bed, that was all. Letting go of the door, he started down the corridor to find her. He had drunk too much — Knudsen had kept him talking until there was no more whiskey in the bottle — and he staggered into a wall before finding his balance again. At the far end of the hallway, the bathroom door was open a crack. A sliver of white light from the bulb above the mirror flared into the shadows. He squinted into the glare and slowed his step. The floorboards creaked, his coat rustled, but the hum of the taps drowned out his unsteady approach.

Reaching the bathroom, he stopped in the doorway and peeked through the crack. Polina was standing in front of the sink, washing her face. She had placed her hands on the edge of the pedestal and was contemplating her reflection in the mirror. She was naked to the waist, and the diamond ring dangled from its string between her breasts, slowly twisting, its facets catching fire one by one. Except for the water spilling into the porcelain basin, there was no other movement in the room. Polina held herself perfectly still. Her hair, wet from her bath, hung to her shoulders in tight clumps. Tiny streams dripped down her forehead, her cheeks, her neck, her chest, glistening in the electric light. Oskar was staring at her, his mouth slightly agape, when he realized that she, too, was staring back at him. Their eyes met in the mirror, and they gazed at each other, framed inside the plane of the rectangular lens. Neither of them flinched. Neither spoke a word. When Polina did finally turn toward him, Oskar lost his breath as her reflection blossomed into her face and glass softened into flesh. He couldn't remember a moment like this before, when they had stood this close and simply looked at each other. Behind Oskar, muted voices echoed down the hall. In the bathroom, the water tinkled and gurgled as it escaped into the drain. The faucet whined.

Then Oskar realized how drunk he was. The floor wanted to tip. He couldn't keep Polina in focus. Swaying on his feet, he spun around and started back up the corridor. The light from the bathroom had blinded him, and he had to peer through a floating image of Polina's face to find their room again. The bed appeared in front of him, then wheeled into a blur as he sat down. He pulled off his clothes. His head hit the pillow. He tried to stay awake and wait for her. But by the time Polina followed him into the room, he was out.

The bed was a single, narrower than the mattress he slept on at home. When Polina climbed under the blankets next to him, he woke up again, enough to grab hold of her, though not enough to open his eyes, and he pulled her against him so tight that there was no gap between them. He would tell her about his conversation with Knudsen and about the merchant ship in the morning. He was too drunk to speak, too exhausted. And Polina, he knew, needed her sleep as well, every bit as much as he did. It had been a long day, and tomorrow would be even longer. The water in her hair was cold, and it soaked the pillow and penetrated his undershirt. Her smell was familiar now—he could focus on it instead of the strange smells inside this hotel. Outside, the wind gusted, and the windows rattled. The wet bedding grew warmer. Down the street, a group of sailors were laughing, and their voices echoed shrilly off the cobblestones. In the room next door, two men were arguing. But the sounds grew ever more distant, and a few minutes later, Oskar was fast asleep.

The last sensation he would remember was the spreading of her wings, and then being borne aloft on Polina's slender back, effortlessly, through a sky drawn, like song is, too, in whispers and ink.

■ ■ ■

Goodbye, Oskar.

When dawn broke, Oskar was standing at the Nielsens' gate in the pouring, icy rain, saying goodbye to Amalia again.

The metallic pulse of Fredrik's saw echoed up the hill from the side of the barn, in rhythm with his heartbeat. His sister's lips brushed his cheek. Her whispered parting warmed his ear. Then he became aware of the hard, lumpy, damp pillow. Had he been dreaming? He woke slowly, shivering. The bed was much colder than it should have been. The blankets had fallen off during the night, and he had been too worn out to notice. He woke because Mads Knudsen had arranged for their passage on a Danish icebreaker berthed in the harbor at Helsingør. The icebreaker was leading a Swedish ship through the naval blockade into the North Sea, and the captain had agreed to take Oskar and Polina as far as he could, then smuggle them onto the merchant ship. Oskar had told himself to wake at the first sign of light — the crew wouldn't wait for them — and that is what his body had done. He reached for the blankets. The salty taste of Polina's hair teased his tongue. Then he realized that he was by himself in the bed, and he opened his eyes. The air was thick and dusky, the hotel was silent. He lifted himself onto his elbow. The room was empty. Polina was gone.

She could have been in the bathroom down the hall again, as she had been last night, but Oskar knew that she wasn't. He sat up onto the side of the bed, rubbed his eyes with his palms. Her bundle of clothes was missing from the floor next to his suitcase. His head ached from the alcohol. His thoughts moved slowly. He stood, crossed to the window.

Outside, the small town was blanketed in mist. The morning was still, the narrow street was deserted. When the hotel door opened beneath him, he knew that it would be Polina. Oskar watched her step onto the sidewalk. Vague recollections tugged at his consciousness. The rustle of fabric when she pulled on her clothes. The scrape of her hands on the floor, searching for her belongings in the dim light. The squeak of leather as she dug through his suitcase for the packets of crowns. And then her voice in a whisper, *Goodbye, Oskar.*

She paused beneath the window, looked up and down the street as if she wasn't certain which way to go. Then, slipping the makeshift bundle beneath her arm, she ducked her head and started walking. Watching her through the glass, in his own way Oskar understood. If she had been able to love him, she would have stayed. She didn't look back, not even a glance, and Oskar never saw her face again. Her footsteps quickly faded, and just like that he was alone. This girl who had led him from his home with his father and sister was nothing but a memory, a name. Polina.

Seagulls screeched down by the strand. When the wind blew, the mist swirled like smoke. This village was on fire. This country was smoldering. There was nothing left for him here — if he tried to stay, everything he held would dissolve in his hands like ash. Oskar thought about counting the money in his pocket. But it didn't matter how much Polina had left him. He would take whatever he had and go. He found his trousers and his shoes, got himself dressed. There was no time left for reflection.

He didn't notice the diamond ring until he was reaching for his suitcase, on his way out the door. He stopped still, opened the case, lifted the ring from the shadows. The old shoelace he had fashioned into a necklace for Polina slipped between his fingers and hung from his hand, catching the weak light. He held the diamond in his palm, gazing at it. Then he slipped the shoelace over his head and tucked the ring under his shirt. The cold stone cut a path down his chest. He had to hurry. He left the hotel and headed silently for the launch. His footsteps chased him down the empty alleyway.

30.

Fredrik wasn't a good driver. He had driven trucks and trac-tors for decades. This was part of his work on the farm. Behind the wheel of an automobile, though, he lacked the same con-fidence. Rather than borrow the car from the Nielsens, he had decided to take his motorcycle instead. It was a BMW with heavy tires. The roads were still icy, even after the rain, which had melted the snow. But the machine would get him to the coast. He didn't have any gloves. He had given them to Oskar. So he wrapped his hands in rags, then kick-started the engine and climbed onto the rumbling, cumbersome ride. At four in the morning, it was still pitch-black. The headlamp barely lit a path in front of him.

Amalia woke to the sound of the motorcycle's engine. The exhaust pipe was loose, and the cylinder fired its syncopated rhythm with a guttural roar. When Fredrik revved the motor, the growl reverberated over the sleeping farm, and the pigs began to bleat. Amalia sat up in bed and looked out the window in time to see her father circle to the top of the driveway then follow a fragile column of yellow light through the gate. She watched him disappear, then got out of bed, stumbled into the bathroom.

When Fredrik reached the coast above Copenhagen, in Hornbæk, his hands were so cold that he had lost feeling in his fingers. Beneath the rags, his knuckles bled. When he stood off the motorcycle, his thighs ached. He leaned the machine onto its kickstand where the asphalt met the dunes, then, bending into his steps, climbed the steep bluff. The sun was rising, and the clouds had begun to clear. By the time he reached the top of the hill, a band of golden sunlight was stretching across the flat, steel surface of the water like a flaming slick of oil. The wind gusted, and tall grass tickled his fingers. The sun carved shafts from the air. He stood still on the hard sand, raised a hand to his brow, and scanned the sea.

Beneath him, far in the distance, a huge merchant ship was skimming through the mercury, as grim as a factory. Diesel exhaust billowed from its stacks, as if the gigantic hull had itself caught fire. He watched it glide across the strait, carving a route between chunks of ice set adrift by an icebreaker. Behind it, the seawater churned in its wake, etching a white tail that betrayed its path. Of course, Fredrik had no way of knowing if this was the ship that Oskar was on, or where this ship was headed. But he held his hand up anyway, into the sky, and waved.

AMERIKA

31.

New York. April 1991.

Across the well-lit gallery, a tall, silver-haired man was standing in front of a photograph labeled with a simple title underneath: *Polina*. It had been difficult for Angela Schmidt to include this particular photograph with the rest of the collection. She understood that it was a defining composition for her father. Without it, she doubted that the publisher compiling her father's work would have been interested in the others, no matter their historical importance. Still, Angela couldn't help but feel some shame. Her father's photography revealed his horror of the war. But — in Angela's mind at least — this image of the girl in his room in Copenhagen exposed him. He had been a part of the atrocity, not just an observer. She watched the man whose gaze was fixed upon the black-and-white portrait, ignoring the crowd in between — the New Yorkers who had gathered here on this Sunday in April. For them, this opening had become a social event. The exhibit had been written up in the *New York Times*. They congregated in small groups around the photographs, hardly noticing them at all, more intent upon one another. A small chunk of the Berlin Wall, emblazoned with green and red and black streaks of graffiti, sitting in a glass case labeled with a date — *9 November 1989* — attracted more of their attention than her father's images. There was something different about this tall man. When she had first caught sight of him, she had mistaken him for a European. Now as she moved closer to him, she realized that, despite his age, he was dressed in the jeans and flannel shirt and worn boots of an American wrangler. In the few minutes she had been watching him, he hadn't once looked away from the photograph.

What a wonderful success, Angela. But Angela barely heard the praise. She smiled at her U.S. editor without taking her in, continued in a straight line toward the portrait of Polina.

"Excuse me," Angela said to the man.

It took a moment for the words to penetrate. When he turned to face the gray-haired woman, the man's eyes registered his recognition. She took note of his weathered skin. When he extended a hand toward her, she noticed how scarred it was before she grasped it. "I knew your father," the man said.

This stunned Angela. Very quickly, though, she realized that the information wasn't a surprise. There had been something intimate in the way this man was looking at the girl in the photograph. "You knew her, too," Angela said, "didn't you?"

The man's mouth formed the semblance of a smile.

"Who was she?"

The man didn't answer. It occurred to him now that he couldn't, not really. He had never been able to define her. He had never been able to capture Polina any more perfectly than Hermann had in this photograph.

"Do you know what happened to her?"

"No. I lost track of her. I don't know if she lived or died." The man's voice was a confusion of accents. He read the progression of Angela's thoughts. "I'm Danish," he explained. "But I left Denmark—"—*during the second winter of the war.* He didn't finish the sentence. He had noticed the scintillation of gems beneath the thin fabric of Angela's shirt.

She followed his stare to her own chest, then raised her eyes again. "It belonged to my father," she said.

The man nodded his head, but he couldn't speak.

Angela took hold of the platinum chain, lifted the pendant from beneath her collar. When she held it in her hand, the man took a half step backward. "I nearly parted with it. When I left my husband, I thought I would need the money." She met the man's gaze. "But I decided to keep it after all, and I'm glad that I did."

The man didn't ask to hold the jewelry. He simply raised one of his twisted hands, extended a callused finger, touched the smooth surface of the sapphire.

"I would like to hear how you knew my father," Angela said.

The man thought about this. Already, this encounter had brought back too many memories for a single day. He had known when he read the notice about the exhibit, before making the trip to New York, that it wouldn't be easy to confront these images from his past. He had long since buried these ghosts, and they wouldn't wake quietly. He hadn't expected, though, that his reaction to the photographs would be so visceral. He looked once again at the image of Polina, standing half naked in the apartment above the bakery in Copenhagen. He remembered this skirt clutched at her waist. He remembered these hands. He remembered her colorless eyes and her broken teeth. The smell of dust overwhelmed him, and for a split second he was standing in the German lieutenant's studio again, following this Polish girl in his peripheral vision, reading her face through the shadows.

"Was he a good man, my father? As you knew him, I mean —"

Angela's voice reached the man from a great distance. When he looked at her again, he had grown older. *War can make criminals of heroes*, he thought, *and heroes of criminals*, and he remembered the day when he had seen Fredrik's name on a list of Danes who had given their lives to the resistance. But he didn't reply. He returned her gaze. Then he turned and left the gallery. Just like that. It wasn't an insult to her. It was the act of a man of few words. Angela didn't realize until he was already gone that she hadn't asked his name.

"Wait," she said, but it was too late.

Oskar pushed through the doorway onto the sidewalk, let the door close behind him. He had to shake the feeling that he was stepping into snow. The photograph of Polina had brought him back to Copenhagen again. Back to the winter of 1941. He hesitated, uncertain of his direction, imagining a maze of cobblestone streets twisting and turning through the frozen city, through the mist, back to the train station. For a fleeting moment, he lay in bed again, in Polina's arms, in the small hotel in Korsør. In a few more steps, around the next corner perhaps, he might find himself with his father and sister one last time, in their little cottage in Jutland. Then a yellow taxi slid past. A truck honked, a couple of pigeons took flight. The cacophony of New York confronted him. He looked upward into the pale sky through eyes made of glass. The sun touched his face. And he continued walking.

Acknowledgments

It took me about three weeks to hammer out the first draft of *Fredrik's Want* — which was this novel's original title. I based the story on what I recollected from hazy childhood tales of my father's uncle, who actually was a brute and a member of the Danish resistance during World War II, but my purpose in writing the book had little to do with this man or Denmark during the war. To me, the story was metaphor. *Fredrik's Want* as I first conceived it was what it is, on a primal level, to be a father, and this was something I had the audacity to believe I could teach to my children. After finishing the first draft, it took almost four more years to turn that rough metaphor into the book it is today, and in that process I learned more from my children about what it means to be a father than I will ever teach them, through this novel or otherwise. I am indebted to both Ray and Melissa, profoundly, not only for their actual work as my most staunch critics but for their love and their insight.

The book also owes its present form to Kim Witherspoon, Lena Yarbrough, and Judith Gurewich.

Finally, I need to mention my debt to my friend Johanna, who showed me what it means to be beautiful.

CRAIG LARSEN *was born in 1963 and is a graduate of UC Berkeley and Columbia Law School. His first novel,* Mania, *was published in 2009. A single father, Larsen has lived in New York and Europe. He currently resides in northern California.*

▣ OTHER PRESS

You might also enjoy these titles from our list:

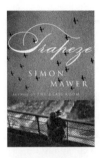

TRAPEZE by Simon Mawer

A propulsive novel of World War II espionage that introduces Marian Sutro, heroine of *Tightrope*

"The book is full of the fascinating minutiae of espionage — aircraft drops, code-cracking, double agents, scrambled radio messages. There's a romance, too... Mawer exhibits a great feeling for suspense, and produces memorable episodes in dark alleyways, deserted cafes, and shadowy corners of Père Lachaise." —*New Yorker*

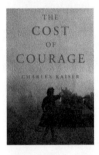

THE COST OF COURAGE by Charles Kaiser

The heroic true story of the three youngest children of a bourgeois Catholic family who worked together in the French Resistance

"A thorough and quite accessible history of Europe's six-year murderous paroxysm... *The Cost of Courage* documents, through the life of an extraordinary family, one of the 20th century's most fascinating events — the German occupation of the City of Light." —*Wall Street Journal*

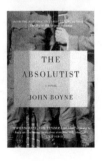

THE ABSOLUTIST by John Boyne

A masterful tale of passion, jealousy, heroism, and betrayal set in one of the most gruesome trenches of France during World War I

"A wonderful, sad, tender book that is going to have an enormous impact on everyone who reads it." —Colm Tóibín

Also recommended:

CROSSING THE BORDERS OF TIME
by Leslie Maitland

A dramatic true story of World War II, exile, and love lost—then reclaimed

"*Schindler's List* meets *Casablanca* in this tale of a daughter's epic search for her mother's prewar beau—fifty years later." —*Good Housekeeping*

HIS OWN MAN by Edgard Telles Ribeiro

From one of Brazil's eminent authors comes a Machiavellian tale, set during South America's dirty wars, where the machinations of a consummate diplomat and deceiver ring dangerously true.

"Nuanced and psychologically incisive...This tale of international intrigue (Graham Greene might provide the best comparison) shows how malleable concepts of left and right, and right and wrong, can be during extended periods of political unrest and military repression." —*Kirkus Reviews* (starred)

BLOOD BROTHERS by Ernest Haffner

Originally published in 1932 and banned by the Nazis one year later, *Blood Brothers* follows a gang of young boys bound together by unwritten rules and mutual loyalty.

"Haffner's project is journalistic, to portray destitution and criminality without the false sparkle of glamour. His skill in portraiture and the depiction of a social milieu is evident." —*Wall Street Journal*

⚏ OTHER PRESS

www.otherpress.com